The Novel's Seductions

The Novel's Seductions

Staël's *Corinne* in Critical Inquiry

Edited by
Karyna Szmurlo

Lewisburg
Bucknell University Press
London: Associated University Presses

Associated University Presses
440 Forsgate Drive
Cranbury, NJ 08512

Associated University Presses
16 Barter Street
London WC1A 2AH, England

Associated University Presses
P.O. Box 338, Port Credit
Mississauga, Ontario
Canada L5G 4L8

The paper used in this publication meets the requirements of the American National Standard for Permanence of Paper for Printed Library Materials Z39.48-1984.

Library of Congress Cataloging-in-Publication Data

The novel's seductions : Staël's Corinne in critical inquiry / edited by Karyna Szmurlo.
    p.   cm.
    Includes bibliographical references and index.
    ISBN 0-8387-5337-X (alk. paper)
    1. Staël, Madame de (Anne-Louise-Germaine), 1766–1817. Corinne.
I. Szmurlo, Karyna.
PQ2431.C7Z96   1999
843'.6—dc21
          98-7650
          CIP

Corinne is an immortal book, and deserves to be read three score and ten times—that is once every year in the age of man.

—Elizabeth Barrett Browning

Contents

CONTENTS

Acknowledgments

My teaching appointment at Rutgers University in the late 1980s put me in continuing contact with an international group of brilliant scholars whose work became an inspiring model of critical thinking and sparked my interests in Staël studies. I am particularly indebted to Madelyn Gutwirth, whom I had the good fortune to meet at this time. Her encouragement sustained me during this project and many others. I wish to express here, my warmest gratitude and admiration for her vision, unfailing generosity, and her invaluable support, both moral and intellectual.

This book would not have come into existence without the foregrounding scholarship of Simone Balayé, the leading Staëlian of our time, whose erudite edition of *Corinne* served as the basis for this collection, nor without Avriel Goldberger's translation which made Staël's novel accessible to English readers. I feel honored to acknowledge the impact of their work on these studies.

Like other works restoring the connections among women writers, *The Novel's Seductions* is, in its essence, a collective enterprise. I am immensely grateful to all the thinkers represented in this volume, to the long-time colleagues as well as to the young critics who were graduate students at the germinal stage of this project, for their enthusiasm, hard work, cooperation, and above all, tolerance of numerous delays and revisions over the past several years. Sadly, Charlotte Hogsett did not live to see the completed book, for which she especially had written the closing essay. I wish to acknowledge here her presence so important for the conceptual structure of the volume.

My thanks go also to the teachers and students, the responsive listeners and questioners, who will take Germaine de Staël's novel to the twenty-first century.

To Mills Edgerton, Director of Bucknell University Press and to Julien Yoseloff, Director of Associated University Presses, I express deep appreciation for believing in this book. I wish to thank the entire AUP staff for an exceptionally constructive collaboration.

Acknowledgments are due to those authors, editors and publishers who allowed me to use, in revised form, all or part of the following seminal texts: Madame de Staël, *Corinne ou l'Italie,* edited by Simone Balayé, Editions Gallimard, 1985. Reprinted with the permission of the editor and the publisher. Madame de Staël, *Corinne, or Italy,* translated by Avriel H. Goldberger, copyright (c) 1987 by Rutgers, The State University. Reprinted by permission of Rutgers University Press. Simone Balayé, "La fonction romanesque de la musique dans *Corinne,*" *Romantisme* 3 (1972); Joan DeJean, "Staël's *Corinne,* the Novel's Other Dilemma," *Stanford French Review* 11 (1987); Marie-Claire Vallois, "Voice as Fossil; Staël's *Corinne, or Italy*: An Archaeology of Feminine Discourse," *Tulsa Studies in Women's Literature* 6 (Spring 1987); "Performances of the Gaze: Staël's *Corinne, or Italy,*" revised and adapted from Chapter Seven in *Subject to Change: Reading Feminist Writing* by Nancy Miller. Copyright (c) 1988 by Columbia University Press. Reprinted with permission of the publisher. "*Corinne* and Female Transmission: Rewriting *La Princesse de Clèves* through the English Gothic," revised and adapted from Chapter Six in *Virtue's Faults: Correspondences in Eighteenth-Century British and French Women's Fiction* by April Alliston. Copyright (c) 1996 by the Board of Trustees of the Leland Stanford Junior University. Reprinted with the permission of the publishers.

Notes on the Contributors

APRIL ALLISTON, Associate Professor of Comparative Literature at Princeton University, is the author of *Virtue's Faults: Correspondences in Eighteenth-Century British and French Women's Fiction* (Stanford University Press, 1996) and of various articles on related topics. Her critical edition of Sophia Lee's *The Recess* (1783–85) is appearing in the University Press of Kentucky's "Eighteenth-Century Novels by Women" series.

SIMONE BALAYÉ, Former Conservateur at the Bibliothèque Nationale in Paris, is the foremost Staël scholar of this era. She is the editor of Staël's *Lettres à Ribbing* (Gallimard, 1960), *Carnets de voyage* (Droz, 1971), and *Corinne ou l'Italie* (Gallimard, 1985). She is the co-editor, with Countess Jean de Pange of the Hachette edition of *De l'Allemagne* (1958–60) and of *Dix années d'exil* (Fayard, 1996) with Mariella Bonifacio. Author of numerous articles, historical and interpretive, on all facets of Staël's work, her *Madame de Staël, lumières et liberté* was published by Klincksieck in 1979 and *Madame de Staël: écrire, lutter, vivre* by Droz in 1994. Simone Balayé presides over the Société des études staëliennes which publishes the *Cahiers staëliens*, a review devoted to the works and careers of Staël and the Coppet Group.

MARGARET COHEN is Associate Professor in the Department of Comparative Literature at New York University. She has published *Profane Illumination* and *Spectacles of Realism,* a co-edited collection of essays, as well as articles on modernity and gender in journals including *New German Critique, L'Esprit Créateur, boundary 2, Cultural Critique* and *Social Text.* Her book *Compromising Positions: The Literary Struggles Engendering the Modern Novel in France* is forthcoming from Princeton University Press.

JOAN DEJEAN is Trustee Professor of French at the University of Pennsylvania. Her recent books include *Fictions of Sappho, 1546–1937* (Chicago University Press, 1989); *Tender Geogra-*

phies: Women and the Origins of the Novel in France (Columbia University Press, 1991); and *Ancients Against Moderns: Culture Wars and the Making of a Fin de Siècle* (Chicago University Press, 1997).

PAOLA GIULI is a Lecturer of Italian and Comparative Literature at Princeton University and Rutgers University. She has written on both eighteenth- and nineteenth-century women writers, feminist theory and deconstruction. Her most recent publications focus on women's contributions to Arcadia, and its representation in literary history. Her book in progress is entitled *Enlightenment, Arcadia and Corilla: The Inscription of Italian Women Writers in Literary History.*

MADELYN GUTWIRTH, Emerita Professor of French and Women's Studies at West Chester University, is now Research Associate at the Alice Paul Center for the Study of Women, University of Pennsylvania. She is the author of *Madame de Staël, Novelist: The Emergence of the Artist as Woman* (University of Illinois Press, 1978) and *The Twilight of the Goddesses: Women and Representation in the French Revolutionary Era* (Rutgers University Press, 1992), which received Honorable Mention in the Louis Gottschalk Competition, American Society for Eighteenth-Century Studies, 1994.

CHARLOTTE HOGSETT received her Ph.D. from Harvard University. She was the author of *The Literary Existence of Germaine de Staël* (Southern Illinois University Press, 1987). Her research interests expanded to American public education in light of contemporary feminist theory and to twentieth-century writers, Marguerite Yourcenar in particular. Her contribution to the volume was written just before her death.

NANETTE LE COAT, Associate Professor of French, Trinity University, has published articles on Volney, Rousseau, the Idéologues and Revolutionary culture. She is working on a book project entitled *Romantic Anthropology: Post-Revolutionary European Writers and the Study of Culture* whose purpose will be to show how a new anthropology emerged from the cultural dialogue between post-Enlightenment, post-Revolutionary France and the new, Romantic Germany.

NANCY K. MILLER is Distinguished Professor of English at Lehman College and the Graduate Center, CUNY. She is the author of *The Heroine's Text: Readings in the French and English Novel, 1722–1782* and *Subject to Change: Reading Feminist Writing*. She is the editor of The *Poetics of Gender,* and co-editor with Joan DeJean of *Displacements: Women, Tradition, Literatures in French.*

ELLEN PEEL is Associate Professor in the Department of World and Comparative Literature and in the Department of English at San Francisco State University. Her major interests are narrative, literary theory, and feminist criticism and theory. Among her writings on *Corinne* is a chapter in her book in progress, *Beyond Utopia: Feminism, Persuasion, and Narrative.*

KATHARINE RODIER is an Assistant Professor of English at Marshall University. Her essays and reviews have appeared in *The Emily Dickinson Journal, Review, American Literature,* and in the collection *Susan Glaspell: Essays on Her Theater and Fiction* from the University of Michigan Press. She has published poems in *Poetry East, The Virginia Quarterly Review, Poetry Northwest, The Antioch Review, Poetry,* and other journals. She is currently co-editing *American Women Prose Writers, 1820–1870,* a volume of the *Dictionary of Literary Biography.*

NANCY ROGERS is the Director of the Division of Public Programs at the National Endowment for the Humanities. She earned M.A. and Ph.D. degrees in French literature from the George Washington University. Her professional experience includes teaching French and Humanities at Howard University, the receipt of an NEH Fellowship-in-Residence at Princeton University, and teaching American literature and language at the University of Tübingen in Germany. She is the author of two books on American English style and of numerous articles on nineteenth-century French literature and women's studies.

NANORA SWEET teaches English and Women's Studies at the University of Missouri-St. Louis. Her essays on Hemans and her circle appeared in *At the Limits of Romanticism* (1994) and in the following 1997 volumes: *The Lessons of Romanticism, Approaches to Teaching British Women Poets in the Romantic Period,* and *European Romantic Review.* She is currently co-editing a volume of essays on Hemans and completing books on Hemans and the bourgeois laureate of Reform.

NOTES ON CONTRIBUTORS

KARYNA SZMURLO, Associate Professor of French at Clemson University, received her Ph.D. from Rutgers University where she organized the first international conference on Staël (1988). Her work has centered on eighteenth- and nineteenth-century French literature with a particular focus on women writers and performing arts. She is the co-editor of *Germaine de Staël: Crossing the Borders* (Rutgers University Press, 1991), Staël's bibliographer, and more recently, an active contributor to the philosophy of language. Her book in preparation, *Performative Discourses: Germaine de Staël,* explores the link between politics and semiotics in the Revolutionary context.

SUSAN TENENBAUM is Associate Professor of Political Science at Baruch College, CUNY. Her areas of specialization are public policy, public finance and political theory. She is the author of numerous articles on Germaine de Staël and the Coppet Group. She is presently working on a book *The Political Thought of Germaine de Staël.*

MARIE-CLAIRE VALLOIS, Associate Professor of French at Cornell University, is the author of *Fictions féminines: Mme de Staël et les voix de la Sibylle* (Anma Libri, 1987). She has written on both eighteenth- and nineteenth-century authors (Montesquieu, Diderot, Chateaubriand and Hugo). She is currently completing a book *Changing Places: Women, Fictions, Revolution (1650-1850).*

VINCENT WHITMAN is a Ph.D. student in English at the University of Connecticut and teaching assistant for the Freshman Writing Program. His main area of concentration is English Romanticism. His B.A. and M.A. in English are from Sangamon State University in Springfield, Illinois. The paper on *Corinne* grew out of the program "Comparative Feminist Criticism" directed by Professor Margaret Higonnet.

Introduction

KARYNA SZMURLO

OVER the last two decades American academia has shown unprecedented interest in Staël's novel. No longer dismissed as a weak exemplar of the genre, *Corinne* is now acknowledged as the productive reply of a woman writer to the feminine condition. Madelyn Gutwirth's pioneering work, *Madame de Staël, Novelist: The Emergence of the Artist as Woman* (1978), followed by Avriel Goldberger's translation of *Corinne, or Italy* (1987), has inspired feminist readers. After a series of major critical initiatives carried on by scholars such as Joan DeJean, Vivian Folkenflik, Charlotte Hogsett, Doris Kadish, Nancy K. Miller, Carla Peterson, Naomi Schor, Marie-Claire Vallois, and Margaret Waller, to name just a few, *Corinne* has become a crucial reference for women's studies, placed on undergraduate/ graduate reading lists.[1]

In response to a growing demand for a more comprehensive exploration tool of Staël's seminal work, the present collection features essays that scrutinize its problematics while providing students and teachers with an updated bibliography. A specific agenda governs the body of contributions prepared by internationally known Staëlians as well as a new generation of critics. Each of the three sections of the volume addresses the communicative, transactional qualities of *Corinne* in an attempt to answer the following sequence of questions: How does the aesthetic substance of the novel act upon readers to achieve the force of a manifesto for social change? How does the novel modify and extend the boundaries of the genre for political goals? What kind of textual/ideological transmutations does the novel bring forth into texts by other literary women? Ultimately, the volume demonstrates through its organization the performative power of Staël's fiction capable of influencing today's women who, almost two centuries after the novel's publication, still experience their own "days of Corinne."

17

The recent explosion of debate on Staël's novel coincides with the elaboration of the poetics of gender and the active search for new emancipatory strategies in language. Feminist critics have discovered in Staël's extraordinary fantasy of gender transgression a heuristic use of multivoicedness efficiently working against existential closure, against women's banishment to the borders of culture. As Corinne takes the stage, she is already an accomplished poet, writer, art critic, actress, translator, improviser, dancer, and speaker of foreign languages. With her access to multiple linguistic registers, Staël's heroine ostentatiously displays an unlimited desire and competence. What is more, in claiming her identity with a country—as the title *Corinne, or Italy* suggests—she invents a supplemental system of references which makes the splendor of meridional nature, Roman architecture, history, literature, and art reverberate to her own grandeur. As Madelyn Gutwirth explains in the introductory chapter, nineteenth-century readers identified the myth of Corinne as an unmistakably revolutionary act. Its cult of a feminine transcendence through art, posited as an aggressive counter-discourse at the very moment of Napoleon's acme of militaristic expansionism, fired up patriarchal criticism to battle the novel ferociously so as to diminish its literary status. Nonetheless, for female readers in France and abroad, Staël's heroine gained prestige as counterpart to "the Byronic hero" and, by analogy, to "Delacroix's (goddess) on the barricades." In violent contrast to the marginality of their own lives, Corinne's megalomaniacal aspirations resounded as a prophecy of intellectual emancipation and freedom.

The novel does more than illustrate gender difference as opposed to social reality. Today's critics, who espouse for feminist goals the Barthian concept of textual *jouissance* as well as Bakhtin's theory of dialogics, view Staël's pleasurable dimension and heterogeneity as symptomatic of feminine writing "in conflict, in conversation, and to some degree, in correspondence with the ideologies it is trying to dislodge."[2] By complicating the heroine's plot with an English lover, the guardian of restrictive patriarchal laws to whom Corinne is irrevocably related by past family ties, Staël structures the novel's narrative as a dialogic exchange which further decenters cultural hegemony. Consequently, the novel's textual energetics arise not only out of the economy of exchange invested in the equation Corinne or Italy, but from the relationship between the protagonists that produces a conversation—in the larger meaning of the word—between countries, cultures, styles, images, and ideologies. This crisscrossing of forces has appealed most of all to recent critics, who have produced extensive analytical material on *Corinne* as the locus of tensions and oscillations between self-assertion and self-regression.

The first section of the collection, "Transgressive Rhetorics of Desire," explores *Corinne*'s relational structure. The opening piece demonstrates how variations in linguistic patterns—in the first chapter of book 1 "Oswald" and the first chapter of book 2 "Corinne at the Capitol"—serve to differentiate the two lead characters while conveying the novel's thematic foci (Nancy Rogers). In the search for an ideal partner, Corinne ironically chooses a wrong supporter who, fearing feminine superiority, misinterprets her art and deserts her. The central antagonism between female desire and nihilizing patriarchal law reappears on many levels of the narrative. While the thematic/stylistic apparatus of poetic improvisations reveals a progressive reduction of the heroine's freedom and expansiveness (Vincent Whitman), the novel's sonorous background, with the interweaving of music and silence, participates in the dialogue between "life and death" (Simone Balayé). Even theatrical performances frame the struggle of gazes as the judgment of patriarchy confronts feminine playfulness (Nancy Miller). Finally, the novel can be read as a disintegration of the aesthetic of sensibility exemplified in Corinne's art by the aesthetic of faithful mimetic reproduction dear to her lover, not only in relation to painting but to the sociopolitical context of post-revolutionary France (Margaret Cohen). All the same, this variety of redundancies echoing the lethal attraction of patriarchy allows for negotiations and a potentially unlimited set of transgressions of gender-specific boundaries.

The second part, "Gender/Genre-Bending," shows Staël's reworking of the novelistic tradition. For years condemned to marginality, *Corinne* is finally valorized in and because of its provocative inadequacies. The text's massive antinovelistic discussions and descriptions seem to convey both a failure of the oral feminine tradition and the problematics of coming to writing. In what she considers as the "*mise en abyme* of the 150 years of the French novel's history," Joan DeJean perceives a revolutionary attempt to dramatize a lack of voice and the impossibility of female authorship in the patriarchal structure.

How then can *Corinne* be said to create a new framework of power for literary women? Reduced to silence, the female author shifts from autobiographical writing—used profusely by the male Romantics—to a curious archaeological form of travelogue where, according to Marie-Claire Vallois, she speaks without putting herself into the position of being called into question as a female subject. In her psychoanalytically informed essay, Vallois finds in *Corinne, or Italy* a displacement of the fictional "I" to a metaphorical double: a country where the stones and voices of the mother's land speak for the heroine. The same archaeological quest emerges as a work of cultural history that challenges the scientific historiography of Staël's time. As Nanette Le Coat argues, the analysis of an Italy densely inhabited by memories offers a modern epistemological perspective on the links between memory, imagination, and place. The category of *souvenirs de l'esprit* transmitting a historical knowledge as sensuous experience, as well as the category of *souvenirs du corps*—in which Corinne's gestures are a living embodiment of the land's traditions—point to a specific concept of history in accord with a feminine perception of human relations. The multilayered, permeable texture of the novel confirms a physical and psychological connectedness with ancient cultures.

Corinne is also a pioneering work of political sociology. After examining the several strands shaping Staëlian theory of the genre, Susan Tenenbaum demonstrates that Staël—who always regarded literature as a surrogate for other mechanisms of social control—has merged in the travelogue, literary theory with her preoccupation as a political theorist. By broadening the scope of a traditionally frivolous genre, Staël makes claims on behalf of her gender, for she sets the novel within a progressivist historiography that ascribes a critical role to women as agents of historical advancement. Drawing on Montesquieu's concept of *esprit général* as a product of the physical and moral causes of each society's unique character, Staël opposes her own pluralistic vision of national differences to Napoleon's imperialistic designs, and successfully articulates a manifesto for international understanding through cultural studies.

The third section, "Genie at Large," reestablishes the novel's distinctive place in the account of literature by women. The magnitude of Staël's influence has been documented in numerous studies on the affiliations with the Anglo-American followers who—while striving for public acceptance and literary fame— modeled their own lives on Staël's heroine or created Corinne- like characters (Jane Austen, Mary Godwin Shelley, Margaret Fuller, Charlotte Brontë, Fanny Kemble, George Eliot, Elizabeth

Barrett Browning, Elizabeth Stuart Phelps, Lydia Maria Child,
Willa Cather, Sarah Orne Jewett, Anna Jameson, among others).[3]
The new findings of this section not only confirm *Corinne*'s
disseminative powers but demonstrate how the issues fore-
grounded by Staël's work are still operative and open to the
future.

The first essay by Paola Giuli on the transient popularity of
Corilla Olimpica (1727–1800) and her crowning in Arcadia joins
the final piece on Marguerite Yourcenar (1903–87), the first female laureate accepted by the French Academy in its more than
350-year history. Charlotte Hogsett recalls the Arcadian incident
in the analysis of Yourcenar's reception speech at the Académie
in 1970, while providing new insights on the "anxiety of influence" phenomenon among women longing for recognition.

Essays devoted to precisely such textual affiliations constitute the core of the following section. April Alliston places
Staël's novel among women's fictions in formal terms. She demonstrates—from a structuralist perspective—that numerous
episodes, characters, and themes in *Corinne* involve direct revisions of *La Princesse de Clèves*. As seen by Alliston, Staël re-
reads La Fayette's seventeenth-century classic through the
earliest example of the English female Gothic, Sophia Lee's *The
Recess* (1783–85). Ellen Peel and Nonora Sweet enlarge the circle of mutual influences as they incorporate Elizabeth Barrett
Browning (1806–61), together with lesser known figures from
the British female canon: the poet Felicia Hemans (1793–1835)
and the cultural critic and novelist Maria Jane Jewsbury (1800–
33). Staël's figuration of a woman poet and the dialectics En-
gland/Italy gave all three writers an operational, critical
language, and structured their metaphoric systems to inscribe
gender and culture.

But how to explain extensive borrowings by a male author
who dominated the nineteenth-century American marketplace
and who deliberately tried to minimize and obscure the significance of Staël's novel? Quoting passages directly taken from *Corinne* by Nathaniel Hawthorne and embedded in *The Marble
Faun,* Katharine Rodier demonstrates that the concealment tactics (omissions and misspellings of Staël's name or names of her
characters), even as they question the authenticity of Staëlian
fiction, disclose Hawthorne's anxiety of female influence. In addition to the conflicting attitude toward *Corinne* and its author,
Rodier analyzes other possible sources for these curious appropriations: Margaret Fuller, "the Yankee Corinna"; Hawthorne's

own sister-in-law Elizabeth Palmer Peabody, who patterned her life after Staël; and his close acquaintance Elizabeth Barrett Browning, whose *Aurora Leigh* was being acclaimed as he began to plot *The Marble Faun*.

The depth of the ongoing response to *Corinne* points to another dimension of Staël's relational writing, that of a dynamic exchange between reader and text. The audience-oriented novel builds a framework of expectations while providing "inferential walks" through a flexible text that allows readers to reconsider the fictional world again and again. Staël's awareness of the audience grows out of her exceptional experience of the *salonnière*. From earliest youth, Louise Germaine used conversational brilliance to charm the best literary minds. Surrounded by the guests of her influential parents—Jacques Necker, Louis XVI's first finance minister, and Suzanne Curchod, the founder of an immensely successful salon—she would engage in verbal scrimmage and discovered the seductive powers of voice. Later, as a witness to the struggle for power in the context of the French Revolution, Staël was particularly interested in speech as it influenced historical events. Her numerous texts not only provide evidence of her involvement in politics, but also show how she masterfully transformed the art of the *salonnière* into an arm of political propaganda. The most striking characteristic of Staëlian persuasion is a reflexive structure with a speaker/hearer (writer/reader) relationship displayed directly. Recurring sequences of dialogue and direct appeals to interlocutors indicate that her texts are heavily discursive and take a specular form which, in Benveniste's terms, represents the "oral."[4]

Staël seems to perceive in these strategies an emancipatory potential, a modern rhetorical-responsive version of social constructionism. Whether she praises the debates of revolutionary clubs or her father's perlocutionary talents tested in the most threatening circumstances, she seeks to emphasize the political effectiveness of mediation. The works of the writers and intellectuals gathered about her in the multinational Group of Coppet best illustrate Staël's rejection of the politics of exclusion and her growing trust in the liberating force of polyphony. This cosmopolitan circle reunited and directed by Staël in Switzerland, where she created a citadel of resistance to Napoleon, would attempt to dismantle the Empire through the passionate intellectual transactions among its members and their exchanges with the external world.

A strong bond links Staël's social background to her successful performance as the novelist who found a militant praxis in acoustic structures. This embodied voice in the written text (not unheard by Staël's own contemporaries), a vibrating "grain of the voice" with an "immense halo" of resonances as Roland Barthes would have it, is what again intrigues readers. First, because of the phenomenon of orchestration and echoing. As Avriel Goldberger points out, the major challenge to the translator of *Corinne* lies in solving the problems of multiplicity of tones and voices.[5] Marie-Claire Vallois also detects in her inquiry into the work's archeology, not only a new critical category of the "authorial voice," as distinct from that of the narratee, but "diverse masquerades" of the myth of voice as understood in its different meanings: patriarchal, maternal, that of the past from beyond the grave, or the oracular, the voice of the future. In addition to this semantic opening, there is in *Corinne* a systematic effort to incorporate hearers as necessary to the speaker's articulation. This dynamic informs not only many scenes of staging and improvisation in which the heroine gives voice before a circle of admirers, but also Corinne's lengthy Roman walks with her preferred addressee, Lord Nelvil. To maintain Oswald's desire, the heroine lavishes upon him a host of stories of Italian art, just like the Arabian sultana Scheherazade, whose enchanting tales prolonged the orgy of voice over a thousand and one nights in an attempt to exorcize the danger of execution.

Furthermore, the novel denounces the incompetency of the interlocutor who ruins the authority of the performative discourse. Oswald looms as an abuser of words, an illusive performer whose rhetoric involves sequences of unkept promises. With a pleasure in scandal, the novelist exposes his tactics of distancing and has him reiterate the acts of desertion. Overwhelmed by a dread of insecurity and irritated by Corinne's talents, he leaves the places of public acclaim, retreats behind columns, and blends in with crowds. Even at the moments of most intense admiration, he repeats physical and emotional dismissal. Unable to decode an identity for the "sorceress alternately disquieting and reassuring," or to distinguish life from fiction, he literally collapses, "losing consciousness."[6]

This strategic demonstration of the nullity of the paradoxical mediator is inscribed in the work's main project: a call for a dynamic response from the audience *in absentia,* spectrally present in the narrative. In this seductive enterprise, the contextual rules that govern productive communication curiously intersect with a specifically female mode of knowing, "contextual rather than categorical," based on "cohering through human relations."[7] To recruit women's desires and interests, the novelist appeals to their innate qualities: a sense of continuity and connection to the world. "Those who are alike understand each other" because of uniquely female attributes: an ability for compassion and the narcissistic desire for identification. This textual mirroring builds a strong communication [*entente à distance*] which breaks frontiers of every sort to create an interwoven system of networks. Only in the situation of an ideological pact does the voice acquire an enigmatic physical power which "acts upon people even when they are unaware of it" and weakens old institutions and prejudices.[8] If we take into consideration that the common grounds determine the reader's ability to decode the text, and that this ability grows with the reader's political awareness, *Corinne* was conceived as a literary gamble addressed to future generations. The novel's readability today results from a prolonged saturation of its language in the anticipatory accents of social change which increased the force of Staël's message and enlarged its circle of respondents.

The essays in this collection thus illustrate the most fundamental imperative of Staël's theory of reception: a dynamic participation of addressees in the act of e-vocation (in the etymological meaning of the word), in which the author's voice must be taken up anew by readers and literally brought alive, amplified in every act of interpretation. Staël's novel teaches this transmission of power. In the instances of highly productive energies, the *improvisatrice* brings back to life generations of poets, writers, and thinkers: her voice—of distinctively public inspiration—gives the effect of being multiple and densely populated. Furthermore, the entire novel can be read as an orchestrated prosopopoeia in which Corinne's voice not only speaks for the abandoned and silenced heroines of the past, but is resurrected itself by a new generation of interlocutors, the wife and daughter of Lord Nelvil, who know how to preserve her feminine heritage.

Staël's demand for mediators able to understand and revive the text with an intellectual energy of their own has been generously fulfilled in the last half of this century. In Europe, Countess Jean de Pange and Simone Balayé, the latter now the leading Staël scholar and promoter of international research, have devoted their lives to the reassessment of Staël's works. In the 1985 Gallimard edition of *Corinne* and in her numerous publications,

Simone Balayé has exposed—with profound erudition—the novel's historical genesis, its Italianism and virtuosity in the use of the arts. On the other side of the Atlantic, Madelyn Gutwirth would reveal the feminist dimensions of Staëlian fiction, producing an outburst of creative readings. This volume's contributions, with their new critical perspectives, multiply *Corinne*'s communicative elements, proudly continuing the novel's effort of literary empowerment.

Seeing *Corinne* Afresh

MADELYN GUTWIRTH

Corinne's Second Coming

STAËL'S novel, as a political and aesthetic embodiment of freedom, remained powerful for most of the nineteenth century. Its heroine, together with her author, came to stand, as Hugo later did on his rock in exile, for the spirit of liberty banished from Napoleon's armed camp of a nation. The realm of the spirit that the Italy of the novel represented was for the Romantics the counter to the temporal realm's perversion of that spirit, and Italy gained thereby in prestige, becoming more and more, for the times, the poet's and the free man's *pays d'élection*. Lamartine, the Poet-Legislator, reflects the quintessential image Corinne and her creator imparted to the Romantic era, one that combined poetry and freedom into a single entity:

> Mme de Staël, a male genius in female form: a spirit tormented by the superabundance of its strength, mobile, passionate, bold, capable of generous and sudden resolve, unable to breathe in that atmosphere of cowardice and servitude, demanding space and air around her, drawing toward her as if by magnetic instinct all who felt a feeling of resistance or concentrated indignation fermenting within them; herself a living conspiracy.... Elite and exceptional creature the like of which nature has not given us a copy, uniting within herself Corinne and Mirabeau![1]

Yet it must be acknowledged that the present collection of essays ratifies an extraordinary resurrection. For although Germaine de Staël's reputation as a canonic literary figure has sustained itself into the twentieth century, she had nonetheless markedly lost ground since the end of the nineteenth century, particularly as a novelist, and more specifically, as author of the all-but-infamous *Corinne*. So much had this been the case that Albert Thibaudet could confidently affirm the novel's demise in 1936: "This work which now seems dead to us was one of the

26

most glorified of works in its time."[2] Thibaudet had nonetheless
to concede that Staël had wielded her very real power over people's minds more for her novels than for her works of ideas.
Delphine and *Corinne* had in fact enjoyed a success and a popularity that were, simply, immense. *Corinne* alone was published
in more than forty editions between 1807 and 1872, tapering
off only slowly after that time. However, critics at the nineteenth
century's end came to complain that Staël's fiction was simply
too time-bound to be deserving of our attention.

Since, as we notice in Lamartine's praise, the novels have been
interpreted almost exclusively as fictional projections of self,
Germaine de Staël's personal reputation has had a decided
influence upon that of her works, and vice versa. Especially is
this true of *Corinne,* which was so insidiously—and meretri-
ciously—identified with her person. And, as we can readily judge
by Lamartine's first phrase, much of the polemical criticism surrounding *Corinne* until this day has turned upon the vagaries
of definitions of gender through time: was the novelist, and what
was deemed her fictional surrogate "truly feminine;" or rather,
was she somehow aberrantly so, leaning rather to an unwelcome
"masculinity"? Those who did and do not deem her femininity
or that of her heroine as problematic read her without fear or
constraint and find in both a source of serious attention. Readers troubled by evidence of what they deem "masculinity" in
both life and work usually end up by viewing her as unnatural,
rebuking her along with "women of her sort," and dismissing
this "pretentious" and "inflated" novel's perversions.[3] In other
words, it is the war of the sexes that has made *Corinne* a critical
battleground. We distinguish this once more in Sainte-Beuve's
waspish comment:

> If I had a young friend to instruct with my experience, I would say
> to him: "Love a coquette, a grisette, a duchess. You will be able to
> tame her, subdue her. But if you are after any happiness in love at
> all, never love a muse. Where you think her heart is, you will find
> only her talent. Do not love Corinne,—and especially if she has not
> yet reached the Capitol; for then the Capitol is inside her, and on
> any pretext, on any subject at all, even the most intimate one, she'll
> mount it.[4]

For canonic masculine criticism, it has become an article of
common cause to mock and belittle Staël's achievement and her
creation in nakedly *ad feminam* terms. But, as we now see it,
this critical harassment, far from being occasioned by her fail-

ures as a woman and an artist, were rather occasioned by her
successes, and by her following among women: by an anxiety
that women might be fired to emulation by *Corinne*.

The Prophecy to Women

Lamartine's goddess of freedom, resembling Delacroix's on
the barricades, was a far cry from the frequently emotionally
torn and timorous Germaine de Staël, but she gives us a proper
measure of her potency as an emblem, both negative and positive, for her era. Of course, the fact that this symbol of liberation
was embodied in a demigoddess did not pass unnoticed by
women. Certainly it was they who read her novels most tirelessly
throughout their numerous printings. Between 1815 and 1845,
these volumes continued to be extremely popular, receiving
much notice from both critics and public. No other novelist in
France whose works were not currently appearing was the subject of as many articles during this spell. "*Corinne* was commonly recognized as superior to *Delphine,* and was coupled with
René as a lasting work of the Empire." It must be added that
"the space accorded Chateaubriand did not compare with that
given to Mme de Staël."[5]

In Sainte-Beuve's 1851 essay on the poet Delphine Gay, he
tells how in the 1820s this pretty young woman had had herself
posed and drawn as a muse, spoke of herself, and was incessantly
spoken of, as a "Corinne." "Mme de Staël's Corinne was then in
fact the great ideal of all celebrated women."[6] In the aftermath
of her pilgrimages to Rome and to the Miseno in 1827, Delphine
Gay made energetic but vain efforts to become France's national
occasional poet, writing verses on the deliberations of the Cham-
ber of Deputies and against the bloodthirsty General Cavaignac.
The great tragedienne, Rachel Félix, had herself painted by Delacroix in 1838 as *The Sibyl with the Golden Branch,* in a persona
resembling depictions of Staël as Corinne more than the actress
herself. If Rachel and Delphine Gay actually enacted such fantasies, we may only guess how many less noticeable readers of
Corinne quietly treasured this triumphant heroine, who formed
so violent a contrast with the women in the society they knew.
That they identified with Corinne's downfall as well is clear, for
did it not make more bearable their own toleration of their me-
diocre lives, to see this genius even more vulnerable than they?
But the impact of the popularity of *Corinne* lay in the visibly

inspiriting effect it had on their self-image. The powerful, seductive, and ephemeral heroine who had fled a living death to find
personal liberation was certainly for many of them the analogue
of the Byronic hero.

Perry Miller tells us that when "Isabel Hill's translation of
Corinne appeared in 1807" (the same year as its publication in
French), it "promptly became a troubling intrusion into all
Anglo-Saxon communities. It was perpetually denounced from
middle-class pulpits and assiduously read by middle-class
daughters in their chambers at night."[7] In 1824, Letitia Elizabeth Landon, a translator of Staël and a poet, published *The
Improvisatrice,* a long meditative narrative, relating a tale reminiscent of Staël's novel and imitative of Corinne's own improvisations, whose third stanza begins, "My power was but a woman's
power; / Yet in that great and glorious dower / Which Genius
gives, I had my part." Among Englishwomen, Corinne's influence
would persist, and Elizabeth Barrett Browning will be prodded
by it in her own creation of *Aurora Leigh* in midcentury,
whereas George Eliot, unable to ignore this vogue, would de-
nounce it as inappropriately self-centered in *The Mill on the
Floss.*

In the New England no less than in the old, or in Paris, Corinne's model became for many thinking women a new version
of female virtue, one linked to accomplishment. As Emerson
would put it, this model of the new woman embodying "tenderness, counsel," was one "before whom every mean thing is
ashamed—more variously gifted, wise, sportive, eloquent, who
seems to have learned all languages, Heaven knows when or
how."[8] This is how it came to pass that in the Boston of the
1840s it was observed that the disconcertingly brilliant Margaret
Fuller had some of the affected airs of a "Yankee Corinna." Fuller
would acknowledge this debt to the hilt, proclaiming that Mme
de Staël's intellect makes "the obscurest schoolhouse in New
England warmer and lighter to the little rugged girls who are
gathered together on its wooden benches."[9] Corinna was a figure
that a lively minded little girl like Margaret could warm to, showing her as she did the value of the life of the spirit in a heroic
woman. She would bypass the histrionic narcissism of this figure because she needed it, could use it to fabricate her own
identity as a being moving toward transcendence. As a creator,
like Staël, of self-aggrandizing fantasies, Fuller would also follow
her example: in one of her rhetorically expressive heroines Emerson detected "a new Corinna with a fervid Southern eloquence

that makes me wonder as often before how you fell into Massachusetts."[10] His intuition was solid, for in fact the South, with its tradition of eloquence, enjoyed an even more intense Corinne cult than the North, and more than a few Southern salons were presided over by a "Corinne."[11]

The cult of a feminine sensibility wedded to gifts and accomplishments could and did easily degenerate into a climate where sometimes pretentious coteries pursued the purely cultural goals of literate discussion or musical entertainment. Yet, at the same time, it certainly encouraged deeper forms of self-development in women, urging their minds and fingers to perform more arduous tasks, and lending greater prestige to their new skills and learning. What the examples of both the celebrated "Corinnes" and the unknown ones illustrate is the hunger of women for a heroic model from whom, despite their daily defeats, they might extract some vital strength.

The Corinne Myth

Beyond all question, *Corinne*'s publication in 1807 established Germaine de Staël's reputation: it was an act. Beyond all else that she wrote, this work consecrated the author's identity as an artist. And in composing it, she had wrung out of her spirit a new myth. But a myth, as Elizabeth Janeway has observed, if it is to deserve the name, must meet some ready collective understanding, and the Corinne myth stands radically apart from ordinary experience.[12]

The classic hero of monomyth "ventures forth from the world of common day into a region of supernatural wonder: fabulous forces are there encountered and a decisive victory is won: the hero comes back from this mysterious adventure with the power to bestow boons on his fellow man."[13] Such a heroine is the gifted Corinne who leaves England for Italy. Her mythic journey contains a sea journey (to England) and is marred by an encounter with a dark power that prevents her triumphant return from the "kingdom of dread." There could be no mythical resolution, however, in sacred marriage, nor through any ritual of father atonement in the myth of the free heroine, in contrast to that of the hero, as Staël saw. The errant daughter remains unwed and unforgiven. The sole remaining mythical ending possible is that of apotheosis. The gods must be seen to embrace what men are unable to comprehend, and Corinne is, at the last, acceptable to the heavens. Only by virtue of some such elevation by death could this myth be salvaged from chaos and some boon to humanity divined in its heroine's odyssey. According to Northrop Frye's formulation, the central myth of art is a quest for a vision of an end to social effort, an innocent world of fulfilled desires, a free human society. Corinne's Italy partakes of the nature of just such an earthly paradise, and its ethos bathes her apotheosis.

The Corinne myth is, then, not one of a dying god, but of a dying goddess, isolated and sacrificed by the order of the world. In lending her Corinne, as John Florio expressed it, all "three good things in a woman, the riches of Juno, the wisdome of Pallas, and the beautie of Venus," Staël also exploited her remarkable moment in history. The fall of the *ancien régime* momentarily toppled all institutions, including the Church. Into the breach caused by the abolition of the forms of faith, the Revolution, without recking what it did, threw goddess worship, as figures of Reason and Demeter replaced the dying God upon its altars.[14] As she saw all about her such embodiments in her own sex of divine attributes previously reserved, in their highest sanctity, to the other, Staël seized the occasion to posit a counter-patriarchal, feminine cult of transcendence through art. This is the revolutionary aspect of *Corinne*. Of course patriarchy had never really died, and in the nineteenth century, goddess worship, except that of Mary and Victoria, was soon banished.

Germaine de Staël did not scruple to capitalize on existing avatars of female power, alien as some of these might have been to her conception of female genius. In the eighteenth-century novel, woman, despite her ambiguous status, was often venerated as a "fecund power. She is Cybele, Pomona, Ceres, all the divinities of the harvest and of fruitfulness."[15] Staël, in her reconciliation between Corinne and Lucile, strove to blend the traditional, purely biological, nurturant powers of a Demeter, a Ceres, or a Mary with those of Athena, Persephone, Artemis, the wise and solitary virgins. The "virginal mother" Lucile is a solitary who learns wisdom, and her wise and gifted half-sister Corinne is generous, loving, and nurturant.

But Corinne, while incorporating the Demetrian myth of female sacrifice, also undermines it by railing, in a very modern spirit, against its murderousness. In *On Literature,* Staël had written some troubled paragraphs about the problematic of grandeur in women:

> The appearance of malevolence makes women, no matter how distinguished they may be, tremble. Courageous in misfortune, they are

timid in the face of enmity; thought exalts them, but their character remains weak and sensitive. Most of those women whose superior faculties have inspired in them a desire for fame resemble Herminia armed for the battle: warriors see the helmet, the lance, the radiant plumage; they think they are faced with force, and with the very first blow, they strike to the heart.[16]

Clearly, she attempts to mitigate any illusion of strength a woman may create by this insistence upon her vulnerability; nevertheless, it is Corinne's capacity to be strong, to be seer and poet, rather than her weakness that makes her unique. For Freud, femininity lay in a latent sexuality that only congress with the male could elicit. For Staël, femininity is a narcissistic polymorphous perversity feeding on both itself and others. It finds worth within, that can either be validated or deprived of validation by others. This is the stubbornly resisting core of *Corinne* that needs to be reckoned with.

We might choose to view this polymorphism of Corinne's, as has been so often done in the past—and has so insistently been the mode historically of dealing with the presence of *ego* in women, as "mere" narcissism. "At once priestess and idol, the narcissist soars haloed with glory through the eternal realm, and below the clouds creatures kneel in adoration; she is God wrapped in self-contemplation."[17] Simone de Beauvoir's characterization in some ways seems to fit the megalomaniacal aspect of Corinne all too well. There is no question that *Corinne* is a myth of female narcissism that any woman might offer herself passingly, of a magical ruling destiny of the spirit. Narcissism has been traditionally the sole licit form of female self-gratification, but what we have in *Corinne* is by no means sheer self-worship: it has a social dynamic. It is not merely an invitation from the woman to others to certify her charms; even more, it is the stance of the self-contained woman, expansively flaunting her charms and inviting the world to share in the pleasure she herself takes in her being. She arouses in others a heightened sense of themselves. Such is the Corinne of the Capitol.

The effect she creates is curiously paralleled in a highly stylized realization of the same form of eroticized female self-love by the early twentieth-century painter Florine Stettheimer, in a dramatic self-portrait. In it, the woman's magnetic power is supremely that of subject, not of object. Hilton Kramer described it as "ornamental and jewel-like, painted against an ice-

blue background, with the figure of the artist reclining with a
bouquet of flowers on a red couch. Everything is exaggerated
and outrageous—a little campy, a little bizarre, yet extremely
powerful in its pictorial effect."[18] Stettheimer the painter paints
herself as a dazzling palette: she adorns her art and is adorned
by it. Corinne is to her creator as the Florine of the portrait is
to the historical Stettheimer: a dream of self affirmed. A similar
campiness attaches to Florine as to Corinne, a parallel use of
the specific period vogues—here of the flapper, there of the goddess—in the search for a figure through which to assert more
fully a female personal force. And perhaps we may glimpse in
these magnifications of self an avatar of a specifically female
narcissism, distinct from the manifold forms it takes in the
male.

Of course, as Simone de Beauvoir admits, "when a woman
succeeds in producing good work, like Mme de Staël . . . the fact
is that she has not been exclusively absorbed in self-worship."[19]
What she has posited in *Corinne* is not only female self-love,
which is important enough, but a related female autonomy and
self-belief that actually allow the heroine to put her talents at
the service of her society. Corinne's condition, at the novel's
outset, is that remarkable state for any woman in the novel:
it is health. Like Beauvoir's intelligent hetaera (and here we
fully grasp the bond between woman's sexuality and her creativity) she resorts to "a more or less fully assimilated Nietz-
scheanism: . . . her own person seems to her a treasure, the mere
existence of which is a boon to humanity. . . . If she sets great
store by her renown, it is not for purely economic reasons—she
seeks in fame the apotheosis of her narcissism."[20]

When the Nietzschean impulse originates in a woman, it has
come automatically to appear ludicrous, and, during the reign
of masculine scorn for female aspiration, Corinne's has been
viewed as playing against our full acceptance of her destiny as
inherently tragic. "Destiny in the nineteenth century is princi-
pally male." In woman, greatness was then felt to be at the least
a social error, at worst a deep flaw, and the hypothesized greatness of a fictional female character by a female author has been
presumption twice over. The victorious woman has been "surrounded by a decor of illusion at once jewel box and prison."[21]

In spite of this seeming entrapment, in its very daring and
presumption, the myth of Corinne took hold and lived for the
nineteenth century. With the entirely transfigured outlook presented by this present collection, we see Staël's novelistic gamble
granted renewed life.

Part I
Transgressive Rhetorics of Desi

Undermining and Overloading: Presentational Style in *Corinne*

NANCY ROGERS

Few are the literary accolades for the style of Germaine de Staël's *Corinne*. Such vaunted nineteenth-century voices as Goethe and Sainte-Beuve complained of its monotony, and although Sainte-Beuve also admiringly referred to the novel as a *roman-poème, Corinne* has hardly been the object of praise for its literary language. Even its admirers, such as Ellen Moers, whose *Literary Women* did much to establish the novel as a masterwork for the elucidation of women's issues, wrote: "The prose of the novel seems to me to have all the flat-footed grace and dignity of some sprightly elephant." She calls it "The novel that Mme de Staël had the brilliance but not the talent to write."[1] Charlotte Hogsett, one of Staël's most recent defenders, while exploring the unity and coherence of Staël's work as a whole, at the same time finds her writing a frustrating challenge: "The reader struggles along, the feminist reader despairingly so, through pages of the style that Paul de Man so accurately said was characterized by 'banality, dissimulation, and self-serving sentimentality.'"[2] And even Madelyn Gutwirth, that graceful explicator of Staël's works, remarks that the author "often [leaves] us wandering in a field of prosey and cliché-ridden abstractions." Gutwirth also finds the dialogues in the novel often exhibiting a "static, frozen quality," and that there are "serious stylistic inconsistencies not altogether foreign to those of *Delphine*."[3] In short, according to almost two hundred years of literary criticism, the woman simply could not write novels.

Yet, discriminating readers usually do not flock to the prose of writers who cannot write. "[*Corinne*] is an immortal book, and deserves to be read three score and ten times—that is once every year in the age of man."[4] Thus proclaimed the young Elizabeth Barrett, who, like so many writers of her century, had her "days of Corinne," an admiring expression that Matthew Arnold attributed to George Sand, but which could represent an integral part of the cultural formation of many a nineteenth-century writer on either side of the Channel. Ellen Moers has traced the seminal influence that *Corinne*—its heroine, setting, themes, and set scenes—had on writers from the Brontës to George Eliot, Willa Cather, and Kate Chopin. These writers not only transposed Staël's characters into their own works but were struck by such exhilarating ideas as the spontaneity of art and love and the determining nature of regional or national cultural values and their effect on personal relationships. In addition, they must have felt the force of Staël's remarkable analytical perspicacity, her ability to understand the psychological natures of her characters, the forces and flaws in their personalities leading them to the inescapable conclusion of the novel. It is hard to believe that this "predecessor of those 'Silly Novels by Lady Novelists' which George Eliot so wittily demolished," as Ellen Moers terms *Corinne,* failed to attract and keep readers through its language as well as through its characters, plot, and ideas.[5] Can form and substance in *Corinne* possibly be as disparate and adrift from one another as has been charged?

Helmut Hatzfeld analyzed the style of one of the key passages of Staël's *On Germany,* in which poetry in France, which Staël finds "classical," is compared to that of other nations, which she sees as "popular." Hatzfeld finds that Staël uses a conservative vocabulary, avoiding neologisms, and determines a parallelism of structures in the passage, with a minimum of conjunctions, an abundance of superlative expressions, and sustained antitheses in the argumentation. Many of these observations are echoed in Danuté Harmon's doctoral dissertation, the only book-length study of Staël's style. Harmon maintains that the primary element of Staël's language is the coordinate structure of her sentences, carried out through the frequent use of *et* and *mais* and "basic to her dialectical thought process of thesis/antithesis/synthesis."[6] She examines other such stylistic aspects of the two novels as Staël's semantic preferences, verb structures, use of comparisons, and metaphors and similes, delineating patterns in the two novels. Yet, this study is curiously detached from the novels themselves, removing linguistic habits from artistic function. Or, stated another way, Harmon's observations and conclusions relate more to Germaine de Staël's mindset and ideology than to what Leo Spitzer referred to as the "philological circle," the circle of understanding or the literary center of a work or a writer's art.

In order to attempt to arrive at the "heart" of *Corinne,* those aspects of Staël's style that form the linguistic center of the work, and to help to determine its enormous appeal to nineteenth-century writers, especially women, we will focus on two key chapters of the novel—the first chapter of the first book ("Oswald") and the first chapter of book 2 ("Corinne at the Capitol"). The subject of the style of *Corinne* as a text is much too vast for an essay, especially given the different kinds of narrative structures—travelogue, epistolary, and poetic improvisation, for example—that give the novel its uniqueness. Yet, a comparison of these two chapters, in which Staël posits her hero and heroine, introducing her readers to the two poles of her narrative, around which the major events evolve and into whose inner beings she wishes to penetrate, should provide insight into how the patterns of language in *Corinne* interplay and resonate.

Joan DeJean has raised one of the crucial questions concerning *Corinne* as a novel: "Is *Corinne* an inaugural or a terminal text, a harbinger of the glorious nineteenth-century novel or a final exemplar of that novel's less glorified precursor tradition, the eighteenth-century novel?"[7] According to DeJean, the question is complicated by the fact that Staël, as a woman novelist at the beginning of the nineteenth century, was faced with a particular dilemma: whether to follow the model of the novels of the first women novelists, such as Madeleine de Scudéry, in which conversation is the starring method of discourse, or to be led down the narrative path of the "genealogical fictions" established by Rousseau's *Julie ou la Nouvelle Héloïse* and perfected by the male masters of nineteenth-century French prose. One aspect of the issue of the predictive or duplicative nature of the text is clearly that of lexical choice, and it is hard to ignore the abstract quality of Staël's nouns and adjectives, thus linking *Corinne* with the novels of the past. Madelyn Gutwirth has explored Madame de Staël's debt to Racine's *Phèdre* as well as the fact that the young Staël was "steeped in the neoclassical taste that informs the works of her time" and "permeated by Enlightenment *clarté.*"[8] And Lucia Omacini, in studying the reaction of Staël's contemporary critics to the style of her novels, demonstrates how Staël's "tics," or "overuse" of certain key abstract nouns, allow the author to accustom her reader to pay more attention to her ideas than to her words. She studies such abstract expressions as *vie, poésie,* and *enthousiasme* in the novels and shows that, far from being gratuitous, these expressions relate directly to Staël's intellectual and psychological universe and are a "positive contribution to the renewal of the language."[9]

The two chapters in which Staël introduces the major players in her novel are notable for the sheer number of nouns used, almost three hundred in the one presenting Oswald and nearly five hundred in that in which Corinne makes her appearance. Unlike her contemporary, Chateaubriand, who began to move the French novel toward concreteness and specificity in his descriptions, Staël chooses to present Oswald and Corinne primarily through nouns denoting psychological, emotional, or moral qualities. Chapter 1 ("Oswald") contains only three categories of nouns that can be considered concrete: those related to people, natural phenomena, and the ship on which Oswald is sailing to Italy. These three categories comprise only a small percentage of the total number of nouns (12%), most of which denote such intangible concepts as health and fortune. The absence of any concrete details about Oswald's appearance—we know nothing about him as a specific individual except his name, title, and financial status—leads the reader to focus attention directly upon his moral and psychological qualities. And what a mixed portrait Staël gives us: noble and spirited, but devastated and made ill by the loss of his father; generous to others, yet caring little for his own happiness; in short, a Wertherian hero, who, with his vacillations, tensions, and melancholia, looks forward to the passionate but lost characters of the "genealogical fictions" of the nineteenth century. It is interesting that the contradictions in Oswald's character are often conveyed through unmodified nouns, as in the following passage, in which such unadorned nouns are italicized:

Ce *contraste*, entièrement opposé aux *volontés* de la *nature*, qui met de l'*ensemble* et de la *gradation* dans le cours naturel des *choses*, jetait du *désordre* au *fond* de l'*âme* d'Oswald; mais ses manières extérieures avaient toujours beaucoup de *douceur* et d'*harmonie*, et sa *tristesse*, loin de lui donner de l'*humeur*, lui inspirait encore plus de *condescendance* et de *bonté* pour les autres.[10]

[This contradiction, entirely opposed to the will of nature which decrees consonance and gradual change as the natural order of things, threw the depths of Oswald's soul into disarray; yet his demeanor unfailingly showed gentleness and harmony, and his melancholy, far from putting him out of sorts, inspired still more sympathy and goodwill toward others.] (5)

This practice has the effect of foregrounding the nouns, forcing the reader to concentrate on Oswald's naked moral character; gentleness, sadness, good-naturedness, condescension, and goodness characterize him, along with a combination of disorder and harmony. One wonders what kind of woman would be able to withstand such a male, rife with internal contradictions. Proper nouns in the chapter, of which there are only sixteen, refer to the name of the hero (Oswald), his rank (Lord Nelvil), and place (Ecosse, Harwich), thus making these concepts central to the chapter and, indeed, to the novel. The chapter on Oswald also contains not a single concrete adjective, not even one of color, leaving Oswald in the gray, sad mists of vagueness. There are twice as many moral adjectives with a negative connotation (*cruelles, coupable, violent*) as there are those with a positive thrust (*active, glorieux, spontanée*), so that the first chapter of this novel produces an effect of negativity, thus introducing the reader to the dominant mode of the text. *Funeste* [deadly], which is one of the adjectives most often repeated in the work, with its connotations of fatality and sadness, is one of the few adjectives that Staël puts in the affective position, as in *la funeste imagination*, thus claiming its prominence in the very first chapter.

"Corinne at the Capitol" also contains a preponderance of abstract nouns (almost two-thirds), but only a small percentage of those refer to the emotions, most of which are positive (*reconnaissance, joie, triomphe*) in contrast to the negative nominal field in the chapter on Oswald. Staël is much more exact in her depiction of Corinne than in that of Oswald, using concrete nouns of place, parts of the body, and clothing; nouns of color, sometimes as adjectives (*cheveux du plus beau noir, tapis d'écarlate*); and nouns denoting specific aspects of the arts (*statues, tableaux, tragédie, vers*). Proper nouns referring to Corinne's famous predecessors, such as Petrarch, Tasso, and Sappho, establish the heroine's lofty, poetic lineage and countermand the absence of her own proper name. The famous introductory portrait of Corinne, as seen through Oswald's eyes, with her deep black hair, an Indian shawl artfully draped around her head, her white dress with a blue band below her breasts, dressed, in short, like a neoclassical sibyl, and carrying her statuesque frame like her Greek predecessors, allows the reader to envision this fascinating, compelling woman. The contrast with the blankness of Oswald's portraiture makes the reader wonder how this colorless, faceless Scotsman could ever presume to be the protector, as he instantly wishes to be, of the celebrated Corinne. For not only is Corinne presented by such adjectives as *supérieure* but the entire adjectival field of this chapter is positive, containing only one adjective that can be considered negative, and that one refers to a Roman man on the street whom Oswald sees as belonging to a *rang obscur.*

Another striking trait of the chapter introducing Corinne is the number of superlative expressions, such as *la femme la plus célèbre de l'Italie* [the most celebrated woman in Italy] and *l'une des plus belles personnes de Rome* [one of the most beautiful women in Rome], that relate to the heroine. In contrast, only one superlative appears in "Oswald," *la plus intime de toutes les douleurs* [the most personal of all griefs], which conveys one of the major negative traits of the male lead, his overwhelming and extreme grief at the death of his father. Corinne, however, is presented in the most glowing of terms, with her gorgeous hair and beautiful voice, *la plus touchante d'Italie* [the most moving in Italy]. Even those surrounding Corinne are afforded the highest degree of favor: her chosen escort, the prince Castel-Forte, is *le grand-seigneur romain le plus estimé* [the Roman lord most respected for . . .], and the women lined up within the Capitol to pay homage to her are *les plus distinguées* [the most eminent women]. Staël's determination to place her heroine at the very pinnacle of her novel and to give her favored status is carried out not only through such adjectival superlatives as those above but also through an extensive use of such intensifying expressions as *à chaque instant,* as in *à chaque instant on la nommait* [he heard her name on everyone's lips]; forms of *tout,* as in *tous disaient qu'on n'avait jamais écrit ni improvisé d'aussi beaux vers* [It was universally agreed that never before had anyone written or improvised such beautiful poetry]; and *chacun,* for example, *Chacun se mettait aux fenêtres pour la voir* [Everyone came forward to see her from their windows]. In this short chapter, there are twelve "true" and nineteen quasi-superlatives, so that both Oswald and the reader are prepared for an extraordinary woman by the time Corinne arrives on her chariot. It is telling that there is only one regular comparative expression in this chapter, implying that Corinne has no peers and can be spoken of in only the highest of terms. Further, it is especially revealing that this one comparison is made by Lord Nelvil, ironically, the only person who can bring Corinne down from the summit. As he listens to the exaltations offered to Corinne by the distinguished assembly of poets grouped in the

Capitol, he finds their description of her wanting: "... il lui semblait déjà qu'en la regardant il aurait fait à l'instant même un portrait d'elle plus vrai, plus juste, plus détaillé, un portrait enfin qui ne pût convenir qu'à Corinne" [... he thought that just by looking at her he could have done a portrait more accurate, true, and detailed, a portrait that would fit no one but Corinne]. Since Oswald's first responses to Corinne are admiration, tenderness, and the belief that she needs the protection of a male friend, his portrait of her would most likely be far different from the glorious one of the celebrated Corinne presented by the narrator. By refusing the poetic, written portraits sketched by the poets of Rome, which, by the way, are not conveyed to the reader, and contemplating the creation of one that is better, Oswald initiates the rejection of the power and truth of others' words that occurs with disastrous effects in the novel; as several critics have noted, the move to silence and away from language, both oral and written, is the path that Corinne follows in this novel. The rejection of the written portrait of Corinne by Oswald thus prefigures his rejection of Corinne herself, based on his interpretation of and reaction to her written "history" or "confession," the turning and determining event in the narrative.

Before leaving the matter of lexis in these two chapters, it should be noted that Staël uses comparatively few adverbs, most of which are neutral adverbs of manner or time. There is a distinct lack of vivid adverbs, especially in the chapter on Oswald, which contains only thirteen adverbs of any variety, and this lack contributes to the colorless nature of the portraiture. Verbs, as well, are essentially dull, and in the opening chapter are most often either static, *faire, dire, savoir,* etc., or variations of the copula (*être*). There are very few verbs of action, which is unusual given that this is a description of a voyage, yet many that relate to Oswald's inner state, such as *souffrir* and *attrister.* One is also struck by the number of reflexive verbs, which, of course, in most cases turn the action back upon the subject and remove a sense of activity from the prose.

The chapter on Corinne displays a more vivid verbal and adverbial field than the one on Oswald; there are more adverbs of manner (*sévèrement* and *énergiquement,* for example), more verbs of motion, and far fewer reflexive verbs and verbs of feeling. An important cluster of verbs in this chapter contains those of the senses—*voir, apercevoir, entendre, remarquer,* etc.—all relating to Oswald and his response to surrounding events. Germaine de Staël thus highlights Oswald's senses and readies him for his initial view of Corinne by having him first hear about her from an unnamed source, then little by little learn more about her superior qualities, listen to the music announcing her arrival, smell the perfumed air around her chariot, and, finally, just as his English reserve tells him to turn away, catch sight of Corinne herself and become captured forever. This deliberate, gradual overcoming of the distance between Corinne and Oswald, achieved primarily through verbs of the senses, enables the narrator to focus on Corinne through the vehicle of the hero, producing a portrait that is extremely positive, except for the one trait that will prevent Corinne from standing alone, Oswald's perception that she "avait imploré, par ses regards, la protection d'un ami, protection dont jamais une femme, quelque supérieure qu'elle soit, ne peut se passer" [had pleaded for the protection of a friend, a protection no woman can ever do without, however superior she may be].

To conclude our discussion of the semantic field in these two chapters, we must note the frequent instances of the copula and of verbs denoting mental actions (oublier, intéresser, devoir, etc.), which give the impression of two personages in stasis. This is especially unusual given the fact that Staël is introducing characters on the move, one on a sea voyage and the other being drawn in a chariot by four white horses. It is thus clear that even in these chapters of movement, the emphasis is on who Oswald and Corinne are, what they think, feel, and experience sensually, rather than on what they do or where they are going.

Staël is devoted to complex sentences, the thrust of which is most often carried forward through the coordinating conjunction et or the subordinating conjunction mais. Of the eighty-six sentences in the two chapters, only eight are simple in structure. However, it is interesting that both chapters open with simple sentences, the direct effects of which are highlighted by the many complex sentences to follow. The first, "Oswald lord Nelvil, pair d'Ecosse, partit d'Edimbourg pour se rendre en Italie pendant l'hiver de 1794 à 1795" [Oswald Lord Nelvil, a Scottish peer, left Edinburgh for Italy during the winter of 1794–1795], establishes the classic "who, when, and where" of a narrative event, leaving only the "what and why" to be discovered, and posits an impressive figure on a trip. The chapter presenting Corinne also opens with a simple sentence describing Oswald, a complement to the novel's opening, for the hero has reached his destination: "Oswald se réveilla à Rome" [Oswald awoke in Rome]. Both chapters thus open under the sign of the male, and the simple sentences focus our attention directly upon him. The only other simple sentence in the opening chapter is one of Staël's generalizing observations: "Il est si facile de se faire avec ses propres réflexions un mal irréparable!" [it is so easy to do oneself irreparable harm through private reflection], which is particularly interesting for the retention to the end of the sentence of the object of the verb, which would normally follow *se faire,* but which here becomes emphasized. The most striking simple sentence in "Corinne at the Capitol" is also the shortest: "Son nom de famille était ignoré" [Her last name was not known]. The importance of this sentence as a theme in the novel can hardly be overestimated.

By far the largest proportion of the sentences are straight narrative statements; only in the chapter entitled "Oswald" do we see the use of questions (three) and exclamations (six). Two of the questions reveal Oswald's inner thoughts and torments as he wrestles with his guilt concerning his relationship with his father. The third is a generalizing question posed by the narrator, which allows Staël to muse upon her hero's behavior: "mais quand on est capable de les [peines] ressentir, quel est le genre de vie qui peut en mettre à l'abri?" [Yet to a person capable of feeling such pain, what manner of life can offer refuge?]. Four of the exclamatory statements occur in Oswald's thoughts, including one after that popular romantic expression of despair so favored by George Sand, *Hélas!,* one in a generalizing maxim by the narrator, and one in the prayerlike wish of the sailors as they bid Oswald goodbye: "Mon cher seigneur, puissiez-vous être plus heureux!" [Kind sir, may you be happier one day!] These variations in narrative presentation, none of which occur in the chapter introducing Corinne, add to the extreme emotionality of the presentation of Oswald. That Staël does not give the reader insight into Corinne's inner being through reported thoughts, by its absence tends to present the heroine as a more straightforward and understandable character.

The most common type of sentence in these two chapters is compound and complex, depending primarily on the conjunctions *et* and *mais,* but also demonstrating more variation than many of Staël's critics have discerned, by the use of *bien que, quoique, puisque, cependant, non seulement ... mais, sans que, car,* and *comme si.* The typical Staëlian sentence in these chapters is loose in structure, a linear and direct kind of sentence in which the writer does not have rhetorical effect as her aim. In contrast to periodic sentence structure, in which the writer loads the beginning of the sentence with anticipatory constituents, which introduce an element of suspense and force the reader to decode the sentence, the loose sentence guides the reader through the use of trailing constituents, in a natural manner. Staël's sentences, while demonstrating this naturalness and directness, are extremely complex, weaving several ideas into their development. In fact, Jacques Barzun might almost have had Staël in mind when he wrote: "The complex form gives and withholds information, subordinates some ideas to others more important, coordinates those of equal weight, and ties into a neat package as many suggestions, modifiers, and asides as the mind can attend to in one stretch."[11] The complexity of Staël's sentences derives from such structures as appositives, participial phrases and clauses, and adverbial clauses. Staël favors, however, long sentences in which several ideas are separated by semicolons. Coordination and subordination are common in these sentences, which most often move in a steady progression to a concluding notion which is quite different from that at the beginning of the sentence. The longest sentence in the chapter on Oswald demonstrates well how Staël lays out and develops her thoughts. The sentence (which has been broken into two sentences by the translator), as outlined below, shows five distinct ideas, whose constituent parts (phrases and clauses) are here set on separate lines:

(1) Personne ne se montrait plus que lui complaisant
                                    et dévoué
        pour ses amis
        quand il pouvait leur rendre service;
(2) *mais* rien ne lui causait un sentiment
                                    de plaisir
        pas même le bien
                    qu'il faisait;
(3) il sacrifiait
            sans cesse
        et facilement
            ses goûts à ceux
            d'autrui;
(4) *mais* on ne pouvait expliquer
            par la générosité seule
            cette abnégation absolue
            de tout égoïsme;
(5) *et* l'on devait souvent l'attribuer
            au genre

de tristesse
qui ne lui permettait plus
de s'intéresser
à son propre sort. (28)

[No one could prove more available and devoted to his friends whenever he could be of help; yet nothing brought him pleasure. Time
and again he effortlessly sacrificed his own preferences to those
of others, but generosity alone could not explain such completely
disinterested abnegation; people were often inclined to ascribe it to
the kind of sadness that kept him from taking further interest in
his own fate.] (3–4)

It is immediately obvious that this is a superbly balanced sentence, opening with two clauses, the subjects of which are negative impersonal pronouns (*personne* and *rien*), placing the real
subject of the sentence (Oswald/*il*) in the middle clause, and
closing once again with two impersonal pronouns (*on* in both
cases). Here we see the typical Staëlian practice of subverting or
undercutting through her extensive use of subordinate clauses.
The first, or main/independent clause posits Oswald as a devoted
and helpful friend, supposedly the sign of a strong, healthy man;
this notion is immediately subverted by the fact that he receives
no pleasure from his actions. The third clause, a new independent one, continues the theme that there is actually something
wrong with Oswald, since he always sacrifices his desires to
those of others, a notion which is furthered by both the subordinate clause (4), which describes the wonderment of others at
this total abnegation of self, and by the final thought that people
attribute this extreme behavior to the kind of sadness that he
is experiencing. The movement from Oswald's generosity to the
feeling that there is something wrong in his psychological
makeup to the concluding notion of a lack of interest in his own
fate allows Staël to present a vacillating portrait of her hero, and
this she achieves in similar sentences throughout the chapter.

The longest sentence in the chapter on Corinne (which becomes three separate phrases in the translated version), while
equally complex, proceeds in a different manner.

(1) L'on voyait
dans sa manière
de saluer
et de remercier
pour les applaudissements

qu'elle recevait
une sorte
de naturel
qui relevait l'éclat
de la situation extraordinaire
dans laquelle elle se trouvait;
(2) elle donnait à la fois l'idée
d'une prêtresse
d'Apollon
qui s'avançait
vers le temple
du Soleil
et d'une femme parfaitement simple
dans les rapports habituels
de la vie;
(3) enfin tous ses mouvements avaient un charme
qui excitaient l'intérêt
et la curiosité,
l'étonnement
et l'affection. (52)

[Her way of greeting people, of thanking them for their applause, revealed a kind of naturalness in her that enhanced the splendor of her extraordinary position. She seemed at once a priestess of Apollo making her way toward the Temple of the Sun, and a woman perfectly simple in the ordinary relationships of life. Indeed in her every gesture there was a charm that aroused interest and curiosity, astonishment and affection.] (21)

Here, the complexity derives, not from subordinating conjunctions that undermine positive ideas, but through a piling up of prepositional phrases and relative clauses, all of which add to the glory of the portrait of Corinne. From the opinion of onlookers in the first clause to Corinne herself in the second and to her charming movements in the third, all elements of the sentence combine to demonstrate the extremely happy effects that the heroine has on those watching her. Although Staël's method of depicting Corinne through complex sentence structure most certainly changes as her heroine undergoes an extreme alteration in the course of the novel, it is important to note the differences in the way she uses complex sentence structure to introduce the two main characters in these opening chapters.

A noticeable lack in the sentence above describing Corinne is the conjunction *mais,* about which much has been written. As Madelyn Gutwirth states: "The language used is in fact very ordi-

nary, full of clichés and, as Goethe noted, of 'mais—buts,' thus
of qualifications," and Danuté Harmon quotes Sainte-Beuve on
the same topic.[12] Harmon herself devotes several pages to Staël's
use of *mais*, seeing it primarily as expressing opposition, and
thus upholding her contention that Staël's thought process, and,
by extension, her style, is basically dialectical. Harmon also
notes several instances of *mais* used in a declamatory or rhetorical sense, but she is convinced that the extensive use of *mais*
complements Staël's frequent use of *et* to link ideas in opposition, a style which she believes derives from "that of J.-J. Rousseau, who was often dialectical, as seen in his *Rêveries du
promeneur solitaire*."[13]

In these two chapters there are twenty-three instances of
mais used to link independent clauses, fourteen in "Oswald"
and nine in "Corinne at the Capitol." Those in the latter chapter
tend to uphold Harmon's contention that Staël uses *mais* primarily for contrast or opposition; for example, in the sentence
"L'émotion était générale; mais lord Nelvil ne la partageait point
encore ..." [There was universal emotion, but Lord Nelvil did
not yet share it in the slightest], Staël highlights Oswald's En-
glishness and his initial hesitation to respond positively to Corinne. The other way that Staël uses this conjunction in this
chapter is to add to or explain further an idea in the independent
clause, as in the following sentence, in which she explains why
even ordinary Italians admire Corinne:

> Oswald regarda l'homme qui parlait ainsi, et tout désignait en lui le
> rang le plus obscur de la société; mais, dans le midi, l'on se sert si
> naturellement des expressions les plus poétiques, qu'on dirait qu'el-
> les se puisent dans l'air et sont inspirées par le soleil. (51)

> [Oswald looked at the man who was speaking; everything about him
> suggested the humblest level of society; but in the south, people use
> such naturally poetic language that it seems to be snatched out of
> the air and inspired by the sun.] (21)

In the chapter introducing Oswald, however, the *mais* is almost
always negative in impact, as in the long sentence outlined
above. Most often the *mais* has a subverting effect and undermines the statement that precedes it, as does the first instance
in the novel: "Il avait une figure noble et belle, beaucoup d'esprit,
un grand nom, une fortune indépendante; mais sa santé était
altérée par un profond sentiment de peine." [Noble and hand-
some, he had a good mind, an important name, independent

means; but his health was impaired by a deep sense of affliction.]
This, the second sentence in the novel, could hardly be clearer
in its depiction of the author's view of the hero (and, by the way,
it is exceedingly difficult to separate Staël's voice from that of
the narrator in this novel); he is a fine fellow, except for one
thing: his grief has made him sick, both physically and psycho-
logically. One more example should suffice to show this subverting function of *mais*:

Il avait cependant un caractère mobile, sensible et passionné; il ré-
unissait tout ce qui peut entraîner les autres et soi-même; mais le
malheur et le repentir l'avaient rendu timide envers la destinée.(28)

[Yet his was a restless nature, sensitive and passionate, combining
all the qualities that might sweep others along, and himself as well;
but unhappiness and remorse had left him hesitant to confront
fate.] (4)

Staël sometimes uses *mais* in this chapter to explain a concept,
without the purpose of subverting; she does so in two instances
by beginning the sentence with the conjunction, as in this
example:

Oswald n'avait pas exprimé cependant une seule fois sa peine, et les
hommes d'une autre classe qui avaient fait le trajet avec lui ne lui
en avaient pas dit un mot. Mais les gens du peuple, à qui leurs
supérieurs se confient rarement, s'habituent à découvrir les sentiments autrement que par la parole. (31)

[Yet Oswald had not once expressed his grief, and those men of the
upper classes who had traveled with him had never said a word
about it. But the common people, in whom their superiors rarely
confide, are accustomed to discern feelings without the help of
speech.] (6)

And, finally, the above sentence also illustrates Staël's penchant
for using *mais* to introduce a generalizing statement in the present tense, which she does on three occasions in this chapter.
The following example demonstrates this usage and shows us
how Staël depends on *mais* to halt a preceding idea and to turn
the reader's attention to another concept, this time a musing
on "sensitive souls":"Lord Nelvil se flattait de quitter l'Ecosse
sans regret, puisqu'il y restait sans plaisir; mais ce n'est pas ainsi
qu'est faite la funeste imagination des âmes sensibles." [Lord

Nelvil imagined that he might leave Scotland without regret since he could not stay there with pleasure; but the funereal imaginings of sensitive souls are not so easily contained.]

The final striking stylistic category that we will consider is Staël's penchant for the generalizing statement or observation, which sometimes takes the form of the maxim so dear to the heart of her mother, Suzanne Necker, whose posthumous published works consisted of "those wise and inapplicable dictums."[14] Even though Staël never acknowledged her debt to her mother in formulating her own approach to the novel, it is clear that she had incorporated the need and ability to draw general conclusions from specific events, actions, or feelings into her narrative style. There are seven examples of the moralizing generalization in "Oswald," almost all of which reflect upon the behavior of the hero, as in, for example, "Quand on souffre, on se persuade aisément que l'on est coupable, et les violents chagrins portent le trouble jusque dans la conscience" [When people suffer, they are readily persuaded of their guilt, and violent sorrow unsettles conscience itself]. Here, the generalizing forms a separate sentence, but often there is a shift from narrative event to generalizing (and the accompanying present tense) within a sentence:

> Il espérait trouver dans le strict attachement à tous ses devoirs, et dans le renoncement aux jouissances vives, une garantie contre les peines qui déchirent l'âme ... ; mais quand on est capable de les ressentir, quel est le genre de vie qui peut en mettre à l'abri? (28)

> [Through a cheerless devotion to every duty, and renunciation of all intense pleasure, he hoped to ward off the anguish that rends the soul. ... Yet to a person capable of feeling such pain, what manner of life can offer refuge?] (4)

On the one hand, Staël usually uses the impersonal pronouns *on, il,* or *ce* to comment on the hero, as in "Il est si facile de se faire avec ses propres réflexions un mal irréparable!" [It is so easy to do oneself irreparable harm through private reflection!] or in the musings on sea voyages, "Il en coûte davantage pour quitter sa patrie quand il faut traverser la mer pour s'en éloigner" [It is much more painful to leave the land of your fathers behind if you must cross the sea]. On the other hand, she twice in this chapter makes specific subjects the topic of generalizations, as in her statement, cited above, on the sensitivities of *les gens du peuple* or her explanatory comment at the end of a sentence on

Oswald that *l'âme se mêle à tout* [the soul enters into everything we do]. In the chapter introducing Corinne, in vivid contrast, the generalizing comment is never directed at the heroine, but instead is used to explain or add details on such topics as the Italians' enthusiasm for the arts, the Romans' taste in art, the importance of music in arousing emotion, and the behavior of people in the *midi,* thus setting the heroine within the larger context of her society. Many complaints have been registered by critics that Staël's use of generalizing commentary in the "travelogue" sections of the novel, when the narrative voice often takes over from those of Oswald and Corinne to educate the reader about the beauties and treasures of Italy, leads to a stilted tone devoid of life. However, in the two chapters under consideration here, the moralizing, generalizing voice achieves what Staël meant for it to do, namely, convince the reader of the deeply reflective nature of her novel. These generalizing statements also allow the narrator to guide the thinking and reactions of the reader to Oswald as an individual and Corinne as an Italian artist, as well as to remind us that we are intended to draw lessons from the experience and personalities of these two characters. Like George Sand, thirty years later, Staël is determined to communicate directly with the reader, to share with her readers her ideas on how the world functions, with the obvious assumption that the reader will agree.

One stylistic trait that is notable by its very absence in these two chapters is the use of simile and metaphor to lend embellishment to the discourse. Such other figures of speech as phonological schemes (rhyme, alliteration, assonance, etc.) and other kinds of tropes are likewise missing as a dominant stylistic trait. This lack of rhetorical flourishes reinforces the grave, reflective aspect of this novel, thus linking it to the many ideological treatises of its author. It would be interesting to see if the same patterns hold for such treatises as *On Germany* (1810), for example.

This survey of Staël's presentational style in *Corinne* enables us to see how variations in linguistic patterns produce very different effects on the reader's responses to the two lead characters. The chapter on Oswald displays an intensely negative field of stylistic traits, conveyed most obviously through a vocabulary of pessimism, death, and melancholia, which predominates and lends a dark tone to the opening of the novel. The lack of specificity about Oswald's appearance and the concentration on his inner, moral qualities, which demonstrate a vacillation between action (helping others) and the inability to care for his own fate, add to the colorless, highly emotional, contradictory atmosphere of Oswald's character and his voyage. This milieu is abetted by the frequent use of the undermining conjunction *mais,* which enables the narrator to set up Oswald as an attractive, wealthy figure, but to show that in reality he is a man who is unable to control his destiny. And, finally, again as we have seen, the moralizing, generalizing voice utilized in this chapter serves to focus on Oswald's negative traits, his dark, intense, "romantic" qualities, which align him with the brooding male characters to come in the nineteenth-century novel.

Staël's introduction of Corinne, in contrast, derives from a very different cluster of stylistic traits, one which we might term overloading or elevating in thrust. Here, the emphasis is on the superiority of the heroine, conveyed through an extremely positive lexical field; of the adjectives that describe the emotional character of Corinne, all are positive. There are very few negative expressions of any kind in "Corinne at the Capitol," and, indeed, the extensive use of superlatives builds up the female lead so that she towers above all others so far introduced. There are no examples of undermining in this chapter, and the generalizing statements serve to elevate the heroine by focusing on the positive relationship between the Romans and the arts, at the center of which she stands. Sentence structure tends to derive its complexity from an accumulation or piling up of prepositional phrases and relative clauses that again serve to enhance the status of the heroine. The only clue to Corinne's downfall is Oswald's perception that she needs someone to protect her, a contention that at this stage we (the readers) dismiss, coming, as it does, from a character who is in no way the equal of Corinne.

There is no doubt that Germaine de Staël was a writer of high seriousness in *Corinne,* one who was committed to telling the tale of the destruction of the woman of genius in a reflective, captivating manner. Her style is thus straightforward and lacking in rhetorical excess, and she varies the patterns of her language, as we have seen, so that her two main characters are presented in quite different fashions. This provides at least a partial explanation of why so many readers, among them some of the most discerning writers of the nineteenth century, were entranced by *Corinne.* For in this novel, despite its too frequent coincidences, the somewhat stilted character of the dialogue, and the intrusion of its pedagogical aspects, two compelling personages are created. The pessimistic, vacillating, Byronic Oswald appealed to the emerging Romantic sensibility. His doubt, disenchantment, interior tensions, and dark nature made him a fascinating figure, especially in contrast to the larger-than-life Corinne, who, like her creator, seems to have one foot firmly planted in the preceding centuries. This neoclassical poetess, mythologized and eulogized, is shown as linked to the past through her artistic lineage and her Sibyl-like traits. Yet, Oswald's reaction to her—that she needs to be protected, that is, dominated—shows the crack in her facade and relates her to Sand's Lélia, a fully Romantic poetic woman of genius who is also destroyed by male passion. In sum, who in her Romantic mind could stop turning the pages of this novel after meeting the dark Oswald and the bright Corinne? The thoughtful, serious nature of Staël's style makes this love story seem of supreme importance, as indeed it proved to be in the development of the novel, especially by women writers.

Laurence Porter has seen a maturation of Germaine de Staël's "thought and style" between *On Literature* (1800) "where her thought is rationalistic, categorizing, and deductive," and *On Germany* (1810), "where her thought has become inductive, impressionistic, and intuitive."[15] *Corinne,* written between the two, shows itself to be on the cusp between classicism and romanticism. This is especially true in the introduction of the two main characters, the Romantic Oswald and the neoclassical Corinne with the inner flaw which will open her to the contradictions, imperfections, and instability of Romantic heroines. In DeJean's terms, then, is *Corinne* "an inaugural or a terminal text?" Our survey of presentational style would lead to a conclusion that *Corinne* partakes of both. With its abstract vocabulary and natural, rational sentence structure, it looks backward, but its haunting Romantic sensibility, the clear relationship between ideas and feelings that it displays, and the nature of its characters, mired in the mysteries of their pasts, propels it to a central, dominating position in the future of the novel, as Romanticism looks forward to Modernism. It is no wonder that the tremors of passion unleashed by this work have caused almost two centuries of readers to experience their own "days of Corinne."

"Remember My Verse Sometimes":
Corinne's Three Songs

Vincent Whitman

WHAT becomes of the protagonist's public speech over the course of *Corinne, or Italy* doubles the trajectory of her personal history. The three public readings of her verse mark stages in a process that begins in popular acclaim and acknowledged cultural influence, and ends in isolation, despair, and premature death; that moves from a triumphant improvisation at the Capitol to a surrogated farewell to her public (and her life) from behind a veil at the Academy of Florence. The primary themes of these oral performances coincide, as to be expected, with the Romantically sweeping themes of the novel itself: history, nature, genius, passion, death. The transformations that occur (on both levels) in the relationships among these themes trace a history in which the progressive attenuation of the protagonist's originally free, expansive, authoritative, and public literary discourse mirrors her physical and psychological disintegration.

The First Song

Corinne first appears at the ceremony and improvisation at the Capitol, where she epitomizes the popular artist/performer. Her talent is recognized and honored. She is lauded in Prince Castel-Forte's introduction as a powerful cultural presence, whose superb artistry, being so particularly the product of Italy and so concerned with national themes, reflects glory of the nation as a whole. The acclaim that precedes Corinne's performance certifies the force of her genius before we hear her utter a word. In fact, Avriel H. Goldberger, in the introduction to her translation of the novel, maintains that in light of such grand claims, "Staël was unwise to give us Corinne's improvisations instead of merely suggesting them." As Staël was not herself a brilliant poet, Goldberger continues, "the author could only fail in attempts to demonstrate her heroine's genius," with the result that "Corinne may at times seem more pretentious than great, and even too good to be true."[1] Goldberger's point is well taken: the "improvisations" themselves, as literary performances, as lyrical texts that must stand or fall on their own merits, do not bear the weight of inspiration and genius imputed to them within the narrative.[2] The populace's adulation of Corinne, the Prince's extravagant paean to her talent, her coronation as poet laureate following her performance: What do we find in the texts themselves to justify such anticipation and response?

One can reply that Staël has managed to give us the texts of the improvisations and to suggest them at the same time. Firstly, these representations are inseparable from our imaginative construction of their performative context, including the large adoring audience, Corinne's visual impression on them (her stage presence), and the music with which she accompanies her spoken song. And more importantly, the improvisations aren't rendered in verse at all but as prose paragraphs that can convey only the literal import of the (nonexistent) poetry, bereft of its imputed musicality (including the unique music Corinne claims for Italian itself), its metrical regularity and energy, etc.[3] Staël's suggestion, then, is that something crucial to the effectiveness of the performance has been lost in translation (both from poetry to prose and from Italian to French), something the reader must supply imaginatively. It is a strategy that perhaps asks us to suspend disbelief much too willingly, and one that begs the question of Corinne's improvisatory brilliance in the same gesture that claims it: This poetry is so sublime it can't even be translated, the narrator says to the reader; take my word(s) for it. But what alternative does Staël have to this rather shifty solution to such a seemingly intractable narrative problem, short of avoiding representation of the improvisations altogether? Although these texts are certainly not instances of poetic genius, a closer look at them reveals how they effectively signify Corinne's distinctive genius nonetheless.

Corinne's spontaneity of invention is fundamental to that genius.[4] As *improvisatrice,* she becomes inspired literally on demand: "*The Glory and Bliss of Italy!* cried those around her in one voice" (26). Obviously, her art requires that she be physically present to her audience. She cannot absent herself from her text because her text is both embodied and evanescent—it comes into and goes out of existence at the same moment. Hers is above all an art of presence. To elaborate on Staël's suggestion, then, any representation of Corinne's improvisation—even if it were great poetry—is bound to be problematical to the point of self-contradiction, a textual arresting of an essentially ephemeral utterance, the sign of authorial absence not quite able to disguise itself as an authorial presence.

Nevertheless, Staël finds ways to suggest the fictional fact of Corinne's powerful presence in the text of the first improvisation. It appears to move as we imagine such extemporaneous compositions must: by a free association of ideas rather than the rigorously structured logic of a predeliberated, worked and reworked written text; and by the accretion of elements that stand as approximately equal in importance rather than the subordinative embedding of elements in a hierarchy of importance. Certainly the various thematic sections are interrelated, but they are deployed by accumulation; there is apparently no comprehensive structure, premeditated or otherwise, into which they are extemporaneously fitted. Corinne's public meditation on "the glory and bliss of Italy" begins with the political glory of the Golden Age, moves forward to the intellectual and artistic achievements of the Renaissance, backward to the Middle Ages and an extended section on Dante, back (forward in time, that is) to the Renaissance and Tasso, Petrarch and other artists and thinkers, on to a section praising Italy's climate and natural beauty, from there to a section on the simple and moderate pleasures of the Italian people, back to the comforting and restorative influence of nature, and then to a pause in the performance.

To say that the discourse drifts is close to fair, but to call it aimless or formless is not. Rather, it flows with remarkable ease and latitude, is freely recursive in both thematic movement and reference to history. It is anything but fragmented or disjunctive. Thematic transitions are unobtrusive, even left implicit at times, but the speaker is continuously weaving the thematic threads, often returning easily in a new context to a topic that had seemingly been left behind. Italian political history merges with the history of Italian genius: "Imagination restored the universe [Italy] had lost"; "In Dante, Italy came back to life in all her power" (27). Genius is in turn stimulated by history: "[Petrarch's] country inspired him better than Laura herself. . . . Working far into the night, he called antiquity back to life" (28). Genius is also vitalized by nature: "Our serene air, our smiling climate inspired Ariosto"; "Artists, scholars, philosophers: you are . . . children of the sun which in turn broadens the imagination, quickens thought, excites courage" (29). And nature mitigates the traumas of history: "Elsewhere, when social upheaval afflicts a land, the people doubtless feel abandoned by the divine powers. But here, we always feel the protection of heaven, we see that it cares about man" (29).

The thematic interweaving continues after the pause. "Struck by [Oswald's] air of sadness," Corinne introduces a new theme and works it into the fabric of her improvisation. Mortality, and the individual's oppressive knowledge of it, is related to the history motif: "Here the ruins . . . the empty places, leave vast spaces for the ghosts to walk"; "All these wonders are monuments to the dead. . . . [T]hey endure and we pass on" (30). She relates the new theme also to the genius motif: "[G]enius is itself numbered among the illustrious dead" (31). Finally, Corinne (hoping to console Oswald) links the themes of death and nature: "The southern peoples picture death in less somber colors than those who dwell in the north. Like glory, the sun warms even the tomb"; "Under this beautiful sky, frightened spirits are less hounded by the chill and solitude of the grave" (31). Despite the eventual appearance of the death theme, Corinne's first improvisation is exuberantly optimistic and celebrates the manifold forms of life in history (especially the abiding presence of the past), art, and nature. Even the thought of death is mitigated by the replete and harmonious vitality of the present moment.

The accretive development of the first song is itself an instance of the productive energies the song celebrates thematically, and its multiplicity of theme and abundance of historical reference constitute an additional, if implied, theme. The song produces the effect of multitude, of being densely populated, with its crowd of poets, thinkers, citizens, and ghosts. Corinne's voice gives the effect of being multiple as well. She speaks not only for but as the whole city.[5] The voice is not in the usual sense of the word impersonal—it is not at all cold or passionless—but under the influence of the distinctively public inspiration that informs Corinne's performance, she appears, as in her experience of certain moments of conversation, to transcend her individual identity:

At times the interest lifts me beyond my own powers, brings me to discover in nature and in my own heart bold truths and language full of life that solitary thought would not have brought into being. . . . I sense full well that what is speaking within me has a value beyond myself. (45)

We can identify an important quality of Corinne's genius in this passage without necessarily crediting its hinted Romantic mysticism: She possesses an expansiveness of sensibility that enables identification with diverse modes of experience, and this empathetic capability is reflected in both the form and content of her art.

This capacity is of course grounded in the particulars of Corinne's history. Her voice is more-than-one not only because she speaks for/as a whole society, but because her identity is culturally dual in the first place. Corinne is Italy, but she is also England, as we learn when her secret is revealed. She is both: South-and-North. This duality helps account for a public and self-sufficient lifestyle exceptional even for Italian society. Corinne is free because she is different, not only from others but within herself. No one person, institution, or even culture can claim her exclusively because she slips out of the categories that must provide the basis for such a claim. Her allegiances can therefore be virtually universal.

During the period between Corinne's first and second improvisations (approximately the first half of the novel), she is completely aware of her increasing emotional dependence on Oswald—and its damaging effects—but is curiously unable to overcome it. "[T]o feel dominated by a single affection as I do can be rewarding only in private life," she tells him. "Loving you as I do does me great harm. I need my talents, my mind, my imagination to sustain the brilliance of the life I have adopted" (90). That *singleness* constitutes the danger above all, and Corinne clearly understands the threat in particular to the public aspect of her life, so crucial to her identity. Oswald's influence is eroding the multiplicity of her engagement with the world, and her protest shows that she apprehends his desire to take her out of circulation altogether. Oswald became conscious of this desire immediately after Corinne's improvisation at the Capitol, when he betrayed his narcissistic wish to reduce the manifold objects of her enthusiasm to a single one: "He wondered if it were possible to be loved by her, to have concentrated on oneself alone such diverse beams of light" (38–39).[6] His jealousy of her public success is revealed at several points during this period, the ardent reaction to Corinne's tarantella provoking a good example: "Well Corinne, what homage, what success! But among all those men who worship you so enthusiastically, is there *one* brave and reliable friend? Is there a lifelong protector?" (93; emphasis added).[7]

We find a model of the sort of mate Oswald has in mind in the segment of Nelvil Sr.'s reflections given in the first chapter of book 8. She is the "faithful wife" who, "according to the laws of nature . . . first among [her husband's] loved ones, must follow him" in death; whose dying husband is "this being who was your all" (137).[8] Although this fragmentary text and Corinne's first improvisation cannot be judged by the same criteria, the two do share a meditative, reflective function, and the differences between them are instructive. Not only is Nelvil's text essentially monothematic—concerned exclusively with "the last days of the sensitive man"—the notion of singularity is privileged throughout. The apostrophe to "[u]nknown communities of God's creatures . . . scattered across the firmament" seems to signify a remarkable openness to the diversity of forms "human" consciousness may take; but that multiplicity is ultimately reduced to homage to the Father, who is the focus of "interests common to all intelligent and sentient beings, whatever the places and distances that separate them" (136). Yet few can attain to the singularity of attention and devotion Nelvil idealizes. "Where," he asks, "is the man who has loved God single-mindedly?" The persistent reiteration of the question indicates that the fragment is really about exclusion rather than inclusion, and ultimately about absence: "If he exists," we should certainly honor that man, but the repeated interrogative, unanswered, suggests that he does not, or that if he does he is not present, and finally that if he is present he will not be for long. He tells his wife and children that they "will go alone now, alone in a world from which [he] shall disappear" (138). The text is itself the mark of his absence.

The Second Song

Oswald tells Corinne his story on their way to Naples, and after hearing it she knows that upon the disclosure of her own he will abandon her; not just because of the past connection between them, but because his story demonstrates how willing he is to sacrifice his own and others' happiness to the Law of the Father, as codified in the grim northern version of social and filial duty. He carries with him at all times a reminder of that duty in the text of his father's reflections, in particular the fragments given in the second chapter of book 12 (229–230). The theme of the first fragment in this section is familiar and appears unobjectionable: Honor thy father and mother. But its message is actually more restricted: Honor them in anticipation of their disappearance. Honor when the time of disappearance itself comes; defer to the authority of their absence, of the "by-gone reign" that nevertheless persists, or should persist, into the present. The child's social choices and relationships, "the small arrangements of private life," should be based on "the science of the past." To "live entirely in the present moment . . . confined there by a dominating passion" is the root of filial error (229). Everything extraneous to that passion the child dismisses as "old-fashioned and antiquated." But such presentness is mistaken. No moment is unique, for "[t]he vast theater of the world does not change actors. . . . [M]an is not renewed; he is simply variable" (229). What has already passed describes a closed circle into which all supposedly immediate experience is displaced. The disappearance of the parents leads ultimately to their transfigured reappearance and the simultaneous disappearance of the present moment, of the moment's presence. For, if the memory of their virtues persists, as the father promises and the text ensures, "next to the vivid colors we use to paint their blessed halo, we would find ourselves obliterated in the very midst of our golden days" (230).

Corinne, reading these reflections to Oswald, is able to discover an internal countertext to this argument for the rule of the absent, one that acknowledges the need for "making allowances in the realm of the social virtues" (230). But this appeal by the father for tolerance is based on his insistence that immediate experience is fundamentally deceptive. The senses participate in this deception, in which "the imagination leads us astray with false glimmers." Multiple sensations, thoughts, possibilities conflict with one another and confuse the subject: "So many dangers . . . so many interests . . . so many unknowns." Tolerance is finally a function of the universal inability to withstand the chaos of the present moment. "[W]here is the man who is blameless" in the face of it? (230). The question is asked and has to be answered within another sort of closed circle: The man "who has never dwelt in the solitude of his own conscience" is not even aware of the question. Only the man who is able to absent himself from the immediate present can hear the question at all and try to answer it.

Corinne knows the operation of the law of duty through its effects on the women of the Edgermond household, including herself, while she resided there. Duty apparently entails the denial of one's own happiness, conformity to stifling social mores, and single-minded devotion to the colorless script English society has reserved for women. Corinne's emotional state as she commences her second improvisation is conditioned by these considerations (and by the fact that she has given Oswald the text of her own story, having elicited his promise to wait eight days before reading it). However, upon beginning her performance "[s]he tried to contain her distress and, for a moment at least, rise above her personal situation" (231). This intention is a useful frame through which to read the second song.

The basic thematic categories of this improvisation are the same as those of the first, but Corinne's attitude toward them—and so her treatment of them—has undergone a remarkable transformation, as have the relations of the themes to each other. Her first utterance, the designation of her themes in relation to the site, hints at this change: "Nature, poetry, and history challenge each other for grandeur in this place" (241). Ostensibly, her list merely figures and praises the beauty and historical significance of the site. But the sentence also suggests a struggle of which the first improvisation was innocent. The beginning of the song at the Capitol was concerned with the nation's historical vicissitudes, but nature, history, and art all combined to produce "the glory and bliss of Italy." Here, these categories are introduced as engaged in a struggle for mastery. We might read this contest simply as a conventional rhetorical device were it not that the idea of struggle permeates the entire second song.

In contrast to Corinne's treatment of the nature theme in the first improvisation (a contrast partly but not entirely attributable to the difference in location), the "smiling climate" gives way to a scene of violent and terrifying natural forces. In the first song, for example, Rome's climate inspires Ariosto's poetry, but here Lake Avernus inspires the legends of the rivers of hell.[9] In place of a natural world that comforts and heals, we find one that rages and horrifies: "The heavy element heaved up by the tremors of the abyss hollows out valleys, raises mountains, and its petrified waves bear witness to the tempests tearing its womb apart" (242). The analogy to the violent turbulence of human passions emerges explicitly in the next stanza.

With the apostrophe to "memory, noble power," the theme shifts to history, but again from a perspective far removed from that of the first improvisation, where the past was a source of comfort and spiritual sustenance. Here it primarily signifies what has been lost "across the centuries," and in particular for the loss of well-being: "It would seem that times gone by are, each in turn, repositories of a bygone happiness. . . . [O]ur souls seem to long for a former homeland that the past brings closer" (242); that is, brings closer but never fully recovers, never transforms into a presence.

The nature theme returns briefly in conjunction with the history motif, but in a way that echoes the idea of struggle for mastery. The Romans who came to the area "hollowed mountains to tear columns from them. The masters of the world, slaves in their turn, subjugated nature as a consolation for their own subjugation" (242). The anguish of Corinne's own situation comprises the subtext of this transformation to powerlessness, and the image suggests that Corinne, who was once in the position of master—crowned by her fellow citizens, in control of her destiny—is, as the narrator tells us earlier, becoming "increasingly enslaved by her love for Oswald" (90). It also suggests that by this subjugation Oswald compensates for his own to the Law of the Father.

In the stanzas that follow, Corinne reflects, as she frequently did in the first song, on the lives of well-known historical figures. But here they are political figures instead of artists: Cicero, Scipio, Marius, Tiberius, Nero. And the unifying principle is displacement/exile—with its attendant themes of crime, persecution, and death—rather than national glory. The idea of exile is acutely pertinent to Corinne's own situation. She is by choice and temperament an exile from her English fatherland. Now because of her growing dependence on Oswald she faces spiritual exile from her readopted Italian motherland as well. (Later, of course, she fails in a desperate attempt to repatriate to England.) The prospect of being left entirely homeless figures importantly in the second half of the improvisation.

As Corinne contemplates the landscape in which these ancient tragedies occurred, history merges once again with nature: "The islands brought forth from the sea by volcanoes were used . . . for the crimes of the old world. The unfortunate people banished to these solitary rocks . . . gazed from afar at the land of their fathers" (243). The first section concludes with an impassioned apostrophe to mother nature, a cry for the reappearance

of the nurturing and consoling element of the first improvisation: "O! earth all bathed in blood and tears, thou hast never
ceased producing both fruit and flowers! Hast thou no pity for
man? And does his dust return to thy womb without making it
shudder?" (243).

As she did at the Capitol, Corinne now pauses, but the contrast
between the two interruptions is revealing: "impassioned applause" suspended the first performance. During the ensuing
pause, she determined to respond to Oswald's sorrow when she
resumed. Here, she interrupts herself, or at least the inter-
rupting forces come from within. The audience is silent as Corinne "reflect[s] on the enchanting scenes around her" and on
"Oswald who was there and who might not be there forever"
(244). At the Capitol, the object of Corinne's attention during
the pause was Oswald's grief; here she communes with her own.

When the improvisation resumes, the narrator tells us (since
the "translation" cannot register the shift), the verse assumes
unprecedented form: "[N]o longer dividing her song into octaves,
she gave way to verses without the usual intervals" (244). Thus,
the midpoint of the middle song marks a change in Corinne's
art from a conventional form to one much more idiosyncratic.
The octave form was of the public domain, and so appropriate
to the communal emotions voiced by Corinne as "Italy." As her
poetic discourse becomes more an expression of private sorrow—although by analogy to national history at this point—
the conventional structure becomes inadequate; these private
emotions must develop their own forms. Thus, though the first
improvisation is marked by an internal break, it is not split
formally as the second is.

The subject of the improvisation following the break is personal indeed: the suffering of historically prominent women
faced with dislocation and (sometimes violent) separation from
the men they love. Corinne speaks "[s]ome memories of the
heart, some names of women" (244)—Agrippina, Porcia, Cornelia. This section introduces a new kind of history into Corinne's
art, one with which she can identify not as the spokeswoman
of a national culture but as a woman convinced that she is destined to share these women's experiences of loss and exile.

Corinne views Sorrento, thinks of Tasso's sister, and then of
Tasso, who "deranged with suffering" came to his sister "to ask
refuge from princely injustice . . . nothing left but his genius"
(244). In the stanzas that follow, Corinne suggests that genius,
once the source of her extraordinary happiness, has become the

source of her extraordinary suffering: not just that great souls suffer greatly but that eventually the great artist's prodigious talent cuts her off from the companionship available to the less gifted, from the possibility of feeling at home in the world, and even from nature itself: "Thus talent, appalled by the wilderness all around, wanders through the universe without finding anything like itself. Nature provides it no echo" (245). The theme of dislocation returns in a new context: "[D]oes not fate pursue exalted souls . . . ? They are exiles from some other region." Corinne continues in this vein "with ever heightening emotion" until, overcome, she faints (245). The final stanza is so agonized, in fact, it is less performance than an outpouring of grief so overwhelming that it removes her from her audience completely (as she has just said genius is removed from the quotidian).

In contrast to the gracious, audience-pleasing reference to scripture that closes the first song, the second ends with terrible abruptness, sounds truncated. And although the geographical features referred to in the improvisation are visible (present) to the artist and audience, not only is the song largely about absence (separation, exile, the isolation of genius, death), Corinne is simply not as emotionally present, with the audience, as she was at the Capitol. She appears to become more alone with her feelings as the song progresses, appears to be speaking only for and even to herself. And finally, this improvisation does not operate through an accretion of approximately equal elements to anywhere near the degree the first one does. An associative train of ideas, free movement from topic to topic, and recursion of familiar themes in new contexts propel this song also. But the intensity of Corinne's despair forces her invention into a channel that flows predominately in a single direction, toward the topos of her private sorrow. It has also subordinated all the song's themes to the overriding one of absence (a cluster comprising exile, separation, and isolation). "The glory and bliss of Italy" was putatively a controlling theme also, but one that allowed virtually unrestricted expansion of creative impulse, diversity of subject matter, and accumulation of equally valued detail. Corinne's new theme does not.

The Last Song

The disasters that occur between the second improvisation and the last need not be recounted here. They precipitate Corinne's physical and psychological decline, her withdrawal from public life, and her loss of ability "to compose as she once did" (368). The catastrophe itself appears to hinge on a series of misunderstandings and missed connections while Corinne is in Scotland. These mechanisms are rather disappointing—the tragic effects do not seem inevitable outcomes of such incredibly accidental causes. If, however, we regard Oswald's obsession with his dead father's wishes as the underlying cause of Corinne's ruin, the catastrophe appears absolutely inevitable. The contest between Oswald's desire for Corinne and his desire to remain obedient to paternal authority is decided conclusively by his father's letter to Lord Edgermond rejecting Corinne as an acceptable mate for Oswald and electing Lucile. Once Oswald reads it, the "absent Corinne" sees that the struggle is hopeless: "She had to fight against the nature of things, the influence of the native land, a father's memory" (331). Oswald's letters to her get briefer, avoid discussion of the couple's future, and eventually betray his resentment of her as the cause of his own unhappiness (335). The mischances in Scotland may function as the immediate cause of Oswald's marriage to Lucile, but after he has read his father's letter he is irretrievably disposed to that choice anyway.

In the second segment of her improvisation at Naples, Corinne voiced only part of the truth when she suggested that her genius was the cause of her suffering. To be extraordinarily talented is always dangerous, but to be as extraordinarily—and as publicly—talented a woman as Corinne threatens disruption of the patriarchal order. Nelvil Sr. affirms as much when he rejects her as a possible mate for his son:

> [S]uch unusual talents must necessarily arouse the desire to develop them, and I do not know what theater would be broad enough for the active mind, the impetuous imagination—for the passionate character, in short, perceptible in her every word. . . . [I]n countries whose political institutions give men honorable occasions to act and prove themselves, women should remain in the background. (329)

The northern "theater" is too narrow to contain Corinne's talent, especially the multiplicity of her talent. She poses a danger to the social institution, to "those prejudices, if you will, that bind us together and make of our nation one body." Nelvil Sr.'s immediate fear is that her "foreign ways" will make Oswald unhappy and lead to his expatriation (329). But more than that, her genius is excessive, threatens to overflow the boundaries of the patriarchal order. The letter to Lord Edgermond is a mechanism devised to bar her from the social structure Nelvil Sr. is convinced her "unusual talents" would destabilize. It is in effect a legal document pleading the case for that exclusion, and its structure is the strict logic of a formal petition: an appeal to the good will of the court, testimony concerning the characters of the parties involved, exposition of the applicable principle of law, a warning of the harm that would follow were the petition denied, and a description of the good that would follow were the petition granted. In its content the letter is an instrument for the enforcement of patriarchal law against a transgressing subject; in its mechanical, closed structure it stands in opposition to Corinne's inclusive and expansive first improvisation.

When Corinne was at the height of her powers, her improvisations were a function of her multiplicity as speaking subject, of her capacity for detachment from any single claim on her allegiance to the degree that she could be artistically engaged on her own terms with the many, fully present yet unabsorbed. By the end of the novel that multiplicity is reduced to a single, attenuated "beam" focused, as Oswald had hoped, on him alone (though he is now absent to her, even at the end when he attends the last song). The audience for Corinne's final performance is "immense," but the song is really for Oswald alone.[10] And she has now been absorbed almost to the point of disappearing altogether. She appears more a specter of her former self than a living woman. She is veiled; she does not (cannot) speak.

She has, however, produced a text that can be spoken for her by another (as eventually Juliette [even Lucile?] will speak fragments of Corinne's text). The themes that populated her previous songs are here, but the transformation that began at the Capitol when she adapted her improvisation to Oswald's sorrow is almost complete. An energetic accretion of diverse poetic elements is out of the question, as every element is subordinated to the theme she introduced for Oswald's sake into her first song. History is now a private history of the injuries and losses that will end soon in death. Though Corinne has made frequent poetic use of the past in her previous songs, now the references are not to names from Italian history but to the past tense of her own glory and bliss: "You have allowed me glory"; "What confidence nature and life inspired in me of old! I believed that all misfortune came from not thinking enough, from not feeling enough" (416). Genius is now indistinguishable from an extraordinary capacity for suffering: "My genius, if it still survives, can be sensed only through the strength of my sorrow." And everything in nature has come to signify her imminent disappearance. Although she does not frame the following passage in the first person, Corinne clearly speaks of herself, and in fact her surrogate speaks it *to* her as to the audience:

> If the wind murmurs, you seem to hear [the angel of death's] voice. At nightfall, great shadows in the countryside are like folds in his trailing robe. At noonday, when those possessed of life see only a calm sky, feel only the beautiful sun, he who is claimed by the angel of death glimpses in the distance a cloud that will soon screen all of nature from his eyes. (417)

What has become of Corinne's literary discourse is the result not of some intrinsic conflict or infirmity, but of the enforcement of patriarchal authority at the site of her public voice. This does not argue that her final text has become *like* Nelvil's. It is different from that as well as from her previous songs: it is the product of the contractive operation of patriarchal law upon an expansive and multiply engaged poetic sensibility. We do find, however, traces of a Nelvilian infection in the last song. As in Nelvil's reflections on death, the poet points to her impending departure, projects the listener into that future, and makes that absence appear a present fact:

> [I]f I win a few tears more, if I still believe that I am loved, it is because I am going to disappear. . . . When spring returns, remember how I loved her beauty, how many times I praised her air and her perfumes! Remember my verse sometimes, for it is marked with my soul. (417)

Within the world of Corinne, this song differs from the first two because it is not ephemeral, a sound that comes into and goes out of being with the moment. This one has at terrible cost been frozen into permanence. Paradoxically, just this arresting revives the threat of the voice's slipping the constraints of patriarchal law. By its very attenuation the voice bears the mark of—re-presents and reproduces—its original power as surely as it bears the mark—shows the wounds—of its suppression. In the trajectory of Corinne's songs, Staël has led us to this imagination: Disembodied, the last of the three will remain in that world, an indictment—beyond overt accusation—of the violent forces that transform a poetry of presence into the signs of absence.

Plotting with Music and Sound in *Corinne*

Simone Balayé

Mme de Staël's ideas concerning music, her tastes, her sensibility, have been studied, but there is more to be said.[1] We would have to tie all these elements to each other and illustrate what links them to literature and other forms of art, to ethics, religion, and to politics in Staël's thought overall. In this far more modest study, I chose to take as my point of departure not the author but her two great novels, *Delphine* and *Corinne,* to seek out the function music plays in them. But I was forced by the facts to recognize it would be impossible to treat them together, because music plays so dissimilar a role in each of them: consequently they could not be studied using the same method.

In *Delphine* Mme de Staël accords music no privileged role; it would be false to say she reduces it to being a mere accessory to the worldly life of Paris. Music emerges as it is integrated into the heroine's sensibility at some moments in the story; it underlines emotional states; it is the "mysterious language" that conveys "indefinable emotions," happiness in love, and waves of dreaminess and melancholy; it expresses the depth of sentiment, and sometimes provokes it. It assumes also that function of recollection dear to Mme de Staël from her youth.[2] When times of pain arrive, music, which has invoked joy and love will evoke only suffering; if it recalls past happiness, it is only to render the present all the more painful, even to the point of itself being experienced as intolerable.

But the greater riches of *Delphine* lie elsewhere. Music doesn't possess the symbolic breadth in it that it will achieve in *Corinne.* A mere walk-on in the first novel, by the second it comes to emblematize the protagonists and their story. We can trace *Corinne*'s dramatic trajectory through its use of music and sound: to illustrate this, we must follow the novel's narrative line to show the enrichment brought to each phase of it by music.

The novel opens upon the voyage Oswald, Lord Nelvil has undertaken from Scotland to Italy. This hero is given to us as a distillate of mourning, solitude, and indifference to the surrounding world, which has lost all reality for him. He lends his attention to no external object, attending only to the sorrow that has eaten at him since his father's death. His life no longer matters to him, and so he accomplishes exploits of the most gratuitous foolhardiness. His relations to others are characterized by devotion, by small favors, even by sometimes heroic acts. Thus he organizes the fight against the fire that nearly destroys Ancona and throws himself into the flames to save those who have been abandoned in their several prisons, the Jews, the criminals, the mad, carrying out his task with great courage, yet somehow without being fully present in these deeds. This fire is a complex episode which marks Nelvil's true entry into the novel strikingly, before Corinne's triumphant appearance in it. The catastrophe is portrayed in its forms, its color, and its movement, and on the auditory level, through Oswald's voice, dominating the tumult, floating over the sailors' cries and the crowd's, their prayers, their broken sentences. The fire itself, described in its color, light, and dynamism, yet remains mute like the hero, neither crackling nor roaring with the vital energy of flame, but, in imitation of Oswald, imbued with disaster.[3] From the start of the book, this non-music of the fire will symbolize misfortune and death, destruction, silence. Only "the voices of nature," the rustle of the wind, the murmur of the waves will do "his heart some good." Thus music does not enter the novel with him. Rather, it frightens him.[4]

Once all has returned to good order in Ancona, Oswald resumes his travels, blessed and admired by all, once more embraced by silence, throwing aside the chatter of the Count d'Erfeuil, the companion chance has given him. And so his trip to Rome continues, lifeless and sad. He sees nothing and nothing is shown us through his eyes. "His imagination, concentrated on his sorrows, could not yet find pleasure in nature's delights or art's masterpieces" (46). Arriving in the city on an evening of gray skies, he awakens next morning to heavens blue and filled with brilliant sunlight.

Then tumult erupts as bells toll and cannons roar. Outside, amidst the joyful noises, Corinne's name flies about; that famed poetess in whose name the coronation of Petrarch at the Capitol is to be repeated. Oswald, intrigued and curious, hears the music that precedes the heroine's processional. She appears in her triumphal chariot as at a Renaissance festivity: a beauty combining fame, grace, and simplicity; she is music and poetry, as Prince

Castel-Forte affirms in the eulogy he presents to her.[5] Then follows Corinne's celebrated improvisation, accompanying herself upon the lyre of the poets of antiquity, as she draws from her instrument "touching and prolonged sounds" (65). At the very moment when she is crowned with the laurel wreath, we hear one of "those triumphal strains that magnify the soul in such a powerful, sublime fashion" (68) that it evokes tears even from the one for whom it is played.[6]

In contrast to Oswald in the catastrophe at Ancona, a foreigner in the midst of a terrified throng, Corinne appears as the queen of the festival, saluted by an entire people who recognize themselves in her, just as she recognizes herself in them. Oswald has not lifted his eyes from her; all is described through him for the first time: until this moment, nothing had been described from his point of view. At the ceremony's end, the protagonists' eyes meet. He even dares to speak to her.[7] The parade, as it reconstitutes itself, separates them and then it disappears. Oswald, as evening falls, walks about alone: astonished and bewildered, without knowing how he got there, he finds himself at the bridge of Saint Angelo.

In place of the brilliance of festivity we have silence; the sun's light gives way to the moon's rays, illumining "the Tiber's pale waves." Statues become "white shadows staring at the passing waves and at time, which no longer concerns them" (69). Oswald, after his momentary encounter with joy, is returned to his original silence and solitude. In this way, the contrast between the protagonists is underscored, symbolizing, among other elements, silence and music in turn, in the first two sections of the novel.

However, Corinne, having noticed the garments of mourning worn by the Scottish lord and surmising his suffering, has fashioned her improvisation so as to associate Italy's consolatory power with her account of its beauties and glories. Herein we find the first sign of the heroine's ambiguity. She is at once Italian and English; we will later learn, when Lord Nelvil himself does, that she has fled England, that is, its judgments and its order, for fantasy; its moral rigor for permissiveness. This double and problematic origin, which is the source of her plenitude, at once connects her to Oswald and alienates her from him. She can understand him, but the reverse is not the case: this will be reflected throughout the novel, in the slightest difference of opinion, as well as in their ways of experiencing one another's character and comportment. We see her, at once constant and changeable, living in the present and not at all in the future, troubled by what she sees of Oswald's inner conflicts. He is himself torn between his desires and his duty, all the more so for having once before betrayed his father and his country for the sake of a foreign woman. Music, a nonspeech, is perhaps the sole mode in which they may both comprehend one another and, often, feel reconciled, beyond words.

Oswald settles down in Rome in Corinne's company, which soon becomes a need for him. He knows nothing of her past and witnesses her peaceful life among her friends, surrounded by all that can embellish existence: letters, art, and friendship.[8] Around her the atmosphere is all music. She sings, plays that harp whose sounds, during Oswald's first visit to her, had filled up a troubled moment of silence. In her garden at Tivoli, the spontaneous strains of Aeolian harps resound, harmonies which seem born of the scents of flowers and of branches quivering in the winds, a music which feeds ceaselessly upon itself and so well emblematizes the poet-improviser (230–31).[9]

This is a time of repose in the novel during which Corinne initiates the man who has begun to love her to the beauty of Rome. In all of its ruins and tombs, the glory of its memories and the mediocrity of its present, Rome allows us a glimpse of the grandeur of hope through the voice of its Sibyl. The lovers' walks take place in a city which appears ever silent: Saint Peter's, solitary and contemplative; palaces deserted; gardens immobile (98–106); and a mood of abandonment everywhere. Corinne shows Oswald what speaks most to their souls, in an attempt to demonstrate how much they resemble one another, despite appearances.

Only the murmuring of the waters can sometimes be heard. In the novel, the sea, the lapping of waves, rivers, fountains, the tumult of waterfalls, all are so many pretexts for considering the passage of time and of the generations, images of the infinite, of life and death. Often Corinne and Oswald watch the Tiber flow noiselessly in its livid, funereal course, concealing, as is believed, ancient treasures in its waters, an image of Rome long gone and promised to its rebirth.

One night, Corinne, soon joined by Oswald, stops at the Trevi Fountain, before that "abundant spring cascading in Rome's midst, appearing like life in this tranquil place"; its murmuring is like "the necessary accompaniment to the dreamy existence led there" (125). In its pool that evening the faces of the lovers are momentarily reflected together; the fountain symbolizes the power of vital instinct; but the reflection dances in waters flowing toward death and separation: a union merely fugitive in the present, already condemned.[10]

During Holy Week, in the course of his solitary walks, Oswald will find other fountains and spaces where life seems doomed: the fountain of the convent of Saint-Bonaventure, on the Palatine, flows soundlessly into a child's tomb (book 10, chapter i). The one in Carthusian cloister, between black cypresses, is a thread of water "one scarcely hears, so slow and feeble is its gushing: one might rightly say that just such a water clock perfectly suits this solitude where time makes so little noise" (256).

Corinne always finds life intermixed with death; whereas Oswald, immersed in himself, finds only death. This is the trap into which he will end up leading the brilliant and vulnerable heroine. The whole of the novel is apparent in this murmuring of waters.

On their very first outing Corinne has led Lord Nelvil to the fountains of Saint Peter's Square, eternally spouting and murmuring in their unchanging stony form, strong and vigorous as the colonnade surrounding them. They are a vital force, like the Trevi, but instead of presaging a sentimental episode, they suggest to Corinne some reflections of an aesthetic order, occasioned by their harmony with the feeling "that a majestic temple arouses in us" (101). The "murmur of the waves" and the sheets of water are linked with the architecture of the square. "A beautiful architectural monument has no . . . precise meaning; and in seeing it, we are possessed by that unformed and aimless dream state that takes our minds so far away. The sounds of water flowing accords with all unformed and deep impressions; they are unvarying as the edifice is ordered; 'Eternal movement and eternal rest' are thus brought together" (101–2). A bit further on, architecture will be compared with "music continuous and fixed" (103), a transposition of that metaphor of "frozen music" that had so struck Mme de Staël in Germany in 1803.[11]

Here we seize how Corinne's reflection assimilates two languages of art which, according to her, owe nothing to nature and in no way imitate it. What is more, they allow one a free range of reverie, from which no moral idea nor any other kind emerges.[12] One might posit that for her the highest arts are music, and then at a lower degree, architecture, because they are the most abstract ones, the only ones that allow thought its fullest freedom, imposing no specific direction at all upon it. This becomes more evident in subsequent conversations and episodes. But it is important that this should appear here, in the conversation in which Corinne initiates Oswald to the beauties of the arts of Italy; what she has to say concerning music and architecture shows how she detaches them from any idea of utility, a concept so dear to Oswald on the planes of religion and ethics, instead thinking of them in terms only of their beauties, purely and gratuitously. Corinne can understand and even share Oswald's viewpoint, while yet remaining no less the defender of art for art's sake, and this becomes a conflict between them, adding one more to all the others.[13]

A fresh conflict erupts between Corinne and Oswald on the occasion of a ball in a Roman palace. The first to arrive, alone and melancholic, he listens to "this dance music which, like all music, makes one dreamy, even if it seems designed only to evoke joy" (146). In this book we often find such rapprochements of festivity and sadness. Corinne appears, brilliant in all her youth and beauty. During the ball she dances a tarantella with the Duke of Amalfi. This dance, like the polonaise performed by Delphine, is not merely a graceful apparition, destined to present her in a favorable light to her lover's sight. Corinne makes manifest her creative imagination in it; as she combines the resources of music, poetry, and the visual arts, she brings "into being a mass of new ideas for drawing and painting."[14] In the "passionate joy" of the dance she "would transmit into her spectators' souls what she felt, just as if she had improvised, played on the lyre, or sketched some forms; all was language to her." She electrifies "the witnesses of this magical dance" and transports them "into an ideal existence, where we dream of a happiness not of this world" (148).

"The exactitude and suppleness of motion," or at other moments its vivacity, express the sensuality of music (148). The man, as victor, first circles around the kneeling woman, and then the roles are reversed as the woman rises: it is then she who dances, triumphant, around him. Corinne lends herself to the voluptuousness of popular dance, so close to primitive instinct, and with her gifts raises it to a level of true art, without freezing it or depriving it of life. The tarantella ends in a rage of joy. Oswald, moved like the others, yet cannot applaud it, discontented as he is with the approval given this woman he wants to keep to himself, in the depths of a Scottish castle. It must be observed that the two parts of the dance are inverted from those of the novel: it is Corinne who will have first circled victoriously about the smitten Oswald, entreating and rebellious; but it is he who will rise up and bring death through his own triumph.

The two are reconciled after a fairly lively quarrel.[15] Their outings are followed by innumerable political and literary discussions that often enough uncover their fundamental differences. Music, opera, and ballet have their place in these conversations, but on this terrain the privileged interlocutor is the Count d'Erfeuil, so that musical criticism fills a lesser role than does music itself in delineating the divergences of sentiment of the protagonists. This is even more true of its relation to the plot.

Ever since coming to Rome, Oswald has been unable to surmount the sadness that assails him when he hears music. To listen to Corinne's song is mostly a matter of contemplating her, "but, if, in the streets of an evening several voices were raised . . . to sing some beautiful strains of the great masters, he would first attempt to stay and listen; then he would wander off, because an emotion at once so searing and so inchoate would restore all his sorrows" (246). Nevertheless, he consents to go to a concert with Corinne.

At her arrival, the laureled poetess is recognized and acclaimed; the musicians salute her with those "fanfares of victory," which make her relive the emotions of her triumph (246). Oswald, jealous of her successes which for him always raise a barrier between them, retires to the back of their loge. Once the concert begins, they are separated. Thereupon follow some reflections about the music, and we are at first uncertain if these come from Corinne or if they are the author's speaking in her stead before moving on to concentrate the reader's attention on the characters. It is possible here, as in other places in the novel, that the reactions sketched in are fundamentally hers. Does Mme de Staël succeed in truly detaching herself from her characters so that they take on their own life? This problem is one we might be tempted to resolve by studying the points of view of the protagonists, of the implied author, and, distinct from the latter, Mme de Staël's own. Perhaps hers is a personality too sensitive, too unquiet to forget itself, to commit—as Jean Starobinski used to say—"literary suicide," the total sacrifice of self that produces a masterpiece; but a failed masterpiece can still be a book abundant with riches.

"Of all the arts," she tells us here, music "is the one that acts most immediately upon the soul" (224–25). The others direct it to one idea or another; it alone addresses the intimate source of being, and entirely alters its internal order. Architecture, a reflection of music, enjoys no similar power. And neither do painting or sculpture, since in seeking to represent something, they limit reverie and guide thought instead of liberating it. "Painting could never content itself with anything as imprecise and musing as sound, since it gives itself wholly in a moment" (225).[16]

Music, quite to the contrary, unfolds itself in time, as a fleeting pleasure that escapes, even as we feel it, leaving behind "a melancholy impression . . . ; the regularity of beat, recalling the briefness of time, calls up the need to take our pleasures in it" (248).[17] It creates a feeling of plenitude: "There is no longer any silence around us, life is full, the blood pumps quickly. . . . We feel within ourselves that impetus that active existence grants us, and so we no longer have to fear those obstacles it encounters in the world outside" (248).

Until this point, we've seen how music would accompany love and reverie, evoking sensuality; it has pointed to the need to enjoy the passing moment and life itself. We see it arousing nostalgia. Here, there is much more to it: a being reaches out to a happiness freed from earthly contingencies because, at its core, it has encountered its creator. Music acts like prayer, as an intercessor between man and God. "What people say of divine grace which has power to transform the heart all of a sudden can apply, humanly speaking, to the power of melody; and among presentiments of a life to come, those born of music are not among those that should most be disdained" (247–48).[18]

There is but one power that equals music: that of the glance. "The look of someone beloved, concentrated upon you and so penetrating your heart that you end by lowering your eyes from so great a happiness: this gleam from another life might engulf any mortal who would stare at it fixedly" (249).[19] The effects of music can be as searing as those of too great a love, of the glance of the beloved, or as unbearable as God's glance. This secondary meaning can easily be glimpsed beneath the primary meaning of this ambiguous text. The course of the concert will prolong the intensity of the lovers' joy. Perfectly attuned, the duet with two voices will bring to their souls "a delectably gentle feeling . . . which could not persist without becoming painful: such well-being is too much for the human frame: it is then that the soul vibrates like an instrument playing in unison that too perfect a harmony would shatter" (249).

This solitary meditation may well take place in Corinne's mind; it is symbolic of a love that devastates through the very excess of joy it bestows; it presages the destruction of its earthly existence and its rebirth in God; in this way, the life cycle comes into play: that of the destruction and rebirth we find at the book's ending.

Italian music is given as an emanation or representation of Corinne herself and the enchantment she holds for Oswald.[20] In it lies the very soul of the heroine, Oswald's initiator not only to the beauties of earthly arts, but through them to another world. Art becomes God made manifest on earth, a means of communication with Him, a prayer answered. Oswald grasps Corinne's gravity and the depth of her thinking and feeling. A "deep emotion" pervades them, "that is magnified with every moment that passes" (250). This concert, begun in disunion, ends in a communion of human and divine love.

With the approach of Holy Week, as Corinne prepares to go into retreat, Oswald falls once again into his original void, out of which she alone, at moments, can draw him. Away from her, he cannot bear the pleasure art bestows.[21] Neither can he stomach worldly company or excessively theatrical religious ceremonies or absurd sermons. The popular stations of the cross from the Coliseum seem less distasteful to him, as does the life of retirement of the convents.

With the *Miserere* at the Sistine Chapel, we hear music resound with great strength for the last time in the story of Corinne and Oswald. Its nature and effect are like a realization of Corinne's meditation at the concert. Then, she listened to a music both "voluptuous and passionate," evoking a near fatal intensity (266). The *Miserere,* commending its "renunciation of the world," will be played out in the fading light of day, beneath oppressive paintings. In the whole of this episode, music is experienced through Corinne, spectacle, through Oswald. At his arrival, he notices only *décor*—a sky "dark and fearsome," worthy of Michelangelo. "Daylight scarcely penetrated the stained-glass windows, which cast shadow rather than light on the paintings; darkness enlarges the figures of prophets and sibyls, already so imposing," all the more. And incense brings its funerary note to this crushing scene: "All sensations prepare one for the deepest of them all: the one that music produces" (265).

Through Oswald's eyes, attention is concentrated upon Corinne, pale and dressed in black, until this point lost in the throng. The music is borne in upon them, aerial and pure. In that moment, she is giving no thought to her lover.

It seemed to him that it was in such a moment as this that one would like to die, if only the separation of soul from body were not accomplished through pain; if only an angel were to come and carry off all feeling and thought, those sparks of divinity that strive to return to their source, away with him on his wings: to die then would then be ... but a spontaneous act of the heart, only a prayer more ardent and better answered. (266)

The *Miserere*'s verses unfold, alternating low, harsh recitatives that depress hope with the celestially hope-filled strains on which it ends, restoring Corinne to thoughts of a gentle, easeful death. Hers will come to her at the end of long tortures.

The passage of time is doubly represented through music and the advance of night. As the night proceeds, the painted figures, before so terrifying, come to appear like "phantoms shrouded in shadows. The silence is deep: a single word would cause unutterable pain in such a mood, where all is intimate and inward ... Each person moves along alone, noiselessly" (267). The procession reaches Saint Peter's. Standing forth by itself, a great illuminated cross lights up the immense nave, the gigantic statues and imposing tombs, and the Pope, garbed in white, the cardinals, the prostrate priests, the throng of the living reduced to the proportions of "pygmies, in contrast to the images of the dead" (267). In the pale light from the cross, Oswald notices Corinne, the only person his glance can distinguish. The silent prayer ends. Suddenly, the church comes to life, becoming "akin to a vast public promenade." Corinne comes toward Lord Nelvil "transported by joy" (268). The charm has been broken. Oswald can comprehend nothing of this rapid fire change of mood, since he remains deep in the mood of religious devotion, and he reproaches that brilliant creature for her too facile return to society.[22]

From this time forth, there will be no more great musical moments, unless we except one in the heroine's tale of her past life. The *crescendo* has been reached. Corinne's initial serenity has gone, to be replaced by an imperfect happiness, punctuated by shafts of grief. The trip to Naples marks the start of the *decrescendo*, as if, for Corinne, the departure from Rome's protection in search of this foreigner constituted a denial of her origins and could only bring misfortune to her. Now she bears her death within her, because she has embraced the one who symbolizes it. "This daughter of the sun, afflicted by secret sorrows, resembled those flowers still fresh and radiant, but that a spot of blight, caused by some fatal sting, menaces with early death" (355).

During the trip to Naples and the sojourn in the Campania everything is organized in terms of two contrasting themes that landscapes and sounds symbolize. After the Roman plain with its deadly fevers, they enter the Campania. The perfumes of its lemon trees act like "a melodious melody" upon the imagination, "invoking a poetic turn of mind, exciting talent and filling it with nature's bounty" (280). Here a new association arises between music and scent, a quasi-sensual link we find two pages later as nightingales perch among roses. "The purest of songs unite with the sweetest of scents: all of nature's charms are drawn to one another" (287).[23] The effect of this association just at the moment when Corinne is uncovering the beauties of the Campania's countryside underscores how music possesses the power of arousing creative genius as it acts upon the senses.[24]

Nature's luxuriance masks its cruelty; the waves break upon the rocks in their fury; a volcano dominates this peaceable land. Naples is nothing but savage yells, songs, and dances; a people wretched and ruddy, possessed of an unbelievable vitality, yet ceaselessly threatened by the waters and by underground fire. Here, in its most lovely province, Italy finally loses its mask of serenity, its dreamy melancholy. And here Corinne will begin her apprenticeship of suffering.

A short while after their arrival in this city which is presented as a sort of caricature of Rome, its restless opposite devoid of gentleness, Corinne goes with Oswald to attend an Anglican service aboard an English war vessel anchored in the port. The whole of this episode takes place in near-monastic silence: the captain's voice, giving orders, echoes throughout the ship, "the firm and smooth voice" of the chaplain, and "muffled voices" that answer him (297). This English orderliness is contrasted with Neapolitan disorder; the simplicity of Anglican faith with the sumptuousness of Catholic ceremony; and in the end, Oswald with Corinne.[25]

This scene initiates the decoding of the past life of them both. Oswald will tell his story on that night at Vesuvius, beside the river of lava, in the somber rustling of starlight, in the whistling of flames and wind, the sole sounds to break the deep stillness that surrounds them with its profound threat to Corinne's life. At the tale's end, the ringing of churchbells wafts up to them, whether sign of life or of death they cannot tell, but at least a reassuring reminder of the existence of God and of humankind. The evil spell is broken, and they rush to leave these infernal regions for that illusory paradise that lies at their feet. Corinne now knows that she must have but little hope, that Oswald will turn away from her when he learns the truth of her past.[26] We need retain here only the central episode. Corinne had lived in Italy until her fifteenth year, when her father, remarried, had summoned her to his side. England is remembered without amenity: its rough climate, the hostility of nature, the howling of the winds in the corridors of a lonely castle, its narrow-minded and vacuous society, the father who has lost all pleasure in life, the bigoted and limited stepmother who forbids Corinne to teach her half-sister Lucile music. Silence reigns in this family circle. Corinne makes music for herself alone; she wanders every day over the countryside. And instead of Italy's harmonious strains, she hears the cries of crows hidden off in the clouds. With her father's death, she falls into an increasingly unbearable silence of the spirit. The longing to flee grips her. Then, one evening, she hears some Italian singers beneath her window. "I cannot express what I felt: a flood of tears covered my face as all my memories were revived; nothing can recall the past the way music does; it does more than bring it to mind, it becomes visible when music evokes it, cloaked in its mysterious veil of melancholy" (384). Corinne is carried away. The nostalgia of exile is replaced by an irresistible attraction.

> I fell into a kind of drunken state, and I felt for Italy all that love itself impels one to feel; desire, enthusiasm, sorrow. I was no longer mistress of myself, and my whole soul was borne along towards my country. I needed to see it, breathe its air, hear its sounds ... If life were ever offered to the dead in their graves, they wouldn't raise the stones overhead more impatiently than I wished to tear off my shroud. (385)

This exultation "caused by music" plunges Corinne into confusion. In truth, music's power is not limited to the recollection of memory: in a moment it renders the past present, is "the past recaptured," whose rebirth will make all the more constricted her life of exile and solitude, so at odds with that happy childhood and adolescence that the twenty-year-old had repressed. Her longing to leave is intense, but the decision remains unmade, as her stepmother has the Italians dispatched, because "it is scandalous to listen to music on the sabbath" (385). It is then that Corinne flees.

A perfume, a painting, possess this power too, though in lesser degree. Before leaving for Naples, Corinne takes Oswald to visit her picture gallery and explains the reasons she has chosen its works. Once again, she is reduced to monologue because Oswald, having misinterpreted one of her remarks, has fallen silent. She shows him one last painting, drawn from Ossian, where we see "the son of Cairbar asleep upon his father's grave," as his father's ghost flies above in the clouds, and the arrival of the bard "who will honor the memory of the dead" (237, 238). Oswald is overwhelmed by memories of his father and his country. What the picture has triggered is continued by music. Corinne takes up her harp and begins to sing Scottish ballads "whose simple strains seem to accompany the sounds of the winds, moaning in the valleys" (238).[27] Softened by nostalgia itself, Oswald returns to loving. Like Delphine and Léonce, he cannot escape music's power. But music's effects upon Corinne are far more powerful, since she is an extraordinary creature, endowed with a fiery sensibility and a creative imagination—Mme de Staël's sole novelistic character to possess such a gift—which destines her to hear voices of this nature more intensely than do others.

Oswald and Corinne return to Rome even more sorrowful than when they left it, and little by little, sadness gives way to tragedy. Corinne slowly loses even the appearance of joyfulness. A reading of the novel through its locales would demonstrate this. As for music, it disappears, except for some brief, nostalgic notes. The heroine has lost her power; swept along by the baleful man to whom she has attached her fate, she finally enters that domain of silence from which she had, passingly, rescued him.

Both resolve to leave Rome. Corinne feels she will never return to it. One evening, she hears a band of Romans walking out in the moonlight, and singing. She follows them, drawn along from one monument to another by their melodies.[28] Music here "seemed to be letting itself be heard to console those who suffered," or to express "the vanity of things of this world," (408) thereby revealing to Corinne how much all her genius, beauty, and celebrity were nothing but illusions in her life. The fleetingness of all that is earthly will visit her spirit in a hallucination, provoked by music, of ruins, the signs of destroyed civilizations, and of modern monuments still intact, yet preordained to their own imminent destruction. Once the singers have dispersed, Corinne goes alone to revisit the Coliseum and Saint Peter's. She imagines the basilica, too, in ruins, "these columns now erect, half fallen to earth, its portico broken, this vault open to the sky" (409). We perceive how the words once pronounced at Pompeii, "ruins upon ruins, tomb after tomb," (300) have now come into their own. As day dawns, she mounts to the cupola and looks out from it at the bell towers and columns, surrounded by the devastated countryside. Through its hallucinatory powers, music has brought forth this vision and given it its depth.

Corinne and Oswald leave for Venice. The first sound that assaults them comes from the cannon, fired three times over the laguna to announce the taking of the veil by a nun. Silence shrouds the lovers, still more completely and more painfully than elsewhere. Gondolas glide over the waters, and one hears nothing but the sound of their oars. Only occasionally do they detect the songs of the gondoliers "reaching out across the canals like reflections of the setting sun" (430). Tasso's verses resound in ancient tones that resemble the monotony of church music. Corinne and Oswald spend hours gliding, for the most part silently, over the lagoon, surrendering themselves to "those vague thoughts that nature and love arouse" (431).

Even this flawed happiness is to end. War recalls Lord Nelvil to England. Corinne, alone and virtually without news of him, goes one day into St. Mark's, where her imagination depicts the scene of her wedding to Oswald. Once more, music provokes a flow of images and a striking fantasy. "All at once, she hears a somber murmuring and notices a coffin that had just been brought into the church." Returning home, she shuts herself indoors. Henceforth, "music occasions no more than a sorrowing shudder in her" (474).[29]

When she travels to England to try to see Oswald, the military band in an inspection in Hyde Park and the national anthem are to her no calls to glory: rather, they give voice to Corinne's regrets at having abandoned Oswald's country. At the last, the ball at the Edgermonds' castle in Scotland will seal Lord Nelvil's engagement to Corinne's half-sister amid sounds of tiresome quadrilles. Oswald remembers the dances of Italy, unsuspecting that close to him in the park Corinne is prey to the cruelty of the festivities and ignorant of his grief over his loss. She wanders at length between the well-lit castle, emitting its traces of music, and the moon's decor on the other side of the stream, so mournful and silent, a frontier symbolizing the rift between two futures still in the realm of the possible. It is her sister's prayer at the tomb of their father that will provide her with the resolution to sacrifice herself: first tempted by suicide, she will choose renunciation, despite her inability to resign herself to it, and retires to Florence. And there, sometimes, a musical air will bring her for one brief instant to something of her former brilliance. Music reappears shortly before her death, as she uses her last energies in teaching Oswald's daughter, who will be her reincarnation on earth.[30]

As I said at the outset, from *Delphine* to *Corinne* the role of music in Staël's novelistic economy had evolved greatly: the affective and psychological associations deepen. But some appear in *Corinne* that are altogether new, and these are precisely those connections with other forms of art which, in turn, come to enrich the perceptions of sentiment and their expression.

Between the end of the year 1800, when she probably began *Delphine,* and especially starting from her trip to Germany in 1803–04 and until 1807 when she finished *Corinne,* Mme de Staël cogitated much over the circumstances of the writer, over problems associated with genius and creativity, over the place of literature and the arts in intellectual and affective life. This explains why the heroines of these two novels, in spite of some few resemblances between them, are so different from one another and cannot live out in the same way an amorous fate ultimately quite similar. Corinne has to assume a doubly difficult destiny, exacerbating Delphine's problems with those that genius presents her. There is no doubt that in 1804. when the concept of her second novel fired up in her mind, she had no idea that she was about to create so extraordinary a personage.

We might read *Corinne* through its paintings, its sculptures, and settings, all that falls into the visual domain. It would be a richer reading than this, and would once more give the lie to the notion of Mme de Staël's ostensible insensibility to the fine arts. We might see how they, too, are integrated into the novel, and what wealth they bring to it.[31] Throughout all that is said about music, we've glimpsed one link uniting them all: that the world is the work of a single thought expressed in a thousand different forms. Music, a form more powerful than any other, leads to contemplation: it is a sort of mediator between the soul and the beauty it sometimes brings into being. The interpreter of human love, joy, doubt, and sorrow, it dreams and it can also escape. It is the tongue in which man feels himself in converse with divinity. "Music, love and religion have about them an admirable monotony, the kind we might wish to extend eternally."[32]

Performances of the Gaze: Staël's *Corinne, or Italy*

NANCY K. MILLER

> What then of the look for the woman, of woman subjects in seeing? The reply given by psychoanalysis is from the phallus. If the woman looks, the spectacle provokes, castration is in the air, the Medusa's head is not far off; thus, she must not look, is absorbed on the side of the seen, seeing herself seeing herself, Lacan's femininity.
>
> -Stephen Heath

> To begin with, men do not simply look; their gaze carries with it the power of action and of possession which is lacking in the female gaze. Women receive and return a gaze, but cannot act upon it.
>
> —E. Ann Kaplan

THE gaze is not simply an act of vision but a site of crisscrossing meanings in which the effects of power relations are boldly (and baldly) deployed. Given Beauvoir's analysis in *The Second Sex* of subjectivity as a way of looking at the world, Irigaray's theoretical work on the politics of visibility in the formation of sexual identity, and the recent work in feminist film theory and art history on the look as a central piece in the production of ideologies of desire, it seems somehow inevitable that feminist critics of the novel would also focus, as I do in this chapter, on the literary representation of the gaze. The regimes of sexual difference, the visual, and the literary relay each other in complicated ways; what exactly do we mean, for instance, by love at first sight?

To what extent does Staël's novel as a feminist text engaged with issues of subjectivity support or unsettle the claim that woman's place in culture is constructed by man's view of her, by a look that emanating from his position of self-identity seeks to circumscribe hers? Can the gaze of a woman writer "speak" the body differently in images that don't "fix her in the frame"?[1]

In *Corinne* where as a performer the object of the gaze takes pleasure in being admired and is at the same time in her own right the producing *subject* of a gaze, one would expect the lines of sight to complicate the structuring effects of the dominant gaze. In the same way, since the staging of Corinne's identity as a woman takes place in scenes foreign to its privileged witness, Oswald (and presumably to its French readers), paradigms of sight in the novel are articulated with codes of cultural reference that, already intertwined, map on to the constructions of sexual difference. The text both dramatizes the power of the gaze to delimit the proper sphere of femininity and offers a powerful resistance to it. Put another way, Staël's novel engages the possibility of an authoritative vision within femininity that refuses the legitimacy of a permanent patriarchal construction. The novel, in this sense, is a book about the fathers as an authorizing, all powerful location and body of intention; about the name of the father, about the fatherland, about the organization of separate spheres in which the letter of the father's law compels the son's desire, and the daughter's seeks to inhabit another, perhaps maternal space. With all this in mind, I want now to track the power of the gaze *elicited by performance*, produced by its effects, and perhaps reopen the question of its sex, or at least of its gender.[2]

Love at First Sight?

Oswald awakens, his first day in Rome, to the sound of church bells and cannons announcing the crowning at the Capitol of "the most celebrated woman in Italy ... Corinne, poet, writer, *improvisatrice*, and one of the most beautiful women in Rome."[3] It does not necessarily follow, however, that such distinction in a woman would predispose him to falling in love. On the contrary, the narrator underlines the fact that "focusing the public eye on a woman's fortune" [*cette grande publicité*] ran counter to "an Englishman's customs and opinions" (19) and explains that in England "the combination of mystery and public notice" would be harshly judged as a violation of social protocol. "Her last name was not known; her first work had come out five years earlier signed only *Corinne*. No one knew where she had lived before or what kind of person she had been" (20). But the Englishman is in Italy. Out of place, observer of a scene to which by definition he does not belong, Oswald quickly becomes a fascinated spectator who anticipates the coronation as though it were a work of poetic imagination. He is dazzled by the performance and when he meets Corinne privately, enchanted by her, but is this a match? What do they see in each other?

The work of the gaze as a gendered and gendering operation of looks from the beginning structures the relations of power and desire between Corinne and Oswald. Oswald sees Corinne for the first time before she begins to speak, while she is still an object of discourse and admiration, and in that moment it is *her* look that inaugurates their exchange: "her expression, her eyes, her smile, spoke in her favor, and one look [*le premier regard*] made Lord Nelvil her friend even before any stronger feeling brought him into subjection" (21). Despite the power of Corinne's self construction as a visible public object—a woman pleased to be admired; despite the extraordinary context of Oswald's first sight; Corinne, in white, dressed like Domenichino's Sibyl, seated in an antique chariot drawn by four white horses—and the "electrifying" effect of this sight on his imagination (22), when Oswald then watches Corinne at the crowning itself, on the stage of the Capitol, he sees only the woman in the performance. Corinne's performing gaze offers the spectacle of genius located in a woman's body, but as spectator Oswald insists on separating the genius from the woman "in the very midst of all the splendor and all her success, Corinne's eyes pleaded for the protection of a friend, a protection no woman can ever do without, however superior she may be. And he felt that it would be gratifying to be the sustaining strength of a person whose sensibility alone made sustenance necessary" (22; Balayé 54). This flagrant gesture of interpretation as self-reference by which the man reads the woman's unexpressed needs in her eyes [*par ses regards*] because she is a woman instantly privatizes the public meanings of a woman's gaze, and installs the couple firmly within the regime of what Monique Wittig in "The Straight Mind" calls "the heterosexual contract."[4]

Oswald's resistance to stepping outside his own categories leaves him fixed in his identity as the judge of woman. This inability to see except *as a man* is, I think, the central piece in Staël's critique of patriarchy, a critique, I should emphasize, attentive to the harm done to its sons as well as its daughters.[5] I will make the further claim that the narrator's insistence on the limits of Oswald's vision of Corinne as a performer is part of what makes the book feminist, or rather makes the question of representation for a feminist reader inseparable from a politics of the gaze. If Oswald watches Corinne like a man, through a legacy of patriarchal looks, the reader, authorized by the narrator's feminist writing, reframes his gaze, rereading as a woman. We might wonder who owns the gaze here?[6]

Paradoxes of the Comedienne

Although in the representation of Corinne's glory the crowning is the event the narrator and Corinne return to as the ultimate euphoric reference of her existence—the moment, in the terms of my argument, in which the performance of an identity creates a productive female gaze—the scene in which Corinne plays Juliet shows more complexly the stakes involved in what Naomi Schor in "Portrait of a Gentleman" has called "the battle of the gazes" in this novel, the struggle between the judgments of patriarchy and the desires of a feminist subject. The performance of Shakespeare's tragedy of paternal prohibitions and fatal visions (translated by Corinne and returned as it seems to the audience to "its native tongue" [*sa langue maternelle*], dramatizes, we might say, both Corinne's need for a theater in which to be seen and Oswald's desire to replace that scene with himself (126; Balayé 134). He will tolerate the praise of the world Corinne elicits only if "the look of love, more heavenly still than (her) genius," is directed uniquely at him (125). Once again, as in the scene at the Capitol, the man needs to separate the woman from the genius in order to consolidate his own identity.

Corinne's perspective involves a different kind of separation. On stage she knows she is acting. She can *see* the effect her acting has upon Oswald, and she splits herself from Juliet within the act of performance itself: "How happy Corinne felt on the day she played that noble tragedy for her chosen friend! How many years, how many lives would be dull after such a day!" (125). In this public moment we see the work of Corinne's *performing* gaze, the field of its mastery, and the scene of her ultimate pleasure: "living for a moment in the sweetest of the heart's dreams." This pleasure—*la jouissance pure*—is not, however, an erotics cut off from her private feelings for Oswald. On the contrary, if "for the authority of art" Corinne would not want Oswald to play a part on the stage in the play with her, she does want him in the audience: she wants him there to see the extraordinary power of her emotional range: "See what capacity I have for love!" (128). The narrator analyzes the complex nature of Corinne's pleasure in performance: it is to experience "all the charm of emotion with none of reality's agonizing distress" and at the same time the reality of emotion's effects: both the pleasure of public recognition—applause, etc.—*and* the satisfaction of laying all that "through the look in her eyes" at Oswald's feet (128, 129). This economy of pleasure resembles the calculus of fantasy that adds the erotic to the ambitious wish Freud assigns to men in the essay on creativity, "The Poet and Daydreaming." I want simply to note here the way in which the fantasy is undermined from within by the narrator's discourse, as it goes on to characterize the object of Corinne's desire: at the feet of the one object whose approval "was more precious to her than glory" (129). This internal subversion is part of the contradiction—the ideological muddle—that inhibits Staël's novel from beginning to end. For like Oswald, Corinne is also tempted by the look of love, and that gaze like the look that judges is embedded in patriarchal plots; not the ecstasy of stasis, the perfect *jouissance* of the moment Corinne exalts in. Thus, the problem here is not simply the sex of the gaze, but its literature.

By its intertext Corinne's gaze *as* Juliet is bound to a pleasure in death: Juliet's lines upon learning Romeo's name, lines reproduced in English in the novel: "Too early seen unknown and known too late!" Like Juliet, Corinne comes to learn that a body is not easily parted from its name under patriarchy's eye even if her own renaming has tried to undo those continuities; she learns very exactly "what's in a name." In the same way, when Oswald comes backstage after the play, staggered by Corinne's performance as Juliet and no longer able to distinguish truth from fiction, he finds himself speaking Romeo's lines in English: "Eyes look your last! arms take your last embrace"; they also suggest that vision under the paternal regime is deadly.

The problem the excess of Corinne's public presence causes the fathers may also be traced to the intimacies of etymological derivations: theater and theory (in Greek) share a root—*thea*—to see: both theater and theory are, then, in this sense scenes of spectating, beholding, contemplating. Now spectators at the various theaters of ancient Greek life (including the events of the polis) were predominantly if not exclusively male; so were the spectators of representation (also known as philosophers).[7] When Corinne is viewed *as theater* by the father and the son, their look articulates and regrounds the position of authority occupied by the figure of that privileged spectator of Greek life.[8] Put another way, the gaze is male when its act of seeing cannot separate itself from these dominant powers; seeing enacts ideology. "The privilege of sight over other senses, oculocentrism," Jane Gallop has argued in her reading of Irigaray's revision of Freud's "old dream of symmetry" through his "blind spot," supports and unifies phallocentric, sexual theory." "Every . . . viewing of the subject," she continues, "will have always been according to phallomorphic standards."[9]

Staël's production of Corinne's performing gaze wants to trouble that conflation of contemplation, theory, maleness, phallic authority by showing the political investments of spectating, the limits of its vision from father to son, and by complicating the notion of spectacle. This double move unveils the stakes of a woman's performance as *theater*—what she by her gaze might give to be seen; and what it would take for the gaze to be received. We might usefully borrow here from Mary Ann Doane's discussion of Irigaray's project to "provide the woman with an autonomous symbolic representation."[10] In her development of the notion of a feminine specificity that would not be an essentialism, Doane points to the distinction (drawn from Plato) that Irigaray makes between mimesis as "specularization" and an earlier "productive" mimesis: this first repressed mimesis, Irigaray writes, "would lie more in the realm of music." In an analysis oddly reminiscent of Kristeva's formulation of the semiotic as a space of rhythm and music that "precedes and underlies figuration and thus specularization," Irigaray imagines the possibility of "a woman's writing" "in the direction of, and on the basis of, that first mimesis."[11] Throughout the novel, Staël shows the productive, transformative power of this mode, a mode systematically repressed by a discourse of what Irigaray calls "adequation," the commensurability of word and thing. The relation between the two modes, the realm of "music" and the severe zones of the gaze will be rehearsed or placed in representation by the figuration of the tension between Italian and English paradigms. Corinne's dancing of the tarantella offers an exemplary case:

> It was in no way French dance, so remarkable for its elegance and the difficulty of its steps; rather it was a talent much closer to imagination and feeling. The quality of the music was expressed by movements that were in turn precise and languorous. As if she were improvising, as if she were playing the lyre or sketching faces, Co-

rinne communicated her feelings directly to the souls of the spectators through her dance: everything was language to her. Looking at
her, the musicians were moved to make the essence of their music
felt more strongly. It is impossible to explain the impassioned joy,
the imaginative sensitivity that electrified everyone watching that
magical dance, transporting them into an ideal existence where happiness not of this world is dreamed. (92–93)

The explosive potential of this physical improvisation, this body
language of immediacy that emerges from a woman's imagination, provides a challenge to the old patriarchal order very much
in the spirit of Cixous's celebrated call, . . . for an "écriture féminine," a women's writing that would bring women "into the
world and into history by her own movement." Staël's text in
fact embodies another, poetic libidinal economy that writes "*the
very possibility of change*, the space that can serve as a spring-
board for subversive thought, the precursory movement of a
transformation of social and cultural structures."[12] But the novel
also tells the fate of that gesture when it is read by the representatives of the old order.

If the Italians, as men who are moved by women, are transported by dance and music into the ideal, Oswald, the Englishman, remains fixed on the threshold of his real: "Trying to
hide his distress, his fascination, and his suffering, he managed
to say: 'Well Corinne, what homage, what success! But among all
those men who worship you so enthusiastically, is there one
brave and reliable friend? Is there a lifelong protector? And
should the vain uproar of applause be enough for a soul like
yours?' " (93). In the end, it seems Staël's (Romantic) recovery
of another mimesis, of a modality of dance and poetry, ecstasy
and transport, fails to achieve its transformative aims because in
the writing of a novel Staël necessarily comes up against genre;
narrative's need for the linear metonymies of story, for the reali-
ties of representation—the demands of Oswald's plot, for instance. (Corinne's persistently somatic relation to performance
is a symptom of that inevitable failure.) It would be a mistake,
however, to conclude too quickly. For in the posterity of the text
that is *Corinne, or Italy* and that contains the story of Corinne
and Oswald, the image that remains attached to Corinne's body,
that we might say becomes the iconography of her representation (reproduced notably on the cover of the folio edition), she
is figured as a transforming presence with her lyre.

Corinne appears on stage a last time in Venice in a production of Gozzi's comic opera, the *Figlia dell'aria*. At the end of the performance, Corinne's character sits on a throne from which she commands her subjects: the audience rises spontaneously to applaud Corinne as though she were a real queen (306). But when the curtain falls, Corinne learns the news she has dreaded since the backstage theatrics of *Romeo and Juliet*: Oswald must leave for England. In the emotional violence of their exchange, Corinne faints, and falling hits her head against the ground. When she comes back to herself, she measures the distance that separates this from their first meeting: "Oswald, Oswald, I was not like this the day you met me at the Capitol. On my forehead I wore the crown of hope and glory, now it is stained with blood and dust" (308). Although Oswald swears on *her* father's portrait, on a "father's name" that their love will continue, the narrator strikes a somber note: "In point of fact, to vanquish love once marks a solemn step in the progress of love: the illusion of its omnipotence is finished" (315). Thus the discourse of the novel comes to elaborate the power of the maxim to shape and regulate behavior.

Suffering and the Specular

The story of Oswald and Corinne shows that as long as woman is on display, however sublime her performance, she will be subject to the rigors of patriarchy; the letter of the father's law Bakhtin calls "the dead quotation."[13] But, as we will see now, paradoxically, it is only in the unfolding of the abjection that Corinne endures when she *stops* performing that we finally take the measure of patriarchy's indictment in this text.

Once Oswald returns to England we witness the figural de-crowning of Corinne, her insertion as object into the regime of the male gaze as the support of representation; and it is precisely at this point in the narrative that Maggie Tulliver, we recall, in *The Mill on the Floss* stopped reading Staël's novel: "As soon as I came to the blond-haired young lady reading in the park, I shut it up and determined to read no further. I foresaw that that light complexioned girl would win away all the love from Corinne and make her miserable." Maggie was a good, stage one resisting feminist reader, who knew enough about images of women in literature to feel sure that this book would not end well for Corinne; and she wishes for "some story . . . where the dark woman triumphs."[14] Was Maggie right to stop reading?

The last five books of the novel display the "miserabilization" of the dark woman Maggie predicted. The reader tracks the fall from the exaltation produced by the tropes of public admiration into the abjection of the woman who now unseen becomes the spectator of staged events in which she does not perform—indeed has no place except that of witness to her own exclusion. The internal insistence on the dysphoric symmetry of these scenes, however, produces a complex reading effect; paradoxically, the melodramatic moments of intense pathos caused by Corinne's "invisibility" give her in the reader's eye and her own the "theater" she needs by representing her peripeteia *as* theater: as scenes of beholding.

At home in England, Oswald reads his dead father's letter of judgment about Corinne and hesitates about what to do. As Corinne waits in anguished paralysis for Oswald to write, she receives the visit of a woman who bears in her body the image of Corinne's internal crisis: "The person entering her room was totally deformed, her face disfigured by a dreadful illness; she was dressed in black and covered by a veil meant to conceal the sight of her from those she came near." The woman, who is seeking charity not for herself, but for the poor, is stunned by Corinne's appearance, and the narrator underlines the irony of their relations: "The poor woman, long since resigned to her own fate, looked at this beautiful person with astonishment . . . Italy's most brilliant person who was succumbing to despair!" (336). This figuration of Corinne brought down from the heights of a performing brilliance to the obscure zones of an object of pity will limn the final stages of the novel in which we read the destiny of the dark woman, as she becomes the woman in black who hides herself from view.

Corinne finally decides to come to England herself. In London, she goes to see Mrs. Siddons perform in *Isabella, or the Fatal Marriage*. Not knowing that Oswald has returned to England, but not wanting to "attract the attention of some Englishman who might have known her in Italy," Corinne arrives at the theater veiled. She chooses a small box for herself "from which she could see everything without being seen" and follows both the play and the actress (who Oswald has said is like her) with absorption (340). But during the intermission she notices "all eyes [*tous les regards*] turning toward a box" (340; Balayé 481). In a flourish of hyperbole that echoes the description of the effects produced by the appearance of the princess of Clèves at the court—"even in England where women are so beautiful, it had been a long time since anyone so remarkable had appeared"—Lucile (her own half-sister) is posed as the specular ideal. But it is not enough for Corinne to compare herself to the *image* of youth and find herself lacking; the degradation of the fall into specular suffering requires another turn of the spiral. Corinne suddenly sees Oswald, and seeing him for the first time since their separation, follows his gaze, which like the others' attaches itself to her sister's body. When the play is over, Corinne again hides herself from the crowd, and from an opening in her box watches Oswald escorting the young beauty from the theater, "the most beautiful person in England through the countless admirers following in her footsteps" (342). Normally an acute, even paranoid, reader of the slightest fluctuation in Oswald's feelings, suddenly faced with the new configurations of desire, Corinne resists interpretation and reserves judgment. Postponing the privacy of the *tête-à-tête*, she chooses instead a scene of public display—the review of Oswald's regiment in Hyde Park—as a theater in which to determine with "her own eyes" the status of his true feelings for Lucile.

In a reversal of positions which makes Corinne the spectator and Oswald the spectacle, as she prepares to go and watch the man on parade, Corinne now worries about her appearance. She hesitates about how to present herself, what to wear; and then suddenly, looking at herself in the mirror and seeing in its reflection her *sister's* face "light as air" decides against display and dresses in black, draping herself in a mantle, Venetian style (346). When Corinne, who is accustomed to being viewed as the *figure* of "Corinne," poet and improviser, and not simply *as a woman*, observes Lucile being seen *as a woman*, she immediately experiences her subjection to the law of the male gaze by seeing herself through it, or mirrored in it. In John Berger's analysis of this effect of vision: "Men look at women. Women watch themselves being looked at. This determines not only most relations between men and women but also the relation of women to themselves. The surveyor of woman in herself is male: the surveyed female. Thus she turns herself into an object—and most particularly an object of vision: a sight."[15] Once Corinne becomes this sight she enters a realm of acute suffering. Cut off from the mobile *jouissance* of performance, through which she defies the conventional inscription of woman's body, Corinne seems to enter the borderline zones of an identity in crisis; the state, neither subject nor object, that Kristeva describes as abjection.[16]

Like the disfigured woman dressed in black who had come to beg for charity, Corinne, in turn, her face protected from sight by the depth of a carriage, watches Oswald. Prancing on horseback, he performs like the hero of a nineteenth-century novel, in honor of the remarkably blond Lucile toward whom once again all admiring gazes turn: "Oswald gazed at her with those looks; they had been turned upon her" (346). The narrator thus underscores in discourse the repetition in plot of the general structure of reversal which organizes the last movements of the novel; emphasis reiterated on still a third level of the text in the narrator's rendering of Corinne's thoughts: "Ah, Corinne thought, it was not like this, no, that I made my way to the Capitol the first time I met him; he has hurled me from the triumphal chariot into the unfathomable depths of sorrow" (347). We may understand the fall from the height of art, from the triumph of Corinne's public, even national performance, to the depths of individual suffering as Corinne's descent into the privatized spheres of femininity. The political economy of this reversal is based in the regime of the look that constitutes Corinne as Woman.[17]

This, then, is the text's feminist knot, or one of them. For Corinne needs not only an interlocutor and a reader, she requires what in Colette's discourse about women and love in *The Vagabond* is called "the eager spectator to [one's] life and [one's] person";[18] and this perforce generates the deadly specular logic of representation; for that spectator tends to believe only what he sees: the woman as sight; or as Woolf has shown, his mirror. The witness who looks and sees without a mirror seems to inhabit a lost maternal plenitude. The novel embodies the conflicted attempt to construct (perhaps *re*construct) a female subjectivity through work *and* desire without a maternal support and *against* the power of the paternal gaze to circumscribe that project within the identity of Woman. Staël's fiction challenges the legitimacy of that power in writing—the narrator's and Corinne's; but at the same time, we are also given to see the cost of protest as it is lived out in a somatic body, the vulnerability of its text subjected to the wounding powers of patriarchy's canons.

Melancholia, Mania, and the Reproduction of the Dead Father

MARGARET COHEN

"'CORINNE,'" continued Oswald, "falling at her feet, 'reign over my life forever. Here is the ring my father gave his wife, the holiest, most sacred of rings, offered in the noblest good faith, accepted by the most faithful heart. I take it from my finger to place it on your own'" (249). If Oswald is moved to give Corinne both his father's ring and a pledge of undying fidelity, it is not for her passion or even for the triumphant public performances which make her national renown. Rather, Corinne wins Oswald's commitment for her skill at portraiture; for her ability to restore a picture of Oswald's father damaged when Oswald threw himself into the water to save "an old man [who] disappeared [*disparut*] under the billows" (247; Balayé 357). Indeed, restoration is perhaps too weak a word for this talent whose power Oswald describes in miraculous terms. After Corinne's intervention, the portrait is "not only mended, but a much more striking likeness than before" (249).

Nancy Miller comments: "We might want to think about this restoration of the image as an emblem of the central gamble at the heart of the novel."[1] I take the portrait episode as my opening emblem because it suggests a motivated relation between Oswald's melancholic attachment to the dead father and his interest in an aesthetics of faithful mimetic reproduction. In the following pages, I want to explore how Staël develops this relation throughout *Corinne*, supplementing Staël's aestheticopsychological analysis of Oswald's case with Freud's comments suggesting mimesis to play a central role in the melancholic psychic economy.

How, I will also ask, does the case of Oswald compare to the psychological needs informing the other aesthetics central to the novel, an aesthetics of sensibility exemplified by the feats which lend Corinne her national renown, although not Oswald's ring?[2]

While Corinnean sensibility has often been read as a momentary feminine escape from the Father's Law, Freud's work on mourning permits us to understand its links to Oswald's pathology of melancholy. Corinnean sensibility bears strong affinities to the state of mania that Freud hypothesizes as the obverse of melancholy. It is, I conclude, resistance only if the notion is conceptualized in psychoanalytic rather than political terms.

Historical issues underwrite my examination of the nexus into which *Corinne* draws aesthetics and psychology: my interest in how collective psychological factors might shape the state of the novel in postrevolutionary France. In particular, I am interested in the period when the children of the Revolution were writing, the July Monarchy, when the realist novel "rose," as it is said, to occupy a dominant position in the literary hierarchy. At this time, however, mimesis was not the only representational possibility valued in novelistic polemic and practice. Notably, the novel claiming to reflect external reality faithfully (nascent realism) was in competition with an avatar of the novel of sensibility (the sentimental social novel), and this opposition was often coded along gender lines: masculine mimesis opposed to feminine sentimentality.[3]

As I argue elsewhere, such an alignment of gender and genre indisputably owes much to events internal to literary history.[4] Nonetheless, the cases of Oswald and Corinne suggest it may also have its roots in upheaval extending across the social field: the trauma of the French Revolution. Certainly, Staël's analysis of Oswald's melancholic attachment to mimesis is uncannily prescient of materialist critics who understand July Monarchy realism in terms of its collective psychological function. In their discussions, realism is read as a vehicle of incomplete collective mourning, an attempt to supplement the void in discursive authority produced by the death of the king.[5]

"One is no longer reading a novel"

The relation of mimesis to sensiblity is at issue throughout the aesthetic debates filling *Corinne,* and notably in the book devoted to the fine arts, "Statues and Paintings." From their first visit to the famous sights of Rome, and then to Corinne's house at Tivoli, Corinne and Oswald explore their aesthetic differences which Staël grounds in material factors: "but their differences here as in everything else had to do with differences of nations, climates, and religions" (146). And from this first visit, Corinne takes the side of sensibility against mimesis, developing its power through ranking the various forms of plastic art.

Corinne's opening gesture is to proclaim the superiority of painting over sculpture. The latter, she suggests, is too closely bound to the brute materiality of external fact: "Sculpture can offer only a vigorous and simple existence to the eye, whereas painting suggests the mysteries of communion with the self, giving voice to the immortal soul through evanescent color" (146). Corinne by no means dismisses sculpture altogether; its value, however, lies in its ability to take the viewer beyond whatever subject matter it may seem to represent:

> Contemplation of those admirable lines and shapes reveals an inde-
> finable divine plan [*je ne sais quel dessein de la divinité*] for hu-
> manity, expressed in the noble face that has been granted to man.
> Through this contemplation, the soul rises to the level of hope filled
> with enthusiasm and virtue, for beauty is one in the universe, and,
> whatever form it takes, it stirs [*excite*] religious feeling in the human
> soul. (142; Balayé 216)

Enthusiasm, excitation, feeling: the vocabulary belongs to a Romantic brand of sensibility where mimetic forms affect the viewer by exciting emotions taking him or her into an exalted world. "An indefinable divine plan [*Je ne sais quel dessein*]," Corinne terms the experience to which mimesis ideally leads, as she uses a phrase which eloquently expresses her opinion that mimetic sculpture's value lies in its power to move the viewer away from external representation. While such sculpture expresses a divine plan that Corinne characterizes with a word evocative of visual procedures of representing external reality, "dessein," Corinne simultaneously qualifies this design with a phrase stressing the undescribable nature of its subject: *"je ne sais quel dessein."*

If Corinne ranks painting above sculpture, not all subjects are, however, equal in her republic of aesthetic forms. Corinne, Staël tells us, "maintained that religious subjects were the most suited to painting" for, Corinne goes on to state, "nothing could replace the benefit of religious painting for the soul" (222–23). Corinne's comments on Titian's "Jesus Christ falling under the burden of the cross" exemplify the power she understands religious art to possess: "Of all my paintings ... it is the one my eyes always go back to, and yet the emotion it brings is never exhausted" (154). Corinne finds paintings which belong to the lesser order of "events drawn from history or poetry," in contrast, to be generally encumbered by questions of subject matter which distract the viewer from what she calls the "pictorial [*pittoresque*]," an adjective she uses to designate the power of the medium itself to excite affect (146; Balayé 222). Such paintings, Corinne states, are

> rarely pictorial. Painters from earlier times wrote the words their subjects were to speak on ribbons issuing from their mouths; often historical paintings would be comprehensible only if this practice had been retained. But religious subjects are immediately understood by everyone, and attention is not diverted from art to the problem of guessing what it represents. (146)

Corinne not only criticizes historical paintings for the fact that their reference to external events undercuts their plastic power, but also points out that, particularly in the case of subjects removed in time, the very ambition of historical painting, the recreation of a time gone by, is a hopeless task:

> Corinne added an observation strengthening her line of thought further still: since the religious feeling of the Greeks and Romans, as well as every other aspect of their mind-set and their spirit, cannot be ours, it is impossible for us to create the way they did, to invent new ideas in what might be called their territory. They can be imitated by dint of study, but how could genius soar where memory and erudition are so vital! (147)

Consequent with Staël's theoretical materialism, Corinne here holds that historical painting can call up the past at best only according to the mode of representation that Walter Benjamin terms allegorical, as a heap of externally accurate details devoid of presence or life (indeed, Corinne's entire discussion of the hierarchy of the arts is pervaded by the Romantic valorization of the symbol that Benjamin's modernist reading of allegory combats). Religious art, in contrast, as well as "subjects belonging to our own history," provide an experience where presence takes precedence over externally accurate but fundamentally dead re-presentation: "painters can tap their own personal inspiration; feeling what they paint, painting what they have seen. They use life to imagine life" (147).

"Rhetoric," Corinne also calls the sentimental, inspiring power of her preferred form of painting: "She claimed that painting like poetry had its rhetoric" (147). Importantly, Corinne repeatedly describes painting in terms borrowed from the verbal arts; thus, we have seen her suggest that "painting . . . [gives] *voice* to the immortal soul" (146, emphasis added). "The opposition between painting and poetry belongs to an opposition traditional since Aristotle between a mimesis which reproduces nature, a given model, and a productive mimesis, which supplements a lack in nature . . . which perfects nature, in enlarging it, embellishing it," Sarah Kofman writes.[6] When Corinne applies a language of verbal expression to visual representation, she works a Romantic displacement on this opposition. For Corinne, the visual arts are not empty as opposed to full mimesis. Rather, they too can become a form of representation going beyond mimesis to "the mysteries of communion with the self" (146).

One further aspect of Corinne's aesthetics of sensibility deserves mention: the fact that while sensibility aims, like mimesis, to blur the polarities between art and life, this blurring takes a different form. The blurring of mimesis has long been criticized as a deceptive illusion: painted grapes which the birds mistake for real. The blurring of Corinnean sensibility, in contrast, occurs through the power of feeling to overcome the boundary separating aesthetic object and its audience; it results in revelation rather than deception. What better example of this blurring than Corinne's triumphant performance of *Romeo and Juliet* where, as Simone Balayé observes, "the audience . . . no longer knows whether it is watching the experience of the real woman or the tragic heroine?"[7] Particularly the novel's self-immersed hero who is moved to his own passionate display:

> Once the play ended, Corinne was exhausted and overcome with emotion. The first to reach her room, Oswald found her alone with her attendants, still dressed as Juliet and, like her, half fainting in their arms. Troubled and confused to such a degree that he could not tell whether he was seeing truth or fiction [*il ne savait distinguer si c'était la vérité ou la fiction*], Oswald threw himself at Corinne's feet and spoke these words of Romeo in English:
> 'Eyes, look your last! arms, take your last embrace.' (130; Balayé 200)

Sensibility overcomes the distinction between art and life through the release of emotion, and brings in its wake a revelation of forces occulted (unconscious?) in the intercourse of everyday life. In this case, the message is not pleasant: Oswald reveals his deep identification with the Fathers which will lead him to act as an agent of Corinne's destruction.

Corinne's interest in sensibility is consonant with a position that Staël advances throughout her theoretical writings on the social value of fiction. "The morality of a novel thus consists in the sentiments that it inspires," Staël writes in the 1810 *On Germany*.[8] She had already developed this idea in the 1795 *On Fictions* as well as in her subsequent *On Literature*. Thus, for example, *On Fictions* declares:

> Nonetheless, the sole advantage of fictions does not lie in the plea-sure they procure. When they speak only to the eyes, they can only entertain: but they have a great influence on all moral ideas when they move the heart; and this talent is perhaps the most powerful way to direct or to enlighten.[9]

Summing up the power Staël attributes to writings inspiring sympathy, Lawrence Lipking comments that Staël sees such works to "link all feeling people together in a human chain; they dissolve the distinctions among eras and social classes, among authors, readers, and fictional characters."[10]

Responses to *Corinne* in the years following its publication would suggest that Staël's novel met its author's theoretical goal. In 1828, Hortense Allart praised the section of the novel where Corinne goes to England in the following terms: "Then one is no longer reading a novel but rather a history [*histoire*]; fiction takes on the character of reality; Corinne is no longer an imagi-nary being, she is a respected, beloved friend, whose pains [*peines*] preoccupy you, torment you, and to whom you would like to devote yourself and your life."[11]

A different impression

"In some respects," Staël tells us, "Oswald's impressions were different" (147). If Staël's melancholy hero, like Corinne, values art for its powerful effect on the viewer, he cannot conceive that this power derives from anything other than its mimetic quali-ties. Thus, he places historical subject matter above religious art, defending his hierarchy with the assertion that the task of art is above all to *represent* life in all its energy and diversity:

> although it is true that a happy combination of color with light and shade produces a musical effect, if it can be called that, painting *represents* life and is called upon to express the passions in all their energy and diversity. (148, emphasis added)

"If it can be called that," Oswald equivocates, making evident his doubts about whether the vocabulary of the least mimetic and most inspiring of arts, music, can be applied to painting at all. And while Oswald agrees with Corinne that the effect of the painting should be immediate, he interprets this requirement as the demand that historical paintings should not be encumbered by overly abstruse subject matter: "when historical events are as well known as religious subjects, they have the advantage of the variety of situations and feelings that they retrace [*retracent*]" (148; Balayé 225). *Retracer*, we notice, is the verb Oswald chooses to describe the relation between art and sentiment. "The emotion it brings [*me cause*] is never exhausted" was how Corinne put the power of the Titian painting that she liked best (155; Balayé 234).

Perhaps unexpectedly, Oswald's belief in the representational power of painting leads him to oppose a *Bilderverbot* to Corinne's praise of religious art. For Oswald, the gap separating the external world at issue in painting and the ineffable nature of the divinity is too great to be bridged by any act of representation: "He believed that thought dare not give Him form, and that in the very depths of the human soul, there is scarcely an idea conceptualized enough, ethereal enough, to reach the level of the Supreme Being" (147). But Oswald's religious *Bilderverbot* does not only derive from his devalorization of exterior mimesis in relation to the abstract world of spiritual exaltation. In addition, it derives from the fact that he endows mimetic representation with a disturbing allure. "I cannot bear the portrayal of physical pain. My strongest objection to Christian subjects in painting is the distress [*sentiment pénible*] we are made to feel by the image of blood" (149; Balayé 226). And he continues,

> Nothing so torments our imagination as bloody sores or nervous convulsions. In such paintings, it is impossible not to look for a precise imitation of reality [*l'exactitude de l'imitation*], impossible not to dread finding it. What pleasure would come from an art made up exclusively of that kind of imitation? It is more horrible or less beautiful [*plus horrible ou moins beau*] than nature herself, from the moment its only aim is to resemble her. (149; Balayé 226–27)

While this passage devalorizes art which is purely representational, "more horrible or less beautiful than nature," it also shows Oswald tremendously susceptible to this art's admittedly ambivalent power. "Horrible" is strong language; "a precise imitation" is something that one both "look[s] for" and "dread[s]."

Oswald's objections to representation in religious art, then, would seem to derive from his susceptibility to its almost insupportable attraction. Mimesis triggers an ambivalent response that we would expect from heavily charged psychic material rather than the elevated realm of artistic exaltation.

Melancholia and mimesis: One step forward, two steps back

What psychic factors might produce Oswald's ambivalent investment in mimesis? Corinne starts to answer this question when she challenges Oswald for failing to appreciate the painterly aspect to painting. "Must he not be faithful to history, and if he is, will his work be sufficiently faithful to the pictorial aspect to painting [*pittoresque*]?" (154; Balayé 233). Corinne's critique of Oswald's interest in "fidelity" might be understood as her objection to his substitution of referential for aesthetic concerns, the fact that he approaches art by worrying about its fidelity to some external phenomenon. But Corinne also makes clear that Oswald's notion of fidelity derives from his attachment to a highly subjective point of reference: "You are only moved by what suggests [*retrace*] the heart's suffering" (149; Balayé 225).

If Corinne links Oswald's interest in mimetically faithful art to his investment in melancholic recall, Staël leaves it to her omniscient third-person narrator to make explicit the psychic trauma underwriting Oswald's aesthetic preference. We come to the picture which Corinne has saved for last, well aware of its power. This is the picture of "Cairbar's son asleep on his father's grave." "The view of this canvas *reminded* him of his father's grave and the mountains of Scotland [*le tombeau de son père et les montagnes d'Ecosse se retracèrent à sa pensée*], and his eyes filled with tears" (157; Balayé 238; emphasis added).

Invoking the charged verb *retracer*, the narrator uses it, as in previous instances in the novel, to characterize Oswald's preferred form of art. But rather than applying it, like Oswald, to a picture's mimetic reproduction of objectively verifiable details or even, like Corinne, to a picture's ability to reproduce the "heart's sufferings," the narrator here uses the verb to designate the centrality of mimesis to the structure of the melancholy psyche. Oswald's fixated imagination is explained as dominated by the repetition of a melancholic primal scene: the son mourning his dead father in a place where the distinction between fatherland and father collapses.

If Oswald's susceptibility to mimetic art derives from the importance of "retracing" in his psychic economy, this explanation would make sense of the ambivalence of his response. In such a response, he displaces the ambivalent affect that accompanies his melancholic retracings from the psychic to the aesthetic realm. And the affect, we note, is ambivalent in the extreme. "Oswald's grief is compounded by guilt," Margaret Waller points out; guilt over how he has betrayed his father.[12] Supporting this explanation is the fact that Oswald describes the painful quality of his psychic suffering with the same term that he applies to the horrifying power of mimetic art ("*je ne puis supporter*"). In the case of the dead father, Oswald sighs:

> "while he was still alive, did not an incredible set of circumstances convince him that I had betrayed his affection, that I had rebelled against my country [*patrie*], against his will [*la volonté paternelle*], against everything sacred on earth." These memories were so *unbearable* [*insupportable*], that Nelvil could not bring himself to confide them to anyone; indeed he was afraid to ponder them more deeply. (4–5; Balayé 29; emphasis added)

For Freud, an ambivalent relation to the lost object is constitutive of melancholia, playing a crucial role in the melancholic's inability to complete the work of mourning and move on. "The self-tormenting in melancholia," Freud asserts in a text written as if it were based on Oswald's case, "which is without doubt enjoyable, signifies just like the corresponding phenomenon in obsessional neurosis, a satisfaction of trends of sadism and hate which relate to an object, and which have been turned round upon the subject's own self."[13]

Freud's analysis of melancholy is further helpful in the case of Oswald because it develops the insight of Staël's narrator that retracing is a gesture central to the melancholic pathology. When explaining why the melancholic fails to transfer his cathexis from an old to a new object, Freud hypothesizes that melancholic attachment derives from a form of object-cathexis where the subject duplicates itself in the object to which it is attached. "The object choice," Freud proposes, "has been effected on a narcissistic basis, so that the object-cathexis, when obstacles come in its way, can regress to narcissism."[14] In his fondness for mimetic art, then, Oswald displaces to aesthetics not only his attachment to the psychic act of retracing but also the structure of the melancholic ego divided against itself. Art and the psyche send back images of each other in a mimetic *"mise en abyme."*

In any mimetic relation, a gap opens up between a representation and its object, and the narcissistic ego-reduplication characterizing melancholia is no exception. Freud writes,

> The object-cathexis proved to have little power of resistance, and was brought to an end. But the free libido was not displaced onto another object; it was withdrawn into the ego. There, however, it was not employed in any unspecified way, but served to establish an *identification* of the ego with the abandoned object. Thus the shadow of the object fell upon the ego, and the latter could henceforth be judged by a special agency, as though it were an object, the forsaken object. In this way an object-loss was transformed into an ego-loss, and the conflict between the ego and the loved person transformed into a cleavage between the critical activity of the ego and the ego as altered by the identification.[15]

The dynamic of Oswald's relation to his dead father conforms to Freud's description of the two faculties produced by the melancholic experience of ego-reduplication. When Oswald meditates on what to do with Corinne, he compares this relationship to his relationship to Madame d'Arbigny in the following terms:

> he remembered being in love, undeniably much less than with Corinne—and the object of that choice could not be compared with her—but still, that feeling had swept him away to *unreflected* acts [*actions irréfléchies*], acts that had broken his father's heart. "Who knows," he exclaimed, "who knows whether he would not be just as fearful today that his son would forget his fatherland and the duty he owes it?" (131; Balayé 201; emphasis added)

Oswald's two movements, I would suggest, demonstrate a psychic conflict resembling that between the "critical activity of the ego and the ego as altered by identification" described by Freud.[16] While Oswald's first movement draws him toward a fusion with "the object of [his] choice," his second movement is to criticize such spontaneous attraction as "unreflected actions" transgressing the Father's Law he has internalized as his own.

A similar double movement characterizes Oswald's behavior throughout the novel; for economy of argument, I return to the emblematic portrait scene. "Oswald's first impulse [*mouvement*]," Staël tells us at the opening of the episode inaugurated by the drowning man, "was to throw himself into the water" (247; Balayé 357). Consonant with Oswald's description of the effect of his actions in the case of Madame d'Arbigny, this unreflected action damages the father, although in this case, it is the dead father's shape rather than the living father's heart. But Staël also incorporates a second reaction in the same mental economy: "Oswald's second impulse [*mouvement*] was to put his hand on his chest to find his father's portrait; it was still there, but so damaged by the water that it was scarcely recognizable. Bitterly distressed, Oswald exclaimed: 'Dear God! You have taken even his image from me!'" (249; Balayé 359).

Here again, then, we find the trajectory I have linked to the melancholic's narcissistic ego split. After a moment of impulsive self-abandon, Oswald takes stock of the fact that his behavior has threatened the Father in some way, although here, interestingly, Oswald abdicates responsibility for the destruction he works on the Father's image, no longer accusing himself, but rather the Father of Fathers, "Dear God." Importantly, while Staël draws together Oswald's gestures by using the same term (she calls them a first and second "impulse [*mouvement*]"), she simultaneously distances them in her narration. The phrase "Oswald's second impulse [*mouvement*]" occurs two pages after Staël has mentioned his first *mouvement*, separated by many other gestures (Oswald's fainting, for example, as well as his being revived by the loving touch of Corinne). Through this displacement, Staël emphasizes that the double movement of melancholic narcissism can unfold across a protracted period of time.

Because of this double movement, Oswald's trajectory throughout the novel resembles nothing so much as a sentimental impasse described in a recent country-western song: "one step forward, two steps back." Repeatedly performing a spontaneous action that betrays the Father, Oswald then imagines his father's critique of the action and responds by getting stuck, unable to complete successfully whatever he had started to undertake.

The inhibiting effect of melancholic repetition brings me to one last form of *retracing* that Staël includes in her nexus of melancholy, mimesis, and the power of the dead father: "reproduction" in the Althusserian sense.[17] Oswald's melancholy relation to his absent father is accompanied by a discourse asserting his interest in reproducing the social order of the father. Thus, Oswald uses the charged verb *retracer* when he speculates on how to accede to the status of father himself. "I want to know what kind of a wife my father planned for me: and do I not already know since I can *retrace* for myself [*me retracer*] the image of my mother, his dearly beloved wife," Oswald reflects (134; Balayé 205; emphasis added). But Oswald's ambition to reproduce the order of the Father is undone by the melancholic nature of his investment in the Father's Law. When Oswald transgresses this Law and then laments his transgression, he certainly reduplicates his position as (erring) son. But by doing so he simultaneously prevents himself from acceding to the position of father, and thereby handing on the order of the Father to another generation. As Waller observes, "Staël shows Oswald as a father's son in order to undermine rather than strengthen the paternal line."[18] Melancholic repetition blocks ideological reproduction.

"The loss of some abstraction . . . such as one's country [Vaterland], liberty, an ideal"

Oswald's investment in an aesthetics of mimetic reproduction, I have been arguing, derives from his relation to the lost object which is both ambivalent (sadistic—guilty) and narcissistic. And if, as we have seen Staël suggest, the case of Oswald is grounded in his material situation, we can also relate it to the material situation of the novel more generally. I refer here, of course, to events just preceding *Corinne* and which the novel represents as present through their conspicuous absence: "At that time it was necessary to stay away from France and its environs because of its wars; it was also necessary to keep distance from the armies who made the roads impassable" (7).[19]

In her representation of Oswald, I now want to suggest, Staël relates his ambivalent relation to the lost father to the state of the bourgeoisie more generally following the death of the king. Indeed, the death of the king immediately precedes the opening lines of Staël's text, which provide the novel with a historical frame as they introduce its hero: "Oswald Lord Nelvil, a Scottish peer, left Edinburgh for Italy during the winter of 1794–1795" (3).

Although Oswald is not a bourgeois but rather a peer, the association of Britain with the bourgeoisie was widespread in France at the time that Staël wrote. I cite here only one example, drawn from contemporary French literary criticism. When Louis Bonald discusses the way in which literature is an expression of society, he remarks, "it is to be expected that the English have excelled in the novel, which offers the painting of family mores considered not in pastoral surroundings, but rather in urban surroundings, and which we call *bourgeois*: for the English, like all Protestant and commercial peoples live largely in domestic society."[20] Britain is the land which cultivates the liberal values dear to the revolutionary bourgeoisie. Notably, it is there that the crucial liberal division between public and private spheres appears in unadulterated form.

In the terms Oswald himself uses to describe his melancholic betrayal of his father, Staël strengthens her analogy between his condition and the state of the postrevolutionary bourgeoisie. "'I had rebelled against my country [*patrie*], against his will [*la volonté paternelle*], against everything sacred on earth,'" is how Oswald describes his past failings in the novel's opening pages (4–5; Balayé 29). Oswald here accuses himself of transgressing a social order similar to the monarchic order headed by the dead king, where *père*, *patrie*, and the sacred meet as one. In this context, the word Oswald applies to his betrayal is significant as well, for "rebel" describes as much collective transgressions of state authority as the individual's lapses from private authority. So, too, Staël describes the way in which the absent father regulates Oswald's behavior in language with political overtones. His father's memory, Oswald tells Corinne, is "a memory that *reigns* with you over my soul" (280, emphasis added).

Further echo of the collective situation of France in the case of Oswald is found in the details of the picture in Corinne's gallery which moves Oswald to tears. This picture by George Augustus Wallis, Jean Ménard tells us, treats an episode from the poems of Ossian, "in which Connal, by moonlight, sleeps on the tomb of his father Duthcaron ... The son does not want to abandon the tomb before his father has received burial rites."[21] A father who has not yet received appropriate burial rites: the painting recalls the situation of the unlaid king whose spirit will continue to haunt France through its turbulent nineteenth century.[22]

That problems of national and ideological identification may be implicated in the pathology of melancholia is a point, interestingly, suggested by Freud. "Mourning," Freud observes, "is regularly the reaction to the loss of a loved person, or to the loss of some abstraction which has taken the place of one, such as *one's country [Vaterland], liberty, an ideal* and so on. In some people the same influences produce melancholia instead of mourning and we consequently suspect them of a pathological disposition."[23] Freud's choice of abstractions whose loss triggers melancholia applies strangely well both to Oswald and to the postrevolutionary period when Staël wrote *Corinne*. During this period, as Staël's own career illustrates, intellectuals in sympathy with the republic struggled not only with how to conceptualize the *patrie* without the *père*, but also with how to explain the deterioration of the revolutionary ideals into imperial rule.

To validate *Corinne*'s association of Oswald's melancholy with the postrevolutionary bourgeoisie is a project beyond this essay's scope. It necessitates extensive historical documentation as well as theoretical reflection on how literature addresses history and on how to apply psychoanalytic concepts to the collective realm. Nonetheless, if the significance of Staël's connection among aesthetics, psychology, and historical trauma must remain at the horizon of my discussion, I have not yet finished elaborating her exploration of this connection in *Corinne*. While Oswald suspends the portrait of the dead father, like the albatross of Coleridge's ancient mariner, around his neck, does Staël represent Corinne's inspired sensibility as escaping from the weight of the Revolution's dead? Why does Corinne retouch the portrait of the father that Oswald was distraught at the thought of losing? Why, as has often been asked, does she restore the authority of the dead father whose law separates her from the object of her desire?

Mania: Corinne

"The most remarkable characteristic of melancholia, and the one the most in need of explanation," Freud states, "is its tendency to change round into mania—a state which is the opposite of it in its symptoms."[24] Is "the content of mania . . . no different from that of melancholia," Freud speculates, or is mania an index of the melancholic's triumph, if only briefly, over the cares which weighted him/her down: "In mania, the ego must have got over the loss of the object (or its mourning over the loss, or perhaps the object itself), and thereupon the whole quota of anti-cathexis which the painful suffering of melancholia had drawn to itself from the ego and 'bound' will have become available."[25] While Freud is drawn to the latter explanation, we also see him describe these two possibilities in such a way that the difference between them starts to fade. In the second case, mania turns out to be only a temporary surmounting of melan-

choly, not a permanent triumph over this form of psychic
relation to the libidinal object: "the manic subject ... plainly
demonstrates his liberation from the object which was the cause
of his suffering, by seeking like a ravenously hungry man for
new object-cathexes."[26]

In his discussion, Freud speculates that "all states such as joy,
exultation or triumph which give us the normal model for mania, depend on the same economic conditions."[27] "Oswald awoke
in Rome. A dazzling sun, an Italian sun, first struck his gaze. ...
He heard bells ringing out from the city's many churches; he
heard canons firing at intervals to announce some important
ceremony. When he asked for the reason, he was told that this
very morning the most celebrated woman in Italy was to be
crowned at the Capitol: Corinne—poet, writer, *improvisatrice*,
and one of the most beautiful women in Rome" (19). *Corinne*
opens at the height of Corinne's mania, literally a triumph, her
apotheosis in a public festival constituting Italy's latterday
peaceful equivalent to the Roman celebration of the same name.
That there is something maniacal to Corinne's success has,
moreover, often been observed, and not always in a favorable
light. Thus, even a critic as well disposed to Staël's heroine as
Gutwirth comments, "Corinne is a heroine stranded between a
fantastic megalomania and its opposite, nothingness."[28]

If Corinne's sensibility conforms to a Freudian mental economy of mania, this state should occur when "the ego must have
got over the loss of the object (or its mourning over the loss, or
perhaps the object itself), and thereupon the whole quota of
anti-cathexis which the painful suffering of melancholia had
drawn to itself from the ego and 'bound' will have become available."[29] Certainly, Corinne was miserable before coming to
Rome; can we attribute her misery to a melancholic fixation on
a lost object such as Freud describes? Might she, for example,
have suffered from a crippling nostalgia for Italy, the lost home
of the mother which would be her feminine equivalent to Oswald's investment in the father's land?

Corinne, however, qualifies the underwriting cause of her unhappiness in somewhat different terms. She would have been
quite happy to remain in England, she tells us, had her stepmother not condemned her to the weak tea of provincial life.
"Had my stepmother been willing to take me to London or Edinburgh, had she thought of marrying me to a man with enough
wit to value mine, I would never have had to give up either my
name or life, even to return to my former homeland [*patrie*],"

she says (265; Balayé 380). Qualifying Italy as her "former home-land [*patrie*]," Corinne marks her distance from it.

In associating her suffering with her stepmother, Corinne clues us in, I think, to another lost object at the root of her mania; an object that draws her closer to "the most personal of all griefs, the loss of a father," suffered by Oswald (3). Corinne's abuse at the hands of her stepmother derives from the fact that her father fails to protect her with appropriate paternal authority, and Corinne also ascribes a decisive role in her sufferings to a second failed encounter with a father.

> "*I love repeating it*, Oswald, that although I had never seen you, I was in a decided state of anxiety as I waited to meet your father . . . *there was so little basis for my feeling that it had to be a warning of my fate.* When Lord Nelvil arrived, I wanted to please him; perhaps I even wanted it too much, and I tried infinitely harder than I should have." (260, emphasis added)

Failing to please the father, Corinne loses both his esteem and the son that was to have been her reward, a gift not only from Oswald's father but also from her own: "I was almost twenty when my father decided it was time for me to marry, and it was then *that my appointed destiny started to unfold.* Our fathers, yours and mine, were close friends, and it was you, Oswald, you who my father hoped would be my husband" (259, emphasis added).

I underline to call attention to Corinne's use of a vocabulary of fatality to describe her encounter with Oswald's father which, she suggests, plays a crucial role in deciding her life.[30] Corinne herself, that is to say, authorizes a psychoanalytic reading of her encounter with Oswald's father, for when viewed from a psychoanalytic perspective, fate becomes trauma, a formative encounter with the real that has already occurred at some moment in the subject's past.[31] Consonant with a psychoanalytic explanation, too, would be the strangely pleasurable affect with which Corinne invests her repetition of the painful real: "I love repeating it."

The Fathers' love, I am suggesting, becomes the object whose loss Corinne neurotically reenacts.[32] And Corinne's rhetoric associates this loss with mourning if not melancholia. She figures her sojourn in England as death and her departure as rebirth into a new life: "were life offered to the dead in their graves, they would not lift off their tombstones with greater impatience than

I felt to cast off my shrouds, and repossess nature, my imagination, and my genius" (268). That Corinne's mania supervenes
following a deathlike period recalls the close link between mania
and melancholia elaborated by Freud. Consonant with Freud's
speculations, too, it is catalyzed by an event which momentarily
allows Corinne to think that her sensitivity to the lost object has
been overcome: "Had my father lived, I would have spent my
whole life caught up in that woeful situation," she remarks of her
miserable existence before coming to Italy, "but he was suddenly
carried off by an accident" (262). In a confusion crucial to the
smooth functioning of the Law, Corinne mistakes the biological
for the symbolic Father and experiences the death of the former
as freeing her from the latter's hold.

In the very terms Corinne uses to describe the alternative
that Italy provides to England, however, we intimate that her
triumphant sense of having freed herself from the weight of the
Fathers' displeasure will not last. At the moment Corinne departs from England, she revises the symbolic power which she
accords her mother's land. She no longer terms it the former
patrie, but rather the home of "the generation of fathers and
protectors" (263). In conceptualizing the positive power of Italy
in such a fashion, Corinne shows that she carries her paternal
household gods along with her even as she makes her escape.

If Corinne is still trying to set straight her failed encounters
with the Fathers, it is to be expected that this setting straight
will occur even less satisfactorily with Italian than English masculinity. Psychoanalysis teaches us that subjects cannot change
the content of what Lacan calls *tuché*, their formative encounter
with the real. The kernel of Corinne's trauma was with an English rather than an Italian father: "your father's land and mine"
is how Oswald characterizes the land where both his and her
fathers lie buried (275). Tellingly, when Corinne expresses her
disappointment with Italian men, she laments their failure to
display the authority that is the province of the symbolic Father.
As she puts it of an Italian whom she loves but eventually leaves:
"I realized that he did not have spiritual strength, and that in
life's difficult situations, it would be up to me to support and
buttress him. At that point there was no further question of
love, for women need sustaining strength, and nothing chills
them like having to provide it" (271).

No wonder, then, the unavoidable lure of the English lord.
"The manic subject . . . plainly demonstrates his liberation from
the object which was the cause of his suffering, by seeking like

a ravenously hungry man for new object-cathexes."[33] In the case of Corinne, however, and consonant with Freud's elaboration of repetition elsewhere, the new object is in fact the old. "What Corinne sees in Oswald," as Waller observes, "is thus a return of the repressed—her paternal heritage."[34] As might be expected from a subject's renewed encounter with an object playing a role in her formative trauma, Corinne's dealings with Oswald plunge her from mania into a melancholy abyss. So, Corinne herself encompasses her triumph in the same trajectory as her subsequent suffering: "he has hurled me from the triumphal chariot into the unfathomable depths of sorrow," she remarks of Oswald when she later sees him prancing before Lucile in "review" (347).

Corinne will try throughout the novel to provide the traumatic scene with a happy ending, as her pursuit of Oswald seeks to set right her failures in the past. But she also realizes, with the neurotic's impotent perspicacity, that no amount of repetition can undo the traumatic primal scene. If only, she laments to Oswald, we had "met *then* and had you loved me, our common fate might have been clear and unclouded" (259–60, emphasis added). Her every effort to erase this trauma ineluctably reproduces it; exemplary of such reproduction is the scene when Corinne spies on Lucile at her father's tomb. "Corinne was about to come forward and ask her sister to restore both her rank and husband to her in her father's name; but her courage failed her when Lucile took a few hurried steps toward the monument [the tomb of Oswald's father]" (356). "[I]n the presence of this grave," Staël continues, "the barriers between them appeared stronger then ever to her mind [*réflexion*]. She remembered Mr. Dickson's words: *his father forbids him to marry that Italian woman*, and it seemed that her father was joining forces with Oswald's and the whole of paternal authority condemned her love" (357; Balayé 504).

Just like Oswald, that is to say, Corinne alternates moments of mania with melancholic self-critique. And Staël extends the psychic reversibility between mania and melancholy to the aesthetic realm. Her hero and heroine each feel tremendously attracted to the form of aesthetic response which the other prefers. While Corinne colludes in the restoration of the father's portrait, Oswald enters fully into the "jeu" of *Romeo and Juliet*. Indeed, Corinne ends her career in a binge of mimesis which makes the restoration of the portrait into trivial work. If forces of sympathy have produced a resemblance between Lucile's daughter and

Corinne ("The little girl looked like [*ressemblait*] Corinne: Lu-cile's imagination had been absorbed with memories of her sis-ter during pregnancy" [386; Balayé 542]), Corinne works on this resemblance to transform Juliette into "the miniature of beauti-ful painting," which is to say, herself:

> One day Lord Nelvil was passing through the room where Juliette was taking a music lesson. She was holding a lyre-shaped harp made for her size, in the same way that Corinne held it, and her little arms and pretty expression imitated Corinne perfectly. It was like seeing a beautiful painting in miniature, with a child's grace tinging everything with innocent charm. Oswald was so moved at the sight that unable to say a word, he sat down trembling. (411)

Once we implicate Corinne's mania in the same trajectory of incomplete mourning as her melancholy, it becomes difficult to interpret the aesthetic expression of this mania, sensibility, as providing an empowering means of resistance to either Oswald's psychic or aesthetic investment in melancholic reproduction. If sensibility is a strategy of resistance to the power of the Fathers, it turns out to be resistance understood in psychoanalytic rather than political terms: psychic energy which reproduces the old repressive relations instead of putting them aside. Supporting such an interpretation would be the fact that Corinne's greatest triumphs of sensibility reproduce the order of the dead father as unerringly as her restoration of his portrait. While Corinne's performance of *Romeo and Juliet* moves Oswald outside of his melancholic self-absorption, it is only to reveal the depths of his allegiance to the Father's Law.

In *Corinne*, I am suggesting, mimesis and sensibility turn out to be two sides of one melancholic pathology. Breaking down these reactions along gender lines, Staël explains their differ-ences by calling attention to the asymmetrical positions of pro-ductive sons and daughters in relation to the Father's Law. While sons initially experience the Father's death as the imperative to reproduce the Law that authorizes their own position, daughters experience it as a release from the Law that their own productiv-ity transgresses. Ultimately, however, the distinction between these gendered reactions disappears. The inability to bury the dead Father drags son and daughter alike into the melancholy abyss.

Part II
Gender/Genre-Bending

Staël's *Corinne:* The Novel's Other Dilemma

Joan DeJean

THE place of Staël's fiction in literary history has never been
clearly established. Is *Corinne* an inaugural or a terminal text,
a harbinger of the glorious nineteenth-century novel or a final
exemplar of that novel's less glorified precursor tradition, the
eighteenth-century novel? For her first major prose fiction, *Delphine,* Staël adopted the epistolary mode perfected in the eighteenth century, for the most part by male novelists, notably by
her literary father Rousseau. *Julie,* Rousseau's master text, established the course that would be followed by the tradition
of the French novel now referred to as great. *Julie*'s ending
announces the death of the circular, uncontrollable epistolary
temporality, and the future novelistic reign of the time of generations, the temporality that is the foundation of family novels,
the genealogical fictions created by those known today as the
masters of the French novel. Staël's choice of the third person
for her second, and final, novel *Corinne* could therefore be seen
as both a prediction of the course of nineteenth-century prose
fiction and a rejection of the first-person forms in which the
eighteenth-century novel had been almost exclusively articulated. *Corinne,* however, makes a most unsatisfactory inaugural fiction.

Before I explain this statement, let me justify this attention
to canonic positioning. Naomi Schor has recently called for a
project of revisionism, an attempt "to denaturalize an all too
familiar [literary] landscape . . . the canon we have inherited
from Lanson and company and transmitted more or less unex-
amined for decades."[1] I agree with her hypothesis that a re-
contoured canon would oblige us to rethink literary, in this case
novelistic, history. *Corinne, or Italy* should displace *Les Liai-
sons dangereuses* (or *Justine*) as the culminating text of the
eighteenth-century tradition, for Staël's immense novel can be

117

read as a *mise en abyme* of the first one hundred fifty years of the French novel's history. This displacement would oblige us to consider the changing place reserved for women's fiction throughout that history.

When Staël adopted the third person for *Corinne,* she looked back to the origin of the modern French novel in the mid-seventeenth century: she resurrected the model for prose fiction developed by Madeleine de Scudéry during the Golden Age of salon activity and of French women's writing. Yet she resurrected this model only to demonstrate that it was no longer viable at a time when the salon tradition had ended and male novelistic models dominated the literary horizon.[2] In *Corinne,* Staël formulated a new dilemma for the novel, to borrow the expression Georges May coined to characterize the rules that delimited the eighteenth-century novel's existence. In his 1963 study, one of the pioneering works whose continued impact has made a volume like the present one possible, May described that novel as poised between the Scylla and Charybdis of impropriety and implausibility.[3] *Corinne* suggests that, for the woman writer, the novelistic dilemma took another form. The woman novelist at the turn of the nineteenth century was torn between two models: a novelistic form created by the first French women novelists and a variant perfected by their male successors. At the heart of this dilemma was the key (w)rite of passage from orality to textuality that Hélène Cixous has characterized as the woman author's "coming to writing."

In *La venue à l'écriture,* Hélène Cixous distinguishes between two interrelated yet radically different moments in the process by which a woman is able to define herself as a writer. The first, her "coming to language" [*la venue au langage*], is a spontaneous, uncontrollable phenomenon: "a fusion, a flowing into fusion, if there is any 'intervention' on my part it is . . . as if I were urging myself 'let it happen to you, let writing go by.'"[4] The second, her "coming to writing" [*la venue à l'écriture*], is an active choice based on a conscious rejection. "I write—woman. What difference? This is what my body teaches me, right away, be suspicious of names: they are only social tools, rigid concepts, little semantic cages (*cages à sens*). . . . My friend take the time to un-name yourself for a minute."[5] Unlike the coming to language, a flowing into and with, the coming to writing is a movement away from, an escape: "Personally, I got out of names rather late. I believed—until the day when writing came to my lips—

in Father, in Husband, in Family, and I paid dearly for this belief/ I paid for this belief with my flesh [*je l'ai payé chair*]."[6]

Cixous's (utopian) vision of these two initiatory experiences may be seen as figuring the two poles of Staël's novelistic dilemma. Cixous's "coming to language" would thus represent Staël's nostalgia for what she considered the original, inherently female creative mode, a style compatible with Cixous's spontaneous oral outpourings. I use "nostalgia" advisedly: Staël was the last true child of the immensely influential salon tradition; the female creativity that flourished in the salons was her actual maternal literary heritage, a heritage she was never fully to receive. Staël's mother, Suzanne Curchod Necker, was known during her student days in Lausanne as "Sappho." She presided over a neo-*précieuse* academy for which she revised some of the founding texts of *préciosité*, including its best known document, the *carte de tendre* devised by the original French Sappho, Scudéry. After her marriage she founded in Paris what has been termed "the last salon of the old society."[7] As a girl, the future baronne de Staël received her informal education in her mother's salon. There, seated at her mother's side, she bore witness to the last pure incarnation of a setting that privileged the genius of conversation with which she, even more than her mother, was gifted to an extraordinary degree. In her writing, Staël continued to reproduce a vision of the female creative experience as a "coming to language."

Thus, according to the legend Staël adopted and promoted (for example, in her 1811 play, *Sapho*) of the figure she considered the archetypal woman writer, Sappho composed orally, effortlessly, instantly. In similar fashion, the seventeenth-century French salon women whose novelistic legacy culminates in *Corinne*—and I think not only of Scudéry but also of less familiar writers like Montpensier and Conti—tried out their ideas first in conversation, and only subsequently passed to writing. Even then they almost always "came to writing" in a mediated fashion, with the aid of a male "secretary," who assumed all the public aspects of literary creation. These literary women had certainly, according to the terms of Cixous's distinction, "come to language," but it could be argued that they had never really "come to writing."

These literary women were in the privileged position of creating within a female literary community, outside the jurisdiction of male literary authority, and without rivalry with male literary models. They did not, therefore, have to come to terms with the inhibiting forces that confronted the woman writer in Staël's day. Attacks on women's writing had become increasingly violent in the course of the eighteenth century. Such attempts to silence the female verb were the essence of Staël's paternal literary legacy. Her biological father, in his own daughter's description, "[could] not bear a woman writer." Necker forced his wife to abandon her efforts at continuing the *précieuse* literary tradition. In an attempt to dissuade his daughter from following the maternal literary example, he mockingly referred to her as "Monsieur de Saint-Ecritoire."[8] Necker unnamed his daughter, removed the mark of her paternity, and renamed her as a writer, although, significantly, *not* as a woman writer. This paternal prohibition was doubled by the attack on women writers made by the male novelist who most influenced Staël, Rousseau. Staël's first published work, *Letters on J.-J. Rousseau,* is a eulogy of her literary father, in which she nevertheless takes him to task, "in the name of women," for having declared women incapable of literary genius.[9] Thus Staël's salon education was counterbalanced by powerful, first-hand experience of the prohibition against women's writing, a *non du père* that eventually led, in *Corinne,* to a rejection of the *nom du père,* or a disnaming process such as Cixous describes.

Rousseau rejected women's writing by proclaiming it inferior to male literary genius. He was thus faithful to critical strategy of his day, for the novelistic standards advocated by critics at the end of the eighteenth century were universally founded on a male novelistic model. These critics rejected the looser construction, the open temporality, the seemingly uncontrolled orality of the prior novelistic model developed by women novelists, a model they pronounced "implausible." They proclaimed instead the importance of novelistic development within a fixed, linear chronology—what Cixous terms "the time of generations," establishing an appropriate association between this temporality and the paternal order.[10] In the nineteenth century, "the time of generations" would engender the novel of education and the family novel, narrative models that reinforce the authority of the Name-of-the-Father. *Corinne* is both a *Bildungsroman* and a family novel, but the structure and the temporality Staël elected for this story of a woman writer ostracized by the paternal order work to undermine both the authority of the family and male literary authority.

Helen Borowitz has made an analysis of Staël's novelistic debt to Scudéry that is as detailed as it is convincing. She devotes particular attention to what her heroine Corinne owes the Sapho of Scudéry's *Le Grand Cyrus*.[11] Her thematic investigation can be extended most fruitfully to the domain of novelistic structure. More than any other factor, Staël's choice of novelistic model explains critical reservations with regard to *Corinne*'s form. Contemporary critics inaugurated this practice—witness Sainte-Beuve's recapitulation of Chateaubriand's often cited *mot*: "perhaps, as M. de Chateaubriand remarked, to make [Staël's] works more perfect, it would have sufficed to take one talent away from her, that of conversation." This opinion is still echoed today. Thus Gutwirth, for example, characterizes as antinovelistic the conversations on literature, the plastic arts, and other subjects that so frequently rupture *Corinne*'s narrative fabric: "The static, frozen quality of these discussions *within a novel* rob the whole of its forward movement."[12] However, the intercalated conversations are the mark of Staël's sense of literary heritage, the continuation of the conversations in Scudéry's novels, a way of keeping the oral, female verb alive in literature. This sign of Staël's allegiance to the original French novelistic model is understandably viewed by post-eighteenth-century critics as an imperfection, for from the early nineteenth century the novel evolved steadily away from Scudéry's digressive, circular temporality, and began to be judged according to its conformity to a model of linear, generational unfolding and progression.

Cixous's distinction between orality (coming to language) and textuality (coming to writing) is particularly appropriate to characterize the dual relationship—on the one hand, to the world of the (literary) mothers, and, on the other hand, to the world of the (literary) fathers—that is central to Staël's presentation of the woman writer in *Corinne*. When we first encounter Staël's heroine, she has apparently already experienced the crucial (w)rite of passage—in Cixous's terms, "to write and to pass through names, that's the same necessary gesture."[13] She has taken the time to "dis-name" herself and to escape from the "semantic cage" of the father's name, and has renamed herself with a name that signifies above all her roles in a community of literary women. Corinne's mother tongue is oral, the art of conversation, the spirit of improvisation. Corinne "comes to language" with her improvisations. Her initial relationship to literary creation is unproblematic, untainted by a sense of guilt or responsibility.

To characterize her heroine's mother tongue, Staël deploys a vocabulary virtually unknown in French before the appearance of *Corinne,* the language of improvisation. While the verb "improvise" is recorded as having been transplanted into both French and English from Italian in 1642, there are few examples of its usage before the early nineteenth century. Similarly, the nouns *improvisateur* and *improvisatrice* are listed as having entered French in the late eighteenth century, but the examples of early usage given are invariably from the first years of the nineteenth century. And in all the early references cited in the Littré and Robert dictionaries, one author's name is predominant, Staël. The vocabulary of improvisation—especially its feminine forms, *improvisatrice* and *improvisation*—is in large part Staël's gift—in *Corinne*—to the French language.

The inspiration for these neologisms dates from Staël's travels in Italy, when she heard some of the legendary *improvisatrices.*[14] She saw male performers as well at this time, but *Corinne* makes it clear that for Staël the improvisatory genius was an inherently female gift: the improvisator who visits Lord and Lady Nelvil in Milan is, in Oswald's words, "not worthy to speak [this poetic language.]"[15] The years in which *Corinne* is set (1798–1803) witnessed the end of the separate world of the salons in which the French art of conversation had been brought to perfection. In Italy, Staël found an oral tradition in which women still excelled, as though the spirit of the salons closed to her by the Revolution and exile were still alive in another guise. The tradition she found, however, was itself doomed; as Staël knew, she was privileged to witness some of the last geniuses of an oral literature already fast dying out. In Italy, *Corinne*'s creator bore witness a second time to the disappearance of a spontaneous female verb. The link she establishes in her novel between the two traditions stands as her testimonial to a vanishing tongue. Corinne herself defines her gift as a variant of the art of conversation: "for me improvisation is like an animated conversation" (84, see also 82). The gift of improvisation also links Corinne to the original literary women, for her spontaneous poetry is, in Staël's vision, the language of Sappho. Like Corinne, Staël's Sapho "improvises" while "accompanying herself on the lyre."[16] The literary woman who gives herself over to improvisation thus becomes part of a centuries-old female tradition of oral poetic creation. *Improvisatrices,* like the *précieuse* muses, speak the language of Sappho.

But then "the most famous woman in Italy, Corinne, poet, writer, *improvisatrice*" meets Oswald, Lord Nelvil, and she is forced to confront the crucial onomastic passage again, and this time she literally "pays with her body." Corinne is ultimately unable to get beyond "Father, Husband, Family." For her, "passion" remains "chained to genealogy," so once she has devoted herself to her love for Oswald, she can no longer remain outside the semantic/social cage of the father's name.[17] Corinne finds herself confronted by the collective forces of a community of dead fathers—Nelvil, Edgermond, even, as a result of her creator's sleight of hand, Staël's father Necker.[18] Corinne is betrayed by her lover not because Oswald is jealous of her celebrity or because he feels more at peace with a homebody than with a literary woman, although those things are of course true, but because of the father's interdiction (*le non du père*). And since the father's interdiction is directed not only against Corinne but against literary women in general, Corinne's fate must be read on the one hand as a warning to all women writers who choose to speak the mother tongue, and on the other as a commentary on the viability of any projected resurrection of original models for women's writing.

For *Corinne*/Corinne, the central problematic is the (w)rite of passage Cixous terms "la venue à l'écriture." The greatest technical difficulty Staël faced in this novel—far more imposing than the recreation of salon discussions on art and history—was the alleged written transcription of Corinne's improvisations. These are the weakest passages in *Corinne,* paradoxically for Staël, improvisational genius and self-proclaimed heir to the great tradition of the female verb. Corinne's improvisations are totally voice-less, without the liberating spontaneity that is the hallmark of what Staël considered the female verb. Furthermore, these allegedly spontaneous creations are almost all the evidence we possess of Corinne's literary genius. When the reader first sees her, she is described as "poet, writer, *improvisatrice*" (49), and while we are told that she has published books (50), we almost never hear of her writing anything. The narrator even explains that writing is contrary to Corinne's genius: "So much restraint was necessary for writing! and Corinne was most attractive when unconstrained and natural" (148).

In the course of Staël's immense novel, her heroine turns to writing only on two important occasions, once before Oswald's marriage, once after it. After his marriage, she composes the "fragments of Corinne's thoughts" (520–26), a disjointed collection of reflections that has nothing in common with the products of oral literary creation. Corinne's first written text is complete, the *aveu* or avowal she composes so that Oswald will know the secret of her past and decide if they can have a future together. Her writing, as she had always known it would, precipitates her downfall. In *Corinne,* for Staël and for her projection, the coming to writing, the attempt to get beyond the belief "in Father, in Husband, in Family," silences the female verb. This is so because it is at this juncture that the literary woman must confront the key obstacle to the survival of the mother tongue, the Name-of-the-Father.

Staël alters dramatically the import of the scene of female revelation when she makes the repressed male name, the name of the forbidden other, not a lover's name, but that of the dead father. Yet the significance of her rescription may not be as plain as it seems. This alteration apparently translates the conflict into oedipal terms since the revelation seems to betray a prohibited desire for the father, but this is to read Corinne's *aveu,* as the princess de Clèves's has been, as though the word could only be used as a synonym for "confession." Corinne's story—which she describes as the *"aveu* that Oswald exacted from her" (277)—corresponds formally to the confessional mode, established both by legal-religious tradition and by literary tradition (especially by Rousseau). Yet the key revelation she persistently defers—her family name and the story of her past involvement with that family's history—is irreconcilable with the notion of criminal activity. Staël rejected the primary significance attributed to the term *aveu* in seventeenth-century legal discourse: "a formal admission of guilt." She thereby rejected, as her precursor Lafayette had, the revelational mode consecrated by male writers, in favor of a prior form of legal acknowledgment, a shift in meaning that makes possible another reading of the significance of the Name-of-the-Father for the woman writer. In *Corinne,* the acknowledgment that precipitates the woman writer's tragedy is a story of a proper name, of the signature and the authority it possesses. Staël's use of "avowal" refers therefore to the original *aveu,* the written text establishing the vassal's loyalty to his lord, a pledge made in exchange for a heritable estate, a text exchanged for another text, the charter on which the lord's signature and his seal stood as a guaranty of the land. Corinne's narrative evokes the genealogy of substitutions on which the *nom du père* is founded. At the time of the repartition of lands that is the basis for the controlling and continuing paternal order, at the origin of the novelistic time of generations, was an exchange in writing; for a declaration of homage and loyalty was given a written proper name, a signature. Thus the *nom du père* established the authority of other paternal names, guaranteeing the inheritances that would in turn guarantee the orderly functioning of genealogy.

The *aveu* in *Corinne* is above all a commentary on the import for the woman writer of both authoritative and confessional exchanges. Corinne's revelation, the name of her father and her familial genealogy, invokes the paternal interdiction against women writers and therefore Corinne's willful violation of this prohibition. Oswald, speaking of his dead father, declares that *"je ne voulais rien faire sans son aveu"* [I didn't want to do anything without his authorization] (312). Corinne's *aveu*, her acknowledgment, is that she is *sans aveu* in another sense of the term, without the authorization of the fathers, for her literary endeavors and for her marriage to Oswald. When she makes the *nom du père* the unspeakable name for her heroine, Staël makes clear all the implications of the original *aveu* in French women's fiction, that of the princess de Clèves.

Corinne's declaration teaches us that all legally binding transfers of authority are exchanges among men, exchanges from which women are excluded because they can never make a valid signature in the paternal script. Because women played no role in the original substitution (homage for land), they are not able to "pledge themselves" in the new *aveu*, what might be termed, after Lejeune, the "confessional pact," that is, the foundation of literary authority in the *nom d'auteur* that guarantees the legitimacy of literary production. An author's signature on his creation is simultaneously a pledge of authenticity and sincerity (like Lejeune's "autobiographical pact"), the gesture by which the author publicly assumes responsibility for his script, and the mark that authenticates his production by revealing its place in his literary genealogy. But for the woman author, Staël demonstrates there can be no *nom d'auteur* in this sense. To sign her production, the literary woman is obliged to use either the name of the father or the name of the husband's father. Either signifies her exclusion from the law of genealogy and the exchanges of property on which it reposes, and therefore reveals her signature to be without authorization. The literary woman may write, attempting thereby to assume authority in the literary *patria*, but she can make no legitimate mark *in the male script* to authenticate her production.

After her *aveu*, Corinne's personal creative gift is no longer able to manifest itself. Her "last song," performed shortly before her death, is a written text rather than an improvisation (580), and she has it sung for her by a young girl (581). Furthermore, the only step she takes to ensure that her legacy will survive her is hardly an authorial act worthy of her original genius. She transforms Juliette, the daughter of her rival and the man who betrayed her, and makes the child over into a miniature of herself. Then she teaches Juliette the song she played for Oswald the day they spent at her villa in Tivoli, and she extracts from her miniature a promise to play the air for him every year on the anniversary of that first visit, using the child as though she were one of Jaquet-Droz's automatons. Thus Staël's portrait of the artist as woman turns female literary creation into a revenge fantasy: Corinne uses her work so that her lover will never be able to forget that he betrayed her because of his fidelity to a paternal interdiction.

Corinne's life writing is an act of revenge on the paternal literary order as well. The name of the Nelvil daughter evokes Rousseau's heroine, and the role Juliette plays is foreshadowed by that confided to Claire's daughter Henriette in *Julie*'s last pages. After Julie's death, the novel's chief representative of paternal Law, Wolmar, stages a dinner in which Henriette, dressed as the dead mother, occupies her place at the table. At the close of *Corinne,* Staël evokes Rousseau's family novel, the most important eighteenth-century French forerunner of the nineteenth-century genealogical fictions that seek to confine woman to a subordinate role in the time of generations. Her evocation of *Julie* in this context makes apparent the motivation behind the father's (Wolmar's/Rousseau's) child marionette, Henriette. She is created in an attempt to bring Julie's threatening female energy under paternal control. Staël reclaims that energy for the woman artist, even though she realizes that, in a novelistic tradition ruled by the time of generations, literary women can no longer come to language. The only creative avenue seemingly still open to them would require them to take possession of their production in that male script, thereby silencing the conversational voice, a lesson borne out by the future of women's writing in nineteenth-century France.

Voice as Fossil; Germaine de Staël's *Corinne, or Italy:* An Archaeology of Feminine Discourse

Marie-Claire Vallois

When asked what he thought of Mme de Staël's latest novel, *Delphine,* Talleyrand's witty remark, "I have heard that in her novel, Mme de Staël depicted us both disguised as women," was to become famous.[1] This bitter jest from a wounded ex-lover evokes, in a few words, the entire mentality of the period, while emphasizing its prejudices. Talleyrand gets even for being feminized by accusing the woman writer of actually being a man. These words constitute one of the first accusations with which Germaine de Staël would be frequently stigmatized: the scandal of "gynandry" or androgyny. If we were to leaf through the stacks of literary criticism concerning Staël, we would read over and over again this same rebuke. This reproach was echoed by another passionate enemy, the Emperor Napoleon, for whom Staël's "monstrosity" consisted of being a "female ideologist."[2] She incarnated a semantic combination of terms that, according to the new Civil Code, were to be naturally opposed. In the post-revolutionary society that was emerging, Staël, as a woman, played a bit too free with words, scrambled letters just a bit too much by ironically entitling herself a "female author" (*auteur femelle*) and laughing about it.[3]

In the preface to the work of criticism that swept her, in spite of herself, into a literary career—*Letters on J.-J. Rousseau*—Germaine de Staël herself agreed that she would have been content if "someone else had described what [she] felt." Entering the Republic of Letters with a critical treatise rather than a typical work of woman's fiction demanded an apology. Nonetheless, she did not conceal the enjoyment that this transgression provided: "but I delighted in the pleasure of recounting this memory and this feeling of enthusiasm to myself."[4] This double declaration—both the denial and the affirmation of her talent as a writer—is accomplished by the contradictory inscription of the prohibition against female writing. This dramatic demonstration of writing's duplicity makes us think, by analogy, of the symptom of hysteria identifiable in the gesture of Freud's patient who, "keeping (as a woman) her dress held tightly to her body, with the other hand struggles to tear it off (as a man)."[5] In this provocative spectacle, a woman exhibits what it is proper to conceal, the play of her bisexuality.

Criticism has not always been so hostile to the Staëlian phenomenon. The reevaluation of Staël, starting at the end of the nineteenth century, obviously must be set in the context of the more general revival of the Romantics. But even in this context the case of Germaine de Staël cannot fail to strike us by its very ex-centricity. She is celebrated not only as one of the Muses of the Romantics, but also as one of their main theoreticians (*On Passions, On Literature, On Germany*), as well as a novelist (*Delphine, Corinne, or Italy*). Nonetheless, the numerous biographies of Staël appearing during this period, while giving her credit for her eclecticism and for initiating this renewal of interest, also betray a strategic shift of critical perspective whose consequences for a woman of letters must be evaluated. This new perspective transforms the author-writer into a "voice." The shift of perspective will be used, as we will see, simultaneously as praise and as dismissal. This should not obfuscate, however, the fact that Staël's writings by their ex-centric specificity force the invention of a new critical category in itself: the category of the "author's voice," which should not be mistaken for the first person of narration. In reading the biographies of Germaine de Staël one cannot help but be struck by how insistently all these critics testify to their constant impression of not only seeing her again, but, particularly, of hearing her. Sainte-Beuve is the first to launch these archaeological expeditions in search of a voice, in pursuit of something dead, lost forever, yet feebly echoed in the writings.[6] As an example, we note that Pierre Kohler concludes his biographical study thus: "she put what was best in her spirit and in her art into these vanished words. Writing, she went on conversing. . . ."[7]

In the tradition of literary criticism classified under the rubric "Life and Works," this sort of commentary tends to "de-scribe" the difference between the sexes, while at the same time reinscribing it, though more discreetly. A woman does not write; she converses, she chatters. Yet this partisan and reductive attitude of criticism indicates an especially troubling insistence.

Why does it seem important in the case of Germaine de Staël to go back to the "living source," to the origin of the text, a text that seems to be only the lifeless remains of a voice whose strange charm echoes from beyond the grave? It is precisely this hollow echo that all those explorers into literary necromancy claim to bring back from their voyage. But is this expedition not doomed in advance to failure? Staël, as we know, almost never uses the voice of autobiography: she rarely writes "I." In *On Germany,* she explains this withdrawal of a personal voice: "Women tend to veil themselves in the cloak of fiction, men in the cloak of history."[8] Women disguise themselves in fiction or romance while men expose themselves in memoirs and autobiographies. The apparent inevitability of this sexual segregation of the genders should not obscure in the female author the strange process of repression and displacement that it implies. Twenty-six years later, composing a second preface to her first writing, *Letters on J.-J. Rousseau,* Germaine de Staël reflected on the extraordinary condition of the Woman of Letters. She consoled herself for the excessiveness of her talents with the thought that no one can blame heaven for having been given "an extra faculty."[9] Certainly it is something extra that the woman author enjoys; writing springs from an excess, a supplementary experience, as Germaine de Staël said in speaking of the novel.[10] This personal logic of the supplement was to shape her theory of the novel in an original manner.

It is therefore proper for the female author (our literary hysteric) to cloak herself in fiction, but should we understand this disguise in the sense of dressing and attiring oneself with jewels to cover something that one does not have, or is it covertly robbing, concealing, and disrobing this monstrous extra that only fiction could enrobe and recount? Fiction and woman in this sense would go together, not according to the restricted economy of the literary institution, but according to an unthinking expenditure and excess. Our hysteric is a creature with not one sex but two; from the beginning she represents the problematic mystery of all feminine identity. And this mystery can only be written as fiction.

Unlike her masculine contemporaries—Goethe, Chateaubriand, or Stendhal—Germaine de Staël would never recount "her story" or that of her heroines through the mirror reflection of a first-person narration. Her memoirs, *Ten Years of Exile,* which are not autobiographical, remained fragmentary and unfinished, as did the diary of her youth: "I wanted to make a

complete journal of my heart, I tore out some of its pages. . . .
Besides, damn the person who can say everything, damn the
person who can put up with reading these faded feelings."[11]

In these few lines Alain Girard sees the rejection of the intimate autobiographical project (*JI* 74). In fact, it does seem difficult for Germaine de Staël to submit herself to the legality of
the identification ritual: "I, the undersigned, Louise, Germaine
de Staël, do hereby testify. . . ." Her refusal of confidential discourse is not so much motivated by a feeling of embarrassment
for her real feelings as it is by their inscription. "As for me, I
was not ashamed of my heart and all alone in the silence of
passions, I felt it beneath my hand still beating for honor and
virtue" (*JI* 76). What is wrong is shifted from the level of feelings
and fixed at the level of the language expressing them. The mutilation and abrupt interruption of the diary thus acquires symbolic value.

Autobiographical writing registers a split between the "I" who
writes and the Me reader-receptor—the split, the phenomenon
of double consciousness identified by Freud as "hypnotic states"
characteristic of hysteria.[12] It is thus not a coincidence that the
names of the two Staëlian heroines, Delphine and Corinne—the
sibyl—evoke, with the mythological connotations, the image of
an inspired woman, one possessed, one other people might call
hysterical.[13] Oracular women, receptacles for divine voices or
inhabited by external voices, become allegories for the Staëlian
feminocentric novel. The woman author is no more able to speak
in her own name than Delphine or Corinne are able to tell their
own story.

And yet she speaks, but without ever putting herself into the
position of being interpellated exclusively as a "female subject,"
as the subjected subject of gender ideology.[14] Germaine de Staël
escapes the trap of autobiography, the ritual of confidence and
penitence performed by an "I," which imprisons once and for
all—the trap of the "I" that could only repeat, as Napoleon would
have it, that anatomy is destiny.[15]

Rejecting the repressive practice of both personal and fictional
autobiography, Germaine de Staël wrote her most famous novel,
Corinne, or Italy, in the third person and as a curious mixture
of romance and travelogue. *Corinne, or Italy,* in spite of its
woman-centered title, presents us, at least at the outset, with
the parallel story of two heroes: a male hero, Oswald, Lord Nelvil,
heir to a great Scottish name, the stereotype of the English Romantic hero, and Corinne the female hero, a poet who lives in

Italy but whose real name and birth remain secret until the middle of the book. After a long and risky journey through Europe, Oswald arrives in Italy where his doctors advised him to go to restore his health and cure the melancholy caused by the death of his father. Once in Rome he is immediately distracted from his sorrows by the celebration of a woman poet, Corinne, the famous *improvisatrice,* who is to be crowned at the Capitol. He is seduced by Corinne's beauty and talents but more particularly by the quality of her voice: he falls in love with her. Corinne offers to show him Rome and falls in love with him. The antique palaces and ruins of Rome and then Naples constitute the romantic, haunting, and ensnaring decor of the love story. Corinne, who is acting as Oswald's private guide to Italy and Italy's spokeswoman, soon lets the ruins speak for her. The story could have concluded with a happy ending if only the female heroine could have continued talking about Italy and kept her own story secret. But once in Naples surrounded by the fumes of the erupting Vesuvius and on their way to the archaeological site of the vanished city of Pompeii, Oswald narrates the story of a past love with a Frenchwoman that, according to him, killed his father. Corinne then cannot help but reveal her own secret childhood story, a story that strangely echoes Lord Nelvil's. She, too, exiled herself in Italy after her father's death. She, too, like Oswald, was guilty of transgressing the father's law. The two heroes have a common past: they lived in the same country; their fathers were close friends and even wanted to marry them when they were still children. But Oswald's father changed his mind when he saw and heard Corinne. This piece of censured familial memory that uncovers their similarities will at the very moment of revelation separate them tragically. For if both heroes have transgressed the father's law, only Corinne remains convinced of the necessity of such a transgression. It is the very inscription of such a story, the female version of the oedipal moment, that will ruin the Roman idyll from then on. Only the pretext of ending the tour of Italy can keep the lovers together. The woman-story then must continue to be censured, and it is replaced by an Italy-story travelogue. This displacement must be analyzed more closely.

Until the end of the nineteenth century, the Bibliothèque Nationale classified *Corinne, or Italy* as a travel guide.[16] This constitutes an eccentricity or de-centering of the romantic subject, of which the female author was fully aware right from the start. "I shall write a sort of novel that will serve as a frame for a trip to Italy."[17] In a curious reversal of the classical hierarchy, the trip to Italy is presented as the privileged subject of fictional writing—the personal fiction serving only as a frame. This displacement of the fictional subject is disturbing because it questions the anthropomorphic hierarchy that is traditional in western fictional writing, where a thing, an inanimate object, cannot take the place of a person (except in the fantastic genre, where the passage from one kingdom to another—inanimate to animate—is the rule).[18] Does that mean that Germaine de Staël's novel should be read under the rubric of fantasy? At first glance, lacking any commentary from the author, nothing would seem to authorize us to do so, unless perhaps it is the figure of the double—person or country—so oddly emblematized in the novel's title, *Corinne, or Italy.*

Germaine de Staël, in fact, titled her second novel, as she had her novellas and *Delphine,* with a feminine first name without a patronym. Unlike the other novels, the erasure of the father's name is here compensated by the vague indication of a place name: Corinne or Italy. This substitution of toponym for patronym cannot help but be problematic for the reader. Is the loss of the paternal reference redeemed by the place name Italy, which, bound to the first name by the copula "or" is, in fact, inscribed as another enigma? A real literary sphinx, does not this fictional entitling speak to the reader with stone words in a landscape of ruins all the better to evoke a woman's secret? From the beginning this riddle seems open to a double solution: one a metonymic performance, Corinne in Italy; the other a metaphoric description, either Corinne or else Italy.

The second possible way of reading—Italy as the metaphorical double of the heroine—is quick to present itself to the traveling hero. In Italy Oswald discovers a mysterious woman; while she reveals Italy to him, he sets out on the quest of loving and knowing her. This romantic key, moreover, was suggested to him by Corinne's attendant and confidant, the Prince de Castel-Forte: "Look at her, she is the picture of our beautiful Italy."[19] A mysterious key nonetheless, for it is not granted to everyone to understand it, since, as the Prince de Castel-Forte says, Corinne is someone "whom it is impossible to imagine when one has not heard her" (57).

The word "heard" [*entendue*] must be taken here in its double sense: in the sense of hearing, but also of interpreting and deciphering. It is a question of reading Corinne's story in that of Italy. There has been a substitution of stories through a delegation of discourse: for Corinne's personal discourse, an autobiographical discourse, is substituted the tourist discourse on which the subsequent delegation of speech depends. In the Italian descriptions, it is no longer the heroine but the "monuments who speak to the soul with their true grandeur" (98).

The heroine's lost voice is inscribed in her stone double: a fossil voice ready to live. The Corinne-monument substitution, moreover, is poetically implicit from the moment of Corinne's first appearance at the Capitol. Does the narrative describe a stone figure carved in an ancient *bas relief* or a being of flesh and blood? "Corinne was seated on this chariot built in the ancient style. . . . Her arms were radiantly beautiful; her stature tall, but somewhat heavy, in the manner of Greek statues" (52). Half-goddess, half-woman, the statue nevertheless begins to live beneath the admiring and loving gaze: "She made one think of a priestess of Apollo coming towards the temple of the Sun, and, at the same time, of a perfectly simple woman" (52).

The tourist trip is thus transformed into an idyll. The statue becomes a woman—a commonplace of that period's literature, some of whose veils Freud lifted in his reading of Jensen's *Gradiva*. The obvious archaeological parallelism between *Corinne, or Italy* and *Gradiva* permits an illuminating comparative development on the theme of voice. *Gradiva* is another magical fiction, the story of a woman of stone who comes to life before the eyes of Jensen's hero and makes him recover his health by the familiar sound of her voice: "I knew your voice sounded like that."[20] This reunion with the beloved feminine voice can only take place, according to Freud's reading, through the loss of the voice of the analyst-doctor that he is: "Gradiva was able to return the love which was making its way from the unconscious into consciousness, but the doctor cannot."[21] Affirming the superiority of fiction over analytic science, Freud in this study nevertheless refuses to assimilate himself into the "total psychiatrist." He rejects the power attached to the institutional "I" of science. But at the same time, he allows himself the right to fiction, the pure fiction of this "classic happy ending, marriage" in Jensen, which cures because it is so strongly romantic. In fact, it is in separating himself from the psychiatrist that he dismisses the reading of *Gradiva* according to a fetishist etiology (a reading privileging the hero's fixation on Gradiva's lifted foot). Thus Freud's more fertile reading becomes necessary: "The case of Norbert Hanold should be described as hysterical, not paranoid delirium."[22] This hysterization of the hero is, however, very discreet, since Freud only provides the key to his reading in a note written in the conditional, the mode of the imaginary.

The Freudian reading, a fictional supplement to the analytic discourse, would consist in revealing the hero's bisexuality, but also simultaneously the bisexuality of the heroine, Zoe-Gradiva, who has become the doctor. This operation of fictional androgyny, moreover, is doubled in the fiction's margins by its repressed opposite, that of a Freud-Gradiva who, losing his sexual identity, receives in return the "voice" of fiction. The hysterical symptom as an "unconscious sexual phantasy that is simultaneously masculine and feminine" is contagious and passes first from the hero to the heroine and then outside the text to include the analyst who secretly becomes hysterical through the pleasure of reading.[23] So Freud, by this fictional detour, is put in the position of speaking, of being spoken, as a woman.

As for Germaine de Staël, she had to publish her sort of novel as a travel guide, and she thus reveals the urgency with which a private story opens onto public discourse, blocking at the same time any possible return to the private. Her archaeological quest does not have *Gradiva*'s happy, familial solution: there is no marriage. The romantic ruins remain palatial monuments, destroyed forever without so much as the outline of a familial roof. Italy remains an open space, knowingly chosen by Corinne as the only one from which she can speak: "You allowed me glory, O you, liberal nation, who does not banish women from the temple" (582).

This exalting of feminine talent seems curious when in the novel the poet finds herself being reduced to silence in order to let the stones speak. It would seem that the Staëlian novel demonstrates almost perversely all the dangers implicit in feminine fiction's strategy of metaphorical substitution. This delegation of the power of speech is not without risk. By assigning to the decor of ruins the task of refracting her image and presence, as if speaking in her name, the heroine not only effaces herself as the subject of the discourse but in the end positions herself as an object of the masculine gaze. Does not the fiction of the touristic narrative, a strategic feminine tactic, risk falling right back into the phallocentric representational trap in which woman is unable to inscribe herself unless it is as an object in ruins, a mutilated object?

Does not the ruin, that broken fragmented object, serve too readily in that worshipping of the feminine body—already lost— only by re-inscribing its presence as mutilation? Pleasure in ruins is part of an androcentric strategy that, while maintaining the fascination of the object of love—and beyond that, sexual difference—denies it by displacing its adoration onto fetish objects: monuments, frescos, statues.[24] This new, melancholy religion of the aesthetic appropriation of the world of shapes makes one feel secure, but it can only reveal the narcissistic investment of the Romantic poet, tourist, or analyst. It is the compulsory route taken by every Romantic author, who, in the depths of exile, can find only the specular double of his own image. The romantic episode at the Fountain of Trevi, stirring the lovers to resume their Roman quest, barely conceals this androcentric and narcissistic dimension of the amorous relationship: "He leaned towards the fountain so he could see better, and his own features then appeared in reflection next to Corinne's. She recognized him and cried out . . ." (126).

This introspective splitting of the individual between two heroes as self and knowledge of self—another characteristic of the modern imagination—according to Staël gives only a partial account of this novel of doubles, *Corinne, or Italy*.[25] In the end Corinne's story is not reducible to that of Oswald. The quest abandoned by the masculine hero at the end of the novel will be taken up again by his wife, Lucile, another English double for Corinne and her paternal sister as well. The novel's riddle does indeed reside, as this proliferation of doubles attests, in the problem of identity, an identity that is the actual "object," initially and forever lost.

The novel, *Corinne, or Italy,* is, in fact, the story of a double voyage. The voyage of exile of the hero overshadows (in the first part of the novel) the heroine's return to her mother's homeland. If it is the father's presence and voice that Oswald seems to have to designate as the goal of his Italian trip, for Corinne it is the mother's. For the heroine Italy is the maternal land, or rather the maternal breast. Corinne both is and is not Italy, which is also her mother. We are in the presence of a new definition of polymorphic identity or a strategy for escaping the Romantic schema. In other words, the Staëlian fiction figures the locus of a loss, the loss of the family patronym, and therefore the loss of the connection of identity that is bound to the name of the father. But, at the same instant, it reveals itself as the locus of another type of privileged connection, one buried more deeply in the memory of civilizations as well as in individual memory. Another narcissism, a primary narcissism that disregards oppositions between person and country, subject and object, self and other, takes the detour of writing to inscribe itself as the archaic relationship with the mother.[26]

A return to origins and a taste for the archaic become clear in other respects as a return to the naming of spaces (the evocative power of the mother as "place name" has been demonstrated by Julia Kristeva) and to the privileging of orality in descriptions.[27] The tourist descriptions only fill the gaps in the adult feminine story—Corinne's story—in order to reorganize, as we have seen, the euphoric space of another story that would resemble that of childhood loves. It would be the story of the infant: the one who does not speak but shows and calls with his or her voice—a child's viewpoint that others will call poetic. The descriptions in this sense are evocation not only in the traditional sense of the word, but also in the etymological sense of "e-vocation" as "calling out" or even as "in-vocation."

It is these tourist designations with their strangely evocative power—the power to evoke archaic place names—that ultimately give the descriptions in *Corinne, or Italy* their real strength. This evocation of the dead ends with the disturbing evocation of the eternal absence in the plot, the mother. Indeed, the tourist discourse would derive its all-powerful rhetorical being from the fact that it ultimately functions as prosopopoeia: that is, as the evocation of a dead person—or rather a dead woman—whom, however, the discourse has made speak and act. The final double, the maternal double, brings together and reconciles all of writing's doubles.

It is certainly this maternal double whom the poet Corinne unceasingly invokes by means of a series of apostrophes opening the first improvisation: "Italy, empire of the Sun; Italy, mistress of the world; Italy, cradle of letters, I salute you" (59). These are invocations to the maternal homeland where the evocation of the past serves less as a signifier than as an alibi for vocalization, for the call, the cry. These are cries of distress by Corinne whose return trip to the mythological past of civilization is poetically akin to the voyage of Chore when Pluto, her lover, steals her from her mother, Persephone/Demeter, to carry her away into the kingdom of the shades and the dead. By playing with mythological connotations, this new playful trick of writing refers to that other quest of a mother for her daughter. Through an infinity of displacements in the linguistic chain, through the impossibility of closing off the naming that is the keystone in the architecture of language, through a perverse game played with her romantic writing, Staël's ultimate goal seems indeed to be the deconstruction—or the ruin—of this privileged cultural edifice that is language as "home." Both in the home of logos that Plato constructed and in the paternal home delimited by Freud, Staëlian writing defines itself as a strategy of exile with no real return.[28] From this perspective, *Corinne, or Italy,* Corinne in Italy, Chore/Persephone calls up the Platonic "Chora," a linguistic articulation completely provisional and essentially mobile, which, "unable to locate itself" except through a "bastard reasoning"—that is, fiction for Germaine de Staël—elsewhere in *Timaeus* finds itself absorbed by the nourishing, maternal space, a space that, "neither a being in itself," nor a projection of the One, is a "being never to be named."[29]

The novel *Corinne, or Italy* produces, in the theater of Romantic literary ruins, the diverse masquerades presented by the myth of voice as understood in its different meanings.[30] First, voice understood in its grammatical sense, the impersonal voice of narration of the travel guide as it presents, in disguise, the story of the heroine. But then the Staëlian feminine novel would also appear to be written in another, grammatical, sense of voice, the passive voice: woman speaking herself, being spoken by the discourse of the Other, the voice of culture, the voice of the father. Giving voice to culture results, however, as we have seen, in a troubling perversion of the narrative apparatus where the in-vocation of the classical past is transformed into an e-vocation of person—the mother. In this last transformation, voice as e-vocation is the calling upon breath to vocalize; it is the first language constituted between mother and child. Feminine literature would here demonstrate its ludic specificity. The role of the Sibyl, her body in a trance applying herself to voicing Apollo's oracles, is thus used in a subversive and playful way. For Corinne, the Staëlian sibyl, voicing Apollo's oracles is a pretext for recalling, as in the older version of the myth, the original possessor of the Delphic oracle—Gaia, Mother Earth. Feminine writing would here operate according to the model of an archaeological quest whose success and pleasure could be achieved only in the mode of theft. The writing of the Staëlian tourist novel is certainly—as criticism has long acknowledged and we must acknowledge—a product of the typically feminine perversion, kleptomania.[31] It has been pointed out that the literary artifact obtained, *Corinne, or Italy,* partakes in the aesthetic of the "ready-made" before any such thing existed. Literature in this sense would discover the veils of its fiction—a fiction where it could only be a question of stealing dresses, a robbery that would disclose, under the travesties of the imaginary, the nothingness of a voice that never stops laughing.[32]

This laughter, however, ends up with more than the last word in the melancholy cemetery of Romantic writings. Among other examples, by way of a Staëlian postscript, there is the example of the kleptomania (masculine this time) in *Mémoires d'outre-tombe*. In order to explain his love for Mme Récamier, Chateaubriand needs the echo of another voice. He inserts in their entirety the love letters sent by Germaine de Staël to the beautiful Juliette, changing neither the heading nor the signature.[33] It is a strange play of echoes, a strange travesty of voice, of this fossil voice that has long haunted and continues to haunt the mansions of the Romantics.

Places of Memory: History Writing in Staël's *Corinne*

Nanette Le Coat

Germaine de Staël's place in literary history is now firmly established, but there has been a considerable tardiness on the part of critics and historians to accord her a niche in the pantheon of nineteenth-century historiographers. Part of this delay is due to the fact that history and literature occupy separate pavilions in our cultural history—an architectural arrangement that is itself an artifact of the nineteenth century. Only recently have the dividing walls been penetrated by a contemporary willingness to challenge disciplinary boundaries, and a new understanding that history writing, like history itself, is a product of social and cultural conditions.

Examination of Staël's history writing has, for the most part, focused on the work that conforms most recognizably to traditional historiographical norms—*Considerations of the French Revolution*.[1] While there is certainly nothing conventional about the work, its subject matter, the French Revolution and Staël's father's role in it, is easily discernible as historical. Yet some of the Staël's most original ideas about history and history writing surface in a book that has not been considered, by conventional standards at least, a work of history at all. In her novel, *Corinne, or Italy*, Staël develops a highly independent position on the relation of memory to history.[2] By embodying her ideas on this subject in a form that was traditionally considered unsuited for serious historical reflection, she challenges consecrated distinctions between "serious" and "imaginative" writing, between historiography and the novel. But Staël goes one step further—she implicitly critiques the scientific historiography of contemporary social thinkers and offers a vision that at once complements and surpasses their own. My task here is threefold: first, taking the writing of C. F. Volney as an example, to show how sensualist philosophy informed a scientific approach to his-

139

toriography—an approach that had some currency at the time
Staël was developing her ideas on history and with which she
reveals some important affinities; next, to show how the profound affiliations established in *Corinne* between memory and
place accord a value to that faculty that challenges a sensualist
epistemology and, ultimately, the positivist view of history that
derived from it; and, lastly, to comment on the insightfulness of
Staël's historiographical perspectives and their relation to our
modernity.

During the mid to late 1790s the most progressive and influential French intellectual milieu was that of the Idéologues.
Gathering at the salon of Helvétius's widow, this varied group
included not only scholars and "gens de lettres," but judges,
high officials, physicians, and diplomats.[3] The Idéologues saw
themselves as carrying on the radical social agenda of the *philosophes*. They were convinced that Idéologie—that is, the systematic study of human perception, language, and thought—could
provide a scientific basis on which to constitute new disciplines
of understanding, inform the structure of institutions, and, ultimately, regulate conduct. At about the same time Staël published her *On Fictions* (1795), the Idéologue Volney, recently
returned from a study tour of the Middle East, delivered an
iconoclastic series of lectures on history at the newly founded
Ecole normale.[4]

Volney and his fellow Idéologues shared the high-Enlighten-
ment tendency toward abstraction, universalism, and rational-
ism. As third-generation *philosophes,* they sought to systematize
and extend Enlightenment social and political theory. Volney's
lectures on history exemplified in many ways these ambitions.
Accounts of the past, in his view, should not only be global and
transhistorical, they should, more importantly, be *scientific.* He
held forth his own *Voyage en Egypte et en Syrie* (1787) as a
model of what scientific historiography could be. This latter
work was hybrid, combining elements of travel writing, political
theory, anthropology, and geography and did not readily conform
to conventional norms of history writing, but its unusual em-
phases—on language, on geography, on a deductive approach—
give us some notion of the new scientific orientation Volney
envisioned for history.

Like Voltaire, Volney was inclined to dismiss much of history
writing as at best, mythopoeia, and at worst, a pack of lies. Much
of his drive to stand history writing on a firm scientific footing
was motivated, in fact, by his distrust of human motivations.

Most historical accounts, he believed, were partisan or self-justificatory and founded on hearsay and unreliable witnesses. There had to be a way to get at the truth of human experience without relying on human beings themselves. One such way was to describe not human deeds (wars, treaties, and marriages) but human institutions, practices, and productions: the military, religious organizations and beliefs, public architecture. Another way was to explain the emergence of these human products through the physical, that is climatic and geographical, conditions under which they were created. Still another way to obviate the necessity of relying on past accounts was to practice a retrospective or "archaeological" approach; to draw inferences about the past from extant architectural and social artifacts.

Volney's account is marked by the enshrinement of scientific objectivity, and this attitude in turn produces some of the text's distinctive features. First is the preferential treatment given to the nonhuman components of a given environment—climate, geography, and architecture figure more conspicuously in his account than human beings. When Volney does present human subjects it is generally not as agents of lived events, but rather as creatures who, over time, display more or less ingenious methods for adapting to external physical conditions. The second distinctive feature of the text is Volney's voluntary self-effacement as writing subject: his dry description of external physical conditions and his equally arid evocation of oriental mores scarcely register his own experience as a traveler in a land radically different than his own. Although his *Voyage* is drawn from personal experience, he rarely uses the subject pronoun "I" and there is, consequently, something abstract and depersonalized about the account—as if the landscape were viewed by some omnipresent, disembodied eye.[5]

Volney's efforts to elaborate a scientific historiography thus lead him to simultaneously broaden and restrict history's purview. He marshals a broad range of evidence—information that we would today characterize as linguistic, geographical, sociological, or anthropological—thereby expanding the definition of the historical. At the same time, however, in his concern for scientific rigor, he radically limits history's compass by eschewing narrative. A schematic outline with categories for various kinds of data replaces narrative as the structuring principle of the account. Volney even tries to discount travel writing's narrativity by dissociating it from the novel. Citing the excess and romantic exaggerations of certain popular travel accounts, he declares: "I believed that as a genre, travel belonged to history and not to novels."[6]

Germaine de Staël's thinking, in many ways, allies her with the Enlightenment as much as with the Romanticism she was so important in promoting. Not surprisingly then her historical vision has some affinities with the perspectives of the Idéologues. Like Volney and Voltaire before him, Germaine de Staël refuses to imagine a history that is merely a litany of the deeds and misdeeds of famous personages. And like Volney, she looks for history's traces not only in written chronicles, but in historical sites and in institutions that reveal the persistence of deeply rooted traditions. She seeks, for example, the effect of ancient religious beliefs on Greek tragedy or the influence of different forms of government on eloquence and freedom of expression.

Corinne was not Staël's first essay in cultural history. *On Literature* (1800) presented an imposing social and cultural tableau, painting in broad strokes the moral and social characters of European peoples as revealed by their institutions and cultural expressions. In *Corinne,* however, we discover a finer-grained study. Staël devises a kind of experiment in which the moral and social values of two distinct cultures are allowed to play themselves out in the destinies of their representatives—Oswald and Corinne. These values are no longer abstract components of national character, but deeply embedded elements of personal psychology. Here, psychology is destiny. But psychology in turn is shaped by national history and character. In a sense what we have then is the collision of two national histories in the personal history of the novel's protagonists. Private and public histories are related in two distinct narrative voices. The story of Corinne and Oswald is narrated in an omniscient third-person voice. The story of Italy, on the other hand, is most often narrated by Corinne, who, in addition to being a poet, muse, and sibyl, is also cast as a historian. She reveals her native Italy's history in two distinct modes. The first mode we might call deictic—she *shows* Italy to Oswald. The second mode is allegorical—she *represents* Italy for Oswald. I would like to begin by turning to the first, more overt way Corinne reveals her country's past and to consider what conception of history is at work in this exposition.

Corinne undertakes to *show* Oswald the sights/sites of Italy, for in so doing, she hopes to bind him to the place. It is her country's beauty and rich history that will "fix" (the term is hers) him in Italy. Her account of the events and personalities that have shaped her country's past emerges not from some master narrative but, rather, from direct contact with the physical setting in which history has transpired. As Corinne directs Oswald's attention to the various temples, villas or public buildings that spread before them, she relates an anecdote or a narrative recalling an event associated with that edifice. In this way each building becomes invested with moral significance. Here is the prison where Catalina's accomplices perished, there is a temple built by Servius Tullius to thank the gods for his rise from slave to emperor, and so on. Each ruin and monument recalls the stories of the people who built and dwelt in it.

Ruins and monuments, however eloquent, cannot tell the whole story. Rome's very geography has been shaped by human actions. The hills are emblematic of the leveling effect of the historical process. What were once distinct promontories are now mere rises. The valleys separating the hills have been filled in with jumbled debris. Similarly, distant periods lie buried under the remains of more recent ones: "You cannot take one step in Rome," Corinne observes, "without bringing together present and past, without juxtaposing different pasts" (72). She likens her undertaking to that of the archaeologist: "In Rome there are many distinguished men concerned only with discovering new relationships between history and the ruins" (72). Like the archaeologist, she must reconstruct the past by discerning its distinct stages and by interpreting the cultural significance of its physical signs. Corinne initiates Oswald into the secrets of Rome by drawing out what the monuments have to say about ancient religious practices, forms of pleasure, and attitudes toward death.

In her archaeological approach, Staël reveals an important affinity with the historiographical methods of Volney. Both attribute a profound significance to the role of place in the determination of history. Both conceive of the privileged place as a locus densely inhabited by historical signs, that is, vestiges of the past. Rome for Staël is like Palmyra for Volney—a forest of signs waiting to be deciphered. Every physical aspect, every hill, river, monument, is a silent bearer of a significance. It is left to the interpreter to sound these mute presences and in so doing reconstitute the past. *How* these signs are interpreted determines, in turn, the nature of the historiographical enterprise. It is here that Volney and Staël part company. If for Volney the task is primarily analytical, for Staël the task makes equal demands on the imagination. This difference is crucial. Whatever the affinities in their thought, Staël's understanding of place and its role in historical interpretation diverges from Volney's in three significant ways. The first is the importance of place in stimulating two faculties that the Idéologues deemed highly unreliable—memory and imagination; the second is the relationship between place and personal identity; and the third is the rapport between the place and the unconscious.

The importance of place is constantly reiterated in *Corinne*. The novel's provocatively unconventional title links its heroine to a nation and a geographical region. Seven of the novel's twenty book headings contain one or more place names and an eighth—"Les Tombeaux, les Eglises et les Palais"—alludes to monuments with specific locations. The reader's introduction to Oswald comes with a discussion of the anguish he feels at having abandoned the places where his father had lived ("*les lieux ou son père avait vécu*" [29]) to come to Italy. And when Corinne is introduced in the next chapter, her identification with a specific place is underscored by the setting in which Oswald first catches a glimpse of her—the steps of the Capitol, this place so fertile in memories ("*ce lieu si fécond en souvenirs*" [52]). In the novel, places are the signifiers and memories, or "souvenirs," are the signified.

It is precisely to such "souvenirs" that Corinne repeatedly alludes while guiding Oswald through Rome. The aspect of the city is, at first sight, staggering in its complexity and disorder. Monument jostles monument, building is piled upon building, ruins are scattered randomly throughout the city. Corinne attempts to make sense of this confusion by recalling the events, personalities, and human activities associated with the various hills, temples, and baths. As she tells Oswald, the memories she evokes are of two different orders: "les souvenirs de l'esprit" and "les souvenirs de l'imagination." The mind's memories ("les souvenirs de l'esprit") are learned; they derive from a vast cultural repository of stories and facts. The imagination's memories ("les souvenirs de l'imagination") are poetic; the physical presence of historical remains inspires a kind of nostalgic identification with the past. While the former are abstract and remote, the latter are immediate, direct, and sensual, bringing with them the intimate conviction of lived experience. Moreover, the two types of memories are complementary. Much of the evocative power of the places that catalyze "les souvenirs de l'imagination" derives from their place names and the names of people with whom they are associated. "We have only the names here now" (62). "'Take me along the Tiber's bank; let us cross the Tiber.' It is as if you were conjuring history by speaking those words," exclaims Corinne (63). These associations depend on previously acquired historical knowledge, or "souvenirs de l'esprit." Historical sites serve not so much as new sources of knowledge, as *reminders* of a knowledge (memories) one already possesses. The novel thus provides a certain model for the way historical knowledge is derived. An inspired and cultivated mind is stimulated by the physical contact with culturally significant objects to draw selectively from the reservoirs of cultural memory. Historical ideas are not only the product of book learning, but, perhaps more importantly, of sensuous experience.

The value Staël attributes to place and to the sense impressions afforded by being "in place" points to a telling difference between her estimation of memory and that of the Idéologues. While both Staël and the Idéologues favored an "archaeological" approach to history because it allowed them to take sense impressions as their point of departure, they did so for quite different reasons. For Staël, the sheer presence of places and things belonging to the past produced sense impressions that could trigger the memory and the imagination—two faculties which she saw as closely linked. Memory was the deepest, most meaningful form of knowledge about the past because it embraced both personal reminiscences and the collected experiences of a culture. But memory was often dormant and inaccessible. The imagination's capacity to simulate experience allowed memory to be reawakened and the bridge to be established between personal and collective experience.

The Idéologues, on the other hand, had quite another estimation of memory. Sense impressions were valued not because they evoked memories, but because they were the first steps in the ideation process leading to reasoned judgments. In the Idéologues' understanding of the thought process, memory and imagination made use of sense impressions and were a more advanced stage in the formation of ideas, but they were also potentially defective links in this process. Destutt de Tracy, the Idéologues' chief theoretician, described how ideas are formed in the third volume of his treatise *Eléments d'Idéologie*. Simple sensation, he asserted, was always reliable and could, moreover, be empirically verified. Memory, however, was more complex. It consisted of combining a present sense impression with the representation of a prior sense perception. In Tracy's judgment, if this representation were erroneous, a false idea might be pro-

duced. He concluded therefore: "the first cause of all error is
the imperfection of our memories."[7] Imagination, as a type of
memory, was equally unreliable. One of the three ways Tracy
defined imagination was as a "sense of living memory which
mistakes remembrances as real and actual impressions."[8] Thus
for the Idéologues, knowledge based on memory was unreliable
because that faculty itself could produce illusion. The only truly
reliable faculty was reason. Great care must be taken that the
initial sensory impressions produced by observation lead to sure
scientific judgments. Observed data, or facts, must be laid out
in logical order. Proceeding in a step-by-step fashion from one
known fact to another, one should, theoretically, be able to construct a properly scientific account of the past without resorting
to memory or the imagination.

The Idéologues' suspicion of memory and imagination is consistent with their ambition to develop a historical discourse that
is at once impersonal and factual. Volney, as we have seen, goes
to considerable lengths to purge his account of any traces of
subjectivity, to describe human history without drawing on human accounts, and to efface, wherever possible, even his own
mediating perspective as historian. Quite the opposite is true in
Staël's *Corinne*. Her heroine's viewpoint is the medium through
which history is filtered. Her subjectivity is seen to enhance and
validate the exposition rather than to corrupt it, a fact that is
gratefully acknowledged by Oswald. "Who ever felt the happiness
I am tasting," he exclaims, "Rome shown by you, Rome interpreted by imagination and genius" (56).

Staël thus departs from the Idéologues in the association she
makes between place and memory. She also differs from them
in discerning a special relationship between place and personal
identity. I noted earlier that Corinne reveals Italy's history in
two different modes. In a deictic mode Corinne shows Oswald
the sites of ancient history. In an allegorical mode she personally
embodies or represents Italy's illustrious past. The allegorical
representation at work in the novel is suggested in the title *Corinne, or Italy*. This association serves a double function in the
plot: it both places and dis-places Corinne within her genealogy.
On the one hand, Corinne is able to allay Oswald's anxieties
about her mysterious past by establishing a distinguished heritage; on the other, she is able to distract him from discovering
her connection with another place—Scotland. But Corinne's association with Italy is through her mother. The suppression or

displacement of Corinne's paternal heritage is revealed in the absent patronymic.[9]

Thus Corinne's presentation of herself and her country's history are partial, selective, and strategic. At stake in these representations is Oswald's love: Corinne is persuaded that if he can be made to love Italy, he will necessarily come to love her. Her gestures, seemingly intended to point out the beauty of the sites, are often contrived to direct Oswald's attention to herself and to locate herself within a tradition. She literally indicates her place in Italy's culture when she points to the niche in the Pantheon that she intends her bust to one day occupy. Significant, too, is the fact that when Corinne feels she can no longer forestall the revelation of her paternal lineage, she stages an elaborate fête at Cape Miseno. The high point of this fête is her own inspired improvisation. The subject—suggested by the assembled guests—is *"les souvenirs que ces lieux retraçaient,"* [the memories recalled by these places (Balayé 348; Staël's emphasis)]. Here the mythology of the place merges with history: "All around you is the land of *Aeneid* where we still seek traces of fictions that, consecrated by genius, have become our memories" (241). Corinne, new Cumaean Sibyl, bears an almost mythic identity with this august site. She becomes the conduit for a kind of unconscious race memory. Agitated by the "force involontaire" of her visions, Corinne succumbs in an ecstatic faint. In moments like these Staël seems to be proposing yet another form of memory—one she might have termed "les souvenirs du corps." Corinne most powerfully represents her culture in the semi-conscious state of inspiration. As her compatriots appreciate—and this is why she is so adulated by them—in her gestures, her poetry, her dance, her improvisations, her way of being, she is the living embodiment of traditions that are as old as the land itself.

Such cultural expressions correspond to what Pierre Nora calls memory. "Memory is rooted in the concrete, the spatial, the gesture, the image and the object."[10] But when Nora speaks of memory, he does so in opposition to history. History is what comes into being when a culture has lost its collective memory. While memory is a living link with an eternal present, history is an incomplete and problematic reconstruction of that which has ceased to be.

Because memory has to do with feelings and magic it accommodates any details it finds appealing; it thrives on vague reminiscences.

These reminiscences are condensed, encompassing and floating, particular or symbolic, and are susceptible to all manner of psychological effects like transference, projection or repression. History, because it is an intellectual and secularizing operation, invites analysis and critical discourse. Memory ascribes a sacred place to reminiscence whereas history tries to oust it from this place. History is always prosaic.[11]

Staël's innovation is to imagine history not as a dead record, but as a vital, sensuous link with the past. In this perspective history and memory are not antithetical. Rather, memory becomes the very soul of history. Corinne's demonstration of physical and psychological connectedness with an ancient culture, her embodiment of memory thus provide a vivid image of Staël's unique historical vision. Within the plot this vision does not go unchallenged. Corinne's performances often produce quite the opposite effect from the one intended; the more successfully she evokes her belonging to her own culture, the more she underscores her difference from Oswald. Significantly, it is in a moment of spontaneity, when Corinne, through her gestures and movements, most vividly demonstrates the physical continuity of culture, that Oswald begins to feel estranged from her. Dancing the Neapolitan tarantella, Corinne "brought to mind the women dancers of Herculaneum" (92). But Oswald is both entranced by her grace and appalled at what he perceives as a lack of modesty typical of Italian women. Oswald's prudery provokes him to speak disparagingly of Italians, and his hurtful remarks bring about his first falling out with Corinne. Indeed, it is most often behavior dictated by unconscious impulses that brings Staël's two characters into conflict. Corinne's atavism and Oswald's involuntary memories create a tension that simultaneously allows glimpses into their deeper psychology.

Oswald's resistance to Corinne allows Staël to explore the relationship between the unconscious and place. Corinne's archaeological approach to a collective past becomes a kind of metaphor for the exploration of personal psychological history. Frequently in the course of their interaction, Corinne inadvertently uncovers what are painful memories for Oswald. This connection is made more or less explicit in one instance. Corinne has just compared her method to that of archaeologists, and Oswald is quick to agree that archaeology is precisely the kind of study that could capture his interest were he composed enough to devote himself to it: "This kind of erudition is far livelier than the type acquired through books," he exclaims; "it is as if you bring back to life what you discover, as if the past reappears beneath the dust that has buried it" (72–73). Metaphorically, Oswald's reticence to engage in archaeology expresses his desire to forget and his fear that clearing away the dust might uncover his own buried and repressed memories.

Staël further adumbrates the parallels between an archaeological approach to history and the exploration of the unconscious in Corinne's topology of Rome. Her depiction of the city anticipates in a striking way a similar topology described by Freud in which he likened the city's aspect to the structure of the psyche. "Forgetting," he writes, "never entails the complete destruction of the memory-trace" for "in mental life, nothing which has once been formed can perish ... everything is somehow preserved," and can in certain privileged circumstances be brought to light.[12] Like the landscape of an ancient city, the topology of the individual human psyche is littered with remnants of the past. While some memories, ruinlike, lie half-exposed to consciousness, others are buried beneath the accumulated layers of experience. In Staël's psychic economy "les souvenirs de l'imagination" are more efficacious than "souvenirs de l'esprit" in bringing memories to the surface because the imagination is both an active and passive faculty and is itself informed by memories. The imagination serves to bridge the gap between forgotten (or repressed) memories and rational consciousness.

As a weapon in her conquest of Oswald, memory proves to be a double-edged sword for Corinne. It cuts between the conscious and the unconscious, between the collective and the personal, but because of its involuntary nature, it is an awkward and dangerous weapon to wield. Corinne seems dimly aware that some memories might alienate her from her lover and that some particular places might evoke these memories. As Simone Balayé has observed, "she scrupulously avoids taking him to catacombs, crypts and dungeons—places which are the antithesis of life, and in which he no doubt would have felt at home, but which she herself feared."[13] Her fear derives not from the lugubrious nature of these places but, rather, from her apprehension that this descent into the underground might subliminally arouse the darker and more melancholic regions of Oswald's mind. But Corinne's appeal to a shared cultural legacy (the Greco-Roman heritage) and the collective memories of a tradition are not as powerful as she had hoped. (Her very use of the word "souvenir" assumes a shared past.) She underestimates Oswald's cultural ties to another place: his fatherland. Ironically, the "places of memory" Corinne does reveal to Oswald raise unforeseen and uncontrolled associations in his mind. What was intended as a distraction, as a way of forgetting becomes, unintentionally, a painful reminder of his alienation from his own culture.

Corinne herself unwittingly encourages these associations by underscoring the relationship between public sites and private dramas. Many of the places Corinne and Oswald visit are the scenes of family tragedies: the Scoundrel's Path where Tullia "trampled her father's body under her horses' hooves" (72), Livia's baths—the site of her infamous poisoning of Augustus, the triumphal arch of Septimus Severus that bears the traces of a bitter rivalry between his sons, the memorial erected in honor of the young Cecilia Metella by her father, or the tomb inscribed with the touching verses of the virtuous young wife, Cornelia. In the presence of these monuments, Corinne observes, "you feel all that is sacred and worthy of respect in family ties" (80). And indeed Oswald does not fail to make such a connection when she shows him the painting depicting the son of Cairbar asleep on his father's grave. His thoughts inevitably, if involuntarily, turn to his own father's grave and the guilt he feels in not fulfilling his last requests.

And so, early in the novel, a pattern of obsessive repetition is established. Each time Corinne and Oswald are brought close by their shared experiences, each time Corinne succeeds in touching his deepest emotions or exciting his historical imagination, Oswald becomes tormented by the memory of his father and distances himself from her. In order to establish a place for herself in Oswald's affections, Corinne must *displace* Oswald's father. That desired displacement is represented in a striking dreamlike image that punctuates the novel's pattern of alternating rapprochement and estrangement. Having spent a day in which they had grown particularly close, Corinne secretly imagines that she has won Oswald's heart. The following morning these hopes are dashed when Oswald sends a formal note to announce that he is unwell. Corinne is sitting despondently by the Trevi Fountain after several days of separation when Oswald comes upon her. "Oswald, pausing there a few moments later, glimpsed the reflection of his friend's lovely face. Such intense emotion gripped him that at first he did not know whether his imagination was bringing him sight of Corinne's shadow just as so many times before it had shown him his father's" (75).

Corinne cannot, however, fully admit to herself her own unconscious desire to supplant Oswald's father in his affections. Indeed, her exaggerated efforts to aid Oswald in his filial cult often amount to denial. On one occasion, she literally restores Oswald's memory by retouching the portrait of his father that had been effaced during his heroic effort to save a drowning man. On another, she takes Oswald to visit tombs: "She did not imagine she might console him; she would not even have wanted to erase from his heart grief rightfully due the loss of a father; but there is something sweet and harmonious in the feeling of sorrow that we must try to make known to those who have felt only its bitterness" (79).

How then are we to interpret the novel's tragic ending? Corinne herself attributes Oswald's definitive rejection of her to the pressing and immediate claims of the dominating social order and what is more—she gives this order its due: "What do memories and imagination mean when one is closed in on all sides by the force and reality of a social order that dominates all the more for being founded on noble and pure ideas?" (278). She thus establishes an opposition between a poetic vision of life, appealing to the imagination and memory, and an ideological (or political) vision predicated on the strict subordination of the individual to social convention. Concurring with Corinne's own interpretation of events, many critics have overlaid this conflict in visions with a gender conflict between a woman of talent (expressing a poetic vision) and patriarchal society (representing the more prosaic, but nonetheless politically dominant, view of life). I generally concur with these interpretations, aspects of which are supported by similar arguments Staël makes in other writings. (The opposition Staël establishes in *On Germany,* for instance, between a romantic outlook and stultifying classicism. Or the untenable position of gifted women described in "On Women Writers" in *On Literature.*) I would like to complicate these interpretations, however, by insisting that Staël not be confused with her heroine. Staël shows us her heroine defeated not only by patriarchy, but by her own failure to recognize the double vector of memory. For memory is not exclusively a source of personal inspiration; it is also the foundation of the abiding traditions and values that inform historically and geographically situated social orders. Corinne's power is also her limitation. Her poetic vision, her capacity for improvisation and physical expression, draw on and represent an unconscious race memory. Yet this capacity to tap her innermost resources simultaneously blinds her to her own contradictory desires. She cannot at once assert the importance of cultural identification and demand that Oswald relinquish his ties. Whatever attraction Corinne and Oswald may have for one another, their values and concepts of social roles are very different. Corinne's tragedy is that Oswald acts according to her precepts, and is as faithful, in his own way, to memory and his place of origin, as she is to hers. Thus Staël's vision is more encompassing, more ironic, and ultimately, more melancholic, than that of her heroine for she recognizes that the private lives of individuals must bear the weight not only of their own pasts, but also that of their cultures. Here, personal conflicts are seen to be not merely the consequence of competing desires, but the product of profound cultural difference. The private sphere is rooted in the broader social and cultural sphere. A conviction of that connectedness is precisely the defining feature of Staël's historiography.

I opened this discussion by outlining some characteristics of Volney's new historiography in order to situate the approach to history that emerges from Staël's *Corinne*. Both Staël and the Idéologues were poised at a crossroads. The early nineteenth century instituted a great divide between scientific and literary culture. The prestige of literature, or to be more precise, traditional humanistic culture, was challenged. In the course of the nineteenth century, historians, and even as we know, some novelists, were at pains to describe their projects and methods as scientific. But even before scientific sociology and historiography announced themselves under the name of positivism, Volney and his fellow Idéologues elaborated methods for the study of human society in which reason, observation, and strict objectivity were prioritized. Staël instinctively resisted this move to scientificity at its very inception. In this she displayed a greater independence of mind than the more widely recognized Romantic historians—Michelet, Guizot, Thierry, or Barante—whose historiographical approach is traditionally contrasted with positivism. Indeed, these historians, as Linda Orr has pointed out, were, ironically, quite eager to jump on the positivist bandwagon.[14]

Staël was skeptical about nascent positivism not in the name of a return to metaphysical or theological modes of thinking, but rather, on epistemological grounds. She boldly asserted that memory and imagination are forms of knowing that supplement and even exceed reason and observation. Memory allows access to the unconscious and the unthought and bridges the gap between the personal and the social. This epistemological understanding has a formal corollary. History is necessarily representation and must recognize itself as such. A mere ordering of facts empties history of its primary human dimensions—the moral and psychological dimensions. As Staël notes in her *On Fictions,* "the full effects of truth are frequently incomplete."[15] The lessons to be derived from the recitation of public events are of little moral significance to the individual: "between the notable events memorialized by history there exist immense gaps in which the trials and misfortunes that constitute most private human lives take place."[16] It is by filling in these gaps, by drawing the connections between public events and private lives, that the "les souvenirs de l'imagination" supplement history and allow the novel to become an alternative form of envisioning the past. The vivid image of Rome's topology that Corinne conjures up for Oswald thus suggests not only a model of the human psyche, but also a fitting emblem for Staël's distinctly modern view of the past. The past, like the unconscious, is fragmented, discontinuous, half-buried, and largely inaccessible, but, every now and then, its dark recesses are illuminated by the historical imagination.

Corinne: Political Polemics and the Theory of the Novel

Susan Tenenbaum

This essay examines Germaine de Staël's *Corinne* as it represents a pioneering literary type: a work of political sociology in the form of a novel. As a narrative adaptation of Montesquieu's method of comparative analysis, *Corinne* exemplifies Staël's attempt to expand the boundaries of the novel as a uniquely modern literary form. In her *On Fictions*, Staël portrayed the novel as a uniquely modern and progressive genre open to further thematic and structural development; yet she simultaneously limited its subject matter to private life and its ethical teaching to "quiet virtue." To read *Corinne* as a political novel is thus to address larger questions concerning Staël's theory and practice of fiction and to confront the inconsistencies and ambivalences that beset her writings. In an attempt to engage these broader concerns, I shall first sort out the several strands of analysis that shaped Staël's theory of the novel, locating *Corinne* in relation to them. I shall then make the case for a political reading of *Corinne* that emphasizes its continuities with Montesquieuian perspectives.

Staël's theory of the novel was largely set out in two works prior to the publication of *Corinne:* her little known *On Fictions* and her celebrated treatise *On Literature*.[1] Staël's complex understanding of the novel as a genre is communicated in both works, though each differs in its focus: *On Fictions* systematically describes and classifies forms of fictional writing; *On Literature* examines the interrelationship between the novel and its social context. In both works Staël's approach to the novel interweaves three strands of analysis, which I shall label the temporal (focusing on the historicity of the genre), the universalist (focusing on the novel's portrayal of common human attributes), and the relativist (focusing on culturally diverse exemplars of the genre). These lines of argument overlapped in

Staël's writings, introducing tensions into her thought that will become fully manifest in *Corinne*. To better appreciate these tensions, I shall proceed to unpack Staël's theory of the novel, discussing, in turn, each of its several strands.

At the core of Staël's theory of the novel lay the idea of the genre's modernity, an idea that embraced issues both of form and content. Designating love as the characteristic subject matter of the novel, Staël constructed an ancient/modern literary dichotomy intended to illuminate the causes which inhibited the emergence of the genre in classical antiquity. Prominent among these causes was an embracive conception of citizenship that denigrated the realm of affective life, relegating woman to an inferior social role, and a pagan conception of fate, founded on an external ethic inimical to the development of individual subjectivity.[2] The novel was a literary product of a distinctively modern tradition rooted in Christian spirituality and introspection which traced back to the elevation of woman's moral and spiritual status during the Christian Middle Ages.[3] Staël thus set the novel within a progressionist historiography that ascribed to woman a critical role as agent of historical advance carrying the spiritual message of Christianity and, more broadly, cultivating the inner life of man. As love came to define relations between the sexes, the individual formerly monopolized by his public role metamorphosed into the multidimensional personality; through the agency of love, his sensibilities were refined and his imagination stimulated.[4] The progressive linkage between Christianity, feminism, and the emergence of "modern" literature was a theme explored earlier by the seventeenth-century *modernes,* in whose tradition Staël must be firmly placed.[5] Recasting the Quarrel of the Ancients and Moderns to suit the circumstances of her day, Staël repudiated the authority of classical models whether in the sphere of politics, rejecting the classically inspired Jacobin veneration of civic virtue, or literature, championing the novel as a truly modern genre without antecedents in classical antiquity.[6]

Staël went on to distinguish the contemporary novel from its immediate precursors (which pursued the theme of love in its historical and allegorical settings) with respect to two features: its realism and its orientation to private life.[7] On this approach, Staël merged her temporal analysis of the novel, focusing on the forces of historical advance that contributed to its rise, with a universalist one, focusing on the telos of human self-realization. Staël linked the novel's realism to the evocation of an essentialist human nature made manifest through historical experience. Rejecting any primitivist impulse to seek human nature in pre-social existence, Staël maintained that through history human nature was enriched and brought to explicit consciousness. Accordingly, she regarded the Revolution as the vehicle that would destroy the vestiges of literary artifice in France, ushering in a "realist" literature that took as its subject the common nature of modern man and woman.[8] For Staël, the novel would serve as an exemplar of post-Revolutionary realism by wedding the narrative depiction of emotional life to an explicitly moral teaching anchored in imagination and sentiment. The association of the novel with both moralism and realism had earlier been a theme of Diderot, and Staël took it over in a continuing attempt to defend the status of the genre in France.[9] By further distinguishing the novel as a genre in terms of the setting of its narrative—the sphere of private relations—Staël united literary theory with her preoccupations as a political theorist. Staël's defense of a liberal conception of freedom, defined as the area where individuals are free from governmental interference, not only led her to regard literature as surrogate for law (the novel serving as an instrument of moral education and social control), but also reinforced her belief that the private sphere was the locus of natural sentiment and self-development. The novel's depiction of intimate relations and emotions accorded it a place of prominence in Staël's new liberal order, masking the tension between her historically contingent conception of privacy and her espousal of an essentialist human nature. The privatized setting and emotional focus of the novel led Staël to distinguish it from other literary genres and practices.[10] Unlike the novel, historical writing takes the public sphere as its focus and contains no moral teachings. Philosophical writing differs from the novel by enlisting the faculty of reason, rather than sentiment and the imagination. Techniques like comparative analysis are, accordingly, out of place in the novel, where narrative development alone must sustain the reader's attention.

The third, or relativist, strand nourishing Staël's conception of the novel coexisted uneasily with the temporal and universalist dimensions of her literary theory. When operating from a relativist perspective, Staël addressed herself to the existence of differences among societies and the causes accounting for the distinctiveness of their cultural products. In this endeavor she proved herself an astute student of Montesquieu, applying his comparative method to the sphere of literature and giving liter-

ary form to his notion of general spirit.[11] Staël's theoretical apparatus is seen most clearly in *On Literature,* where she deployed
Montesquieu's scheme of physical and moral causes to illuminate the divergent literary styles of England, France, Germany,
Italy, and Spain. Her investigation concluded that England offered the most fertile ground for the development of the novel
owing to its northern climate (inducing melancholy and introspection) and social practices that placed a high value on privacy
and domesticity.[12] Ironically, Staël regarded Italy as least hospi-
table to the genre, citing the Italian's licentious habits as incompatible with the novel's distinctive focus on love. To examine
Corinne against the backdrop of Staël's earlier theory is to confront a number of marked discrepancies. Most notably, *Corinne*
stands out as a political novel despite Staël's insistence that the
genre's distinctive subject matter was private life. Staël's identification with the private sphere threaded through both the temporal and the universalist strands of her literary theory. A
public/private dichotomy undergirded her aesthetic (and political) polarity between the ancients and the moderns, informed
her conception of human nature, and provided a critical
grounds for differentiating history from the novel. Yet despite
this considerable investment in a theoretical apparatus linking
the novel to the sphere of intimate relations, Staël went on to
write a novel that was profoundly political in intent and
execution.

Before turning to *Corinne*'s immediate political purposes, I
shall first discuss the novel on the level of symbolic representation. Specifically, I shall explore the ways in which the novel's
heroine symbolized the transcendence of the public/private distinction that formed the scaffolding of Staël's literary theory.
Corinne's role as *improvisatrice* provides the point of departure. As *improvisatrice,* a spontaneous improviser of verse, Corinne operated and attained her glory within an aesthetic sphere
that was extrapolitical or "private" in character. Throughout the
novel, Staël portrayed the aesthetic sphere as the dominant force
in Italian life, informing the spontaneous character of social
intercourse and relations between the sexes, the visual splendor
of Italian Catholicism, and the genius of Italian poetry and art.[13]
Less felicitously, Staël described the eclipse of politics by aesthetics as a principal cause of Italy's servitude to Napoleon, setting
up an argument that would considerably complicate the public/
private distinction central to her literary theory.

For Staël, who had identified modernity with the rise of the private sector and who had regarded literature as its agency of moral education, the valuation of the political in *Corinne* represents a notable departure. Italy offered the case of a pre-liberal society yet to achieve in the political sphere the freedom it enjoyed in the aesthetic. The novel must, then, be viewed contextually: its moral purposes here take on an explicitly political coloration. The genre serves as an instrument to redirect aesthetic energies in political directions.

Nowhere is Staël's indictment of Italy more strikingly conveyed than in Corinne's coronation, a scene that enlists political ritual in the service of aesthetic glory, directing public opinion towards aesthetic rather than political achievements. Despite Staël's laudatory portrait of her heroine, she nonetheless made clear her regret that great political deeds were not equally a focus of public acclaim:

In their present situation Italians are allowed but one glory: the fine arts. Their vivid sense of this form of genius should give rise to many great men, yet mere acclaim is not enough to bring them forth; only intense life, lofty concerns, and an independent existence nourish thought. (20)

With this observation, Staël alluded to the political lesson of *Corinne*: an independent and accountable political sphere was a necessary component of the modern state. Italy, possessing an egalitarian, open and aesthetically rich social life, exemplified Staël's vision of modernity, yet was censured by her for its accommodation to Napoleonic despotism which annihilated political liberty as it preserved social freedom.

In *Corinne* Staël portrayed her heroine as an agent of social redemption. Corinne's inspired odes alluding to Italy's glorious past were intended to awaken its citizens' dormant civic consciousness; her poetic images of ancient Rome and the medieval Italian republics served as metaphors of lost dignity and inspirations to national rebirth. Corinne's invocation of classical politics, with her juxtaposed images of former grandeur and modern political decadence, intertwined ancient and modern imagery irrespective of Staël's larger views on the course of historical and literary progress. Staël's breach of her earlier temporal principles was compounded by the violation of her public/private dichotomy as reflected in the actions of her heroine. Using aesthetic instruments to attain political ends, Corinne bridged both spheres as the central character of a political novel directed against Napoleon's system of conquest.

A second element in Staël's theory of the novel—the genre's depiction of an "essentialist" human nature—was similarly compromised by the political character of *Corinne*. The nature of Staël's attack on Napoleon led her to emphasize the recognition of the particularity and difference rather than human similarity. Staël's indictment of Napoleon took as its model Montesquieu's representation of despotism as a form of rule characterized by "equality in slavery."[14] Applying this model to Napoleonic designs for European hegemony, Staël posited a conceptual link between the principle of uniformity and a closed and compulsive system of empire. This, in turn, led her away from universalist theories of human nature, with the potential of lending intellectual support to hegemonic rule, and toward a relativism that championed the pluralistic expression of national cultures. Montesquieu once again proved a strategic intellectual ally; his theory of moral causes and his concept of general spirit enabled Staël to articulate a vision of societal differences with which to oppose Napoleon's imperialistic designs.

Perhaps it is an exaggeration to claim that *Corinne* is the *Spirit of the Laws* rendered as dramatic narrative, though it is undeniable that Montesquieu's magisterial treatise exerted a singular influence on Staël's most celebrated work of fiction. Two aspects of Montesquieu's method would provide the theoretical scaffolding of *Corinne*. His theory of causation sought to identify the determinants that combined to form a society's distinctive character; these comprised physical causes like climate and terrain, and moral causes which included religion, law, custom, commerce, and style of thought. The relative importance and nature of these determinants differed in the case of each society and could be discovered only after investigation and comparative study. This theory of causation formed the basis for the second Montesquieuian concept to be appropriated by Staël: The "general spirit" of a nation was the product of the totality of its physical and moral causes. It accounted for the unique character of each society and undergirded Staël's defense of national independence and cultural heterogeneity.

Staël's use of the Montesquieuian concept of general spirit is immediately encountered in her treatment of character in *Corinne*. The novel's focus on the emotional life of its protagonists and on the special capacities and tribulations of the woman of genius cannot obscure the fact that character in *Corinne* is largely defined by "national" character.[15] This approach is initially conveyed in the full title of the novel *Corinne, or Italy*. Notwithstanding Corinne's hybrid national origins, she is presented as the product of Italian upbringing embodying traits Staël portrayed as distinctive to Italy; Corinne is spontaneous, open, intuitive, direct. If Corinne's English heritage accounted for her attraction to Oswald, her lover's character nonetheless contrasted markedly with her own and reflected the traits Staël ascribed to the English as a nation: tradition-bound, melancholy, proud, and honorable. Oswald's future wife, Lucile, typified English womanhood in her modesty and domestic preoccupations. Lastly, d'Erfeuil represented both the rigid, supercilious character Staël associated with the reactionary French aristocracy, and the enduring traits Staël more broadly associated with the French nation: wit, sociability, elegance, and an attitude of cultural superiority.

It is significant that the characters in *Corinne* display little growth or development; throughout the novel they continue to operate within the conventions of their national type. For example, despite Corinne's tireless efforts to impart to Oswald the spirit of Italian liberality, her lover remains encapsulated in the expectations of an English gentleman. Such conformity to the dictates of national character testified to the novel's "realism," offering an ongoing illustration of the operation of Montesquieu's general spirit. The political implications of this approach to character were not lost on *Corinne*'s readers: by insisting on the diversity of national character types, Staël simultaneously challenged the legitimacy of the empire. More subtly, she warned against a susceptibility to regard other societies as inferior to one's own. This propensity, Staël suggested, was particularly acute in the French and served to nourish the Napoleonic spirit of conquest. Characteristically, d'Erfeuil's observations of the world were redolent of national prejudice, as were his condescending remarks to Corinne, "Lovely Corinne, for pity's sake, do speak French, you are truly worthy to speak it" (37). Even the admirable Oswald was not immune from national bias in his reading of national character: "infidelity itself is more moral in England than marriage in Italy" (97). Against this portrait of national rivalry, hegemonic aspirations, and biased standards of judgment, Staël posited Corinne as a symbol of pluralistic nationalism. Her heroine celebrated the uniqueness of each society, offered a balanced assessment of its accomplishments and its deficiencies, and advocated mutual understanding through cross-cultural study and exchange.[16]

Corinne embodied the Montesquieuian comparativist, now cast in the dramatic roles of guide (through Italy) and voyager (to England). These dramatic pretexts allowed her to unpack the concept of general spirit by describing the determinants which defined the unique character of each society and its members. The novel's plotlines continually dissolve into socio-political exegesis as Corinne introduces Oswald to the diverse causes that shaped Italian life. In chapters devoted to art, architecture, literature, music and religion, Corinne not only shares with Oswald and the reader her intimate knowledge of an unfamiliar culture, but makes the case for Italy's unique hierarchy of social causes in which aesthetic forces predominate. The interplay of social and physical determinants was central to this argument, as Corinne pointed to the close relation between Italy's aesthetic genius and its beneficent climate and terrain. Italy's aesthetic bent, Corinne continued, accounted for a general disinterest in the practicalities of public life and shaped a social structure that was egalitarian and open.[17] As a visitor to England, Corinne again emphasized the importance of physical determinants in shaping the national mind (a harsh climate nurtured British melancholy), yet the focus of her attention was on Britain's unique configuration of moral causes. The spheres of law and custom predominated as molders of British character: the former inculcated a legalistic spirit among the British and promoted civic-mindedness; the latter nourished a countervailing attachment to privacy and domestic pleasures.

With these observations Staël violated her own precepts concerning the inappropriateness of comparison as a technique in the novel.[18] These features of *Corinne* were symptomatic of a more profound shift in Staël's conception of the novel: Staël's embrace of the political as an appropriate subject of the novelist's attention. In her earlier *On Fictions*, Staël argued that the future of the novel as a genre lay with expanding the palette of human emotions beyond love to include "ambition, pride, avarice, vanity."[19] Yet she continued to confine the novel to the realm of private morality, a demarcation intended to preserve the genre's integrity and literary status. *Corinne,* with its openly political message, represented a break with this posture. Such intellectual readjustments are not uncommon to Staël's literary and political writings, and represent ever-shifting resolutions of the tension between the universalist liberal and relativist perspective that competed for her allegiance throughout her career.

By broadening the scope of the novel, Staël simultaneously staked a claim for her gender. In *On Literature* she heralded a sexual division of labor for post-Revolutionary France which *Corinne* subtly subverts, "Perhaps it would be natural that, in such a state, literature properly-so-called would become the natural province of women and men would devote themselves only to higher philosophy."[20] Both author and heroine are public figures operating in a world of fame and influence, not purveyors of the "quiet morality" Staël had earlier associated with the novel. Staël appropriates the nonliterary discourse of political philosophy to literary ends. Montesquieu provided the model for her indictment of Napoleon and, correspondingly, for her vision of a pluralist international order. Yet Staël's Montesquieu passed through the prism of *Corinne,* an *improvisatrice* who crossed the borders of public and private spheres to create a new framework of power for the literary woman.

Part III
Genie at Large

Tracing a Sisterhood: Corilla Olimpica as Corinne's Unacknowledged Alter Ego

PAOLA GIULI

IN spite of the author's disclaimer that "the name of Corinne should not be confused with that of Corilla, the Italian *improvisatrice* everybody has heard of," Staël's *Corinne, or Italy* can be read as the feminist reappropriation and reinscription in literary history of the story of Maria Maddalena Morelli Fernandez (1727–1800).[1] Of humble origins, Corilla Olimpica rose to such prominence that the most powerful European crowns, including Joseph II of Austria and Catherine of Russia, coveted her performances. The acme of her career was nonetheless her being crowned "poet laureate" in Rome at the "Capitol of the capital of the world," the first and last woman poet to receive such an honor.

Corilla's supporters hoped that her Capitol crowning would be part of a larger attempt to revitalize Arcadia's image and outlook by celebrating the most visible exponent of a new poetics of enthusiasm.[2] But with the accusations (familiar to historians of women's literature) of her being an inadequate mother, a sexually promiscuous woman, and a plagiarist, Corilla's seemingly inevitable literary fame began being undermined at the very time of her triumph.[3] Staël's feminist revisionist gaze reinterpreted Corilla's story according to Staël's liberal Romantic concerns and proposed it as a monitory image of the ephemeral nature of female literary stature in a patriarchal society, at the same time salvaging it from the ravages of time and prejudice.

By exploring the intertextuality of Corinne's and Corilla's stories, we will come to a better understanding of "the ways female subjectivity is construed in the public sphere" and of the forces shaping the production, reception and canonization—the sense of creating and being part of a tradition—of the female artist's work. While most commentators now agree that *Corinne* symbolizes the impossibility of professional and personal fulfillment for the woman of genius in a patriarchal society, issues such as the interpretation of the national symbolism in the novel and the use of improvisation as a medium of the protagonist's genius still remain.[4] By reading *Corinne* in a historical setting, as the reinterpretation and reinvention of the story of Corilla Olimpica, the representation of Italy with regard to the position of Corinne in its society no longer seems artificial. In this same context we begin to understand the importance of improvisation to Staël's defense of female literary achievement.

Textual correspondences and historical similarities between Corilla and Corinne's stories beg the question of the exegesis of Staël's note to book 14, which in fact is frequently quoted as sanctioning the lack of connection between these two figures. Staël's crafty wording allows for an interpretation of the footnote that excludes a connection between Corinne and Corilla, for the purpose of deflecting certain criticisms, while at the same time conceding Corilla's implication. Critics whose valuative criteria equated women's public performance to immorality and a woman's pursuit of literary talents to societal upheaval, could only be more incensed if encouraged to look into the life and work of Corilla and the controversy surrounding it. Although very little in the novel, as Schlegel noticed, has anything to do with the Greek Corinna, this canonized and nonthreatening muse of Greek poetry—only *nominally* present in literary history (i.e., represented only by a *name* reappropriated by patriarchal tradition)—contributes to the novel's acceptability.[5]

While most commentators who knew about Corilla made the connection between Corilla and Corinne's Capitol triumph, few (most notably Gennari) indicated Corilla's story as a factor in the genesis of Staël's novel and none studied in detail the implications of such an identification.[6] If nineteenth-century analyses were blinded by the ideology of femininity founding them, contemporary analyses are hindered by the rarity of documents by and about Corilla, and by the total lack of a recent reevaluation of this historical figure.[7] In her thorough study of *Corinne*'s genesis, Gennari wrote: "Corilla is really Corinne's older sister: when speaking of the latter, immortalized by Staël's imagination, one necessarily evokes the former, nowadays forgotten." Although she does not consider the significance of such a relationship to the economy of the novel, Gennari offers a precious introduction to the "traits and attitudes which Corilla lends Corinne." With the help of manuscripts and rare materials by and about Corilla, one can gain a more articulate picture of this very emblematic sisterhood.[8]

By the time Staël came to Italy and began to write *Corinne,* in 1805, Corilla was still widely known, if not generally admired. *Célèbre* is the word most commonly used by Staël's contemporaries to describe Corilla in their works: among them were some of Staël's friends (Schlegel, Bonstetten) and authors whose work was widely known (Lalande, Casanova, Count d'Albon). In particular, we know from Balayé that Staël brought Lalande's *Voyage* with her to Italy. She also corresponded with Teresa Bandettini Landucci, the heir to Corilla's poetic laurels; corresponded and met with Melchiorre Cesarotti, who had been an admirer of Corilla; and had written poetry in her honor. More importantly, Staël was in contact with two of the most prominent figures in Corilla's own life, warm supporters of her crowning: Prince Gonzaga and Abbot Godard. The latter is the man who, on 31 August 1776, pronounced a prose eulogy in honor of Corilla during the crowning ceremony (a function carried out by Castel-Forte in Staël's reinterpretation). Godard welcomed Staël at the Arcadian Academy almost thirty years later, on 14 February 1805.[9] Gonzaga is Corilla's mentor and lover (Staël's Castel-Forte and Oswald in one), who accompanied her by hand to receive her Capitol crown, but eventually left her to marry someone else. Just a few months after the controversial Capitol crowning, Gonzaga was Mme Necker's guest in Paris, where Corilla's story did not fail to be at the center of conversation. At a very young and impressionable age, ten-year-old Germaine Necker probably heard for the first time a story she would never forget.[10]

A comparison of Staël's description of Corinne's Capitol crowning to documents on Corilla's own crowning belies Staël's half-hearted denial of any intended allusion to the Italian poet. Most details of Corinne's crowning correspond to the descriptions of Corilla's crowning in the *Atti della solenne coronazione,* the official acts of the actual event, published in 1779, and in letters and diary entries of Italian and foreign (including French) participants to the ceremony.[11] The location and the description of the room where the ceremony took place, the characterization of the dignitaries, and the very succession of events, culminating in Corinne's laurel crowning and even the topic of Corinne's improvisation and her physical and emotional aspect would seem parallel to those of Corilla. By making Corinne clearly identifiable with Corilla, Staël makes a bold statement on an issue—the legitimacy of a woman's crowning as a poet laureate at the Capitol—that had divided Italian and European public opinion for half a century, and that during the following eighty years was going to be settled once and for all to the detriment of the improviser.

Reviews of *Corinne* reveal how hostile public opinion was to the ideological implications of considering Corinne a realistic character, modeled on a viable, indeed historical, example of femininity. If *Corinne* was a commercial success, it was also a book condemned almost unanimously by the critics. The reason for the book's success with the public was quite simply its sentimental value. Admiring readers, even men, complimented the author on the emotional value of her most dramatic scenes (those of the lovers' separation and of Corinne's death), which had succeeded in bringing them to tears. Professional critics, though, saw and feared the book's progressive message. Given an ideology of sexual roles that predicated that women could only be "shy and respectful daughters, . . . loving and virtuous wives, sensitive and tender mothers" and consequently that "a woman who distinguishes herself for qualities other than those [proper] to her sex" ran counter to the general principles governing nature and the world order, Staël's critics focused on the gender of the protagonist in order to prove that the novel was but an improbable and immoral fantasy. As one critic put it: if women like Corinne existed "all order would disappear from civilized society." From such a conservative perspective, readers had great interest in denying the plausibility of the novel and therefore in ignoring the connection with Corilla.[12]

Staël's friends were left with the difficult proposition of proving the plausibility of the novel without conceding to the realism or the desirability of a character like Corinne's. They ended up presenting contradictory claims, at the same time maintaining and denying that Corinne could be interpreted as the representation of an actual and existing female character and female type.[13] The connection with Corilla was therefore in turn invoked and negated. August W. Schlegel's 1807 treatment of *Corinne*'s relation to Corilla can be taken as emblematic of this strategy. On the one hand, he refers to a historically gendered character and event—Corilla and her crowning—in order to prove the plausibility of Staël's character; on the other, he drops the comparison without further analysis and ultimately bases his justification of Corinne's character on its ideal nature. "One should understand," Schlegel writes, "that Corinne remains an *ideal* improviser. Someone like her probably never existed."[14] In so doing, Schlegel neutralizes the threatening, subversive elements of a gendered historical interpretation by presenting Corinne as an example of romantically ungendered and ideal (therefore unattainable) perfection. In order to assuage the anxieties produced by the book, Staël's defenders joined her accusers in concluding that such a woman, such a poet, such a heroine as Corinne was not of this world.

Corinne as a Realistic Character

The discrepancies between Corilla's story as narrated by traditional historiography and Staël's story of Corinne are the measure of Staël's revisionist reappropriation. As the novel reveals, the very same qualities contributing to the improviser's success also caused, in classically tragic fashion, her ultimate downfall—professional pride and ambition being women's ultimate hubris in a patriarchal society. *Corinne* reinterprets the vicissitudes of Corilla's life and presents them as the epitome of the emotional and intellectual isolation of an exceptionally gifted woman.

Corinne's self-trust, self-reliance, and radiance at the moment of her coronation—epitomizing her proud sense of entitlement—correspond closely to Corilla's character and attitude. Abbot Benedetti, who saw Corilla up-close during the crowning ceremony, described her as tall, beautiful, and as proud as a queen.[15] As Staël writes of Corinne, Corilla wore a long white tunic at the ceremony, which exposed her beautiful arms and emphasized her tall, full, imposing figure and regal bearing (21). Charles Brack, an acquaintance of Corilla, in a note to his French translation of Burney's *Musical Journeys*, published in 1809, wrote: "[Corilla] was a tall woman with a majestic bearing, fiery eyes and an imposing glance. Jealous and proud of her poetical talents, she believed she was superior to all the improvisers, her contemporaries." Burney commented on Corilla's musical abilities: she played violin and sang "supremely well." Endowed with unusually expressive eyes and musical ability, Corilla shares in the characteristics that Joan DeJean defines as Corinne's Sapphic character; she was in fact often referred to as Aspasia and Sappho in one, as Ademollo pointed out.[16] Indeed in light of Corilla's multifarious artistic achievement, Corinne's "superabundance of gifts" (she plays the harp, she dances, she paints, and she writes and translates) should not weaken the novel's credibility, but rather foster it.

Standing tall and self-assured, Corinne appears in the novel "as a priestess, joyously devoting herself to the cult of genius" (32). Just as Staël writes of Corinne, Corilla too was devoted to the cult, that is the cultivation, of her genius and talents. Her poems and letters show professional pride, confidence in her talents, and unabashed conviction in a woman's right to pursue a literary vocation to the highest level of competence and recognition. Corilla, like Staël, believed that no one can blame heaven for being invested with or taking full advantage of "an extra faculty," and that it was in fact a person's right to pursue and "parade" it to the world. In a rare 1761 document, now at the Biblioteca Nazionale in Rome, Corilla writes in justification of her poetic activity and of her institution of the *Ordine dei Cavalieri Olimpici*: "Isn't it true that every man aspires to happiness and does all that is in his power to be so? . . . One cannot therefore condemn my desire to be happy by baring my talents to the world and by pursuing all possible means to cultivate them."[17] Six days before her crowning, Corilla showed great dignity and courage, when, in response to some vicious attacks against her she sang: "Together with humility / I need noble pride / she won't ascend to the Capitol / who has cowardice in her heart."[18]

Both Corilla and Corinne are estranged from their families. They achieve literary recognition at the price of forsaking their pasts and creating for themselves a new identity—a unique, and therefore at times despairingly isolated, space. Corinne leaves her mother and sister, Corilla her husband and child. Their adopted pseudonyms are the new literary identities by which they hope to be known and remembered. No one knows Corinne's real name; she signs her published works and her personal letters with her pseudonym (20). So did Corilla. It is most remarkable how much Corilla's literary persona took over her life. Not only did she unmistakably sign herself "Corilla" to friends and strangers alike, but official documents bear her literary name. What is most emblematic, her tombstone in Florence bears this Latin epitaph: "Corillae Olympicae ossa hic iacent" [Here lie Corilla Olimpica's bones]. In life as in death, Corilla and Corinne refuse their patronymic. In life as in death, they want to be identified with their literary achievement. Their last thought is for the glory they have reached, the pride of their lives: the Capitol crown. Corilla mentions it in her will, Corinne in her last, testamentary, letter to Nelvil: "My ashes are to be taken to Rome first; have my coffin taken along the road my triumphal chariot once traveled, and rest a while in the same place where you gave me back my crown" (409–10).[19]

While Corinne's choice for independence, in spite of isolation, is described as heroic in Staël's novel, contemporary satires and later critical works condemned Corilla's pursuit of literary interests as a disgrace. She was accused of abandoning her husband and three-year-old son "to follow her ambition," and was stigmatized as an unfit and immoral woman, a monster of egotism in fact. Nevertheless, the circumstances of Corilla's decision have not been investigated or clarified. We are only told that information about Corilla's spouse (Fernandez, a Spanish gentleman at the court of Naples) "is not the most flattering." Commentators never took into consideration that women in Corilla's time had no custody rights, since their own legal status equalled those of children under the *patria potestas;* nor did they see any contradiction between the alleged story of Corilla's heartlessness toward her son, and the story of her great love and devotion to her sister's daughter.[20]

What matters to us here is that the story of Corilla's unhappy marriage was typically exploited by her enemies and by nineteenth-century historiographers. Corilla's situation was not explained or investigated, but it was conveniently left to stand as a harsh indictment of Corilla's character and morality, which in turn implied, as it is customary in the history of women's writing, a devaluation of her work. Corilla's coming to writing and to artistic expression was seen as the unnatural act par excellence because of its supposed uprooting of the very essence of femininity: maternal instincts.

By portraying Corinne as an unmarried and childless woman, Staël steers free of the harsher criticism that would have otherwise befallen her heroine, so as to be able to focus the reader's attention on the vital aspect of the artist's anticonformist choice of independence. If unfortunately very little is extant in Corilla's writing which might shed some light on her feelings and motivations in leaving her husband and child—presumably, like Corinne, she "found it painful to discuss [the course of her life]" (37)—we find the artist's "move away from home" reinterpreted in Staël's novel as a distancing from the dehumanizing constrictions of a socially imposed life style. On leaving, Corinne thinks: "The universe would be mine, if I no longer felt the parching breath of malicious mediocrity" (265). It is her desire to escape the confinement of a petty conformist existence that inspires her to leave and live a full intellectual and emotional life. Her stepmother's callous and insensitive attitude makes Corinne's break with the past all the more desirable and acceptable.

Unable to raise children of their own, both Corilla and Corinne left their spiritual and material legacies to their sisters' daughters. Corilla deeply cared for, educated, supported, and eventually legally adopted her sister's daughter, whom she left universal heir to all her worldly possessions and works. In creating Juliette, Staël made of this relationship a symbol of female artistic patronage and heritage; a symbol of the possibility of a legacy being handed down, if not on the written pages of history, then on a personal level, from generation to generation, from woman to woman, from teacher to pupil—in the spirit of contemporary Italian *affidamento*.[21]

The most significant mark of Corilla and Corinne's sisterhood is nevertheless the Capitol crowning. A highly prestigious honor, the crowning was historically and symbolically subversive of the ideology of feminine restraint, self-effacement, and literary inferiority. Consequently, and not surprisingly, the crowning was bitterly opposed. The accusations and aspersions raised against Corilla on account of the crowning caused first Corilla's dejection and ultimately the erasure of her name from literary history. Staël rewrote Corilla's story in order to show that her crowning was legitimate and that her fall was caused by social prejudice, and not, as her enemies alleged and historiography prescribed, by her unworthiness. *Corinne* exposes the paradoxical nature of women's literary vocation in a society where the very same characteristics necessary to its recognition—determination, ambition, self-confidence—could be used to undermine it. Although Corilla did not die of sorrow, but of old age, her career ended as tragically as Corinne's: with her voice silenced, her name erased from the public eye, her Capitol crown "stained with blood and dust" (308).

The Crowning as a Historical Event

The artistic prominence of the crowning scene at the beginning of the novel has already been noted by generations of critics. What is even more conspicuous is that the crowning functions in the novel not as a *telos,* but as an *archè.* It is presented as an undisputed beginning: the axiom, the premise that founds the book's discourse and analysis. No matter how astounding the fact of the crowning appears to us—and appeared to Corilla's contemporaries—what interests the author is not so much the heroine's acts of epic conquest, but the forces shaping her fall and demise. The fact of some women's intellectual excellence and success is taken for granted. The legitimacy of the crowning is never questioned; on the contrary, it is emphasized. The novel instead exposes the process by which even the voices of the most prominent women could eventually be silenced and suppressed by societal prejudice.

The comparison of Staël's descriptions of the reception hall "that had been made ready to receive [Corinne]" to the *Atti*'s description of the "Sala Capitolina" in which Corilla was crowned, offers a measure of how closely Staël followed historical documents in writing her novel.[22] Corinne's arrival at the Capitol is squarely based on the *Atti*'s description of Corilla's entering the *Sala Capitolina*. The textual resemblance is so striking that it deserves to be fully quoted:

> At the presence of select and numerous spectators, [among which] princesses, noblemen and distinguished foreigners, Corilla arrived at the *Palazzo Consolare*. She was received by appointed *Cavalieri*, by the Pope's Swiss Guard, and by the Pope's Red Guard. She entered the *Sala Capitolina* (the main Capitol's hall) at the sound of a thrilling symphony of drums and trumpets and was saluted by applause and cheers of 'long live Corilla!' (*Atti* 37 ff.)

Staël's description of Corinne's crowning seems hardly coincidental:

> Thrilling music sounded before the triumphal procession came into view.... Many Roman noblemen and a few foreigners led the way for the chariot bearing Corinne.... Everyone shouted: Long live Corinne! Long live genius! Long live beauty! ... A fresh burst of music was heard as Corinne arrived; the canon roared and the triumphant Sibyl entered the palace that had been made ready to receive her. (20–21)

Although both Corilla and Corinne enjoy a ritualistic and ostentatious crowning ceremony—both are saluted by cannons, drums, and trumpets, celebrated by Italian as well as foreign noblemen and ladies—only Corinne enjoys a glorious triumphal procession, during which she is showered with signs of approval and admiration from the whole Roman community. Corilla's procession had to be cancelled in order to avoid the taunts and

riots her bitter antagonists had threatened. Among the attempts
to undermine the event, there had already been a letter by the
"Letteratura Romana," a Roman literary organization, re-
questing that the Pope withhold his favor; a letter from Abbot
Cancellieri, to his fellow Arcadians to mobilize them against Corilla; and lampooning satires, libels, and threats of physical violence to Corilla and her supporters. The language of the
opposition was couched in some of the most sexist and vitriolic
terms scholars of women's history are to encounter.[23] A few days
before the ceremony a mock crowning took place in front of
Corilla's window where a prostitute was brought and crowned
with laurels.

Corilla's enemies almost succeeded in their pursuit. The Pope
considered conferring only a diploma to Corilla, avoiding the
publicity and *éclat* of a ceremony. Corilla urged that the ceremony be carried out as planned, but asked to be dispensed from
the triumphal procession, as we learn from a letter that Giovanni Cristofano Amaduzzi, a highly reputed Classicist and a
friend of Corilla, wrote on the very day of the crowning, 31
August 1776:

> Corilla alone has been able to defend her cause, since most of her
> supporters have abandoned her and her closest friends are
> crushed. . . . At this point one could say that she owes this honor to
> nobody but herself. . . . A letter of hers written according to the most
> solid principles of religion, strength, reason and generosity, not only
> swayed in her favor the Pope's decision, but accelerated its execu-
> tion. Modesty and prudence have prompted her to ask the Pope to
> dispense with the public procession to the Capitol. She had her wish,
> in spite of the contrary efforts of the *Conservatori*.

Corinne's triumphal procession is symbolic of an overwhelming approval of the ceremony that Corilla lacked.[24] By portraying
the ceremony as a triumph, Staël discredits all injurious innu-
endoes and debasing accusations regarding its legitimacy and
elevates it to the high pedestal of pure self-assertion and
achievement. "No longer a fearful woman, [Corinne] was a priestess, joyously devoting herself to the cult of genius" (32). Staël
stresses the Dionysian aspect of Corinne's crowning as a celebration of the woman artist's self-confidence, self-determination,
and pride. With a bold and strong language that could not but
irritate the proponents of a traditionally restrained role for
women, she creates an image of female authority that was to be
extremely influential in the history of women's writing.

Not only did Staël follow Corilla's friends' interpretation of the event, as it is demonstrated by her use of the *Atti,* which represents Corilla's supporters' views, but she also showed the gendered dimension of Corilla's predicament that not even her friends could or wanted to see. As the narrator comments: "As soon as Corinne took her seat, the poets of Rome began to read the poems and odes they had written in her honor" (22). These poetical homages showed "a pleasant mixture of images and mythological allusions which could have been addressed over the centuries to any woman renowned for her literary talent, from Sappho's day to her own" (23).[25] Besides being an implicit criticism of a certain kind of flowery, conventional Arcadian poetry, the comment also points to a lack of understanding on the part of Corinne's supporters, who have not been able to grasp and depict the unique value of Corinne's achievement to her age. The text of *Corinne* purports to fill in this gap by showing the extraordinary qualities and sacrifices required of a woman who, in Corilla and Staël's times, boldly and proudly chose to take on such a prominent literary persona.[26]

Symbolic and Historical Import of the Capitol Crowning

In open defiance of the widespread opinion that the only woman ever crowned at the Capitol was not worthy of the laurels bestowed on Petrarch and Tasso before her, Staël has her heroine pronounce these words during the improvisation on "The Glory of Italy" (Corilla had improvised on "The Glory of Rome"): "Why am I here at the Capitol? Why is my humble forehead to receive the crown that Petrarch wore. . . ? Why . . . if you love not glory enough to reward with *an even hand* those who worship her and those who have attained her!" (27; my emphasis).[27] Read in the context of the fervent debate in Rome, Italy, and Europe over Corilla's crowning, Corinne's words can be seen as an implicit reproach of those who questioned the merit of the woman of genius on the basis of sexist prejudice. Since the crown testifies to the glory and fame of a poet, as demonstrated by its illustrious previous recipients, Petrarch and Tasso, the Romans' choice of Corilla could not but be dictated by her merit and achievement. Why would Corilla otherwise be crowned, if not because her supporters loved glory *with an even hand* (i.e., a hand that did not discriminate, not even on the basis of sex)?[28]

To understand the full extent of Staël's vision and defiance in presenting such an interpretation of the events, one needs to keep in mind how vast and fierce the opposition had been to the crowning of a female author as a poet laureate at the Capitol. By an examination of the documents relating to the history of Italian improvisation, of the Capitol crown, and of Corilla, one discovers that the crowning was a highly prestigious honor.[29] It had been bestowed on only three authors in four hundred years and to no woman. The crown was conferred in recognition of a poet's cumulative achievements and fame. Corilla was crowned both for her merit as an improviser and for her written works. Hence, crowning Corilla meant acknowledging a woman's literary excellence and challenging male cultural hegemony. Aspiring to, pursuing, and accepting an honor that entailed a public recognition of her preeminence as a poet in the Republic of Letters ran counter to society's ideology of women's decorum.

Consequently, the crowning turned many of Corilla's admirers into critics. Of those who had hailed and praised Corilla's performance, few stood by her side at the moment of the crowning. Accusations of Corilla's unworthiness ranged from the less personal and milder ones, contending that she was a good poet, but in her own secondary and feminine way, and therefore undeserving of the honors bestowed on Petrarch and Tasso—which conveniently ignored that another less prestigious male poet such as Perfetti had also been crowned—to the most odious and abrasive ones, that attacked Corilla's morals and character and climaxed in the unsubstantiated, but often reported, accusation that Corilla had usurped the crown by fraud.

By the time Staël wrote *Corinne,* Corilla enjoyed some repute, but the opinion prevailed that she had not deserved the crown. Casanova, for example, expressed his admiration for Corilla's gifts, which had allowed him to enjoy the Italian language as he had never before, but his fervent admiration stopped short of the Capitol crown: "Corilla was crowned poet laureate at the Capitol. The same place was chosen where our great Italian poets received their laurels, and it was a great scandal. In fact, although Corilla's achievement was unique in its genre, since it did not consist of anything but a beautiful ornament, it did not deserve to partake of the honors so rightly bestowed on Petrarch and Tasso."[30] Casanova's objection to Corilla's crowning on the ground that her poetic merit was nothing but "ornamental" reveals the gendered bias against Corilla. In conformity with the preconceived notion of its being supplemental, derivative, and secondary, women's art was categorized as ornamental or conversational and in any case peripheral. Corilla's poetic grace and fame remained undisputed so long as they were presumed to be firmly bound to the present.

Staël's story reflects on the crucial period in Corilla's life, the crowning—now being reappropriated with a vengeance—and Corilla's subsequent fall from public favor, and takes this tragedy to represent the woman writer's predicament. Corinne's dejection and death epitomize the demise of the female genius through containment and restraint (domestication and the gendered dichotomy of private and public) and finds its correspondence in the desolation of Corilla's ostracized and persecuted days of the post-Capitol Laurea and, most importantly, in the erasure of her name from literary history.

If they earned for her a Capitol coronation, Corilla's ambition and sense of entitlement also caused her ultimate downfall. The Capitol crown, which Corilla was granted for being the most acclaimed, loved, and admired improviser of the century, should have been sufficient to win her eternal fame; instead, it paradoxically undermined her reputation.[31] Although many of her former critics offered Corilla homage at the time of her second trip to Rome in 1786, a slow erosion of her reputation took place after her death. By 1839 it was definitively decided that Corilla did not deserve the crown, although she was still praised as one of the greatest poets and improvisers of her age. By 1887 all was lost. Ademollo, author of what is at present considered a definitive study on Corilla, presented the crowning as nothing but a cheat; without offering the criticism of even one of her poems, he denied any poetic merit to Corilla, except, perhaps, for a great dramatic presence that enchanted her listeners. The reactionary sexual politics of nineteenth-century Italy completely annihilated any recognition of Corilla's literary genius. She was branded and doomed to appear in specialized dictionaries as merely a curiosity, her poetic triumph as an improviser an inexplicable freak, if not a case of the corrupting charm of the femme fatale. So complete was her reversal of fortune, that in his 1926 history of the Italian literary academies Maylender singles out the moment of Corilla's coronation as the very mark of the Arcadian Academy's incipient decadence.

A Crown "Stained with Blood and Dust"

At the acme of her literary career Corilla also touched the zenith of her isolation. The time following the crowning was a time of personal tragedy and loss for Corilla. Although she received expressions of admiration from people as prominent as Catherine the Second of Russia, she felt shunned and abandoned by many of her friends and society in general. Corilla had to flee from Rome, where the mob's sentiments had been raised against her, and her very life was in danger. Her letters to Amaduzzi in the years 1776–77 are a touching cry for help from what is described in *Corinne* as "the abyss of despair." She is distraught by the fierce and demeaning opposition to her, she is dejected for being isolated from society's applause and recognition. In the days following her controversial crowning, she wrote to her friend Giovanni C. Amaduzzi: "last year I lived happy, [in harmony] with society; now, with my immortality, I live alone, and I am the object of insults and derision." She even got to the point of regretting ever having accepted the crown: "I cannot be grateful for a crown that has created my unhappiness and obscured my glory with all its shameful consequences . . . and has gotten me everybody's hate." About Gonzaga, who supported her crowning, but abandoned her in the wake of the scandal following it, she wrote: "true friends endeavor to make a woman happy. They do not bring her to despair . . . for a sterile laurel covered with the most atrocious bitterness. Ambition without heart is devastating."[32]

Ill and depressed, abandoned by her lover, her acquaintances, and all but a few friends—this is the Corilla on whom Staël draws the final curtain in her novel. Even though Corilla eventually recovered from this despair caused by persecution and isolation, as we have seen, her reputation never completely did: quite the contrary, it experienced a rapid involution after her death. Staël perceptively ended the story at the footsteps of the Capitol throne. The moment at the end of the crowning ceremony when Corinne drops her crown upon meeting Oswald's glance is symbolic of the global focus of the novel—Corinne's loss of her poetic gift and of literary recognition.[33]

The novel describes the heroine's sense of personal loss and dejection when obliged to retire from society's applause and recognition. After giving up her performance to comply with Oswald's jealous desire, Corinne withdraws into depression and confesses: "I miss what I was: . . . I was rather proud of my talent, I enjoyed the success, the glory; my ambition sought approval even from people of no interest to me. But now I do not care about anything. . . . I am profoundly disheartened" (227). Like Corilla, Corinne also will eventually leave Rome, the site of her triumph, her peace of mind forever lost, her crown "of hope and glory, . . . now stained with blood and dust" (308). Unlike Corilla's histories, the novel identifies the cause of the heroine's unhappiness not in her supposedly excessive or unfeminine professional drive, which allegedly led her to obtain an honor she did not deserve, but in societal prejudice.[34] As *Corinne* indicates, the fall from the glory of the Capitol crown to relative obscurity is the work of patriarchal prejudice, the law of the father, represented in the novel by Lord Nelvil, Oswald, Lady Edgermond, and England in general.

With true prophetic wisdom, Corinne predicted her demise at the very moment of her triumph. After noting that the crowning ceremony was a recognition of her fame and talent, she exclaims: "So, if you [Romans] do love glory, *who so often picks her victims from among the victors she has crowned,* then take pride in the centuries that saw the renaissance of the arts" (27; my emphasis). The parenthetical non sequitur acquires meaning and cogency only in the context of Corilla and Corinne's stories. The Italian Renaissance hardly needing any apologist, it seems Staël was trying to soften the dramatic and accusatory impact of the sentence by disguising it. Like Cassandra predicting her own death, like a sibyl using a coded language— but unlike her knowing its cipher, possessing it and not being possessed by it—Corinne reveals she will be the victim of her glory: a woman could not choose glory and remain a woman. As Gutwirth remarks with regard to Lamartine's perception of Staël's artistic activity: "Only her immodesty allowed her to express her genius. Immodesty is, of course, unfeminine: ergo, genius is unfeminine. Having unsexed herself she is no longer a woman, but only a sexless (that is not male) poet."[35] Lamartine's judgment of Staël epitomizes the woman writer's dilemma: Ultimately the judgment is used to undermine the artist. The price to be paid for glory is first, one's peace of mind, and then glory itself.

When on her death bed Corinne writes her last poetic composition, she reveals that in spite of all the grievous consequences, she does not regret her choices. Recollecting her Capitol triumph and the poetic enthusiasm which had led her to it, she exclaims: "No, I do not repent of that generous exaltation. No, the tears watering the dust that awaits me do not spring from that source. Had I devoted my resounding lyre to the celebration of the divine goodness manifest in the universe, I would have fulfilled my destiny, I would have been worthy of heaven's bounty" (416). Corinne regrets not having been able to pursue her career and cultivate her talents the way she felt she had the right to; she regrets having been robbed of "the celestial bliss made of enthusiasm" that inspired it. The reason for her unhappiness was not, as late-nineteenth-century readers of *Corinne* would claim, her professional choice, her ambition, her poetic exaltation. Her tragedy was that of abandoning the pursuit of that for which she was created, that for which her whole soul strove: her poetry.

Enthusiasm and confidence used to inspire her to follow her calling, to pursue her poetic vocation ("What confidence nature and life inspired me of old! I believed that all misfortune came from not thinking enough, from not feeling enough" [416]). She followed her vision with pride and courage as far as she could and where no other woman had been before, or would ever be again: at the Capitol throne; only to realize, to her dismay and anguish, that glory would turn into despair, since the qualities necessary to her professional fulfillment damned her in the eyes of the world. Rejected because of the very talents that constituted her pride and her reason to be, Corinne dies. Her poetic self could not survive without that love that kindles poetic enthusiasm: not just romantic love, but the love of the public and of her community. Inspiration dried up when the poet realized that her confidence in her own talents would not be enough to sustain her; that thinking, studying, and striving would actually elicit from her public the opposite of the desired response.[36]

Corinne's last pathetic appeal to her nation acquires, therefore, a tone of bitter irony. She sings: "you have allowed me glory: oh liberal nation who does not banish women from its temples, you who do not sacrifice immortal talent to passing jealousies, you who ever celebrate the expressions of genius, victor without victims, conqueror without spoils, drawing upon eternity to enrich time!" (416). Corinne's words are not a general tribute to Italy, as most commentators maintain, but one specific to those liberal intellectuals in the nation who had supported her crowning, believed steadfastly in her, and never abandoned her: her friends, people like Castel-Forte. Though these were people of rare quality (Castel-Forte is defined as "a man of uncommon wisdom"), their numbers and their influence were not enough to spare Corinne. The woman thanking her supporters for their benevolence, for the glory accorded her is the woman whose head, by her own admission, was in the dust: a woman sacrificed to those jealousies she decries, a victim of her own glory.

Italy: How "Liberal" a Nation?

By reading *Corinne* in the context of Corilla's history, we clarify from a feminist perspective what the "Italianness" of Corinne means in the novel.[37] Staël's Italy is no utopia with respect to the place of Corinne in its society. It is an idealization only insofar as it does not present Italian criticism of Corilla's poetic merit. Rather, consistent with the representation of cultures along national boundaries, and with the purpose of making of Corinne the representative of Italian genius, Staël chose not to give Corinne's Italian critics a voice in the representation of the heroine. The novel makes explicit the reason for this choice in Prince Castel-Forte's concluding speech at Corinne's crowning: "There is no doubt that Corinne is our country's most famous woman," he said, "and yet her friends alone can describe her; for the soul's qualities must always be divined when they are genuine; if some empathy does not win us inside, fame's glitter can prevent this recognition just as surely as obscurity" (24). Staël's novel is a tribute to those elements in the nation who had the clarity and the openness of vision to bestow a woman with one of the highest honors of the time. In this respect, *Corinne* can be seen as representing the new poetic ideals of a group of enlightened progressive Arcadian and Francophile thinkers (including Gonzaga, Pizzi, Amaduzzi, Godard), who were Corilla's greatest supporters.[38] Because of the reactionary backlash of postrevolutionary Italy and France, those liberal ideals were dying out, and with them, the fame and respect of women like Corilla and Corinne.

Considering the controversial status of Corilla's reputation, especially with regard to her Capitol crowning, and considering the growing influence of a conservative front in both France and Italy, Staël's choice of a representative of Italian literary genius was politically charged and very daring.[39] How averse a portion of the Italian intelligentsia was to this idea is demonstrated by Ugo Foscolo, the most influential Italian man of letters to comment on *Corinne*. In an 1817 draft of his *Gazzettino del bel mondo* he accused Staël of "founding historical events on fables and of describing Italy with a thousand inventions." The crowning of a woman poet at the Capitol was the only fact Foscolo produced in support of his accusation: "I see metaphysics transformed into a female poet and crowned in our days at the Capitol in front of a crowd of people and of princes, without a single diplomat or journalist ever being able to report it." Since we know that a crowning did happen at the Capitol, that diplomats and gazetteers did report it, and that Foscolo could hardly have been ignorant of these facts, Foscolo's statement may only be understood as a failure to acknowledge and validate the event.[40] Of course there is a chronological discrepancy between the time of the actual crowning and the time of the action in the novel: almost twenty years. But time is a relative concept; the very same crowning that was considered current by Schlegel was instead ideologically so distant from Foscolo it might as well have never happened for him. Ultimately what matters to Foscolo is that anyway in *his day and age*—early nineteenth-century Italy—such an "abstruse" event as the crowning of a woman poet at the Capitol could not and did not happen.[41]

On Improvising

If we consider the novel as a statement on "the ways in which female subjectivity is constituted in the public sphere," the figure of the improviser may be seen as a powerful symbol of the predicament of the female genius/writer—the oral nature of her art a symbol of the transience of her fame and of the caducity (ephemeral nature) of her work. *Corinne* embodies the tragedy of the woman artist and writer: the difficulty for even the most talented ones to leave a mark, a permanent trace, a legacy. Nevertheless, I would argue that the issues at the heart of the novel do not hinge on the subordination of oral to written, of improvising to writing, as suggested by some commentators.[42]

Not only were Corinne and Corilla published writers, but improvising was not necessarily considered an inferior expression of poetic talent. Opinions regarding the value of improvising in relation to writing varied. Some considered improvisation a higher and more challenging art form.[43] Indeed improvising ability was held in the highest esteem when Perfetti was crowned poet laureate in 1725. The very fact that an improviser was chosen for two consecutive times (Perfetti and Corilla) to be the recipient of the prestigious Capitol Laurels should also be an indication of the reputation of this medium. While opinions regarding the value of improvising with relation to writing varied, what remained a constant was the hierarchal opposition of the male to the female. If the male improviser owed his success and reputation only to his poetic genius and stamina, the woman improviser owed it to an involuntary ability if not to her quality of enchantress.[44] So, while it had been perfectly legitimate to crown Perfetti as a poet laureate on the basis of his improvising ability—indeed, he was unquestionably considered a veritable genius for it—in Corilla's case that very same improvising ability was instead presented by some as the mark of her inferiority as a poet.[45]

It may be argued that it was exactly because of the excellence and predominance of women that improvising, as well as Arcadia (where most improvisers were helped and promoted), eventually—and as a direct consequence of Corilla's laurels—were stigmatized as "effeminate" and therefore *ipso facto* inferior and secondary. By upholding an improviser, in fact the very one who, with her "glorious" crowning at the Capitol initiated a reactionary backlash, Staël takes a clear stand on the issue of the worth of Italian women improvisers and of the legitimacy of the honors attributed to them.

Corinne results, at least in part, from the consideration that Corilla's triumph and crowning were appearing less and less realistic and could hardly be repeated. An anecdote regarding Teresa Bandettini Landucci, by most considered the legitimate heir to Corilla's poetic laurels, is significant in this regard. According to some, in 1795, the year in which Corinne was supposed to have been crowned, an attempt was made to crown Amarilli at the Capitol, but it failed. On the day of the planned crowning, Teresa Bandettini Landucci, Amarilli in Arcadia, had just finished her impromptu answer to the examination topics, when an onlooker, Abbot Gagliuffi, got up from the audience. Having been allowed to speak, he allegedly "repeated, in equally beautiful Latin, the verses Amarilli had improvised." Amazement and confusion ensued. The planned crowning had to be aborted.[46] Lancetti refers to this episode as hearsay (the only certain fact being that Amarilli was never crowned at the Capitol), and we do not find it repeated by any other source. Yet, whether Amarilli was really thus humiliated or not, the story's symbolic power is plain to see: it embodies the prevailing ideology's desire to silence the woman improviser, and it is representative of the climate against which Staël's book was set.

At a very delicate transitional moment in the history of women, Staël wrote a novel that spelled out what was at stake in the fight over women's rights: not only their present happiness—that is, their intellectual, artistic and emotional fulfillment—but their very inscription in history, the possibility of leaving a mark, of creating a tradition, which would legitimize and empower future generations. The novel can therefore be read as a statement on the phenomenon of the transience of female fame, whose most glaring example at the time of Staël's writing was to be found in the vicissitudes of Corilla's reputation and fame. This poet's striving, working, and suffering, her devotion and dedication to her work, and her vocation were being forgotten. Evolving instead were images of Corilla as a corrupted femme fatale; as a degenerate mother and wife, unworthy of the honor that had been bestowed on her; or as an unambitious, "domesticated," and nonthreatening woman.[47] *Corinne* allows a feminist reappropriation of the story of Corilla, affording sympathetic insight into the issues at stake in Corilla's literary career, such as is not offered by any literary history or monograph. The crowning at the Capitol is an even more powerful symbol than we have previously acknowledged, because it unmistakably recalls and reaffirms with a generosity of vision a historical event that opposing forces had undermined and were in the process of completely erasing from the pages of literary history.

Corinne and Female Transmission: Rewriting *La Princesse de Clèves* through the English Gothic

APRIL ALLISTON

THROUGH correspondences with earlier women writers that cross the borders of national tradition, Germaine de Staël's *Corinne, or Italy* revises received conceptions of both national and gender boundaries. The novel's working out of interconnected problems of transmission—represented as inheritance, education, literary tradition, and history—as well as of women's place in the modern nation-state, is effected largely through its revision of Marie de Lafayette's *La Princesse de Clèves*. This revision shows significant traces of the eighteenth-century English phenomenon that Ellen Moers calls "female Gothic." One of the earliest Gothic novelists, Sophia Lee, similarly inscribed revisions of key episodes from Lafayette's work. By revising aspects of her countrywoman's canonical novel through allusions to the female Gothic, Staël perpetuates the gestures of her predecessors in both nations toward an alternative feminine cross-generational form of literary transmission, one that differs both from a patrilineal model of literary tradition and from any notion of maternal legacy modelled upon it. The result is the creation of a particularly Romantic version of feminine transmission in particular, one that subverts conceptions of *patrie* and of literary tradition that tend to place women in a status of exile within the cultural heritage of their own nations.[1]

As a reformulation of the solutions offered in *La Princesse de Clèves* to the problem of female transmission within a patrilineal society, *Corinne* retains the earlier novel's primary couple, the mother-daughter dyad, in the relation between Lucile and her mother.[2] The description of *Corinne*'s antiheroine as exemplar of English feminine virtue strikingly resembles that of Lafayette's French princess. Physically, Lucile presents the same perfect blank of fair skin and blond hair that make up the nondescript princess, distinguished by the same excessively modest reserve and described in the same terms of "brilliance." For both characters, the culmination of a secluded education by a widowed mother is an entrance at the age of sixteen into the public arena (for Lucile the London opera house instead of the royal court) as the greatest heiresses of their respective nations and the central focus of society's collective gaze (341–43).[3]

What first attracts the hero of Staël's novel to its heroine's foil is precisely that unbroken and exclusive connection to her mother, consisting of a severe education in virtue, for which the princess of Clèves is famous (e.g., "he was lost in a dream of the celestial purity of a young girl who, always at her mother's side, knows nothing of life but daughterly affection" [317]). And in fact the function of Oswald's marriage to Lucile is to preserve that maternal connection unbroken, just as the prince of Clèves is chosen by his future mother-in-law to continue in her role of educator in feminine virtue after her death.[4] Lucile secures Oswald's "interest" (*intérêt*) when she agrees to the marriage, not by expressing any desire for it, but by demanding that it not separate her from her mother. The mother, meanwhile, expresses her satisfaction with the match by pronouncing herself "well replaced" (379).

While Lucile resembles the princess of Clèves in the primacy of her relationship to her mother, Staël's most important revision of the earlier work is to replace this mother-daughter relationship within the very patrilineal frame that Lafayette had de-emphasized as much as possible.[5] Lucile, unlike the princess, is heiress to a true patrimony. She is specifically named as heiress to her father's estate, and when her future husband first catches sight of her, alone and unchaperoned as the princess is when first seen by Clèves at the jeweler's shop, she is on that heritable estate rather than in a place of public exchange. Instead of seeking to match the incomplete set of jewels that form the princess's maternal inheritance, she is absorbed in reading a book (317, 353). The book she is reading is not named, but only one of Lucile's books is ever named, and that is her copy of the same paternal precepts that were handed down to Oswald. Lucile's copy constitutes the main relic of her private funerary shrine to this, her "second father," who praises her feminine virtues and designates her as the perfect wife in his inscription to the book (350). The book is thus a paternal parallel to the princess's maternal jewels; it is movable property that is passed down but does not constitute a patrimony proper, a legacy that must remain incomplete unless the daughter fulfills its destination by living up to its image of perfect feminine virtue.

Lucile is thus literally inscribed in the father's will, not only in the dedication to the memorial book of precepts, but also in the other apotheosized form of inscription that traces the patriarch's ghostly word over all the novel's landscapes: the providential signs that seem to spell out the fate of Corinne and of her relationship with Oswald. In that moment where he first sees Lucile reading the book in the park of her estate, she is marked in Oswald's imagination as the tableau of feminine virtue upon which the gaze of male desire is destined to come to rest: "his imagination set in motion just a short time ago by eloquence and passion, enjoyed the picture of innocence, and seemed to see around Lucile some sort of modest aura that was deliciously restful to the eye" (319). This vaguely described "aura" is reminiscent of the "cloud" that Corinne has by this time already read as the expression of a paternal heaven's condemnation of her relationship with Oswald, and that appears again, as she predicts, at the moment of her death. The providential writing represented by this "cloud" and aura is the international language that all three protagonists know how to read.[6] Thus Staël re-inscribes the characters' relationships, more specifically, in the writing of the father's will *as providence*—which includes that word's other early sense of "inheritance." In both senses, "providence" is precisely the writing that Lafayette had suppressed. Not only does M. de Chartres' presumable real estate and will go entirely without mention; the organizing force of events in *La Princesse de Clèves* is remarkably neither the providence that drives romance nor the chance whose operations distinguish other early novels, like *Don Quixote,* from romance; rather the sense of fatality that pervades it derives from the foregone conclusion of maternal history and its endless specular repetition in the process of its transmission from mother to daughter.[7] This specularity survives in *Corinne* in the relation between Lucile and her mother.

The daughter as mirror is not a simple mirror of specularity, but rather a mirror of speculation: one that gives back the mother's image "with interest," with something added. Ellen Peel has shown in "Corinne's Shift to Patriarchal Mediation" that Lucile's repetition of her mother's prayer indicates that Lady Edgermond "conscientiously follows patriarchal rules" by using her daughter as "a vicarious source of virtue."[8] More specifically, for her dying mother to be redeemed by God, the daughter must *exceed* her maternal model in virtue. While this relation of speculation resembles Mme de Chartres' demand that her daughter be more perfect than any other woman (including, by implication, herself), it has here been specifically inscribed as the *devoir,* the debt, of a specifically *paternal* will that is written in the heavens, in the grave that is also a graven book, and in the landscaped park of the estate (320; Balayé 455).

The shift in *Corinne* from Lafayette's fatality of maternal destination back to a plot organized by the paternal providence of romance is mediated by the subgenre of Gothic romance that intervenes historically and strategically between the two works. The Gothic mother, when she is not dead or absent, tends to become monstrous because she is always a double of the father, and hence a usurper of paternal "providence." The stepmother appears so frequently because she expresses, in the characteristically Gothic logic of the double, its double truth about the mother: in the patrilineal family, she is *at once* dead or absent *and* an intruder, a usurper of the patrimony and of patriarchal powers. This, of course, is precisely the (step)mother's condition in *Corinne.* Lady Edgermond is a Gothic Mme de Chartres: she not only controls a daughter through education in virtue, but theatrically "kills" a stepdaughter, exiling her from the fatherland (*patrie*) and performing that exile as a literal entombment within it.

While in *Corinne* the paternal estate as the daughter's inheritance returns from its repression in *La Princesse de Clèves,* that estate is anxiously preserved from the ruin characteristic of Gothic patrimony through Staël's Gothic strategy of doubling. Ruination, and the paternal threat it expresses, is displaced onto the stepmother, who serves as the father's dark (female) double, just as her castle does to the civilized paternal estate:

> Living quite close to the seashore (*bord de la mer),* we often felt the north wind in our castle: at night I used to hear it whistle through the long hallways, and by day it marvelously fostered our silence when we were together. (255; Balayé 367)

In this sentence, Staël reunites all the traits of the Gothic stepmother in the description of her castle: the pun on *mère/mer,* associating the maternal with the cold, tempestuous, overwhelming and dangerous force represented by the sea, the silencing of the daughter by this dark maternal force, the fragmentation of its enclosure, the mournful monotony of a domestic life that is compared to an imprisonment and a haunting.[9]

The Gothic re-inscription of the maternal order into the paternal framework of providence constructs the boundaries of that framework as those of empire, extending them beyond the borders of the estate and the state to contain and exploit that which they exclude. Thus in Sophia Lee's *The Recess; or, A Tale of Other Times* (1783–85), the heroines must, like the princess of Clèves, go in search of a "match" in order to realize their maternal inheritance; but whether they go to Jamaica, to Ireland, or to their own maternal kingdom of Scotland, they always find that somehow they have never escaped the enclosure of England; they always find themselves back in the Recess.[10] Although much has been written about the association in *Corinne* of England and the North with the paternal, and of Italy and the South with the maternal, of Corinne's (or *Corinne*'s) effort to reconcile the two or to return to a utopian life in the mother country, the problem is not one of an opposition or separation between the two "places."[11] The solution, therefore, is neither one of reconciliation between the two worlds nor of retrieval of a lost maternal paradise.[12] For the problem of *Corinne*'s geography is the problem of empire, one of lack of separation and of the enclosure of the "mother country" within the patriarchal empire as a place of exile.[13] While patrilineal borderlines define both gender and nationality, they also enclose and appropriate aspects of what they define as other, while simultaneously leaving open possibilities of transgression.

What distinguishes the roles of the primary characters in *Corinne* from one another is thus no longer as much a matter of difference of sex as it was in *La Princesse de Clèves*, where the situation of a daughter as receiver of a problematic maternal inheritance was set in contrast with the agency of possession and transmission belonging to a Clèves or a Nemours within the masculine bias of the feudal social order.[14] While Oswald plays both of Lafayette's masculine roles—Clèves and Nemours—to Corinne's and Lucile's differing interpretations of the princess, his most significant role in Staël's rewriting of the earlier novel is that of the princess herself.[15] His response to Corinne echoes that of the princess to Nemours, when he argues that he cannot be hers, although he is unattached, because to marry her would be to transgress the plot laid out for him by his father (275, 277; *PC* 172). And he gives that response because the same curse, nearly word for word, has been uttered upon him by his father as the one uttered by Mme de Chartres upon her daughter:

> Seeing that his wife would not be happy in England, my son would soon find himself uncomfortable here. He has all the weakness sensitivity (*la sensibilité*) inspires, I know that. So he would go off to settle in Italy, and *if I lived to see that expatriation, it would make me die of grief.* (330; emphasis mine)

After the father's death, the son reads the paternal declaration that his own expatriation would have killed his father, were he still alive to see it; just as the princess hears her dying mother declare that her daughter's "fall," were she to live to see it, would be the one thing that could make her glad to be already dead (*PC* 68). The threat that transmits the paternal debt is thus patterned on a model of maternal transmission—which itself, however, had been modelled on a patriline transmission that was already structured like a debt. The effect of this detour, this doubling back of fictions of patrimony, is to debunk the patrilineal transmission of property as a fiction of the perpetuation of agency or empowerment and to expose it as a bond of indebtedness upon which the interest due is perpetually increasing. In *La Princesse de Clèves*, maternal transmission models itself upon patrimony in being also structured like a debt. Indebtedness itself becomes the only legacy transmissible through maternal lines, in the absence or suppression of the property and agency that is the content of patrilineal transmission. Corinne's retranslation of maternal indebtedness into the terms of patrimony offers the Gothic revelation that it, too, is finally *constituted* in indebtedness, and not simply structured, as debt. This re-translation also entails a translation of the terms of a "fall" from feminine virtue into those of "expatriation"—or exile from the *patrie*.

The fatherland, like its son and heir, Oswald, bears in *Corinne* the marks of Staël's translation from the terms of femininity. The reason given by the old Lord Nelvil for fearing his son's expatriation is the weakness of sensibility. Although in the "moral geography" of Richardson's *Sir Charles Grandison*, one of Staël's favorite books, Italy is the country of sensibility, "a location for the excesses of feeling" according to John Mullan, this only shows how little those excesses are capable of containment by the boundaries of national character.[16] For sensibility is one of the chief distinguishing marks, not only of Italy in

Grandison and of Oswald's character in this novel, but more generally of English national character in European eighteenth-century discourse.[17] It is precisely the quality in Oswald that makes him not merely comply with, but *exceed* the father's will, pay back the debt of patrimony with the "interest" of sensibility.[18] M. Dickson, by showing him the letter in which Oswald's dead father translates the curse of Mme de Chartres, "assaulted the most sensitive (sensible) places in Oswald's heart" (331; Balayé 469). The son's response to this attack on his sensibility is, like the princess's, to exceed the demand that is made: "However fleeting that wish may have been, I wanted to comply before I knew you, as a kind of expiation, as a way of extending the power of his will [l'*empire* de sa volonté] beyond death" (235; Balayé 341; emphasis mine). The interest paid by (feminine) sensibility on the debt of inheritance complicitously locates agency in the "will" (*volonté*) of the dead, thus legitimating the inheritance received. As the imaginary agency of the dead extends beyond the grave, it also extends the *patrie* beyond the plot of inherited real estate and even beyond the borders of the nation, so that it becomes an *empire* whose law of patrilineal transmission extends over those countries excluded by its borders.

Italy, "deprived of independence by unfortunate circumstances," has thus come under the dominion of the law that lays down the simultaneously inclusive and exclusive borders of the *patrie* as empire (113).[19] Its association in the novel with the maternal and with the feminine generally, rather than separating it from the fatherland, is in fact the very quality that "pays the interest" that supports the fatherland as empire. Paternal will and feminine sensibility come together to produce the *circonstances malheureuses,* the plot that continues to deprive Italy of her independence. These "circumstances" appear to be ineluctably decreed by a paternal providence, but at the same time require, in order to maintain that appearance, the determination of a reader who will authorize the ambiguous signs traced upon the heavens. Corinne—or Italy—is just such a reader, as is evident from her insistence on determining the meaning of what she reads in the heavens as the paternal writ of her own banishment:

'As I was gazing at the moon, it hid behind a cloud, and that cloud had a deathly look. I have always known the sky to look paternal or angry, and *I tell you,* Oswald, tonight it condemned our love.'

'Dear friend, the only omens on man's life are his good or bad deeds, and have I not this very evening sacrificed my most fervent desires to a feeling of virtue?' (196; emphasis mine)

Oswald here seems to oppose an order of active self-determination to Corinne's order of a paternal fatality, but the terms of his reply undermine the force of his own assertion and secretly reinforce Corinne's. He begins by stating that the only auguries of the life of *man* [*l'homme*] are his own actions; Oswald seems to mean the "generic man," but in fact males are the only group for whom virtue, in the classical tradition of *virtus*, would indeed have been "active."[20] The example with which Oswald supports his precept about "gender-neutral" virtue is that of his own avoidance of action in the name of "sentiment" and "virtue." Like a typical eighteenth-century sentimental hero, then, Oswald adopts a feminine virtue that denies female desire and passively preserves female chastity in order to maintain patriarchal "honor" intact.[21] By "proving" his precept of gender-neutral virtue with the example of his own feminine virtue, Oswald demonstrates that the feminization of masculinity actually brings both genders all the more rigidly into the terms and under the law of the dead father whose will is apotheosized as providence—and thus proves Corinne too sure an augurer.

Italy's relation to the masculine order represented as empire and as English must be understood in the terms of the Gothic, that genre of sentimental fiction as characteristically English as sensibility itself was said to be.[22] In her chapter on *Corinne* in *Literary Women,* Ellen Moers asks a basic but important question: "Why Italy?" She points to eighteenth-century conventions about English and Italian national character in *Sir Charles Grandison,* and concludes convincingly that Staël and Richardson are working with the same conventions about national character: "for married happiness and domestic virtue, England is undoubtedly the place; but for love outside of marriage, go to Italy." She notes in passing that Ann Radcliffe, like her predecessor Walpole but without his personal experience of the place, also chose Italy as the setting for her Gothic novels, even though the Gothic style in architecture is not much in evidence in its actual landscape, as compared with that of the northern countries. Moers closes with a reference to the fact that *Corinne* winds up in northern Italy, "cold as the rest of Europe," and like the North even graced with a Gothic cathedral—precisely not the Italy of sunshine and free love that had been Moers's answer to the question of setting.[23] But Radcliffe's interest in Italy, for that matter, had nothing to do with either sunshine or free love, and even Corinne seems to be in pursuit of a fusion of "northern" with "southern" characteristics. Staël's Italy is, as Moers suggests, an English Italy—in that it is an ambiguous territory split between the Italy of Richardson and the Italy of Radcliffe. This split within Italy does not, however, as Moers further implies, repeat in simple geographic terms the same line of division between North and South that separates Italy from England on the map of Europe, for the central Gothic ruin in *Corinne* is neither the cathedral in Milan nor the paternal estate in Scotland; rather it disintegrates at the heart of Rome itself, appearing to Corinne's imagination in her proleptic vision of St. Peter's in ruins (286).

The key to the significance of Corinne's seemingly unmotivated vision comes near the novel's close, when Oswald and Lucile, touring northern Italy, visit the cathedral of Milan, "Italy's masterpiece of Gothic architecture, just as St. Peter's is for *modern* architecture." At that point the narrator actually quotes Horace Walpole, the first Gothic novelist, on the difference between Gothic and modern churches: "to build modern temples, the popes used the wealth they had obtained through the piety inspired by the Gothic churches" (396; translator's emphasis). In other words, St. Peter's represents a kind of "interest" on the Gothic; it is built with the financial interest (*richesses*) paid in expression of the religious interest (*dévotion*) inspired by Gothic architecture (Balayé 556). This interest is a legacy that ultimately replaces and destroys the "real" inheritance, the Gothic churches themselves. The vision of St. Peter's in ruins projects the English Gothic associations of Catholic abbeys falling into ruin after the dissolution of the monasteries onto the central edifice of Rome as an empire of fragmentation and of death, already undergoing the disintegration in the process of its own transmission.

That Oswald is threatened with exile from within the patriline empire just as much as Corinne is, is dramatized in the act of narrating his history: he concludes the narrative and the chapter by lamenting his inability to escape the "conscience" that is his introjected dead father—that is, his containment within the fatherland as empire even when he is standing in sunniest Italy. Mount Vesuvius, the scene of the narration, is a phallic abyss that is called the "fatherland" (*patrie*) of the Neapolitans—of the quintessential southern Italians, the inhabitants of the "country in Europe most favored by the sun." Within the same page it is also referred to as "the empire of death" (206; Balayé 303).[24] To the extent and in the moment that the sunny south becomes a *patrie,* it too becomes just another territory of the paternal empire of death from which Oswald cannot escape, lying as it does under the continual threat of the uncontainable abyss, Vesuvius. And yet within its domain he remains in exile from it: the scene closes with his anguished wish that the ground would open up to let him enter (*pénétrer*) into the land of the dead, which is the true fatherland (231; Balayé 336). The abyss is *itself* the patrilineal script: Oswald compares the words he reads in the public papers at the moment of his return to England, "Lord Nelvil has just died," to the threatening fire of the volcano. The referent of those printed words, necessarily uttered after the death of Oswald's father and thus after his own succession to the title, contains an inherent ambiguity that identifies Oswald with his dead father. He has become at once the haunted and the haunting. The fiery letters are always before his eyes, "haunting [him] like a ghost," yet their effect is also to transform *him* into a ghost, the shade of his father, as the haunting paternal script actually erases him. Thus he repeats his father's written words, incapable of using his own: "next to the vivid colors we use to paint their blessed halo, we would find ourselves obliterated in the very midst of our golden days, in the midst of the triumphs that most dazzle us" (228–30). The death of Oswald's father—his penetration into the empire of death, his eternal inaccessibility to dialogue—gives his words the fixity of a written will, and makes a specter of the son left behind to wander the map like a restive ghost.[25]

Corinne is in exactly the same position within the paternal empire as Oswald, differences of gender and nationality notwithstanding; the only real difference between them is that she resists. What makes that difference? The difference of gender, though confused and challenged throughout the novel, does momentarily ground Corinne in Italy, even if that ground is only a stage formed by the verge of a precipice. Her maternal inheritance consists of a position within the empire of the father that, although not her own ground, nevertheless allows her to stage a fiction of escape. This ground is precisely what Oswald lacks, as he explains to her at the end of his story: "how could courage triumph, when it cannot even hold out against conscience which is its source." Courage—will, self-determined action (*virtus*)—needs the ground of "conscience" to stand on, by which is here meant freedom from the threat of those fiery fixed characters announcing the father's eternal removal beyond the reach of the son's own discourse. By naming this missing ground "conscience," Oswald is again using not his own language but that of Corinne, who has just suggested that he use her heart—her feminine sensibility—as the grounding that might replace conscience: "judge yourself in my heart, take it for your conscience" (228–31). Yet the difference made by Corinne's maternal inheritance is an unreal estate, a precipice that cannot provide either of them with a sure foothold.

The question of what Corinne has that Oswald lacks leads to the question of what Corinne wants. Attempts to answer that question have been almost as various as the speculations in response to Freud's question about women—and perhaps they are versions of the same question. The suggestions of recent feminist critics tend to characterize Corinne's desire, one way or another, as a nostalgic desire for wholeness, something consonant with the desire to remember a primeval mother or rediscover a mother country, as expressed notably in Gilbert and Gubar's *The Madwoman in the Attic*.[26] Peterson observes that Staël invented, with the Schlegels, the Romantic project of a reconciliation between Northern and Southern aesthetic sensibilities, and argues that Corinne fails to enact with Oswald, or to embody within herself, that ideal union of opposites; instead she both enacts and embodies her failure by falling into madness and fragmentation.[27] Miller puts forth that the wholeness for which Corinne struggles is specifically maternal: "the unconditional love of the mother, the dead mother who named her and who mapped out her destiny . . . a lost maternal plenitude"; she echoes Peterson in blaming Corinne's failure to realize her desire in part on the lack of the very thing she is supposed to be seeking, "maternal support."[28] Read in this way, *Corinne* expresses a nostalgia for the princess of Clèves, who haunts the novel as the daughter whose dead mother both named her and mapped out her destiny by appointing as her husband that very "man who could love like a mother," the ideal male Miller proposes as the obscure object of Corinne's desire.[29]

To understand Corinne's desire as nostalgia for a plenitude that never was, however, is to mistake the ground of her resistance to patriarchy. Moers answers the question of her desire more obliquely, with the remark that "all she gets is what she deserves—Italy." But Corinne certainly doesn't get the Italy of free love that Moers had identified earlier in her essay; she ends up instead with the Gothic Italy, as Moers herself implies at the end of her chapter without making it explicit. Quoting Lucile's question to Oswald, "*Où donc est votre belle Italie?*" she leaves the reader free to follow through its implications on her own.[30] The answer that Moers leaves out is written in that patriarchal script associated with Lucile, and its logic is that of empire. That the North (England) is associated with the father and with the patriarchal order, while the South (Italy) is an idealized mother country, and that Corinne, her own origins divided, seeks in her relationship with Oswald to chart a union between the two, cannot be denied. But the charter she would enact is not one to establish a reunion out of separation, or unity out of opposition, but rather one that would renegotiate the boundaries defining the union that already exists under the patriarchal "empire." For just as the North is fatherland and the South mother country, they are both, finally, the same place of exile, borderlands of a single empire united in imagination, first by the tradition of Rome, then by the ambition of Napoleon, and always in the ruinous Gothic edifice of patriarchy. The system of patrimonial transmission that holds edifice and empire together does so by writing "maternal plenitude" out of existence, and rewriting it as a myth of paradise (happily) lost. The mother as "the perfect *destinataire*," as Miller calls her, the ideal addressee who names her daughter and plots her destiny, is already inscribed by the patriarchal writing as a substitute father, a pretender—like Lady Edgermond, like Lafayette's Madame de Chartres, whose naming and destination of their daughters put dead ends to the daughters' own plots. Maternal destination is of a piece with patrimonial transmission, and Corinne's "failure" in fragmentation, while hardly a happy fall, is the only possible form of her resistance to the wholeness of its empire.[31] Thus Corinne, in losing sunny Italy, loses herself as its coherent, specular image, for as more than one writer has observed, she is early identified as "*l'image de la belle Italie.*"[32]

What Corinne wants is named in a single word: she identifies it herself as *sympathy* (*sympathie*). Sympathy is at once what she offers and what she elicits through her improvisational art; sympathy is what she needs from her lover (e.g., 24, 44, 369).[33] Staël's use of sympathy is borrowed from earlier women writers like Lee, but she alters it significantly. She not only invents "Romanticism" as a term, but here also helps invent one of its central moves, the substitution of "imagination" for the Enlightenment "sensibility" as the term set in uneasy opposition to "reason."[34] Imagination is "the source of her talent," and for Corinne it cannot be separated from sensibility; this is what keeps Corinne's imagination "feminine," even while the talents to which it gives rise place her in the prophetic and heroic role that the Romantics typically gendered masculine. This "gender confusion" causes her deep suffering, because imagination, as a more actively creative sympathy, remains a masculine-identified property (74). That feminine sensibility which is inseparable from Corinne's imagination is what binds her to the patriarchal relations that define sensibility as feminine, making her susceptible to the Gothic fall from feminine virtue made more terrible by its becoming a fall from heroic masculine heights: "he has hurled me from the triumphal chariot into the unfathomable depths of sorrow [*l'abîme des douleurs*] (347; Balayé 489).

In Italy, Corinne is in the Italian state—not the state of one who possesses one's own country, but of one who wanders dispossessed among the ruins of empire (18).[35] Not only is sunniest Naples a nation deprived of independence in an "empire of death," where the ground threatens every moment to open, but it also stonily excludes the living. In Rome itself, Corinne is in the situation of the ancient Roman women mourning their husbands, haunting the sunny landscape as if it were they who were the shades, by mourning their own imprisonment on the wrong side of the river Styx, in exile from the land of the dead heroes (244). By going to haunt the patrimonial estate in Scotland, therefore, Corinne does not change her state, but only gives a plot and place to the state she is already in.

Staël transforms Coulommiers, Lafayette's Baroque pavilion, into a Gothic castle whose patrimonial ground is a frightful precipice. Her heroine's position there is not that of the princess of Clèves at Coulommiers—mistress of the estate, the role filled here by Lucile. It is rather that of the male intruder whose desire leads him to trespass: Nemours. Like Nemours, Corinne arrives unannounced and allows her steps to be guided by chance [*au hasard*] through the park, concealing herself in the garden, like him, from the view of those within (353; Balayé 499; *PC* 120). Whereas this attitude allows Nemours on both of his visits to *watch* the princess through the architectural frame formed by her pavilion (as well as to overhear her *aveu*), Corinne's perception of what passes within the castle is confined to the sense of hearing. While giving her Nemours' active, "masculine" desire, Staël does not give Corinne his mastery of the gaze, his strategy of fixing the object of his desire in a visual frame. Through this rewriting of the Coulommiers scenes, she articulates feminine desire in a language other than the specular.[36]

A servant has to tell Corinne what she cannot see: Lord Nelvil has opened the ball with Lucile, "*the heiress to this castle*" (353; emphasis Staël's). The reader, however, gets a full description of what Corinne cannot see, which turns out to be another scene rewritten from *La Princesse de Clèves,* in which the duc de Nemours dances with the princess, the great heiress who is making her first court appearance (*PC* 120). Staël's narrator characterizes this dance as an unremarkable performance in which Lucile's reserve detracts from her dancing and bores Oswald— quite a contrast with the spontaneous murmur of admiration caused by the spectacle of the princess with Nemours. Lafayette, with a narrator elsewhere quite capable of reporting interior events, frames the dance entirely from the perspective of its spectators (*PC* 53–54). Although Staël also makes her dancers the focus of a collective gaze, she does not report the audience's response, concentrating instead on the thoughts and feelings of the dancers. What becomes crucial in Staël's rewriting, ultimately, is not the gaze, but rather a sensibility unavailable to the senses. "Corinne would have tasted some moments of happiness still could she have known what he was feeling then" (353). If she could know the feelings of the beloved separated from her by the walls of the estate, she would have the pleasure that the duc de Nemours takes from overhearing his beloved's confession of her secret feelings, or from watching her gazing at his own portrait and wrapping his tournament colors around his cane— all spectacular evidence of how he is loved (*PC* 155). Instead Corinne remains aimlessly wandering the garden paths, feeling herself a foreigner on paternal soil, where no providence guides her steps to the evidence she seeks. In the logic of paternal plot—upon the grounds of which providence and real estate become one—it makes perfect sense that without paternal authority for her destination (the castle, with Oswald in it), the very ground beneath her feet is missing ("the ground gave way under her feet" [353]).

Lacking the grounds for desire that allows Nemours to "steal" the evidence of the princess's love for him, Corinne is rather in the position of Lee's heroine, Ellinor, in that author's rewriting of the Coulommiers episodes from Lafayette. She is in the eighteenth-century Gothic position of the virtuous heroine of sensibility who "incessantly hovers on the verge of a precipice" (*R* 3: 150–51). Thrown instantly into the uncertainty in which

Nemours finds himself only later, she begins as he does his *second* trip to Coulommiers, wandering passively in the garden and hoping that the beloved will come out. Whereas Nemours then gets a view of the princess that gives him a pleasure beyond description, Corinne finds herself literally on the verge of the princess's (and Lee's) precipice, where mothers place their daughters in the very act of teaching them how to avoid the fatal *faux pas* ("Corinne had only to take one step to plunge into eternal oblivion," [354; *PC* 155]). In that position she not only hesitates, like Nemours, over what strategy to pursue, but hesitates even over her own desire, just as Ellinor does on the threshold of Lady Pembroke's gallery, her own desire lost in the hesitation between the precepts of virtue and the plausibility of the fiction she has framed to conceal her desire to see her lover's portrait ("she herself did not know what she wanted," [354; *R* 2: 288]). Moving nevertheless like Nemours from hesitation in the garden to a determination to break through the architectural frame and speak with the beloved, Corinne approaches the window where, unlike him, she finds her view blocked. Like Lee's heroine, on the other hand, she encounters the living voice of her lover instead of the expected sight. The sound of Oswald's voice gives Corinne a joyous emotion that is described in terms of ineffability similar to those used by Lafayette to convey what Nemours feels on getting sight of the princess ("The voice of the one we love: indescribable thrill!" [355]).[37] Here the evidence of passion is no longer the name, the verbal signification of speech, but rather the pure sentiment conveyed by the tone of the lover's voice.[38]

The language of sensibility is the only one by means of which Corinne could be supposed to know what Oswald was thinking, and it does indeed convey to her a pleasure parallel to that experienced by Nemours. But the effort to translate Nemours's active desire from the specular language of patriarchy into the audible one of feminine sensibility only turns Corinne definitively into a ghost. At the moment that Corinne becomes a specular object, a *vue* glimpsed by Lucile, she becomes a specter. Recognizing Corinne as the sister who passes for dead in and on the patrimonial plot, Lucile is convinced that she has seen a ghost. The whole scene, with its potential for a translation that would transcend, through the channels of sensibility, the need for patrimonial ground and for the framework of its real estate, is closed again in the twinkling of an eye within the patriarchal frame of reference: "she was convinced that her sister's image had appeared walking toward their father's grave to reproach her for forgetting it." Corinne's "apparition" has the same frightening effect as Nemours's appearance does upon the blonde beauty within the château, who causes the servants to flock around her, thus precluding communication (355; *PC* 156). And no wonder, since for the princess the sight of Nemours breaking into her pavilion was also tantamount to seeing a censorious ghost: that of her mother/husband. The heroine's transformation into a ghost thus completes Staël's Gothic re-inscription of female desire into the patrimonial plot through a double translation of Lafayette via Lee. The plotting masculine subject whose agency is thwarted by the woman's transformation of him into a painting is first translated by Lee in terms of a plotting feminine subject (Ellinor) whose agency is thwarted by her ghostly position of survival beyond her narrowly defined feminine virtue. Staël retains Lee's plotting feminine subject, but the heroine's agency is here thwarted by her ghostly position *as* the mother (in relation to Lucile) whose death works in the service of paternal will to keep the daughter in line.

Corinne's last act corresponds to the princess's: both leave their legacies as they disappear into the abyss of a final frame. It is a correspondence that emphasizes difference, however. Corinne does not follow the princess's example in leaving examples of virtue; Oswald is the one condemned to mirror her exemplarity in the novel's final lines (302–3; *PC* 180).[39] Instead, Corinne leaves the example of her talent—the new Romantic term she thus successfully substitutes for virtue in the end.[40] But the transmission of female talent, like that of inimitable examples, is a paradox—as is all transmission through female lines within a patrilineal framework. Where the only model of transmission is patriline debt, how can maternal transmission escape the terms of debt and of speculation, avoid becoming the mere specular image, the reflection, the horrid specter of patrilineage? What Staël gets from Lee's reading of Lafayette is first of all the refusal to recognize bloodlines as the proper path of inheritance. The princess does not reproduce motherhood; she leaves her inimitable examples to the reader alone. Lee represents her own novel's transmission by closing it with an exchange transacted between the dying Matilda and an unknown young woman. Staël further elaborates Lee's strategy of female transmission by detailing and doubling the means through which Corinne manages to transmit, not exemplary virtue, not her own fictional plot of escape, but her talent—what she hoped would enable her to enact a successful female plot, and may still help the strangers who receive it.

Having failed in her own life plot, Corinne's first plot of transmission is to become, not a substitute father—which is to say a Gothic mother like Lady Edgermond or Mme de Chartres—but rather a Gothic father: a ghostly father who reduces Oswald to a mere double. Lucile's introduction of her daughter to Oswald "as timidly as if she had been a guilty woman" takes on its full significance only when considered in the context of the sentence that follows, which explains Juliette's resemblance to Corinne by observing that Lucile's thoughts had dwelt upon her sister during pregnancy (385–86). A child's physical resemblance to someone other than the husband is the first evidence, in Gothic romance particularly, of legitimacy or its opposite—a wife's infidelity.[41] No wonder Lucile is timid: her child's physical resemblance to another may "suggest" Oswald's emotional unfaithfulness, but it proves her own.[42] This is in keeping with a medical belief of the period that the imagination or desire of a pregnant woman was dangerous in that it could impress itself upon the developing fetus.[43] The force of Lucile's errant *imagination*—the French word used is the same as the source of Corinne's talent, with which the heroine had tried to replace feminine virtue, and which she alone has developed in Lucile— has thus made Corinne the true *father* of Juliette (Balayé 542).

The character of the *héritage* that Corinne transmits to Juliette relies on cultivating through education the Gothic doubling of her appearance, and is thus tainted with possession, as others have observed.[44] This then is Corinne's terrible revenge upon Oswald: first, she robs him of paternity—he has no son, and Corinne is the father of his only daughter, so that he becomes a dead end to his sacred patrilineage.[45] Having diverted his family from the patrilineage, she binds its members to herself through relationships that remain outside the patrilineal script. She is Juliette's illegitimate father and Lucile's substitutive mother, without merely usurping the paternal role because, neither wife nor mother, she is not "wedded" to the father.[46] In this way she contrives to exert a form of agency, even though it is only the agency of haunting. She does this, moreover, without losing her claim to that paternal sympathy without which she would lose her title to any agency at all. By disowning her agency she is able to claim absolution from the heavenly Father on the grounds that she herself has wreaked no active vengeance. Although she adopts with Lucile and Juliette the patriarchal strategy of transmission used by Lady Edgermond and Mme de Chartres, she nevertheless interferes with its specular reproduction of feminine virtue by replacing it with talent as the legacy thus transmitted.

A biographical explanation for Staël's apparent insistence on the inescapability of patriline transmission could be located in the author's ambivalent identifications with biological and literary fathers who disapproved of writing women.[47] Staël and *Corinne* are also informed by a larger cultural context, however, that includes the English "female Gothic" emphasis on women's entrapment in paternal estates that nevertheless literally crumble in the dysfunctional process of their own transmission.[48] The Gothic and other novels of sensibility also explored modes of resistance to such entrapment, as in the previously mentioned ending of Lee's novel, where the only hope held out for a form of female intergenerational transmission that would avoid the patriarchal strategy of "cloning" or "possession," as Ellen Peel puts it, is enacted between women who are strangers, bound neither through patrilineal kinship relations nor through alternatives that merely imitate them.[49] The Gothic thus offers a key for interpreting the multiple and contradictory acts of female transmission that make up the novel's ending.

Corinne's plot for passing on her talent to Lucile and Juliette by making them ghosts of herself is offset by the contrasting one she creates in the performance of her last song. The figure of the unnamed young girl in white (*blanc*), her face a blank upon which suffering has yet to leave any trace, tempers, instead of mirroring, the song's "*sombre*" words. While the performance is a memorial at once of Corinne's talent and of the suffering that robbed her of it, it also refuses to imprint that history of loss upon the next generation. Although the girl repeats Corinne's words, her blank face cannot mirror her history of suffering and seems too fresh even to receive the "impression" of pleasurable sensibility that her performance makes on the audience. This last spectacle is staged so that its vengefulness will fall on Oswald alone. Seeing only a "cruel apparition," he is compelled to mirror the suffering it represents (415). The girl's own public performance of talent involves a repetition of Corinne's words that nevertheless leaves her free, unlike Lucile or Juliette, of both the marks of specularity and the debt of speculation.

And if the members of her audience see a ghost in the veiled figure hovering behind the girl, they see it from that Gothic distance that allows them to enjoy the apparition, assured that *they* are free of its curse.[50] Staël's readers, however, have only her words, veiling the spectacle of Corinne's suffering with a hopeful blank.

Corinne and the Woman as Poet in England: Hemans, Jewsbury, and Barrett Browning

ELLEN PEEL AND NANORA SWEET

GERMAINE de Staël's *Corinne ou l'Italie* was published in 1807 and immediately circulated in England in the original and as the hasty, anonymous translation *Corinna, or Italy*. Staël's novel quickly established itself as the book that would most influence British women poets in the early and mid-nineteenth century. Its heroine was half-English herself, after all, and her life and career brought her into conflict with an English culture that distrusted feminine sensibility and disapproved of feminine publicity. Staël's woman laureate and her elaboration of a feminine aesthetics of difference influenced English women poets of the later Romantic period such as Felicia Hemans (1793–1835), Letitia E. Landon (1802–38), and Maria Jane Jewsbury (1800–1833), writers who are only now being recovered for literary study.[1] *Corinne* was also read avidly by Elizabeth Barrett Browning (1806–61) and has since been recognized as the chief literary influence on Barrett Browning's blank verse epic *Aurora Leigh* (1856). Staël's impact on each of these writers is intensified by their further influence on one another.[2]

Germaine de Staël had experienced difference and the distrust that accompanied it—both as a woman and as a foreigner. Despite her stunning accomplishments, being a woman still exerted a powerful, and often restrictive, influence on her life. Her sex was a major reason that her beloved father mocked her aspirations to be a writer, that her political and literary efforts were ridiculed, and that Napoleon's ire against her was exacerbated.

The sense of being a foreigner also pervaded Staël's experience. Although she was born in Paris, her parents were Swiss (and Protestant as well), and she married a Swede. The feeling of being an outsider in France was brutally impressed upon her when Napoleon exiled her. Moreover, she made long journeys to various countries and thus was frequently an outsider in other countries as well as France.[3]

Staël was not simply a woman but also a feminist, though she wavered at times. While not taking an active part in the women's movement of her day, in *The Mannequin* (1811) Staël satirized sexist folly, and elsewhere she explicitly protested women's oppression, as in "On Women Writers," a section in her book *On Literature Considered in Its Relationship to Social Institutions* (1800). According to Charlotte Hogsett, Staël's feminism surfaced in her unconventional choice of genres and in her struggle—not always successful—to forge a woman's language. Finally, she was a feminist in that she "not only broke with conventional femininity herself, but created popular heroines who did the same."[4]

Staël's feminist preoccupations and her persona as outsider sometimes converged. Ellen Moers says that in *Corinne,* while the novelist "does not argue for an adjustment of marriage to female requirements,"

> her point is to show that regional or national or what we call cultural values determine female destiny even more rigidly, even more inescapably than male. For as women are the makers and transmitters of the minute local and domestic customs upon which rest all the great public affairs of civilization—a perception she derived from Montesquieu—so women suffer more, in their daily and developing lives, from the influences of nationality, geography, climate, language, political attitudes, and social forms.[5]

In *Corinne, or Italy,* the heroine's sex is crucial to the text, for the novel suggests the possibility of a female aesthetic and celebrates Corinne as a specifically female artist.[6] It also makes clear that many of Corinne's sufferings result from her being a woman: because of her sex, she cannot have both love and artistic vocation. Meanwhile, Corinne's foreignness seems egregious in England because of her Italian birth and her inability to repress her "Italian" spontaneity and creativity. She learns of her alienness soon after arriving in England, when her stepmother reproves her for quoting Italian love poetry—and for speaking at all (253). Corinne's Italian birth and habits make her an exile in England, just as her sex metaphorically makes her an exile in patriarchy.

Corinne is a feminist, though at times a timid one. She fights for her right to express her genius, and, eschewing a patronymic, choosing her own name, she enjoys great independence. Along with her deep love of *la belle Italie,* she also shows concern for other women and wittily lashes out at English society for smothering their potential. Corinne became an inspiration to thousands of nineteenth-century women who were struggling to improve their lot.[7]

Her role as mediator is sometimes forced upon her by her position as an outsider who must appeal to an insider. Her mediating also takes a more voluntary form, springing from the comparatist's motivation of elucidating one culture to another. She values William Shakespeare as much as she values Dante Alighieri, and she translates *Romeo and Juliet* into Italian, which she considers its mother tongue, *sa langue maternelle* (Balayé 194). A speaker of French as well as English and Italian, she eagerly strives to reach across national and linguistic boundaries in general. In fact, as Madelyn Gutwirth observes, at times Corinne acts as "mediatrix to humankind," connecting humanity with transcendent realms.[8] In short, Corinne became both a feminist and a comparatist through her complex celebration of difference, which grew all the more powerful when valued as a paradigm by those who read the novel.

Hemans, Jewsbury, and Barrett Browning strove to establish themselves as poets and women of letters in the very setting that distrusted Staël and Corinne—the England that exiled Corinne as a young woman and gravely challenged her powers in maturity. These English women poets emulated Staël by nourishing themselves on the continental sources that Staël's heroine prescribed for Oswald and Europe, especially Italy and its art, architecture, topography, history, and literature. This essay traces in three of Staël's English followers the metaphor of genderized place, a metaphoric Italian landscape and culture that *Corinne* depicts as feminine and feminizing. For Hemans and Jewsbury, who wrote in England and under English constraints, the Italianate aesthetics of *Corinne, or Italy* became an indirect but potent means of feminist cultural critique. To Barrett Browning, who left England to write in Italy, *Corinne* offered the more explicit paradigm of the feminist comparatist.

Hemans and Jewsbury: The Woman Poet, "or Italy"

That book, in particular toward its close, has a power over me which is quite indescribable; some passages seem to

give me back my own thoughts and feelings, my whole
inner being . . .
—Felicia Hemans

In the margin of her copy of *Corinne,* Hemans wrote, "c'est
moi." She often emphasized her Corinne-like national background, half-British and half-Italian.[9] Her activity as a translator
from five modern languages enriched her work with continental
culture, while her provincial settings (Wales, Liverpool, Dublin)
and professionalized marital status (as "Mrs. Hemans") established her safely as a poet of domestic retirement. Unlike her
successor Barrett Browning, Hemans never traveled to Italy or
the Mediterranean South. Instead, she sustained in England the
Corinnian legacy that Staël's heroine bequeathed to her lover's
English daughter (and her niece) Juliette.

During Staël's 1813 stay in London as the literary "lion" of the
season, Staël and "Corinne" were regularly conflated in English
reports. For English women writers, the writer-character "Corinne" became code for the female literary career in its heights
of celebrity and dangerous exposure—in its social value, that is,
and tragic risks. However equivocal as code, as text *Corinne* was
invaluable, and it nourished Hemans's poetry at three interrelated levels: notes, allusions, and aesthetics. First, Hemans regularly enriched her text with epigraphs, headnotes, and footnotes:
on fourteen occasions she brings Staëlian text to bear on her
own, eight times from *Corinne.* Second, Hemans regularly alludes to the triumphs and countertriumphs of Corinne's tours
and odes: the obligatory catalogs of celebrated art works, exiled
Italian poets, shrines in Rome and on the Campagna, and Neapolitan sites such as Virgil's tomb and the villas of proscribed
Roman matrons. Third and most pervasively, Hemans adopts
the aesthetics of Staël's defeated Italy, its fragmentation and fe-
cundity, and applies them to her own studies of history.

As Carla Peterson remarks, in *Corinne* Staël attempts "nothing less than the formulation of a new Romantic aesthetic," one
that is as recognizable in Hemans's poetry as in *Corinne.*[10]
Staël's aesthetic of feminine Italianate beauty pervades her book
in these signal forms: the processional (especially Corinne's inauguration, the catalogs in her odes, and religious and funeral
processions); the floral landscape and ambience of Italy, ranging
from perfume to plague; and Italy's architecture and art.[11]

This aesthetic is liquid, colorful, insinuating, and sensuous;
it is perishable, nonutilitarian, destablizing. In Staël's words, it

is "evanescent," "fleeting"; "the murmur of this immense fountain"; and "the musical charm" of Italian words "independent of
meaning" that calls "flowers to mind" (75, 43, 164–65). In its
presence, Oswald is beguiled from the icy grip of Northern duty
and revived. But then, feeling unmanned, he attacks Italy for
the emasculation that it brings: its men, he says, "have no
strength of character"; yes, answers Corinne, they "prefer life"—
and they consider women's desires (98, 102–3). Both characters
acknowledge these as the effects of political defeat and fragmentation. In these circumstances, women seem to "gain ascendancy
over men" (102)—a false stabilization, for Italy disintegrates
under foreign Northern control and Corinne disintegrates in
contact with Oswald and her own English past. The text as a
whole is unstable—and it is dialectically prolific. It affirms and
denies its values throughout, vibrating at the very last with love
and revenge.[12]

Hemans's first Staëlian works are also her first adult publications. *The Restoration of the Works of Art to Italy* (1816) and
Modern Greece (1817) are progress poems through Italy and
Greece that resemble the improvisational catalogues of Corinne's early poems. These and Hemans's subsequent odes on
British royalty sustain her Corinne-like self-selection as a female
laureate; and early reviewers like the Tory *Quarterly Review*
enlisted her talents in such a service.[13] Hemans privileges an
aesthetics of the South, of Italy and beauty and the feminine,
mingling into them the Northern melancholy of Oswald. These
aesthetics make for a view of history as fragmentation but also
as persistence, what Corinne calls "the eternal mobility of man's
history" (72). For Hemans, such a view of history accurately
describes the temporalities of empire and the feminization to
which we all are heir, whether through defeat, the displacements
of marriage, emigration, and exile, or death, the vanishing point
in life's long funeral procession. The Northern gloom in Hemans
is countered by a Southern optimism in the hardy perennial
flowers that, in *Modern Greece* for instance, supplant Sparta's
ruins.

The Restoration of the Works of Art to Italy is a substantial
intertext of poetry and prose that recounts the return of artwork
plundered by Napoleon. The poem's introduction establishes an
Italy recognizable from *Corinne,* with "myrtle-vale" and "laurel-
grove," Virgil's tomb and Tasso's poetry.[14] The war-ravaged Italy
that Hemans presents in her tour is the one that Staël avoids
when she sets *Corinne* before Napoleon's triumph. As if to say

that her *Restoration* is a sequel to Staël's, Hemans cites many works that appear in *Corinne,* such as the Apollo Belvedere and the Laocoön.

Restoration's verse and prose—six hundred lines of running couplets and eight textual notes—are devoted to an analysis of Italian history encoded in gendered aesthetics. The poem's epigraph from Vincenzio da Filicaja depicts a rapine in which Italy is woman, her artwork her charms, her charms her dowry; a rapine in which dowry is plundered and woman abandoned. Hemans underscores her analysis of Italy as woman and as plunder with a headnote describing the "rapacity" of the French conquerors (*PW* 103). Here, the "charms" among which Corinne once led us a tour have themselves been set in motion; they are being returned, but can never be fully restored. Soon, in a quiet but decisive transformation Hemans turns the "restored" art objects, stone "trophies," into a curtain of feminine beauty and into light as evanescent as flowers and as deceptive as a veil:

> Those precious trophies o'er thy realms that throw
> A veil of radiance, hiding half thy wo,
> And bid the stranger for awhile forget
> How deep thy fall, and deem thee glorious yet.
>
> (*PW* 104)

Although restored, these works are not restabilized as monuments of glory; they remain detached, deceptive, hiding the full extent of Italy's sexualized "fall."

In Hemans's progress poems on Italy and Greece, displacement becomes the motive power of art and finds the processional its chief figure. Italy and its works of art draw pilgrims in an unending parade: "Still, still to these shall nations bend their way" (*PW* 104). And both *The Restoration* and *Modern Greece* close with processionals led by distinctly incomplete or evanescent artworks. In the first, Raphael's unfinished painting of the *Transfiguration* leads the artist to his grave. In the second, Hemans proposes Minerva's perishable "awning" as a more accurate emblem than the Elgin marbles of Greek aesthetics: "embroidered in many colors," this "peplus" was traditionally conducted through Athens "till it had made the circuit of the Acropolis" before being returned to the Parthenon (*PW* 171n36).

With her narrative poem "The Widow of Crescentius" (from the 1819 *Tales, and Historic Scenes*), Hemans enters the debate that murmurs throughout *Corinne* on the strength or frailty of the flower as code for the feminine.[15] Hemans associates her heroine with Italy, "Fair is her form, and in her eye, / Lives all the soul of Italy!" (*PW* 129). She begins her poem with a floral epigraph from *Corinne*: "*L'orage peut briser en un moment les fleurs qui tiennent encore la tête levée*" (*PW* 127). In *Corinne* the passage occurs as a response by Corinne to an Oswald who feels "already bent over the grave by suffering and misfortune": The storm can in a moment break the flowers who again hold their heads raised. The passage is ambiguous: the flowers are broken and transitory ("briser en un moment") and they revive and recur ("tiennent encore la tête levée").[16]

Resisting a stable interpretation, the motto from *Corinne* epitomizes the novel's own oscillating representations of the feminine. Early in Staël's book we hear of "elegant flowers" that "still survive" painted in Livia's baths, scene of her purported plot against Augustus (69). Midway, Corinne and Oswald while walking near Naples have "crushed the flowers underfoot, freeing the perfumes deep within" (195).[17] Hemans's text will entertain its motto's ambiguity of fragility and strength in woman. In a fatal triumph, "The Widow of Crescentius" will bring its heroine back from crushing exile and into a potent political role, one that like Livia's involves the assassination of an emperor.

The "Crescentius" in Hemans's tale is a tenth-century Roman who tries to revive the ancient republic but instead is betrayed and executed by the Saxon emperor Otho III.[18] Hemans focuses her tale on Crescentius's wife Stephania and her swift transformations from bride to widow and from widow to assassin. By the end of part 1, Stephania is a political widow facing exile, "a blighted flower." Like the Staëlian flower in the storm, she must "break" and be "scattered—ne'er to re-unite" (*PW* 130). In part 2, however, Stephania returns disguised as a boy minstrel who uses her mysterious music to gain Otho's confidence. She poisons him and, after revealing her identity, goes to her own death. The Staëlian flower that was crushed rises again to distill from its soft airs (fragrance, music) a poison to kill an emperor before it again is crushed. In the discourse of Staël and Hemans, failure—of flower, woman, or republican values—by its very transitory quality predicts further recurrences of victory—although only if reproduced, portrayed (painted in Livia's bath), and broadcast like seed.

Hemans buttresses her poem with other texts from *Corinne*. As in *The Restoration*, Hemans speaks in part 1 of "The Widow" of Italian works of art displaced by history: "fair forms that sculp-

ture wrought" torn from Hadrian's tomb for use as artillery and
then lost in "time's abyss or Tiber's wave" (*PW* 128). Here Hemans adds a footnote from *Corinne* that reinforces the latent
power in Italianate aesthetics (*PW* 133n4). In the passage, Corinne speaks to Oswald of "beautiful monuments of art" that "lie
hidden beneath" the Tiber: imagining that "a sharper eye" could
see them, she remarks on "the indescribable emotion that constantly comes to life in Rome" (83). This river of dissociated
fragments recalls the "veil of radiance" in Hemans's *Restoration,*
where plundered/returned artworks swirl in a fluid medium,
where energy predominates over matter.

   In part 2 of "The Widow," Hemans alludes again to *Corinne,*
this time to Corinne's Naples improvisation (*PW* 243) and its
evocation of the Neapolitan littoral as a site of feminine and
feminizing exile. This "bright, enchanted coast," writes Hemans,
has lured many an exile, including the great republican Cicero.
It now harbors Stephania, who will command its seductiveness
for herself, in the insidious music (or poetry) that seduces
Otho—"Deep thrilling power in every tone," a "voice" of "murmurs deep" (*PW* 131–32)—and the poisoned vintage that kills
him. Stephania will be executed, but Hemans clearly wants to
highlight the resurgent energy of this subversive minstrel who
is a woman poet. She closes her poem with one more allusion
to *Corinne.* The heroine's grave, "Thy dark and lowly bed" (*PW*
133), will be lost to history; but we can assume that, like the
Roman art that Corinne senses beneath the Tiber, this poet-
heroine will continue to vibrate with the "indescribable emotion" of "genius." Then, in the final work of her 1819 *Tales,
and Historic Scenes,* "The Death of Conradin," Hemans refers
to *Corinne* again as she works to shift political energy from an
executed Ghibelline prince to his dolorosa mother. Here Hemans cites directly from Corinne's Naples improvisation to depict the exiled Roman matrons (*PW* 148).[19]

   While Hemans enacted the role of Corinne in England, her
friend the poet and critic Maria Jane Jewsbury portrayed and
discussed the dilemma of the Corinnian poet and *salonnière* in
English society. Jewsbury wished to act as a woman of letters
and depended on the model of Staël to do so.[20] Her first book,
Phantasmagoria (1825), satirizes literary fashions and ambitions but also praises Staël and Hemans as women with serious
literary pretensions. That Jewsbury suffered from authorial ambitions and disappointments of her own is clear; after a visit
to the pleasant but patronizing William Wordsworth, she was

paralyzed by a psychosomatic illness, from which she recovered after spending the summer of 1829 with Hemans. In "Women's Love" Jewsbury notes that, though her contemporaries might debate sexual equality or inferiority, "geniuses" like Shakespeare and Staël regard such quibbling "with contempt and indifference" (*PH* 1:113). Later in her book, Jewsbury shows herself knowledgeable about Staël and Coppet's debate over whether history or geography forms culture (*PH* 1:294); and she praises Hemans's experiments in the ballad form (*PH* 2:25n). The satirical seriousness of *Phantasmagoria* seems a drier English version of Staël's equivocal style in *Corinne*.

Jewsbury's 1830 book *The Three Histories* experiments most explicitly with the transplanting of *Corinne* to England. This triptych of novellas—"Histories" of an Enthusiast, a Nonchalant, and a Realist—regards from different angles the burning question of Staël's novel: whether it is possible, especially for a woman, to live a life of Romantic sensibility in England. The implied answer is that it is not, but Jewsbury's playful and piquant use of the entire tonal repertoire of eighteenth-century English fiction (satire of course, but also the humor of Smollett, the picaresque of Fielding, and the sensibility of Sterne) leaves all in question. The nimbleness of Jewsbury's critical method remained useful when, in the early 1830s, she became the lead reviewer for *The Athenaeum*. There she addressed the "problem" of the woman writer, for example, in a review of Hemans who, she says, combines masculine and feminine in the woman poet as "the power of beauty."[21]

The central character of Jewsbury's 1830 "The History of an Enthusiast" is, as Norma Clarke says, "a composite of Felicia Hemans and Maria Jane Jewsbury out of Madame de Staël's Corinne."[22] Julia is "a compound of Italian passion, English thought, and French vivacity" trapped in a provincial English town, where she is encouraged to "throw those intense, dreamy, passionate Germans away" (*TH* 79, 58). Like Corinne, Julia would choose the laurel crown even though warned that "from its leaf poison is distilled" (*TH* 25). Her guiding spirits are Staël, those promoted by Staël (Goethe, Schiller, and Petrarch), and Shelley (*TH* 59). Her experience in the provinces of England and in London (where she is lionized) convinces her that the only place for a woman poet is "among Frondeurs and Girondists" (*TH* 114). Like Staël and Corinne, Julia needs "the converse of the great world" to be a writer; but the exposure, gossip, and criticism of the literary world sap her spirit (*TH* 69). Offered a stay with a girlhood friend (whose husband cautions her that she "had better continue to *be* poetry" than to write it; *TH* 47), Julia sets sail instead for the continent with fresh medicaments from "Dr. Morphinus" (gossip may have told Jewsbury of Staël's addiction to opium), vague intimations of death, and plenty of introductions in Switzerland. As in *Corinne,* England has managed to exile its Romantic woman writer; as in *Childe Harold* 3, the Romantic exile sets out in the direction of Coppet.

Corinne's influence on Jewsbury's *The Three Histories* is not limited to characterization and theme. Like Staël's novel, "The History of an Enthusiast" is a third-person narrative studded with a telling sequence of its heroine's compositions: letters, journals, poetry, and selections from her commonplace book. These texts accommodate Julia's evolving subjectivity and painful learning in ways that Jewsbury's satirical prose will not. Writing in her journal about provincialism and "love," the adolescent Julia affirms in herself "the burning hope of self-emancipation" and success in the literary world (*TH* 69). The heroine's name alludes to the possibility of the female subject entailed in "Julie" (Rousseau's heroine, influential on Staël), "Juliet" (acted in *Corinne*), and "Juliette," the name of Corinne's subjective legatee and, if Nancy Miller is right, of Corinne herself.

On the heels of Julia's tentative gains and foreboding future, Jewsbury's "The History of a Nonchalant" portrays the woman of Romantic sensibility as object rather than subject, a woman who *is* rather than *writes* poetry. In this "History," Jewsbury draws the portrait of "Egeria," the nymph of the Campagna that Hemans's nineteenth-century biographers accepted as a description of the poet.[23] In Plutarch's *Life of Numa* Egeria is spoken of as consort and wise counselor to Numa, the pacific second king of Rome. In *Corinne* Staël points to Egeria as "the deity of upright men: conscience examined in solitude" (79). In "The Widow," Hemans cites Plutarch and attributes Rome's loss of power to the disappearance of Egeria's "sacred shields" from the Temple of Mars (*PW* 129, 134). Jewsbury's Egeria retains very little of the Plutarchan aspect in Hemans and Staël and derives instead from Ovid's *Metamorphoses* 15 where, as Numa's widow, she *becomes* her grief, a fountain of refreshment for others.

The protagonist of "The History of a Nonchalant" is a young Englishman, a skeptic and aesthete who goes to Rome and, at "the ruined shrine of the nymph Egeria," meets "an Italian artist and his sister, English by the mother's side and uniting in different ways much of the two countries in their characters" (*TH* 192). In her national mixture and poetic qualities, this "Egeria" is a Hemans or a Corinne. Here is a portion of Jewsbury's description of her, one freely applied to Hemans by nineteenth-century biographers: "She was a muse, a grace, a variable child, a dependent woman,—the Italy of human beings" (*TH* 193). Here is Italy in all of its defeated, dependent state yet still able to "subdue."

Like Oswald, Jewsbury's character Charles is beguiled by his guide to Italy and lingers with her; unlike Oswald, he marries her despite paternal disapproval. When the couple sinks into poverty, Egeria offers to turn her poetic "genius" to money-making; but the conventional Charles would "sooner have died" than "live upon the money earned by a woman—that woman my wife" (*TH* 198). Indeed, the result of the couple's poverty is that Egeria, and not Charles, dies. Taken to England for treatment, she is surrounded by flowers and poetry, still blessing Charles, her "gaoler, whose fetters were so fragrant and soft" (*TH* 206).

In Hemans and Jewsbury, Egeria has two aspects—as a subject, she is an articulate, Plutarchan political guide; as an object, she is an immanent, Ovidian fountain—and these are aspects of *Corinne* as well. Staël's equivocal model does not, after all, allow us to sustain the notion of an independent woman poet laureate or Egerian guide to "conscience" in England or in Italy; but neither does it allow us to ignore her influence as a figure for the motive force of a history that draws us in its processional of defeat and victory, division and reunification, North and South, masculine and feminine. The triumph is that in Staël and her English followers this performance has been re-written in a feminine key, in which the business of living in history is shown to be a matter of displacement and change, of fragmentation and flow. It is so for everyone, male as well as female, emperor as well as widow.

As in its key figures, floral and processional, the aesthetic of *Corinne* entails recurrence as well as change, and the key to recurrence is reproduction. Rousseau's Julie becomes Staël's Juliette who is then reproduced in Jewsbury's Julia. Hemans is emulated by Letitia E. Landon who then translates Corinne's odes for the most available English edition of Staël's novel. A further study of these women and their influence on subsequent writers in England (such as Barrett Browning and George Eliot) would be a study of the stubborn reproduction of Corinne in the setting that distrusted "Corinne" as author but embraced her as book.[24]

Barrett Browning: The Feminist Comparatist

> [W]hat Mme de Staël passed on to her disciples was a heady
> sense of cutting loose from custom, an intoxicating aware-
> ness of the possibility of otherness in the human condition,
> resting on an unsentimental perception of its varying forms
> in various societies.
>
> —Ellen Moers

The similarity between Germaine de Staël's novel *Corinne* (1807) and Elizabeth Barrett Browning's epic *Aurora Leigh* (1856) is no coincidence, for the former exerted a strong influence on the latter, an influence that constitutes a paradigmatic event in literary history. The English author called *Corinne* "'an immortal book' that deserved to be read 'once every year in the age of man'."[25] Because Barrett Browning had acutely felt the lack of female poets to emulate, she found a welcome fictional model in Corinne, one of the first novelistic heroines to be represented as a poet. Barrett Browning, as creator of Aurora, also found a welcome extraliterary model in Staël, creator of Corinne. Nor did the flow stop there, for the English author in turn influenced writers like Emily Dickinson. As Sandra M. Gilbert and Susan Gubar say, "Barrett Browning, while looking everywhere for 'grandmothers,' became herself the grand mother of all modern women poets in England and America."[26] These processes of influence can themselves serve as paradigms for other women writers who seek foremothers.

Both texts build a metaphorical system in which the social construction of sexual difference and the social construction of cultural difference stand for each other. Nationality plays a crucial role in both texts. In each, the poet-heroine is born in Italy of an English father and an Italian mother who dies early. The girl spends part of her youth in England, where she is reared by a rigidly unsympathetic Englishwoman—Corinne by her stepmother, Aurora by her aunt. Both heroines eventually flee gloomy England for sunny Italy, where they find fulfillment. Corinne, for instance, apostrophizes the southern land: "You have allowed me glory: you, the liberal nation that does not banish women from its temple" (416).

For Barrett Browning, the experience of being a woman was both constraining and empowering. Sometimes constraint and power came from the same source, as in her relationship with her father. Angela Leighton has observed that Barrett Browning "would have found corroboration for her own emotional idealisation of her father" in *Corinne,* where difficult love for a strong father, though attributed to a son (Oswald) rather than a daughter, represented Staël's feelings.[27] A similarly mixed influence can be traced to the chronic health problems that first descended on Elizabeth Barrett when she was fifteen. Her status as a female member of the upper middle class made her invalidism seem unremarkable and perhaps even contributed to that invalidism if it was a form of hysteria. Oddly enough, though, being an invalid did give Barrett Browning a modicum of power, for it gave her freedom to read and write, and it eventually gave her a respectable justification for her move to Italy—away from her dominating father.[28]

Barrett Browning's move south made her a foreigner, but she came to love Italy so much that it became a new homeland for her, one that she often celebrated in her poetry. Barrett Browning lost the sense of belonging in the land of her birth; according to Dorothy Mermin, she hated England's "rigid distinctions of gender, nationality, and class." At times, the writer linked her experiences as a woman and a foreigner, using the metaphor of foreignness to represent her exclusion from male poetic tradition.[29]

Turning to Barrett Browning as a theorist, one finds that her feminism had its roots in her youth, when she was a willful girl who chafed under the ideology of femininity and under the inferior education allotted to members of her sex. Drawing on autobiographical notes she wrote in childhood, H. Buxton Forman reports in his introduction to *Hitherto Unpublished Poems* that young Elizabeth Barrett

> regarded it as her one great misfortune that she was born a woman. She says that in those days of childhood she despised nearly all the women in the world *except Madame de Staël*—she could not abide their littlenesses called delicacies, their pretty headaches, and soft mincing voices, their nerves and affectations . . . One word she hated in her soul,—and the word was "feminine." (xxxvii; emphasis added)

These notes reveal nascent feminism in her hatred of traditional female roles, but they betray a callow belief that all women must be conventionally feminine (except herself and Staël). Although Barrett Browning was never to take much part in the feminist movement of her day, she outgrew most of her youthful elitism and became a feminist through her keen sense of women's problems under patriarchy.

Her feminism branches out in a variety of directions in her writing. The writing is permeated by the theme of how a woman can create herself as a poet, a process that, for this poet, culminated in *Aurora Leigh*.[30] Like Staël, but in an individual way, Barrett Browning defied the standard concept of genres suitable for women authors. She deviated from the sonnet convention established in the Renaissance, for she addressed sonnets to a male writer (her husband-to-be, Robert Browning) and to another female writer (George Sand).

Barrett Browning took the especially bold step of writing an epic—*Aurora Leigh*. And in making her epic resemble a realistic novel of contemporary life, she further challenged generic conventions by mixing the traditionally male epic genre with the novel, a genre more accessible to female writers. She also took a feminist stance by making her epic heroine a writer and by writing, in *Aurora Leigh* and elsewhere, on subjects believed unsuitable for ladies, particularly women's sexuality.[31] In addition to discrediting the chivalric quest and rescue story by "thwarting [Aurora's cousin] Romney's grim determination to be a rescuing knight," *Aurora Leigh* displaces it with another plot: "the daughter's quest for the mother. Here women are both subject and object, men little more than distractions."[32] In these ways and others, *Aurora Leigh* epitomized Barrett Browning's feminist poetics.

From an early age the author's wide reading included the works of various foreign authors in the original languages. Admitting the dubious morality of contemporary French fiction, she nonetheless read it avidly, and without her father's knowledge. In her youth, she read *Corinne*—three times—and read a translation of Staël's history of the French Revolution. Her concern with foreign cultures also emerges in her letters, her poems extolling the Italian risorgimento, and her poems protesting American slavery. It is noteworthy that Deirdre David reads *Aurora Leigh* as an expression by its author of concern for mediation.[33]

For Barrett Browning, as for Staël, exile from a patriarchal figure made her all the more feminist and comparatist. Barrett Browning's father could not literally exile her as Napoleon did

Staël, but his tyranny had the same effect. Elizabeth Barrett's elopement to Italy with Robert Browning simultaneously broke her father's prohibitions against leaving him geographically (by going south for her health) and against leaving him emotionally (by acting on her desire for someone outside the patriarchal household). Significantly, it was in Italy that she wrote *Poems Before Congress,* which was denounced in England as both unpatriotic and unwomanly. And it is fitting that it was in Italy that she wrote *Aurora Leigh,* her most substantial work, a work that depends on the sex/culture metaphor.

Aurora's life is deeply tinged by the fact that she is a woman. In her youth she must endure an inferior education that stresses busywork:

> We sew, sew, prick our fingers, dull our sight,
> Producing what? A pair of slippers, sir,
> To put on when you're weary—or a stool
> To stumble over and vex you . . . "curse that stool!"
>
> (*AL* 52; 1.457–460)

Aurora Leigh gives a vivid representation of the obstacles, such as prejudice, that later face the woman struggling to become an artist. Even Aurora's cousin Romney, when he is about to propose to her, criticizes her literary aspirations:

> . . . Women as you are,
> Mere women, personal and passionate,
> You give us doating mothers, and perfect wives
> Sublime Madonnas, and enduring saints!
> We get no Christ from you,—and verily
> We shall not get a poet, in my mind.
>
> (*AL* 81; 2.220–25)

As a foreigner, Aurora has experiences that closely parallel Corinne's, especially in patriarchal England, where both girls' Italian fire is quenched. Aurora leaves off saying her "sweet Tuscan words" (*AL* 50; 1.387), and, burdened by her experience as an outsider, she follows Corinne's lead in referring frequently to Dante—like Aurora, an exile from Florence. As in Staël's novel, the intensified sex/culture metaphor means that exile from Italy is also exile from the motherland.

Considered as a theorist, Aurora emerges as a feminist in her concept of herself as a female artist. To Romney she makes the simple, powerful statement: "I too have my vocation,—work to do" (*AL* 89; 2.455). She rebels against the confines of conventionally feminine education and insists on earning her own living as a writer. She also evinces feminist values in the close bond she eventually forms with Marian Erle, whom others scorn as a fallen woman. In proposing that Marian and her baby boy come live with her, Aurora envisions a nonpatriarchal household (*AL* 282; 7.122–25).[34]

Aurora's feminism also blossoms in her gradual development of a female aesthetic. At the core of this aesthetic lies her discovery of a muse, a discovery recognized by various feminist critics, though they explain it in different ways. According to Leighton, it is "sister" Marian (*AL* 251; 6.449) who becomes the muse, while in Helen Cooper's reading the heroine finds inspiration in muses who are male, even Miltonic, but not intimidating. And Joyce Zonana explains how Aurora, realizing a muse need not be an objectified other, finds a muse in herself. All three interpretations pay tribute to Aurora's skill in evading traditional androcentric notions, which would reserve the muse for male poets.[35]

We have seen that Staël's *Corinne,* while a popular success, also became more than that, for it made a fundamental contribution when women's literature was first beginning to establish its power as a tradition. When Barrett Browning set out to write an epic, she could have found a safe model in John Milton—a canonical male Englishman. Instead, she made the feminist and comparatist gesture of choosing outsiders as models. It is significant that most of the books that strongly influenced *Aurora Leigh* were written by people who were female, foreign, or both.[36] It is particularly significant that Staël, both a woman and a foreigner, wrote the novel that provided the paradigm for *Aurora Leigh*'s representation of the sex/culture metaphor in general.

Similarities between *Corinne* and *Aurora Leigh* have been stressed in this essay, but key differences also exist, especially between the endings. While the two were written in different genres, in different countries, the dissimilarities stem particularly from the specific historical circumstances that molded the two texts. The growth of feminist values between the writing of the two books made Barrett Browning's text more optimistic than Staël's in some ways. Corinne loses her lover, loses most of her creative ability, and dies a broken woman; in contrast, Aurora wins her lover, remains an artist, and looks forward to a fulfilling future.

No single explanation can account for the differences, but one important factor is the influence of *Jane Eyre*. Jane's lover is blinded in a fire, an experience that—combined with others—makes him less proud and better suited to marry Jane as an equal. Aurora's lover undergoes similar suffering, with a similar result (though Cora Kaplan reports in her introduction that Barrett Browning claimed to have forgotten *Jane Eyre* when writing *Aurora Leigh; AL* 24). Among the foremothers available to Barrett Browning was Charlotte Brontë, who could imagine an ending in which a man lost power and a heroine gained it, making them equal. In short, the feminist ideals of Staël and Corinne helped make possible the feminist practice of Brontë and Jane, Barrett Browning and Aurora.

With the freedom of literary characters, Corinne and Aurora bring the sex/culture metaphor into its sharpest form. Meanwhile, as an author Staël exemplifies the pioneering feminist internationalist, and Hemans, Jewsbury, and Barrett Browning follow the model and give it new life in their own ways.

Nathaniel Hawthorne and *The Marble Faun:* Textual and Contextual Reflections of *Corinne, or Italy*

KATHARINE RODIER

> Yes; we will follow in her track, and be such men as she is a woman; if, indeed, men can, like women, make worlds in their own hearts. . . .
>
> —Germaine de Staël

> For, nobody has any conscience about adding to the improbabilities of a marvellous tale.
>
> —Nathaniel Hawthorne

IN 1859, six years into a seven-year expatriation from the United States, Nathaniel Hawthorne and his family fled what he deemed the "charmed and deadly circle" of Rome for England, where he would complete a manuscript begun in Italy, the story of "the communion of a crime": *The Marble Faun,* first published in London as *Transformation* (1860) (4. 213; 320).[1] En route, after leaving Geneva by lake steamer, Hawthorne jotted in his travel journal yet another description of a local cultural landmark; as Nina Baym remarks, the full but static images that dominate Hawthorne's European notebooks, and which fortify in turn his late fiction, could today be preserved "much less laboriously with a camera."[2] But the specificity of this Swiss entry seems far from photographic: "Our course lay nearer to the northern shore, and all our stopping-places were on that side. The first was Coppet, where Madame de Stael (sic) or her father, or both, were either born, or resided, or died, I know not—and care very little" (14. 554). A glance into one of his well-used tourist guidebooks could have apprised Hawthorne that at Coppet neither Germaine de Staël nor her father, Jacques Necker, was born; that each in fact had lived there in exile; that only Necker had died

221

there; and that both daughter and father were entombed on the château grounds. Perhaps at this late stage of Hawthorne's sojourn, Coppet was just one too many sights for him to see, let alone register.

His apparent lack of interest may bespeak his world-weariness after eighteen entrancing but often appalling months in Italy, during which his eldest daughter nearly succumbed to "the malaria" or "Roman fever": Hawthorne blamed other concurrent lapses in "journalizing" on his own lingering contagion by "the lassitudinous Roman atmosphere" (14. 477; 551). Perhaps his response to Coppet occasioned as well a characteristic instance of self-irony—the urge to undermine his own precise elaborations with mock confusion, to deflate with one cursory swipe of his own pen the self-importance of writing so much dense prose. Or perhaps Hawthorne knew full well the history of Coppet, but for reasons of his own preferred to deny that knowledge. In any case, whether studied or genuine, Hawthorne's admitted indifference toward Coppet disavows a literary legacy which *The Marble Faun* betrays, for it was at Coppet, as his children's governess noted, that Germaine de Staël wrote her most popular novel, *Corinne, or Italy* (14. 866n). In truth, Hawthorne apprehended this work both in its substance and its influence, as his transformation of its familiar images into his own dark intrigue confirms.

Paradoxically, by seeming to overlook Staël's place in his own writings, Hawthorne may signal how profoundly her domain impressed him. Refocusing Harold Bloom's views on artistic influence, Margaret Higonnet proposes that a male writer grapples with "anxieties of indebtedness" to a female precursor primarily by effacing or denying this potentially problematic inheritance. In other words, what Higonnet terms a "blind spot" is symptomatic of an essential conflict particularly true for writers in Hawthorne's nineteenth-century marketplace: even as the heir embraces female paradigms to enrich the passion or emotional authenticity of his own discourse, he simultaneously risks his claim to the high artistic canon—traditionally defined as "masculine"—by incorporating into his work elements of "female" texts, sentimental or sensational, often disparaged as trash.[3] Without mentioning Staël by name, Hawthorne nonetheless shades references to her novel throughout *The Marble Faun,* among them at least two direct allusions, including a scene at Trevi Fountain which any of *Corinne*'s avid readers would recognize. While at points he seems to impugn Staël's descriptive veracity, his romance reflects no close textual study of her narrative. Rather, *Corinne* appears in *The Marble Faun* more as a spectral text, whose themes suffuse but by no means fix Hawthorne's own creation.

Conventional studies of influence tend to focus on the presence of apparently circumscribed or clearly demonstrable intertextual allusions. But postmodern theories of identity and textual instability enable a more profound inquiry into the range of shifting influences over an artist's production. A text which acknowledges a precursor may incorporate the writer's fluid readings of that primary referent, but also his multiple or conflicted readings of that text's cultural manifestations as interpreted and performed by other readers as well as other writers. Extraliterary forces or intervening textual treatments like reviews, tributes, imitations, or parodies can also determine a writer's interpretation of a seminal text, even if the writer never actively studies the original text as a model. Hawthorne's response to *Corinne* embodies a diffuse but remarkable awareness of both the novel and its effects on its readers, which may have included himself, but definitely included much of his society. Seen in this light, his concern to obscure Staël's significance—curtly in his notebook, more ambiguously in *The Marble Faun*—may in truth reveal how inescapably the American author, a celebrated but financially unsettled artist in his own right, labored in the monumental shadow cast by the convergence of Germaine de Staël's persistently popular fiction and her personal fame.

As several critics point out, *The Marble Faun*—which juxtaposes artists and copyists, original and derivative creation—most resembles *Corinne ou l'Italie* in its broad design. *Corinne* chronicles the ill-starred romance between its eponymous protagonist, a part-Italian, variously gifted genius and renowned *improvisatrice,* and the puritanical Oswald, Lord Nelvil, a Scottish peer whose misinformed but dutiful decision to marry Lucile, Corinne's blonde, equally beautiful, benign, and fully British half-sister, ensures the happiness of no one. Estranged from Nelvil, Corinne loses her art and ultimately her life. In "Hawthorne's Literary Borrowings," Arlin Turner maps the parameters of his subject's overt appropriations from Staël's novel: most notably, like his predecessor, Hawthorne uses amply drawn Italian cultural sites to stage his characters' critical discussions on art, love, and the relative demands and consolations of Protestantism and Catholicism, highlighting Roman Carnival scenes.

Turner also notes that, "In *Corinne* Hawthorne found precedent . . . for presenting the unhampered life of unmarried women of artistic temperament in Rome."[4] But while Hawthorne describes Hilda, an accomplished copyist, as "free to descend into the corrupted atmosphere of the city" as she would not be in America, "unhampered" seems inaccurate to characterize fully the lives of either Hawthorne or Staël's women, variously pursued by secrets, by anguish, and in the case of Miriam, Hawthorne's vibrant young painter, by a madman (4. 54).

According to Turner, Jane Lundblad, and others, Miriam may be modeled on Corinne, with her brilliance, her uncertain past, and her tragic passion.[5] Developing many of Turner's other observations, Lundblad further surmises in *Nathaniel Hawthorne and the European Literary Tradition* that Hawthorne had long known Staël's works. She sees Miriam as the latest of his *Corinne*-inspired dark women, including *The Scarlet Letter*'s Hester Prynne and *The Blithedale Romance*'s Zenobia. Hawthorne's predilection for featuring impassioned brunettes, often opposed to less problematic fair heroines, dates back through his tales to his early reading, particularly of Sir Walter Scott's romances, which Staël's writing also influenced.[6] In fact, he might have first read *Corinne* in translation during his youthful addiction to romances of all sorts. As Lundblad explains, Hawthorne subordinates his delineations of the female artist and the country of Italy—which Staël essentially conflates, as her title signifies—to his great strength, storytelling, and preoccupation with the contingency of sin, expressed in this instance through a *felix culpa* theme and a plot far more intricate than Staël's, if not more Gothic, featuring twisted catacombs, a Capuchin's corpse, and a "fatal fall" (4. 170). Suspecting that Hawthorne's borrowings were not conscious examples of what Dale Spender terms polish, plagiarism, or plain theft, Lundblad concludes instead that Hawthorne's personal confrontation with the land that Staël so famously rendered may have revived for him an earlier, if now diffuse, impression of *Corinne*, shaping in turn his own perceptions, determining his own version of Rome through a process Spender might define as aesthetic kleptomania.[7]

To be sure, as Higonnet observes, "all speaking and writing consist in verbal loot." And throughout *The Marble Faun*, Hawthorne freely admits artistic influences, also admitting that "[h]e designed the story and the characters to bear, of course, a certain relation to human nature and human life, but still to be so artfully removed from our mundane sphere, that some laws and properties of their own should be implicitly and insensibly acknowledged" (4. 463). In evoking Italy, Hawthorne was a relative latecomer to what Sandra M. Gilbert describes as three hundred years of literary tourism, joining those "poets and novelists who read the sunny, ruin-haunted Italian landscape as a symbolic text, a hieroglyph, or perhaps more accurately, a palimpsest of Western history, whose warring traces seemed to them to solidify in the stones of Venice and the bones of Rome."[8] In 1859, Hawthorne somewhat ironically proclaimed, "[E]verybody, now-a-days, has been in Rome," able, finally, to list himself among the privileged ranks (4. 70). In a literary sense, "everybody" for Hawthorne included his acquaintances Robert and Elizabeth Barrett Browning, as well as presences like Milton, Dante, and Byron, whose "Childe Harold's Pilgrimage" in Canto 4 paraphrases passages from *Corinne* (9n). Clearly, his notion of "the massiveness of the Roman past" assumes literary precedent as well as "Etruscan, Roman, Christian . . . antiquity." But in fusing an "evanescent and visionary" revision of prior texts, historical and fictive, with the "texture of all our lives," Hawthorne may as likely have confounded as confessed his connections to the mundane sphere, preferring to work his own artful and airy sleight-of-hand rather than to enumerate his sources (4. 6). According to his self-professed aesthetic, Hawthorne might have buried a literary debt as an "implicit and insensible" way to acknowledge it. In effect, his appropriations from *Corinne* could have been unconscious or conscious and consciously blurred, as his craft dictated. Confronting an Italy a half-century more lionized, and more tarnished than Staël's, Hawthorne might have been possessed by an ironic spirit of artistic competition, compelled to exploit what he admired in her text as the foundation for an Italian romance surpassing hers in complexity and resonance.

As he playfully details in *The Marble Faun*'s preface, Hawthorne already counted himself guilty of artistic larceny. The "Author" claims to have "laid felonious hands" on "spoils" from artist Paul Akers's studio to include in his romance; "committed a further robbery upon . . . the production" of sculptor William Wetmore Story; and thought of "appropriating" Randolph Rogers's bronze door and—"were he capable of stealing from a lady"—Harriet Hosmer's statue of Zenobia to provide works for his fictional sculptor Kenyon. His ostensible *politesse* regarding Hosmer could mask his pilfering of another female artist's "designs" (4. 4). In any case, it was a likely ruse for the mind that contrived the bogus identity behind "Rappaccini's Daughter," M. de l'Aubépine; the unreliable Coverdale of *The Blithedale Romance;* and the "long whim-wham" of "Wakefield" (9. 135). Accordingly, Hawthorne's obvious references to Staël's *Corinne* may decoy readers from dwelling upon its more subtle and more profound emanations throughout *The Marble Faun,* thereby enhancing the illusion of original composition while concealing its schematic derivation.[9]

Describing both *The Marble Faun* and *Corinne* as "fictions unsuccessfully wed to Italian travelogues," Philip Young overstates both Staël's attitude and Hawthorne's conceivable backlash, declaring, "It is hard to think he was much taken with [*Corinne*], which is slightly hysterical and stridently feminist." As Ellen Moers more equably estimates, Staël's novel, in which marriage and female genius apparently cannot meld, "is not, in any polemical sense, a feminist work."[10] While fundamentally conservative and confirmed in his distrust of human extremes, Hawthorne was no one-dimensional reactionary. He did espouse firm notions of female propriety idealizing his wife Sophia, a gifted artist and writer who "positively refuse[d] to be famous, and content[ed] herself with being the best wife and mother in the world" rather than expose her talents for *The Atlantic Monthly* (18. 204). But Rome's turbid atmosphere may have complicated his adamance:

> The customs of artist-life [in Rome] bestow such liberty upon the sex, which is elsewhere restricted within so much narrower limits; and it is perhaps an indication that, whenever we admit woman to a wider scope of pursuits and professions, we must also remove the shackles of our present conventional rules, which would then become an insufferable restraint on either maid or wife. (4. 54–55)

Conceivably, for Hawthorne but also for his wife, Corinne's tragedy affirmed the gravity of this tension between public and domestic demands upon women.

And even if bothered by *Corinne*'s feminist slant, or its incitement of "sentimental ecstasy," Hawthorne could still find much in the novel to engage him. Many of Staël's concerns anticipate his major themes.[11] If *Corinne* were among his earliest reading, perhaps it helped mold those thematic preoccupations. As Staël writes, and as Hawthorne's oeuvre attests, "Observation of the human heart is an inexhaustible source of literature" (52).

Given his skeptical fascination with his Puritan heritage, Hawthorne might pause over Staël's remark: "Duty, the noblest destination of man, may be distorted, like all other ideas, into an
inoffensive weapon by which narrow minds silence their superiors and their foes" (106). Nelvil's righteousness and Corinne's
"enthusiasm" (13, 17, 23) suggest two recurrent types in Hawthorne's work, polarities equally cut off from "a vast deal of human sympathy," like Richard Digby, "The Man of Adamant," or
the fervent Catharine in "The Gentle Boy" (4. 40). Similarly, the
author of "Roger Malvin's Burial" could himself have written,
"When we suffer we readily convince ourselves that we are guilty,
and violent griefs bring pangs even to the conscience itself" (5).
Hawthorne, daunted at first by the challenge of recording the
inexorable past in Rome's stony presence, not unlike Staël,
might observe, "The study of history can never act on us like
the sight of that scene itself" (31). His own evaluation of the city
would corroborate the precision of *Corinne*'s representations.
Moreover, Hawthorne might approve Staël's descriptive touches,
particularly her fondness, like his own, for haunted moonlit
perspectives:

> In the midst of these reveries he found himself on the bridge of St.
> Angelo ... The silence of the scene, the pale waves of the Tiber,
> the moonbeams that lit up the statues till they appeared like pallid
> phantoms, steadfastly watching the current of time, by which they
> could be influenced no more; all these objects recalled to him his
> habitual train of thought ... (18)

In many regards, then, *Corinne* parallels Hawthorne's "habitual
train of thought." But these very correspondences may have
urged the aging writer, who had not completed a new romance
since 1853, to a more complex synthesis.

Inspired equally by Rome as a realm of tumbled marble and
as a "poetic or fairy precinct," and bent on evoking the reality
of fantasy by conflating the two spheres, Hawthorne might locate
in *Corinne* an already viable plot to enrich, however negative
his own judgment of its depth, however current his familiarity
with Staël's novel (4. 3). In a very basic sense, *The Marble Faun*
enlarges upon *Corinne*. Read as an extrapolation, intentional or
not, of Staël's narrative, Hawthorne's romance, in which *two* sets
of troubled lovers intersect, literally multiplies the interactive
dimensions of the earlier work. As Miriam's pursuer steals into
the plot, *The Marble Faun* suggests *Corinne*'s classic triangula-

tion of incompatible desires, but Hawthorne's addition of Hilda and Kenyon as a complicitous couple meshed in problems of their own compounds this scheme considerably. Designing his romance as fundamentally four-sided also enables Hawthorne to examine a single problem from not necessarily compatible points of view, serving his own multivalent sensibility.

Moreover, Hawthorne parcels out *Corinne*'s concerns among his ensemble often without regard to the gender distinctions Staël determines. In *The Marble Faun*, the sculptor Kenyon loses his art in pursuit of his beloved, much like the female artists in both books, and the beautiful Donatello embodies the native traits of Italy, charging the intrigue with an exoticism perhaps intended to rival Corinne's, but evoking a more deeply shaded pagan past. Hilda shares with Kenyon aspects of Nelvil's cool inflexibility and his reverence for his fatherland. In some instances, Hawthorne conflates *Corinne*'s thematic frictions in a single character. John Michael argues that as Hawthorne's "Catholic characters become more Protestant in their moral anguish, his Protestant characters become more Catholic in their adherence to accepted truths and established institutions." Ironically, Hilda's New England Protestant morality drives her to seek solace in a Catholic confessional, a fusion impossible in *Corinne*.[12]

In opposing Hilda to Miriam, Hawthorne more than replicates *Corinne*'s archetypal juxtaposition of dark and fair women; he draws them together through the image of Beatrice Cenci's suffering, even as he draws them as sharply different temperaments. Witnessing the death of Miriam's tormentor, the virtuous Hilda is herself subsumed in mystery, vanishing because of Miriam's agency. Like Miriam and Corinne, Hilda also becomes an object of passion, albeit through Kenyon's somewhat restrained attentions. *The Marble Faun* also complicates *Corinne*'s already-complicated motif of double confession, through which Nelvil and Corinne disclose in turn their pasts: Nelvil earns Corinne's acceptance; her honesty effects his alienation. In Hawthorne's exploration, both Miriam and Hilda suffer for withholding confessions, yet both rightly anticipate Kenyon's limitations as a confidant. Both women eventually communicate their dark concerns, but unlike Corinne, each receives assurance, however problematic, of her lover's constancy. Paradoxically, for Hawthorne, confidence seems not only a key to redemption, but also a necessary danger, a risk inherent in human connection. In ways, then, *The Marble Faun* reads like

Corinne, but like *Corinne* refracted, diffracted, and shaded through a prism of smoked glass—through Hawthorne's complex vision of Rome's "black reality" (4. 429).

Further amending its forerunner, *The Marble Faun* adds to the nationalistic portraits *Corinne* defines, incorporating a presence not as yet pervasive in Staël's turn-of-the-century Rome: the American. Staël, who called the United States "the vanguard of the human race" and "the future of the world," had serious investments, ideological, economic, and personal, in the new nation. She also confessed to a wealthy young American, John Izard Middleton, that she modeled Lord Nelvil upon him.[13] Like Nelvil, Kenyon thinks often of his homeland, but like Hawthorne he belongs self-consciously to the new world where supposedly "there is no shadow, no antiquity, no mystery, no picturesque and gloomy wrong, nor anything but a commonplace prosperity, in broad and simple daylight" (4. 3). Regularly identified in crowd scenes—along with the beggars, French soldiers, and suspicious monks who also characterize a Rome more populated and more corrupt than Staël's—Americans intrude throughout Hawthorne's cosmopolitan Italy, casually but insistently. In one instance:

> there arose singing voices of parties that were strolling through the moonlight. Thus, the air was full of kindred melodies that encountered one another, and twined themselves into a broad, vague music, out of which no single strain could be disentangled . . . [and] incited our artist-friends to make proof of their own vocal powers. With what skill and breath they had, they set up a choral strain—"Hail, Columbia!" we believe—which those old Roman echoes must have found exceedingly difficult to repeat aright. (4. 163)

To render an authentic contemporary Rome through an authentic contemporary romance, one which reflects his own experience as well as a changing world, Hawthorne again departs from what may be Staël's precedent, modulating her impulse to define national character into figures largely his own. Miriam, for example, while resembling Corinne in many ways, possesses a murkier and even wider cross-cultural heritage. As Hawthorne democratizes Staël's nationalistic distinctions, distributing "Italian" passion and "British" reason in varying degrees among his characters, male and female, he also reiterates that his artists are foremost working artists, "free citizens," not glorified performers or public possessions (4. 132). Even the cosmopolitan Miriam, reportedly connected to an aristocratic family of Southern Italy, maintains a studio full of works-in-progress, as do Hawthorne's Americans. Corinne, crowned at the Capitol for her brilliant improvisations, seems not to labor to produce her art: we see her gallery, but not her workshop.[14] Able to view his "commitment to democracy" in a more international light by 1859, Hawthorne in *The Marble Faun* may diffuse accordingly the rigid types characteristic of *Corinne* while nonetheless privileging his own Yankee pragmatism.[15]

In truth, however, Hawthorne's ostensible problems with Staël's novel may lie less with its text than with its context. *Corinne,* in its original French and in translation, had alike enthralled Europeans and Americans, especially women, since it first appeared in 1807. Printed in forty editions within sixty-five years, *Corinne* colors works by nineteenth-century writers as diverse as Stendhal, Elizabeth Barrett Browning, George Eliot, and George Sand. As Perry Miller relates, Staël's tale in its 1807 translation "promptly became a troubling intrusion into all Anglo-Saxon communities. It was perpetually denounced from middle-class pulpits and assiduously read by middle-class daughters in their chambers at night." Among its American readers was the fifteen-year-old Sophia Amelia Peabody of Salem, Massachusetts, who would in 1842 marry Nathaniel Hawthorne. T. Walter Herbert remarks that the novel "became an organizing force in her moral and aesthetic consciousness and a medium of communion with her sisters, including spiritual sisters like Sarah Clarke and Connie Hall." Across the United States, *Corinne* became more than a best-seller or literary antecedent: it became a furor, inciting female readers to emulate its heroine and its creator, which, as Moers explains, evolved largely into a single identity. Captivated by Staël's artistry, insight, and achievement, American readers inaugurated *Corinne*-style salons from north to south.[16]

Within the decades of *Corinne*'s literary ascendancy, which spanned most of his life, Hawthorne struggled to merge his personal vision and expression with the demands of the American literary marketplace. Graduating from Bowdoin in 1825, Hawthorne spent the next twelve years dependent on relatives while puzzling out his craft in his mother's garret in Salem. As a professional writer, he met limited financial success. But determined to support his art and his wife-to-be, Hawthorne accepted an appointment to the Boston Custom House in 1837, the first of many unsatisfactory undertakings, including a stint at Brook Farm, the Transcendentalist commune. So began a lifetime of

financial unpredictability, of often tedious outside employment
alternating with concentrated periods of writing. His notorious
dismissal from the Salem Custom House in 1849 prefaced the
production of *The Scarlet Letter* (1850), which earned him some
measure of fame, but no real profit. In fact, economic concerns
sent the Hawthornes to Europe in the first place:

> Only one of [Hawthorne's] published works brought him any finan-
> cial security at all, and this was not a novel but the campaign biog-
> raphy of his college friend, Franklin Pierce, which he composed
> immediately following Pierce's nomination for the presidency in
> 1852. . . . [H]e . . . saw in it the promise of deliverance from the un-
> certainties of the literary marketplace. He knew that if elected Pierce
> would show his gratitude with a lucrative patronage appointment.
> The new President offered him the hugely profitable consulship at
> Liverpool, and for several years the post spared Hawthorne further
> efforts to satisfy a popular taste from which he felt increasingly
> estranged.[17]

Essentially, Hawthorne counted on the savings from the appointment to finance later years devoted exclusively to writing and
to his family. During the years in Europe, he monitored developments in the American literary scene, frustrated by the self-
imposed but apparently necessary delay in his return to his art,
hoping that the long moratorium would not stagnate his ability
to compose original and penetrating fiction.

While investigating art as job in an increasingly pragmatic
young nation, Hawthorne also consistently professed respect for
certain European models, among them Spenser, Shakespeare,
and Bunyan, suggesting his own interest in earning posterity as
well as prosperity through his primary vocation. But as Robert
Weisbuch generalizes, "[I]n American admonitions against imi-
tating the thoughts of any other man, that other man is eventually and inevitably defined as an Englishman."[18] In his young
nation, Hawthorne's avowed influences were allied with a bur-
densome British past, one which artists demanding a self-
consciously American culture sought to overthrow. Complicating his ambitions further was the tendency among mid-nine-
teenth-century intellectuals to devalue his chosen genre, fiction,
and to champion instead poetry and philosophical prose as the
legitimate vehicles of serious thought. In addition, in the indus-
trializing United States, writing became a somewhat suspect oc-
cupation, for its practice was less productive than business.
Hawthorne's literary debates with convention and their attend-

ant demands radiate, then, in both historical and contemporary, and apparently incompatible, directions. How to be a novelist in America and be taken seriously? How to create authentic art that both sells and lasts?[19]

For Hawthorne, caught in this web of contradictory influences, Germaine de Staël would perhaps loom larger as rival than as influence. Her *On Germany* stood among the major European works that provoked American thinkers—notably George Ticknor of Harvard, a cousin of Hawthorne's editor, William D. Ticknor—to explore the German influences that helped form and reform contemporary American thought. Applauded also by the intelligentsia for connecting literature to politics in *Literature Considered in Its Relation to Social Institutions,* as well as by popular readership for her romantic novels, Staël clearly stood among the European "living dead" who inspirited *both* elite and mass culture in nineteenth-century America, an incontestable presence even more remarkable for being female.[20]

Capable of disparaging efforts by his fellow scribbling men, even men he respected, like Thoreau, as well as his own work, Hawthorne most famously aimed his invective at female writers. These "public women," whom he identified early in his career as "ink-stained Amazons" in a prophecy of their threatened conquests, emerged later as the "d———d mob of scribbling women" he decried in an 1855 letter from Liverpool to William D. Ticknor, disgusted by what he saw as their sentimental excesses, yet envious of their relative success (17. 304).[21] But as he revealed in a subsequent letter, these women writers could in part redeem themselves in his eyes. Of the American author Fanny Fern and her sensational tale of female artistic independence, *Ruth Hall,* Hawthorne contended:

> The woman writes as if the devil was in her; and that is the only condition under which a woman ever writes anything worth reading. Generally, women write like emasculated men, and are only to be distinguished from male authors by greater feebleness and folly; but when they throw off the restraints of decency, and come before the public stark naked, as it were—then their books are sure to possess character and value. (17. 308)

According to Leland S. Person, Jr., American culture also stigmatized *male* authors as "emasculated men," for it tended to gender authorship as female. In a sense, then, Hawthorne's image of the scribbling women is a self-image, embodying his own uneasy attempts to balance the public and private. As James D. Wallace argues, "[I]n looking at the writing of women he knew and read, Hawthorne saw the abstracted quality of his own writing, and ... his response to them was structured by his satisfaction and dissatisfaction with his own accomplishments." Public women were public reminders of Hawthorne's own predicament. Although Staël died when Hawthorne was only thirteen, her presence through the life of her work, especially through *Corinne*'s continued sales, may have haunted him relentlessly as an example of success, as a touchstone for his own shortcomings, as a model for scribbling women everywhere, and as a reminder of the humiliating "necessity for wooing customers and making a positive impression on the public."[22] And Staël's publicity in writing notwithstanding, her notorious *amours* would give the reserved Hawthorne more to condemn her for than bad taste.

Further amplifying Staël's power for Hawthorne, beyond her success or reputation, was her presence as enacted by public women whom he knew personally, whose associations with Staël may have swirled into the mixed admiration and anxiety these women instilled in him. Most notably, his stay in Rome may have conjured for Hawthorne the living spirit of Margaret Fuller—writer, editor of *The Dial,* reformer, informing presence at Brook Farm, supporter of the Italian revolution, and eventually the lover of an Italian count—killed in a shipwreck returning from Italy to America in 1850. In Concord, "the most intelligent, articulate, and passionate woman Hawthorne ever knew" had played unruly friend to the Hawthornes early in their marriage; Fuller's 1839 Boston "Conversations" had enraptured a younger Sophia.[23] In 1840, another Concord resident, Ralph Waldo Emerson, deemed Fuller a "new Corinne":

> he sketched out what a Corinne-figure comprised: tenderness, counsel, one before whom every mean thing is ashamed—"more variously gifted, wise, sportive, eloquent, who seems to have learned all languages, Heaven knows when or how,—I should think she was born to them,—magnificent, prophetic . . ."

Less charitably, William Henry Channing saw Fuller's appearance as the "Yankee Corinna" as an affectation, the sort of pretense that would annoy Hawthorne, whose ambivalence toward this Corinne-figure is much debated. Commonly characterized as a "native Corinne," Fuller came to valorize Staël more as an intellectual model than as a flamboyant *artiste.* In "Woman in the Nineteenth Century" (1845), Fuller clarifies her attitude to her alleged idol:

> De Staël's name was not . . . clear of offense; she could not forget the woman in the thought; while she was instructing you in the mind, she wished to be admired as a woman; sentimental tears often dimmed the eagle glance. Her intellect, too, with all its splendor, trained in a drawing room, fed on flattery, was tainted and flawed; yet its beams make the obscurest schoolhouse in New England warmer and lighter to the little rugged girls who are gathered together on its wooden bench. They may never through life hear her name, but she is not the less their benefactress.[24]

Nonetheless, Fuller's affiliation with Staël probably enhanced neither in Hawthorne's estimation. Paula Blanchard argues that Hawthorne's explosion over Fuller in his 1858 Italian notebook expresses his anger toward his own image of her, rather than a residual fury at the woman herself. In this passage, he refers to her Donatello-like husband as "half an idiot" and links her alleged intellectual decline to the liaison he calls an "awful joke." Like those of Corinne and of *The Marble Faun*'s artists, Fuller's "powers . . . of production" apparently diminished in the face of love, proving her for Hawthorne "a very woman," an image he claims to prefer (14. 155, 156, 157).

Regardless of Hawthorne's possible uneasiness or resentment toward Fuller, dating back to their awkward connection in Concord, she designated him "the best writer of the day" in an 1846 treatise on American literature, in which she pronounces, "Books which imitate or represent the thoughts and life of Europe do not constitute an American literature. Before such can exist, an original idea must animate this nation and fresh currents of life must call into life fresh thoughts along its shores." In the same essay, she seems to promulgate Hawthorne's own dilemma, declaring, "No man of genius writes for money; but it is essential to the free use of his powers that he should be able to disembarrass his life from care and perplexity." She herself dreaded life as a "paid Corinne." Perhaps Fuller's praise for him as an American original, the acuity of her insights, and her own integrity of vision, combined in recollection with her Corinne-image and other irrepressible traits, unnerved Hawthorne, particularly as he feared losing his own productive powers after his long publishing hiatus. Perhaps his Italian experience drove home to him her loss. At any rate, in Rome, he was compelled to remember her, as his notebook blast proclaims. Possibly tinged with remorse, Hawthorne's vivid if troubling memories of Margaret Fuller may have clouded his inception of *The Marble Faun,* a difficult fusion he preferred not to announce.[25]

Closer to his own hearth, Hawthorne knew another Staël advocate in the person of Fuller's promoter, his sister-in-law, Elizabeth Palmer Peabody, who espoused many of Staël's principles, approving when her younger sister read a "French novel" like *Corinne* because of its author's impeccable intellect. In 1824, Peabody wrote to the adolescent Sophia, "Madame de Staël made no distinction between the sexes. She treated men in the same manner as women. She knew that genius had no sex." According to Louise Hall Tharp, Elizabeth Peabody "decided that she must pattern her life as closely as possible after Madame de Staël."[26] Like Fuller an educator, reformer, and "public woman," Peabody was also an entrepreneur of intellectuals and artists, and an initial publicist of Hawthorne's talent. Rumored to have shared an indefinite romantic bond with him before he settled on Sophia, Peabody helped Hawthorne procure some of his civic employments, a generosity that may have fostered in him both gratitude and resentment, for these jobs supported his family, but reminded him that he could not sustain them with his art. In 1850, he wrote, "Ill-success in life is really and justly a matter of shame. The only way in which a man can retain his self-respect, while availing himself of the generosity of his friends, is, by making it an excitement to his utmost exertions, so that he may not need their help again."[27] And although fond of his indefatigable sister-in-law, Hawthorne found her liberal extremism irritating. Even across the Atlantic, Peabody piqued Hawthorne by soliciting contributions from him for concerns he did not share, and by what he construed as her continual attempts to mother Sophia, implying his inadequacy in caring for her. Both indebted to and impatient with Peabody, whose many enthusiasms originated in part with Germaine de Staël, Hawthorne may have submerged this association in the ambivalence *The Marble Faun* suggests toward *Corinne.*

Through his other sister-in-law, Mary Peabody Mann, Hawthorne knew yet another American Corinne, Julia Ward Howe, who like Staël and Fuller had also preceded him in visiting and writing about Italy. One of the stunning, well-to-do Ward sisters—Louisa Ward Crawford and her family grew close to the Hawthornes while among the Anglo-American artists there—Howe, combustibly married to Samuel Gridley Howe, "the phil-

anthropist of blind people" and somber abolitionist, had lived
happily apart from her husband in Rome (17. 277):

> The all-curious Mrs. Howe,—Julia Ward Howe,—who wrote poems
> in Italian and made speeches in French, studied Hebrew [in Rome]
> with a learned rabbi from the ghetto where he had to be within the
> walls by nightfall. This minor Margaret Fuller, more of the world
> and less of the mind, who was later a great founder of clubs for
> women and for whom "causes" were the breath of life, was already
> an *improvisatrice* and a singer at musical parties that brought the
> Anglo-American visitors together.[28]

The accomplished Howe, later Fuller's biographer, recorded
some of her Italian impressions in her volume *Passion-Flowers*
which, as Wallace explains, Hawthorne in 1854 admired as the
musings of a distinctly American voice, the sort of praise Fuller
had accorded his work. But he questioned Howe's publication of
what he saw as "domestic unhappiness," asking, "What does her
husband think of it?", identifying more strongly with the apparently exploited spouse than with the exploiting artist (17. 177).
In 1857, before leaving for Italy, Hawthorne criticized her again:
"she has no genius or talent, except for making public what
she ought to keep to herself—viz. her passions, emotions, and
womanly weaknesses. 'Passion Flowers' were delightful; but she
ought to have been soundly whipt for publishing them" (18. 53).
Wallace sees in Hawthorne's response to Howe a mélange of his
conflicted attitudes regarding women writers and their propriety
as artists.[29] Conceivably, this coalescence encompassed Howe's
resemblance to the cause-driven Peabody, to Fuller, and to Staël's
privileged *improvisatrice*, torn between the demands of art and
the demands of marriage, but remaining in some fashion "delightful." It anticipates as well the mixed message *The Marble
Faun* delivers regarding *Corinne*.

As Joyce Warren indicates, Hawthorne's career as a public
man in Europe in his later life brought him into contact with
greater numbers of public women, some of whom perturbed
him, but many of whom he grew to esteem, perhaps accounting
for his dual considerations of female ambition in *The Marble
Faun*.[30] In particular, he admired two of Margaret Fuller's cote-
rie, who were themselves friends, and whose lives each suggest
a revision of Staël's *Corinne*. In the American sculptor Harriet
Hosmer, Hawthorne may have seen a permutation of *Corinne*

he approved: a woman who survived by emphatically *not* trying to serve both art and love:

> "I am the only faithful worshipper of Celibacy," [Hosmer] wrote, "and her service becomes more fascinating the longer I remain in it. Even if so inclined, an artist has no business to marry. For a man, it may well be enough, but for a woman on whom matrimonial duties and cares weigh more heavily, it is a moral wrong, I think, for she must neglect her profession or her family, becoming neither a good wife and mother nor a good artist."[31]

Modeling *The Marble Faun*'s female artists in part on Hosmer, Hawthorne has Miriam appreciate the "many women, distinguished in art, literature, and science—and multitudes whose hearts and minds find good employment, in less ostentatious ways—who lead high lonely lives, and are conscious of no sacrifice . . .": a quiet tribute to one who seems to have learned from Corinne's tragic example (4. 121).

But Hosmer's friend, Elizabeth Barrett Browning, undoubtedly afforded Hawthorne an even more perplexing interpretation of *Corinne*. Although never physically robust, Barrett Browning, like Sophia Hawthorne, exchanged an early life of illness for a strong marriage, motherhood, and international travel. Although reticent by nature, she dedicated much of her writing to public concerns, including Fuller's last cause, Italian independence. Of Barrett Browning, Hawthorne wrote, "It is marvellous to me to see how so extraordinary, so acute, so sensitive a creature, can impress us, as she does, with the certainty of her benevolence" (11. 301). Notably, her hugely popular "novel-poem" *Aurora Leigh* (1857) is itself an "extended debate with *Corinne*," which Barrett Browning called "an immortal book." Significantly, *Aurora Leigh*'s revision of *Corinne* ends happily: the surviving artist "has her career *and* her man," not unlike her creator.[32] Hawthorne may have reconciled his vision of the extraordinary, acute, sensitive, benevolent wife of Robert Browning with her status as best-selling author and student of Staël by developing another blind spot—in other words, by not seeing her as a poet at all. Early in his acquaintance with the Brownings, Hawthorne dismissed Barrett Browning's art by confusing it with her husband's. A kindred confusion would surface when Hawthorne considered Staël's Coppet: "we found the Casa Guidi . . . It being dusk, I could not see the exterior, which, if I remember, Browning has celebrated in song: at all events, he has called one of his poems the 'Casa Guidi Windows'" (14.

300).[33] After Hawthorne's death, Sophia's edition of his Italian notebooks restored this poem to its rightful author (14. 810n).

In truth, *Corinne* had possessed Hawthorne's male acquaintances, too. Foremost among them was George Stillman Hillard, Hawthorne's friend, his one-time landlord, and his attorney. Initially, Hillard had impressed Hawthorne as an editor of his revered Spenser; the two men probably met through Elizabeth Peabody.[34] Hillard also authored the 1853 travel guide *Six Months in Italy*, which, in Brigitte Bailey's words, "describ[es] Italy as a feminized landscape with feminizing effects on its inhabitants."[35] Dedicating the book to Thomas and Louisa Ward Crawford, Hillard praised Staël among his "Writers upon Italy," proclaiming, "The great and lasting popularity of 'Corinne' renders it superfluous to dwell at any length on its characteristic excellences, or to quote from its inspired pages." One of the guidebooks Hawthorne relied upon in his European travels, *Six Months in Italy* may have greatly influenced *The Marble Faun*. For example, Hillard writes, "He who has seen Italy only in winter has but halfseen it: he has seen the reverse side of the tapestry,—a transparency by daylight." In *The Marble Faun*, Hawthorne embeds a strikingly similar image: "The gentle reader, we trust, . . . is too wise to insist upon looking closely at the wrong side of the tapestry, after the right one has been sufficiently displayed to him, woven with the best of the artist's skill" (4. 455).

Hawthorne also seems to develop a longer description from Hillard's guide, once removed from *Corinne*:

The Fontana di Trevi is in the heart of Rome. A mass of rocks is tumbled together at the base of the façade of an immense palace. In a large niche, in the center of the façade, is a statue of Neptune in his car, the horses of which, with their attendant tritons, are pawing and sprawling among the rocks. On either side . . . is an allegorical statue, and above the head of each of the statues is a bas-relief. All this is in bad taste,—an incongruous blending of fact and fable, chilled by the coldest of allegories; but it sounds worse in description than it looks to the eye . . . As we look, we begin with criticism, but we end with admiration. . . . This is the scene of the moonlight interview between Corinna and Oswald, as described . . . in the novel; and to this day, whenever the moon has touched the trembling waters with her silver rod, the mind's eye sees the shadows of the lovers resting upon the stream.[36]

One English translation of *Corinne*'s scene at Trevi Fountain reads:

> On the evening of the fourth day of this cruel absence, the moon shone clearly over Rome, which in the silence of the night looks lovely, as if it were inhabited but by the spirits of the great. Corinne ... left her carriage, and oppressed with grief, seated herself beside the fountain of Trevi, that abundant cascade which falls in the centre of Rome, and seems the life of that tranquil scene. Whenever its flow is suspended, all appears stagnation.... [I]n Rome, it is the murmur of this immense fountain, which seems the indispensable accompaniment of the dreamy life led there. The form of Corinne was now reflected on the surface of the water, which is so pure, that it has for many years been named the Virgin Spring. Oswald, who had paused there at the same moment, beheld the enchanting countenance of her he loved thus mirrored in the wave: at first it affected him so strangely that he believed himself gazing on her phantom, as his imagination had often conjured up that of his father; he leaned forward, in order to see it more plainly, and his own features appeared beside those of Corinne. She recognized him, shrieked, rushed towards him ... (35–36)

In *The Marble Faun*'s version of this scene, Hawthorne describes the setting much more specifically. In fact, he echoes many of Hillard's details, noting the fountain's configuration of Neptune and his attendant "Tritons" beneath "a great palace-front" of "niches and many bas-reliefs.... At the foot of the palatial façade, was strown, with careful art and ordered irregularity, a broad and broken heap of massive rock" (4. 144). Like Hillard, Hawthorne moves from criticism to admiration, remarking "the absurd design of the fountain, where some sculptor of Bernini's school had gone absolutely mad, in marble," then the "artificial fantasies, which the calm moonlight soothed into better taste," finally relenting: "after all, it was as magnificent a piece of work as human skill had ever contrived" (4. 144). Following vivid comparisons of the fountain by night and by day, one of Hawthorne's pragmatic Americans speculates on "what could be done with this water power ... in ... our American cities" (4. 145).

When Hawthorne actually alludes to *Corinne*'s Trevi Fountain scene, he continues to echo Hillard:

> "I have often intended to visit this fountain by moonlight," said Miriam, "because it was here that the interview took place between

Corinne and Lord Neville (sic), after their separation and temporary estrangement. Pray come behind me, one of you, and let me try whether the face can be recognized in the water."[37]

Leaning over the stone brim of the basin, she heard footsteps stealing behind her, and knew that someone was looking over her shoulder. The moonshine fell directly behind Miriam, illuminating the palace front and the whole scene of statues and rocks, and filling the basin, as it were, with tremulous and palpable light. Corinne, it will be remembered, knew Lord Neville by the reflection of his face in the water. In Miriam's case, however (owing to the agitation of the water, its transparency, and the angle at which she was compelled to lean over), no reflected image appeared; nor, from the same causes, would it have been possible for the recognition between Corinne and her lover to take place. The moon, indeed, flung Miriam's shadow at the bottom of the basin, as well as two more shadows of persons who had followed her, on either side.

"Three shadows!" exclaimed Miriam. "Three separate shadows, all so black and heavy that they sink in the water! There they lie on the bottom, as if all three were drowned together." (4. 146–47)

Following Hillard's recommendation, Hawthorne does not dwell on *Corinne*'s characteristic excellences, if he perceived any, nor does he quote from Staël's inspired pages. Instead, he revises the scene, seeming to correct what he perceived as an inaccuracy, reading shadows instead of reflections in the fountain's waters, mirroring his first-person observations of Rome as mediated by Hillard. Hawthorne's version transmutes a repeated image and useful ambiguity from *Corinne*'s original French— Rome's "*illustres ombres, l'ombre de Corinne*": spectres and shadows, shades and shapes—but distorts other details, suggesting no more than a casual examination of the text, or none at all. Adding a third presence, the form of Miriam's pursuer, Hawthorne signals the enlarged theater of his drama. Apparently envisaging a broader but also more realistic portrait than Staël's, Hawthorne is himself less than precise in invoking the prior text, misspelling as is common the name of Corinne's lover, "an orthography which has always made trouble, though it is a fair representation of what the French ear hears when the name Neville is pronounced."[38] In *Corinne,* it is Nelvil who sees Corinne's image in the water, then his own, which she in turn recognizes as they appear side by side. Hawthorne's choice of "interview" to describe the lovers' encounter sounds distinctly like Hillard, as does his elaboration of "the shadows of the lovers" which concludes Hillard's vignette. In short, Hawthorne appears to know his Hillard better than his *Corinne,* perhaps to the extent of ignoring Staël's original text, deferring to its interpretation by an American male he personally knew and trusted—one he associated with a literary patriarch like Spenser—rather than to Hillard's more problematic source. If not a more credible reference for Hawthorne, Hillard's text may have been a more convenient one, a possibility that further implies Hawthorne's insouciance toward *Corinne.*

Significantly, Hawthorne had already recorded a version of this scene in his Italian notebook. Relating a "moonlight ramble" about Rome with Sophia in April 1858, he describes a drama scripted by Hillard, ghostwritten by Germaine de Staël (14. 180):

[W]e soon came to the Fountain of Trevi, full on the front of which the moonlight fell, making Bernini's sculptures look stately and beautiful; through the semi-circular gush and fall of the cascade, and the many jets of the water . . . are of far more account than Neptune and his steeds, and the rest of the figures. We descended to the edge of the basin, and bent over the parapet, in order to ascertain the possibility of Lord Nelville's (sic) having seen Corinne's image in the water, or if she could have seen his (for I forget which it was) at their moonlight interview. It could not have happened. The transparency of the water, permitting the bottom of the basin to be clearly seen, its agitation, and the angle at which one looks into it, prevent any reflection from being visible. The moon, shining brightly overhead and a little behind us, threw our black shadows onto the water; and this is what Lord Nelville or Corinne would have seen, but nothing else. (14. 180)

Hawthorne's amnesia over which of Staël's characters saw whom actually captures the range of *Corinne*'s reunion scene, where Corinne and Nelvil *both* eventually see one another in the water. In *The Marble Faun,* Hawthorne edits his recollection of *Corinne* to emphasize a female priority in the scene, corresponding to Miriam's command of the Trevi legends. Prompted perhaps by Hillard's concrete depiction, Hawthorne then asserts his own command, rendering a Trevi Fountain he declares more authentic than Staël's. But in concluding *Corinne*'s scene "could not have happened," Hawthorne unwittingly reveals his own complicity in Staël's vision. It could not have happened at all, of course, because Corinne and Lord Nelvil are purely fictional identities. Nevertheless, Hawthorne accepts the reality of this illusion, even as he tries to subvert it by insisting on the reality of his own re-vision of the famous scene, set in a romance conceived upon blending fantasy and fact. Like the public women he knew who enacted versions of Staël's story, Hawthorne ironically becomes a literal follower of Staël, perhaps in spite of himself, unknowingly casting himself in *Corinne*'s shadow, as he may also have cast its shadows throughout *The Marble Faun*.[39]

In *The Marble Faun*'s penultimate chapter, the American sculptor Kenyon meets such an imposing female, one of a "host of absurd figures" in the Carnival parade (4. 446):

> There came along a gigantic female figure, seven feet high, at least, and taking up a third of the street's breadth with the preposterously swelling sphere of her crinoline skirts. Singling out the sculptor, she began to make a ponderous assault on his heart, throwing amorous glances at him out of her great, goggle-eyes, offering him a vast bouquet of sunflowers and nettles, and soliciting his pity by all sorts of pathetic and passionate dumb-show. Her suit meeting no favor, the rejected Titaness made a gesture of despair and rage; then suddenly drawing a huge pistol she took aim right at the obdurate sculptor's breast, and pulled the trigger. The shot took effect . . . covering Kenyon with a cloud of lime-dust. (4. 446)

In this clash, which is also a courtship, the "rejected Titaness," a dethroned deity, ultimately bests the sculptor not through pathos or passion, but by throwing the matter of his art back in his face, "thus transform[ing] him into one of his own dusty-white statues."[40] In effect, competing with a formidable female turns Hawthorne's artist into an "absurd figure" himself, part of a chaotic public spectacle far from the claims of his professed vocation. Perhaps Kenyon's plight signals Nathaniel Hawthorne's deeper personal conflict as he neared what would prove his career's end, having confronted for years the stubborn spectre of Germaine de Staël, gowned in the "swelling sphere" of *Corinne*'s popularity. As if knowing his readers would compare his Italian romance to its renowned predecessor, which in fact they did, Hawthorne does it first, incorporating his own sometimes veiled comparisons throughout, his intentionality difficult to verify. And although allusions to Staël's novel clearly surface in his romance, any intertextual alignment between these two primary works would have been complicated for Hawthorne by his knowledge of mediating texts like Hillard's, as well as by the extratextual interpretations of *Corinne* that pervaded his culture. In *The Marble Faun*, Nathaniel Hawthorne both effaced and elaborated the artistic model of Staël's novel, a transformation that simultaneously reflects the author's sense of *Corinne*'s vast cultural dominion and the complexity of his own resistance.

Marguerite Yourcenar: Daughter of Corinne

Charlotte Hogsett

Prologue

1794: Bright Roman sunshine lights the way for a horse-drawn chariot to bear Corinne, "poet, writer, *improvisatrice*," to the Capitoline Hill to be honored in a ceremony of ancient origin.[1] Dressed like Domenichino's Sibyl, applauded, introduced with great praise, she improvises a hymn to the "glory and bliss of Italy," accompanying herself on the lyre. A senator places the crown of myrtle and laurel on her head, as trumpets proclaim her triumph.

1981: Under the cupola of the French Institute, Quai Conti, Marguerite Yourcenar, the newest member of the French Academy, enters, wearing a black robe designed by Yves Saint-Laurent and, around her head, a white shawl. She delivers her acceptance speech, according to custom, the eulogy of the academician whom she replaces among the forty "immortals," Roger Caillois. They, along with such eminent public figures as the President of the French Republic, respond to her words with a standing ovation. A glowing response is given by the academician who had worked most diligently for her election, Jean d'Ormesson.[2]

Two centuries separate these two events, not to speak of their difference in status—the one imaginary, the other historical. Yet a number of commonalities suggest that the second of the two women, Marguerite Yourcenar, is a literary daughter of the other, Corinne, the creation of Germaine de Staël. This af/*filia*/tion (the word itself derived from the Latin language both writers knew and admired), beyond time and factuality, manifests itself most clearly in a gesture commonly disparaged in the case of male artists and more sardonically mocked in that of females—the pursuit of glory.

Yourcenar and Staël: Affiliation by Circumstantial Evidence

In her acceptance speech of 1981, Yourcenar did not fail to mention the historic moment it marked: The French Academy was receiving the first (and, as of this writing, only) female member in its history, dating back to 1636. Tempted, she says, to step back to usher in the shades of her female predecessors who had not been deemed "immortal," she names three such writers, of whom the first is Germaine de Staël. But this is what she says: "Madame de Staël would no doubt have been ineligible because of her Swiss parentage and her Swedish marriage: She had to be content with being one of the best minds of the age."[3] This comment is strange for a number of reasons. The verb tense of the first sentence draws attention: Why "would have been" instead of "was"? The conditional (Yourcenar uses the pluperfect subjunctive with conditional force) implies not that the Academy sometimes considered women only to reject them, but rather that the Academy simply never discussed the matter at all. The tense leaves open the possibility that, throughout these nearly four hundred years, among women writers there have been those whose work merited membership, had the Academy been willing to judge their cases. Yourcenar does not stress this idea, using the word "maybe" twice within a few lines as she alludes to it. As the accepted daughter views the excluded mother, it is relevant to ask which of these situations was in fact the case. Had the Academy considered women for membership, or had it not?

The truth is somewhere between the two possibilities suggested here. At its inception, the question of whether or not women were to be admitted was indeed not even discussed.[4] Not until 1702, sixty-seven years into its existence, were women even allowed to attend public meetings of the group. Yet from fairly early in its history, persons both within and without the Academy began to call for the admission of women. Probably the first of these was Gilles Ménage. Not a member of the Academy himself, in 1690 he wrote *Historia Mulierum Philosopharum,* hoping that examples of erudite women of the past would lead the Academy to admit women.[5] His proposal to that effect did not meet with success. A few years later, in 1695, La Bruyère is said to have remarked that he would have preferred to see Dacier's learned wife elected to the chair her husband was to occupy.

During the eighteenth century, a series of *salonnières* helped their male friends, but never themselves or each other, to become "immortals." D'Alembert, during his tenure as secretary of the Academy, proposed the creation of four places especially for women, without result. Further fruitless moves toward admission of women occurred occasionally in the nineteenth century. The feminist/socialist journal *Gazette des Femmes* sent a request to the French Institute for opening admission to women. Prosper Mérimée proposed George Sand for membership in 1862. Thirty years later, in 1893, the novelist Pauline Savari applied for membership but was refused, the Academy "considering that its traditions do not permit it to examine this question."[6] When, in 1910, forty-six members of the Institute (including the French Academy and four other honorary groups) requested that the question of women be considered, the Academy referred back to its 1893 decision as a precedent for its refusal, pronounced in early 1911. Among other women considered was Colette, who, as Yourcenar herself states in the acceptance speech, departed from the route to election by refusing to make visits to academicians expected of potential members. But apparently the question was not raised seriously again until in the late 1970s, when the Yourcenar campaign began.

Thus, Yourcenar's implication that consideration of Staël was a purely hypothetical matter is misleading, while her use of the conditional again in speaking of George Sand is actually wrong. The "daughter" appears, in short, to be dismissive of a history of attempts to have women writers included in the Academy. It seems that the empathy of a successful daughter for unsuccessful predecessors is limited.

Even more strange, however, are the excuses Yourcenar is quick to suggest to the Academy (which, after all, had not asked her to supply them) as the reasons why Staël did not become an academician. In referring to her ancestry and to her marriage to a foreigner, Yourcenar is on shaky ground indeed, since factors very similar to these were major obstacles to her own eligibility. Yourcenar was born in Belgium, not in France; her mother's family was Belgian. While she never married, her home from before World War II until her death in 1987 was in Maine, with her lifelong companion, the American Grace Frick. She became an American citizen. Powerful politicians, most notably perhaps Valéry Giscard d'Estaing and the then minister of justice, also an academician, Alain Peyrefitte, were enlisted to neutralize those facts which, moreover, Yourcenar herself minimizes or explains away in the introduction to the Pléiade edition of her novelistic oeuvre.[7] Bizarrely, Yourcenar mentions as justifications for why Staël was not included in the Academy those very reasons which might well have excluded her, thus drawing attention to and yet implying a distinction between their situations.

Beyond these likenesses/differences, several circumstantial similarities seem almost uncannily to link these two writers. For each, the father provided a fundamental and formative influence, while the mothers were either absent (Yourcenar's mother dies shortly after her birth) or perceived negatively (in the case of Staël). They were both travelers, the nomadic Yourcenar much more enthusiastically and willingly than the exiled Staël. If one tracked their journeys on maps and then superimposed them, the lines would cross and overlap, particularly if one added trips Staël planned or considered—to the United States, to the Middle East. To their journeys correspond works inspired by them. Each writer projected books which would have taken place in the Middle East—Staël, an epic based on the adventures of Richard the Lion-Hearted, Yourcenar, a life of Omar Khayyam—works eventually abandoned for the same reason, ignorance of the languages involved.[8] They both wrote in a variety of genres, both expository and fictional, dramatic and narrative. Neither practiced autobiography with any particular predilection, preferring to speak through historical or imaginary characters. Each woman was born in one country, wrote in the tradition of a second, and yet spent many years in others. Thus both lived in a voluntary or imposed exile and found themselves enriched and yet pained by separation.

Finally, the form of public recognition fantasized by Staël underscored still another commonality between these two writers: their knowledge and admiration of the ancient world and the continuing presence of its heritage. To be sure, Yourcenar would no doubt have deplored the melodrama and self-aggrandizement of the scene Staël created for a character in many ways her alter ego, had she ever discussed it. The flamboyance of Staël contrasts markedly with Yourcenar's controlled and haughty discretion. But the literary roots of both writers extend into antiquity. Yourcenar built a major work on bits of information concerning a Roman emperor in *Memoirs of Hadrian* (OR 287–515). Staël placed her heroine in a situation all the more heady for its ancient tradition.

The crowning of poets with myrtle and of military leaders with laurel was already commonplace for the poets of the Roman

Golden Age, who derived the practice from Greece, but it was apparently Domitian who established, from about 86 C.E., the custom of holding a laureate ceremony on the Capitoline Hill. Abandoned under Theodosius, the crownings were revived during the Renaissance. Petrarch was honored on 8 April 1341. Tasso was chosen for coronation in the spring of 1595, but died before he could actually receive the crown.[9]

As for the episode that places Corinne on the Capitoline, two events from Staël's first trip to Italy seem to have inspired it directly, no doubt adding to her resolution to follow classical and Renaissance precedents. First, she was invited to membership in the Arcadian Academy in Rome, a group inclusive of both sexes and of distinguished tourists passing through the city, as well as of Romans and Italians. Geneviève Gennari has recounted the incident, also underscored by Simone Balayé, on the basis of the remarks Staël made in the journal she kept as she traveled.[10] While the Academy was not without its excesses or, apparently, its comic side, being received into membership seems to have been an honor to which Staël was not insensitive. The episode has its poignancy today—this inclusion in a minor foreign academy of a woman not to be honored in any such way in her own country both because of her sex and of the political disfavor she was incurring.

Second, and resonating with the first, was the coronation, in 1776, of the celebrated *improvisatrice* Corilla Olimpica, who not coincidentally had also become an Arcadian academician. While in Italy, Staël was fascinated with the art form of improvisation, to the point of making it one of Corinne's major genres. She had occasion to witness several "improvisers" and apparently listened with keen interest to the story of the coronation of Olimpica, doubtless recounted by, among others perhaps, the abbé Godard, who had been in attendance at the event. The ceremony had been held at night for reasons that are no longer entirely clear. Despite the contrast between the sunlight bathing Corinne and this darkness, still a woman had received the laurels on the Capitoline Hill.

The Arcadian incident and that of Olimpica are reflected especially in two episodes of Staël's novel. The first is of course the Capitoline scene, a happy triumph with only foreshadowings of the sorrows to come. The darker episode—understood literally and figuratively—occurs in the final chapter of the book. Corinne decides to recite her latest—and it turns out last—verses at the Academy of Florence, but the moment falls at a time of her life when her sorrows turn what might have been a triumph into a bitter comment on her loss of her lover, and with it, that of her health and will to live. Corinne is, in fact, unable to deliver in person the poem she has written for the occasion. So it is that the woman writer's aspiration to recognition confronts the reality of her exclusion from it in much the same way that the opening comments of Yourcenar's acceptance speech at least introduce the somber history of women and the French Academy.

Yourcenar and Staël: Spiritual Affinity

The circumstantial evidence linking these two writers draws attention to, though it neither explains nor even implies, a spiritual affinity, the longing for and efforts toward public recognition of their writing. It was perhaps this desire for glory, strongly attractive yet perceived as somehow unbecoming, that unleashed the strange acknowledgment/denial of linkage in Yourcenar's acceptance speech. While sketching an instinct to step back so that Staël and others might enter before her—as well as thanks to her—Yourcenar extended a metaphorical elbow to push them back by offering pretexts for the exclusion.

The keen desire for recognition is acknowledged early on by both writers in works implicitly linked with the comments they make on their days of reward. The subject of Corinne's improvisation on the Capitoline is "the glory and bliss of Italy," the very words reminiscent of one of her earliest works, *On the Influence of Passions* (1796), of which the first chapter is entitled "On the Love of Glory." Nearly thirty, embarking upon her literary career energetically and yet with some misgiving, Staël bespeaks her own longing for recognition:

> Of course there is inebriating enjoyment in filling the universe with one's name, in existing so much beyond oneself that it is possible to blind oneself about both the space and the duration of life. . . . The soul is filled with a proud pleasure by the habitual feeling that all the thoughts of a great number of men are directed toward you; . . . The acclamations of the crowd move the soul both by the reflections they inspire and by the emotions they stimulate: All these lively forms, then, in which glory presents itself must carry youth away with hope and enflame it with emulation.[11]

The obviously ambitious young writer hardly dares to hope that the glory for which she yearns may actually be within her grasp.

In fact, it is to herself as much as to others that she addresses this book, aimed at demonstrating the superiority of "the resources to be found within oneself" over those passions whose satisfaction requires the cooperation of others: "It is myself also that I have tried to persuade," she candidly comments.[12]

In like manner, Yourcenar's subject matter, her eulogy for Roger Caillois, seems to draw her thought back to her own nascent career. Caillois had, as it happened, had some small influence on that career, Yourcenar recalls. During the war, exiled in South America and in charge of a small review, Caillois accepted and published an essay by Yourcenar, then herself already in North America. That essay, Yourcenar felt in retrospect, included what she and Caillois had in common and what was to become the very foundation of her own writing, "this respect that he felt for everything having to do with the transmission of myths, with their changes in the hands of successive generations, and with the great truths about human nature that the poets have clothed in them" (DR 15). This reference to myths is the first of several clues suggesting that Yourcenar was looking back not only at her career in general but quite specifically to a certain decisive moment in it. The clues come in the form of those aspects of Caillois's many interests and topics upon which Yourcenar chooses to comment.

Two more are to be seen in her discussion of his *Games and Men,* in which he divides games into four categories. Yourcenar mentions all of them, but pays particular attention to two, mimicry (including carnival, theater, masks, and disguises) and vertigo (DR 24–25). The fourth surfaces when Yourcenar comments on the fascination with stones evident in Caillois's late work. He found the "purer object" he sought in stones, she says, in, for example, the diamond, "which, still buried in the earth, carries within itself all the virtuality of its future fires" (DR 43).

The presence of these four elements—myth, disguise, vertigo, and stones—suggests that Yourcenar was thinking of her 1935 book, *Fires,* about which, in fact, Yourcenar herself said, upon the occasion of its 1969 republication, "This *masked ball* [emphasis added] was one of the stages of my awareness" (DR 27). Ambition is a central theme of this series of short pieces based for the most part on classical myths (OR 1043–1135). Yourcenar's ambition is implied especially in the final piece, entitled "Sappho, or Suicide." This Sappho bears the name of the great Greek poet, but her art is not that of the writer but of the acrobat. This activity associates her with Icarus, a character with

whom Yourcenar had been fascinated since her first book of
poetry, published in 1921 under the title *Garden of Chimera*.[13]
In her use of this figure she had no doubt been influenced by
Symbolist poetry, particularly that of Mallarmé for whom the
poet, in "The Windows," is an Icarus who soars "at the risk of
falling for all eternity." *Fires* ends with four brief maxims in
which Yourcenar declares her intention to "beat a record," to
establish herself within and beyond poetic tradition itself. Over-
weening as this ambition may have seemed in 1935, it must
have appeared less out of reach in 1981, as Yourcenar delivered
her unprecedented acceptance speech at the French Academy.
She had indeed "beaten a record." Thus Yourcenar's expression
of her ambition was metaphorical rather than direct, but no less
clear than that of Staël. Both women linked their moment of
triumph with their early longing for such glory.

Resistances

In the early works are reflected concerns each writer experienced even as she expressed her ambition; the acceptance
speeches indicate how the now mature artist was dealing with
those concerns. In both cases, these concerns have to do with
the place of love in the life of the artist and with the status of
the artist as woman. The young Staël included in her early *On
the Influences of Passions* an apparently heartfelt chapter on
love as a passion whose very irresistibility warns one to be wary.
Her thoughts on love were evidently linked in her mind with
the plight of women, for it is in this context that she comments:

> Nature and society have disinherited half of the human race;
> strength, courage, genius, independence, everything belongs to men;
> and they surround the years of our youth with homage, only to
> amuse themselves with overturning a throne, as one permits chil-
> dren to command, certain that they cannot force one to obey.[14]

Clearly Staël is thinking not only of amorous interactions in
these lines, but also of the part her sex as well as her sexuality
was going to play in the unfolding of her life as an artist. These
matters were hardly resolved by the time she wrote Corinne's
scene on the Capitoline. She does not have Corinne treat the
matter directly; rather, she imagines that, pausing for applause,
she notices the melancholy Oswald and, under his look, bends

her discourse toward the thoughts she perceives in his mind, for she "was impelled to meet his need" (30). More dramatically, a bit later on, Corinne's turning toward Oswald causes her crown to fall. Thus does Staël figure the problematic role of the personal in the career-building of the woman writer.

Yourcenar viewed the personal as no less problematic than Staël did, though her manner of treating it was less overt. Sexual orientation and sexual identity are major concerns in *Fires*. Indeed Yourcenar states that the source of inspiration for the book is a great love which her writing was intended to "glorify" or to "exorcise." That the first of its "prose poems" features Phèdre, traditionally a figure of forbidden love, and that the last centers on a figure named Sappho suggest that Yourcenar was writing to "glorify or exorcise" her sexual identity and its relation with her writing identity (*OR* 1049). Her biographer, Josyanne Savigneau, demonstrates that Yourcenar's unrequited love for the homosexual André Fraigneau was at the heart of the "crisis of passion" that inspired the book.[15] The second and third pieces focus on Achilles and involve transfers of sexual identity. Yourcenar follows the tradition that Achilles was disguised as a girl by his mother Thetis in order to elude the death to which he was vulnerable because of his mortal/human constitution. (Later, when he kills the Amazon warrior Penthesilea after he has lost his beloved friend Patroclus in battle, it is that friend's face he sees when he lifts her helmet. The man who as a boy had been disguised as a girl sees a man where there was a woman.) Achilles says that his cross-dressing was the opposite of a disguise. Thus whereas disguises are ordinarily intended to veil identity, Yourcenar is suggesting that in fact they reveal the true self—an idea she was to repeat in her 1981 speech. Clearly a variety of sexual identities and orientations are at work in this book, inextricably related to the emergence of a writing career.

Misandre, the female companion of Achilles, feels buried alive in her body, weighed down by it, a prisoner of her breasts. She watches Achilles flee, as light and as strong as an eagle, toward "everything she would not become" (*OR* 53). When, still dressed in women's clothing, he lands upon the ship that will take him to war, the narrator comments, "No one suspected that this goddess was not a woman" (*OR* 55). Only the man disguised as a woman, not the woman herself, may hope for a godlike destiny. The immutability of this attitude in Yourcenar's thought is demonstrated by her references to George Sand in the Academy acceptance speech. Sliding dangerously close to making a remark about Sand that applies equally well to herself (as she did in her comments on Staël, noted earlier), she states "George Sand would have been scandalized by the turbulence of her life, by the very generosity of her feelings that make her a woman so admirably woman" (DR 11). It seems that not only the scandal of Sand's life (Yourcenar speaks as if the "scandal" of her own sexual reputation had not been an obstacle to her election) but indeed her very femininity made her ineligible. To borrow Yourcenar's own formulation, Sand's error was to have failed to disguise her womanness. Yourcenar obviously viewed feminine gender status as incompatible with, or at least as problematic for, becoming a writer. Whether one can "beat a record" in the domain of literature as a woman seemed to her to be very doubtful indeed.

When Glory Comes

The subtitle of Josyanne Savigneau's biography of Yourcenar is "The Invention of a Life." Beatrice Ness has also pointed out the uneasy coexistence of "truth and mystification" in Yourcenar's self-presentation.[16] It is as if "Marguerite Yourcenar" is a fictional character created by Marguerite Yourcenar (the name itself an anagram of Marguerite de Crayencour forged by the young Yourcenar and her father, Michel de Crayencour) as surely as Corinne was written into existence by Germaine de Staël. Thus the affiliation between Staël and Yourcenar can be seen not only in their avowed desire for glory but also in the gesture of veiling that desire by pushing forward and standing behind creatures to whom they attribute it, rather than claiming it as their own. Yourcenar's diffident reference to "this uncertain and floating self, this entity whose existence I myself have questioned, and which I feel defined only by the several works I have happened to write" (DR 10) is less an expression of a postmodern sensibility than of this invention of personae to engage in activities with which one might otherwise feel uncomfortable.

Further, and as if to put the self at one more remove from the longed-for light of glory, each of these characters, the one no less fictional than the other, chooses male literary figures through whom to speak. For Yourcenar this act is not surprising, not only by reason of the subject the occasion itself imposed but also because it had been her career-long method to privilege male characters and traditionally male concerns. Staël, on the other hand, tended to favor female characters, but Corinne's subject matter on the Capitoline, depicted as not chosen by her but suggested, if not imposed, by the crowd, led her to foreground male figures.

Thus as the woman writer walks into the light of public recognition, she finds herself squarely within male literary tradition. The impact of this positionality is threefold. Both these writers, separated by so much time and, after all, temperamentally quite different despite the resemblances between them one can easily establish, come as if by some linguistic gravitational force to express these three insistent themes. This similarity makes a striking commentary on the affiliation between the two of them and suggests a female tradition not entirely submerged by but rather emerging from the dominant discourse around them.

The first theme, then, is self-expression through male characters. Staël has Corinne especially center on a discussion of Dante in her improvisation. Of the dozen or so paragraphs devoted to Italians, mainly writers but including also artists, explorers, and philosophers, fully eight are devoted to Dante alone. In her description of him, the recurring preoccupations of Staël herself continually surface. She speaks particularly of his exile, his longing for glory in his own country, his death far from home, the transformation into poetry of his emotions, and the power of his imagination to reformulate the world he saw according to his own vision. It is equally clear that as Yourcenar describes the career of Roger Caillois, it is of her own that she continuously thinks. Of his *Games and Men,* the work so linked in her mind, as indicated above, with her own early *Fires,* she says: "[S]omething suggests to me that this axial book is at the same time a turning point: Caillois already is inscribing here these diagonals that he was going to reinforce in every direction later" (*OR* 25). In like manner, after *Fires* Yourcenar had explored and strengthened lines already suggested. A bit later in her discourse, the association Caillois/myself is made more explicitly.

> Without comparing myself the least in the world to this great mind, I experienced at about the same time something of the same rupture. These years were those when, searching the past for a model one might imitate today, I imagined as still possible the existence of a man capable of "stabilizing the earth". . . . (*DR* 31–32)

This reference to an early moment in the elaboration of her Hadrian indicates how present to her thinking was her own career as she detailed that of her subject. At the moment of glory, even if it is necessary to speak of someone else, it is of oneself one thinks and to one's own career one gives witness.

The second theme is death, not surprisingly in the case of Yourcenar, since she was delivering a eulogy, more unexpectedly in that of Staël because of the very optimism of her theme, "the glory and bliss of Italy." The whole content of her improvisation is positive—sunshine, the acclamation of the crowd, music, color. Only in this setting, in fact, could Staël have been able to imagine connecting the words "glory" and "bliss" with the conjunction "and," since from early in her career she had warned herself that for the woman glory may destroy happiness. But her fantasized Italy is the native land of the woman artist. Here and here only can her ambition and her personal satisfaction coexist.[18] Yet one thinks of Poussin's pastoral landscape where perplexed shepherds read the inscription on a tombstone: *Et ego in Arcadia.*

Indeed, when glory is the subject, the thought of death is never far away. Glory depends, to use Staël's early formulation, on forces outside oneself, and further has its own existence beyond the reality and even the lifespan of the person enveloped in its aura. To think of one's glory is to think of the form of immortality it confers and thus to think of one's own death. Yourcenar begins her eulogy thus: "This homage, given by the one who comes to the one who is leaving, dispels, like a great healing wind, any puff of vanity on the part of the newly arrived, and obliges him to make wise reflections about himself" (*DR* 12). To think of one's death is to face also, for Yourcenar, the eventual effacement even of one's glory. When we praise the dead, she says, quoting her own Hadrian, we prepare him for "centuries of glory and million years of being forgotten." She figures this erasure of glory in a striking image: "geological layers of time . . . innumerable particles of duration flowing ceaselessly like sand, and piling up on us who will no longer be" (*DR* 13). Nor does death leave undisturbed the magic Italian world of Germaine de Staël. The glorious beings whose praises she sings are also dead, of course. Beyond that, the sight of the bereaved Oswald turns her from the exaltation of her performance to the thought of death.

> All these wonders are monuments to the dead. Our idle life is scarcely noticed; the silence of the living is a tribute to the dead: they endure and we pass on. . . . All our masterpieces are the work

of those who are no more, and genius itself is numbered among the illustrious dead. (30–31)

If one can speak only through a male tradition and if glory itself is subject to death and an insistent reminder of it, the honored writer not surprisingly begins to look elsewhere for a more satisfactory and durable grounding for her own life and her own work. It is finally to nature that Staël and Yourcenar turn. The thought of death is easier to face in Italy, claims Staël.

Under this beautiful sky, frightened spirits are less hounded by the chill and solitude of the grave along with so many funeral urns. . . . One surrenders less fearfully to nature, of whom the Creator has said: "Consider the lilies of the field, how they grow; they toil not, neither do they spin: and yet I say unto you, that even Solomon in all his glory was not arrayed as one of these." (31)

Yourcenar's point of reference is not that of Staël, the Bible, but rather the work of Caillois himself, especially insofar as it corresponds to the direction of her own mature thought. The very theme of her eulogy is that of Caillois as "lover of stones" (*DR* 16). Having arrived at the culminating point of his career, we learn from Yourcenar that Caillois demonstrated a certain "indifference to the human" and indeed to all forms of life.

Even the tree scarcely moves him, in spite of the almost fossilized dragonflies that he went to see, as I did myself, in the botanical garden of Orotava; he loves it especially as an incorruptible fragment transformed by millions of centuries during which all that was juice, sap, and delicate vegetal fiber has been transmuted or has flowed into amber, agate, or opal endowed with an almost mineral endurance. (*DR* 37–38)

Just as her Zeno had "dreamed of the silent cogitations of stones," wherein truths so deep that they are shared by the human with the animal and the mineral may be found (*OR* 728), so also as Yourcenar takes leave of Caillois she says, "Dear Caillois, I will think of you again while trying to listen to the stones" (*DR* 50).

The silent world of natural phenomena beckoned these writers at the time of their careers when they could present their personae for the bestowing of a great honor. The glory of speech walked a path to speechlessness. This silence, however, is for neither writer the frustration of incapacity nor the thwarting of talent. Rather it is the discovery of a *locus* for the grounding of oneself and one's work beyond time. It is as if these two women writers meet in a place no longer bound by a culture which, because dominated and defined by men, is not an entirely comfortable ambience for the development of a woman's talent, whether because the social construction of women molds her gifts into forms unlike those of men or because the male world itself is not uniformly receptive to work which comes from women. If the context of culture, no matter how revered it may be (and certainly Staël and Yourcenar pay culture their deepest and most sincere respects), proves finally unsatisfactory, then nature must be the setting for creativity. The foundation of the human in the natural, Staël and Yourcenar might well—and perhaps rightly—have argued, is a human and not uniquely a female ideal. But it is not a matter of indifference that contemplation of glory led both of these women to ground their thought in nature. That their ideas, different in so many ways, should find themselves as if irresistibly pulled in that direction demonstrates a profound affiliation and suggests their membership in a culture not at ease in the culture whose homage they sought and won.

Notes

Introduction

1. For full references and an extensive list of publications, see the general bibliography at the end of the volume. Detailed bibliographical sources concerning Germaine de Staël and the Groupe of Coppet have been compiled in *Cahiers staëliens* 40 (1989): 89–137 (Simone Balayé and Anne Amend) and 46 (1995–94): 115–44 (Simone Balayé, Othenin d'Haussonville, and Jean-Pierre Perchelet). A list of the novel's editions, pertinent correspondence, and interpretative studies, may be found in Simone Balayé's edition of *Corinne ou l'Italie* (Gallimard, 1985). See also my chapters on Staël in *French Women Writers, A Bio-Bibliographical Source Book* and in *A Critical Bibliography of French Literature: The Nineteenth Century*. As this book goes to press, I note a major bibliographical source, Pierre H. Dubé's *Bibliographie de la critique sur Madame de Staël (1789–1994)*. Among most recent publications of great impact in America the following should be noted: major chapters devoted to *Corinne* in Margaret Waller's *The Male Malady: Fictions of Impotence in the French Romantic Novel* (1993), Doris Kadish's *Politicizing Gender: Narrative Strategies in the Aftermath of the French Revolution* (1992), Joan DeJean's *Fictions of Sappho* (1989), Nancy K. Miller's *Subject to Change: Reading Feminist Writing* (1988), and Carla Peterson's *The Determined Reader: Gender and Culture in the Novel from Napoleon to Victoria* (1986). Ellen Moers's groundbreaking work *Literary Women: The Great Writers* (1976), with the chapter "Performing Heroism: The Myth of Corinne," restored the lost connections between Staël and other women writers. The year 1987 was exceptional in Staël research. Avriel Goldberger published her translation of *Corinne, or Italy,* and Vivian Folkenflik completed the first English "general reader," *An Extraordinary Woman: Selected Writings of Germaine de Staël.* In addition, new revisionist studies appeared: Charlotte Hogsett's *The Literary Existence of Germaine de Staël* and Marie-Claire Vallois's *Fictions féminines: Madame de Staël et les voix de la Sibylle.* The first international conference on Germaine de Staël in America, organized at Rutgers University in 1988, provided the impetus for numerous MLA, NEMLA, and Nineteenth-Century French Studies panels. The collection of essays, *Germaine de Staël: Crossing the Borders* edited by Madelyn Gutwirth, Avriel Goldberger, and Karyna Szmurlo, grew out of this ferment and featured several contributions examining *Corinne* in the light of current feminist and literary theory. In 1996, Avriel Goldberger made available to readers of English Staël's second great novel, *Delphine,* and is presently translating her memoirs, *Ten Years of Exile.*

2. I quote the call made by Mary Jacobus for a new feminist poetics in her *Women Writing and Writing about Women,* as paraphrased by Patricia Yeager in "The Dialogic Imagination," 969.

3. On this subject consult, in particular, Ellen Moers, *Literary Women*; Paula Blanchard, "Corinne and the 'Yankee Corinna'"; Madelyn Gutwirth, *Madame de Staël, Novelist,* and Avriel Goldberger, introduction to *Corinne, or Italy.*

4. Emile Benveniste in his *Problèmes de linguistique générale,* 2:79–88. Consult also Gérard Gengembre and Jean Goldzink, "Républicain, as-tu du style? ou écriture et politique dans les *Circonstances actuelles.*" Staël's philosophy of language is developed extensively in my "Speech Acts: Staël's Historiography of the Revolution" and "Pour une poétique des langues nationales."

5. In her essay "Germaine de Staël's *Corinne*: Challenges to the Translator." Even Napoleon, Staël's most aggressive persecutor, had to acknowledge the haunting power of her voice while reading *Corinne* on Saint Helena: "I can see her, I can hear her, I can sense her, I want to run away, . . ." J. Christopher Herold, *Mistress to an Age: A Life of Madame de Staël,* 344.

6. Germaine de Staël, *Corinne, or Italy,* trans. Avriel Goldberger (New Brunswick, NJ: Rutgers University Press, 1987), 99, 127. Our primary sources in this collection are Avriel Goldberger's translation, indicated in the text by pages only, and Simone Balayé's edition *Corinne ou l'Italie* (Paris: Gallimard, 1985), indicated by page, Balayé. Only in a few instances were other editions consulted for contextual reasons.

7. Nancy Chodorov, "Gender, Relation, and Difference in Psychoanalytic Perspective in *The Future of Difference,* 14. See also her *Reproduction of Mothering* and Jessica Benjamin's "A Desire of One's Own: Psychoanalytic Feminism and Intersubjective Space."

8. The consecutive quotes are from Staël's *De l'influence des passions* and *Essai sur les fictions* in *Oeuvres complètes* reprinted in 2 vols., 130, 69; and from *De la littérature,* 1:62. Translations are mine.

Seeing *Corinne* Afresh

This introduction, drawing on materials developed far more extensively in my book, *Madame de Staël, Novelist: The Emergence of the Artist as Woman* (Urbana: University of Illinois Press, 1978), reworks material from its final chapter. All translations are mine.

1. Alphonse de Lamartine, "Les destinées de la poésie," in *Oeuvres complètes,* 1:32–33.

2. Albert Thibaudet, *Histoire de la littérature française,* 54, 51.

3. This would be the case with Lamartine, who in 1871 would turn against his earlier enthusiasm for Staël and her kind, "The charming timidity appropriate to her sex and her age, that modesty of the soul, as blushing as that of the body, never came to light in her. . . . Only this grace was lacking to her spirit, but this grace would have meant that she would have remained silent. People felt the want in her of that innocence of the genius who does not know his own powers and doubts himself: they forgot this in hearing the charm of her virile improvisations. For she was no longer a woman, but a poet, and orator." *Souvenirs et portraits,* 220.

4. Juliette Decreus-Van Liefland, *Sainte-Beuve et la critique des auteurs féminins*, 75.

5. Marguerite Iknayan, *The Idea of the Novel in France*, 32–33.

6. Sainte-Beuve, *Causeries du lundi*, 2d ed., 3:387.

7. Perry Miller, introduction to *The Writings of Margaret Fuller*, xxi.

8. Ibid., xix.

9. Ibid., xxi.

10. Ibid., xx–xxi.

11. I have long been indebted to Professor Anne Firor Scott of Duke University for this piece of lore. This piece of social history deserves greater scrutiny.

12. Elizabeth Janeway, *Man's World, Woman's Place*.

13. Joseph Campbell, *Hero with a Thousand Faces*, 30.

14. For an account of Jacobin reaction to this phenomenon see Lynn Hunt, "Engraving the Republic. Prints and Propaganda in the French Revolution," and my *The Twilight of the Goddesses*, chaps. 6 and 9.

15. Pierre Fauchery, *La Destinée féminine dans le roman européen du dix-huitième siècle*, 555.

16. Staël, *De la littérature*, 2:341–42.

17. Simone de Beauvoir, *The Second Sex*, trans. H. M. Parshley, 595.

18. *The New York Times*, 20 February 1973, 22.

19. Beauvoir, *The Second Sex*, 599. Even Staël's waspish biographer supports this: "Her object was not merely to exhibit or justify herself; rather it was to criticize a society that stifled generous impulses and discouraged half of mankind (the feminine half) from developing its gifts." J. Christopher Herold, *Mistress to an Age*, 199.

20. Beauvoir, *The Second Sex*, 541.

21. Jean Starobinski, *Portrait de l'artiste en saltimbanque*, 69–70. The previous quotation is also from this source.

Undermining and Overloading: Presentational Style in *Corinne*

1. Ellen Moers, *Literary Women*, 179n, 173.

2. Charlotte Hogsett, *Literary Existence*, 152.

3. Madelyn Gutwirth, *Madame de Staël, Novelist*, 187, 183.

4. Cited in Moers, *Literary Women*, 173.

5. Ibid., 174.

6. Helmut Hatzfeld, *Initiation à l'explication de textes français*, 77–84; Danuté Harmon, "The Antithetical World View of Madame de Staël," 189.

7. Joan DeJean, "Staël's *Corinne*: The Novel's Other Dilemma," 77.

8. Gutwirth, *Madame de Staël, Novelist*, 167, 175, 209.

9. "Quelques remarques sur le style des romans de Mme de Staël," 233–34 (my translation). Omacini writes: "Pour la première fois jusqu'ici, le 'mot' semble s'imposer en tant que 'signe' laissant filtrer la pensée de l'écrivain et l'influence du contexte social qui lui est propre" (219).

10. *Corinne ou l'Italie* (Paris: Gallimard, 1985), preface by Simone Balayé, 31. Unless otherwise indicated, all citations are from this edition. All translations are from the recent translation by Avriel H. Goldberger, *Corinne, or Italy* (New Brunswick, NJ: Rutgers University Press, 1987).

11. Jacques Barzun, *Simple and Direct*, 156.

12. Gutwirth, *Madame de Staël, Novelist*, 198. "J'ai vu notés au crayon, dans un exemplaire de *Corinne* une quantité prodigieuse de *mais* qui donnent, en effet, de la monotonie aux premières pages." Cited in Harmon, "Antithetical World," 189.

13. Ibid., 196.

14. Hogsett, *Literary Existence*, 58.

15. Laurence Porter, "The Emergence of a Romantic Style," 129. Porter focuses on Staël's use of abstract nouns and her intellectual response to Goethe's *Werther* in *De la littérature* in contrast to the "affective response" emphasized in her discussion of *Wilhelm Meister* in *De l'Allemagne*. He concludes: "This rapid, acutely responsive transformation of Mme de Staël's thought and style prepares and exemplifies the transition of European thought from the Enlightenment to Romanticism" (140).

"Remember My Verse Sometimes": Corinne's Three Songs

I would like to thank Prof. Margaret Higonnet for her extremely helpful criticism and suggestions regarding this essay.

1. *Corinne, or Italy,* trans. Avriel H. Goldberger (New Brunswick, NJ: Rutgers University Press, 1987), xlvii. All parenthetical citations are to this work.

2. See Joan DeJean's forceful criticism of the improvisational passages in "Staël's *Corinne:* The Novel's Other Dilemma," 84. The supposed transcriptions are "the weakest passages in *Corinne* . . . totally voiceless, without the liberating spontaneity that is the hallmark of what Staël considered the female verb."

3. For a discussion of what Ellen Peel calls the contradiction produced by Staël's rendering of purported poetic texts in prose, see Peel's "Contradictions in Form and Feminism in *Corinne ou l'Italie*," 292.

4. Kathleen McGill's "Women and Performance: The Development of Improvisation by Sixteenth-Century Commedia dell'Arte" provides some illuminating historical background for the art of the *improvisatrice*. McGill notes that "the development of repertory improvisation in the theater occurred simultaneously with the appearance of women performers on the [commedia dell'arte] stage" (59). She goes on to dispute the dominant critical assumption that these actresses' improvisational techniques were merely derivative and imitative of academic (i.e., masculine) poetic practice (65–68). Rather, their techniques were "those available to the culture the women themselves inhabited, the popular culture of orality" (68). McGill concludes that these women's artistic choices point to "the social and psychological preferences of women performers for nonhierarchical, multiple process"—to "conversation in preference to dialectic" (69).

5. The description of Corinne as she approaches the Capitol, "dressed like Domenichino's Sibyl" and resembling "a priestess of Apollo making her way toward the Temple of the Sun" signals the oracular function of her improvisations (21). Like her mythological predecessors, Corinne both speaks and is spoken through; she is inhabited by voices, in the plural. In the myths the voices are divine, but Corinne's meditation tends more toward the secular and humanistic, though it is in a sense transcendental nonetheless: The voices comprehend national history and culture and at times articulate a Romantic type of collective introspection.

6. Ominously, Oswald begins to affect Corinne's discourse at their first social contact. During the gathering at which Oswald speculates on the possibility of winning her exclusively for himself, Corinne "would break off at the
most brilliant point of her conversation, disconcerted by his outward calm,
uncertain whether he approved or secretly blamed her" (38).

7. See also, for example, 124, and 127.

8. How to read Corinne's attitude toward this imbedded text (and the one
in book 7, chapter 2) is problematical because Staël's own attitude toward it
must be problematical. The passage is, of course, taken from her father's
Course on Religious Morality, and while Staël expresses great admiration for
the wisdom and sensitivity of that work, the fact that parts of it function in
the narrative as a basis for Oswald's surrender to the will of his dead father—
thus of his decision to marry Lucile—must suggest some ambivalence on
Staël's part.

9. Corinne alludes to other connections between myth and landscape that
hint at the nature of her own situation: Aeneas's descent into the underworld
and his companion Miseno's death at the hands of Triton for challenging the
gods in song. Two stanzas on, Corinne recalls the legend of Pliny's death on
Vesuvius, where he is consumed by the flames he came to study.

10. We learn that Corinne "seemed to take a livelier interest in writing since
Oswald had come," and that she wanted the final performance "to leave to Italy
and, above all, to Lord Nelvil, a last farewell that would recall the time when
her genius shone in all its splendor." Corinne wants the performance to enact
for Oswald in particular the contrast between what she is and once was (and
in fact it performs this gap by splitting Corinne into two persons): "[S]he
wanted the ungrateful man who had deserted her to feel once more that he
had given the deathblow to the woman who in her time knew best how to love
and how to think.... Perhaps she wanted to remind him of her talent and
her success before she died, indeed of everything she was losing through unhappiness and through love"(114).

Plotting with Music and Sound in *Corinne*

This essay was originally published in *Romantisme* 3 (1972): 17–32. The
editor would like to express her thanks to Simone Balayé for her permission
to reprint, and to Madelyn Gutwirth for her translation and adaptation.

1. Fernand Baldensperger devoted a chapter to it in his *Sensibilité musicale et romantisme* as did Léon Guichard in *La Musique et les lettres au
temps du romantisme.* Jean Ménard published a substantial article, "Madame
de Staël et la musique," and Marie Naudin produced "Madame de Staël, précurseur de l'esthétique musicale romantique."

2. *Delphine,* part 3, letter 21 and part 2, letter 5; hereafter referred to by
part and letter. The sounds of nature are treated similarly (see 6.1). As to
music as a spring of action, it appears quite clearly in the episode of Léonce's
marriage (1.37).

3. Later on we observe how he will reveal to Corinne, as they confront
Vesuvius's river of lava, the story that has disrupted his life and will destroy
their future.

4. *Corinne ou l'Italie,* ed. Simone Balayé (Paris: Gallimard, 1985), 37. Subsequent parenthetical references are to the same edition. "He dreaded those

ravishing harmonies that are pleasing if we are melancholic, but oppress us when we are in genuine pain. Music awakens memories that we were trying to quell" (246). We find passages of this sort in *Delphine*: "My soul was in no state to bear it: it brings back all my memories too vividly" (5.3), and also (3.44). Or, finally, Mme de Staël herself after the death of her father: "Poetry, music, these inexhaustible sources of gentle melancholy, attack my heart painfully with a bitter emotion." In *Manuscrits de M. Necker*, preface to Madame de Staël, *Oeuvres complètes* (Paris, 1842), 288.

5. There he will claim, for example, that "Corinne's poetry is an intellectual melody" (56).

6. When, later on, she appears to the acclaim of a concert hall, the musicians, caught up in the popular enthusiasm, will play "fanfares of victory" (246). Oswald, henceforth her professed lover, will see her moved to tears once again, but his jealousy impels him to dare reproach her for her emotion. This being a second panel of the story, a quite different one, where the same triumphal music now evokes only sorrow.

7. He does so in Italian, and she answers in English in so convincingly insular an accent that he is surprised by it. Voices in *Corinne* have much less importance than they do in *Delphine*.

8. This was a form of existence that Mme de Staël had uncovered for herself (Rome, 30 April 1805): "I cannot describe how the way of life here, musical, poetic, picturesque and ethereal, has revealed a new source of ideas and feelings to me." Letter to Claude Hochet in *Correspondance générale*, Béatrice Jasinski, ed., 5:545.

9. It must be observed here that Corinne exercises her creative faculties in literary, poetic and critical domains, then in the dance, and to a lesser degree in the novel, in painting, and drawing. In music, she invents her accompaniments in the process of improvising her poetry. Mme de Staël had not initially decided whether or not to make Corinne a writer. At the beginning, she had limited her to the recital of poems written by others. See Simone Balayé, *Les Carnets de voyage de Madame de Staël*, 113.

10. See two other commentaries about this reflection: Simone Balayé, "Absence, exil, voyage" and Jean Rousset, *L'Intérieur et l'extérieur*, 215–16.

11. A verse by Fontanes quoted in the text. See Simone Balayé, *Les Carnets de voyage*, 78–79.

12. Mme de Staël knows there is such a thing as imitative music, but this is not the sort she loves best. She prefers the expressive. All this should be studied more seriously than has been done until now. See *De l'Allemagne*'s chapter on "Des beaux-arts en Allemagne," 3:356 ff.

13. All their conversations might well be scrutinized closely. Geneviève Gennari poses the problem in *Le Premier voyage de Madame de Staël en Italie et la genèse de 'Corinne'*. It is claimed that Mme de Staël's views are probably better represented by Oswald's than by Corinne's. Matters are probably subtler: this notion comes of a preconception according to which Mme de Staël remained utterly insensitive to the arts in general, and in particular to the visual. Corinne, in this optic, would be expressing ideas dear to Schlegel and others. Far more certain is it that this quarrel expresses a conflict within Mme de Staël herself, who, in any case, was acquainted with Diderot's aesthetic ideas. A study of the function of the fine arts in *Corinne*, on the model of what we're attempting here with music, would certainly produce other perspectives.

14. It is natural that she should give that intellectual dimension to Corinne's talent for dance. This idea is a familiar one to Mme de Staël and her circle. See, mainly, Kirsten Holmström, *Monodrama, attitudes, tableaux vivants.*

15. He stops seeing her and, in his offensive letter attacking the character of the Italians, Corinne's compatriots, gives vent to his jealousy a few days later.

16. "The effect produced by pictures must be immediate and rapid, like all the pleasures produced by the fine arts." Mme de Staël's eye appears not to examine any play of line and color; she rather follows a moral line of thought. Yet, she feels the other facet: "The happy combination of color with chiaroscuro produces . . . a musical effect in painting; but since it represents life, we ask that it express the passions in all their energy and multifariousness" (225). We return always to the idea that visual arts limit thought rather than free it.

17. An idea related to what she says of rhyme, also a measure of time, indicating "memories and hopes."

18. Another quotation relevant here: "It seems, as we listen to pure and rapturous sounds, as if we were prepared to learn the Creator's secrets, to comprehend life's mysteries. No words can convey this sensation, for words lag behind initial impressions, just as translators of prose follow the footsteps of poets" (248–49). Words themselves, like visual art, place limits on the soul. But once assembled, they can in their own turn free it with their melodies.

19. Here she is certainly not thinking about the trials of poetic composition. She understands the writer's problems better than the musician's, but she cannot be ignorant of the latter. She knows perfectly well that poetic inspiration comes up against problems of conveying language adequately, in translating feelings via inadequate words.

20. The music we hear in *Corinne* is Italian; it comes from Pergolesi, Allegri, Paesiello, Zingarelli. For Mme de Staël it conveys better than does German music life's primitive energies. We have to compare her statements here with those in *De l'Allemagne;* it does not follow from this, as some have hastily concluded, that she dislikes German music: simply, she finds it too complicated and learned, drawn as she is by simpler, more natural and spontaneous forms.

21. "Poetry, painting and music, all that embellishes life with an inchoate hopefulness, was painful to him everywhere but by her side" (259).

22. Among the differences that separate them, there is surely one in their vital rhythms: she responds with immediacy, whereas he is moved but slowly; externalizing with trouble, he follows Corinne's mercurial changeability with difficulty, understanding it but little. A discussion then ensues between them concerning the relative merits of Catholicism and Protestantism. Mme de Staël ably defends them both, leaving the last word to the Protestant; but this stand provides the occasion for Corinne to proclaim the beauty of the gratuitous.

23. Here we are not far from those correspondences Mme de Staël will have much to say about in *De l'Allemagne,* notably in the chapter "Du sentiment de la nature." And there are other traces of this in *Corinne* as well. The association between music and perfume recurs in *Delphine, Sapho,* and *De l'Allemagne.*

24. Thus it is that Mme de Staël gladly had music played to her as she wrote. Her daughter Albertine tells how she composed *De l'Allemagne*'s chapters on enthusiasm while listening to Mozart.

25. A host of other, primarily visual details sustain this demonstration, in which silence plays so important a role. See Simone Balayé, *Les Carnets,* 120ff.

26. Between Oswald's story and Corinne's the festival at Cape Miseno is placed, with its joyful peasant dance (counterpart to the Tarantella, danced in Rome) but which Corinne no longer has the heart to engage in fully, as well as her second improvisation.

27. We take note here that this ballad is the one cited by Simone Balayé, *Les Carnets*, 404–5. This ballad, sung by Mme de Staël in her youth and then by her daughter [Allan Ramsay's 'Lochaber no more', tran.] seems to have been the same as Corinne's.

28. "The ideal language of music harmonized nobly with the ideal expressed in monuments" (408).

29. There will be an echo of this scene in Florence, at Santa Croce, where Corinne is finally alone. At Saint Mark's a funeral is being celebrated; at Santa Croce, prayers are being said for those long dead and buried.

30. So we have seen emblematized the cycle of destruction and rebirth I spoke of above. This passage may remind us of the end of [Goethe's] *Elective Affinities*, published in 1809.

31. *Editor's note: For the most comprehensive analysis of the paintings and sculptures, consult Simone Balayé, "Du sens romanesque de quelques oeuvres d'art dans *Corinne* de Mme de Staël," in her *Madame de Staël: écrire, lutter, vivre*, 111–35.

32. Staël, *De l'Allemagne*, 3:380.

Performances of the Gaze: Staël's *Corinne, or Italy*

This essay is an adaptation of chapter 7, *Subject to Change: Reading Feminist Writing* (New York: Columbia University Press, 1988).

1. Mary Ann Doane, "Woman's Stake," 34.

2. It also seems worth stressing the point that most discussions of the gaze and its sex assume a heterosexual paradigm of white male dominance. The question of the female gaze within this economy (and outside its politics) is now beginning to be elaborated. This reading of *Corinne* is one piece of a possible reworking of the concept. Joan DeJean has proposed a modeling of the female gaze as an act of memorialization beginning with Sappho. See also the work of Mary Ann Doane and the collection of essays by German feminists, *Feminist Aesthetics* (1985), several of which address this issue.

3. *Corinne, or Italy*, trans. Avriel Goldberger (New Brunswick, NJ: Rutgers University Press, 1987), 19. Subsequent references by page number are to the same edition, and occasionally—as indicated—to the French text *Corinne ou l'Italie*, ed. Simone Balayé (Paris: Gallimard Folio, 1985).

4. Monique Wittig, "The Straight Mind," 110.

5. Like Charrière writing at the end of the century (*Caliste*, 1788; *Mistress Henley*, 1784), Staël builds here on a line of inadequate men in the novels of eighteenth-century women writers. Oswald joins Riccoboni's Alfred, Ossery and Marquis de Cressy, Tencin's Barbasan and Comminge, as a man insufficiently aware of the superiority of the woman in love with him, and blind to his own flaws. This double blindness sometimes reverses itself in the end, but more typically, recognition of what has been lost comes too late. At the same time, Oswald belongs to the heroes of his own generation, that of the *mal du siècle*; Adolphe, of course, and most famously, René. He is, in Margaret Waller's apt phrase, a "mâle du siècle," whose malady has as crucial symptoms the

inability to assume the life plot set out for him by the paternal maxims; and anguished impotence in the face of the requirements to form a couple and take his legitimate place in the social text.

6. This framing vision of the man's refusal to be moved by a spectacular performance that leaves him instead fixed as the judge of woman is rewritten in Charlotte Brontë's *Villette*. When Lucy Snowe and Dr. John ("that cool young Briton!") watch at the theater in Brussels the "marvelous sights: a mighty revelation," a "spectacle, low, horrible, immoral" of Vashti (Brontë's translation of the French actress Rachel), Lucy in ecstasy at the performance discovers that the doctor is really a man: "'How did he like Vashti?' I wished to know. 'Hm-m-m' was the first scarce articulate answer . . . In a few terse phrases he told me his opinion of and feeling towards, the actress: he judged her as a woman, not an artist: it was a branding judgment" (New York: Penguin, 1983), 399, 422. There is a homologous effect in *The Princess of Clèves* when by the narrator's perspective the reader is given to see the "chain of three men" watching the princess contemplate Nemours's portrait. Michael Danahy, "Social, Sexual, and Human Spaces in *La Princesse de Clèves*," *French Forum* 6, no. 3 (September 1981): 219.

7. In her sharp and witty introduction to a special feminist issue of *Paragraph* (Autumn 1986), Diana Knight reviews Geoff Bennington's play on the derivations of theory and the procession as the "locus of theory" through Woolf's speculation on the "procession of educated men" in *Three Guineas*. I am grateful to Helen Foley for her remarks on theory and theater.

8. Thus as Oswald—in Rome—contemplates the production of *Romeo and Juliet*, he worries about loving a superior woman. Like his father, he fears her excess: "she was too remarkable in every domain" (125). Like Staël's novel, the text of a woman's excess overflows (literary) categories: "elle était trop remarquable *en tout genre*" (Balayé 192).

9. Jane Gallop, *The Daughter's Seduction*, 58.

10. Doane, "Woman's Stake," 31.

11. Luce Irigaray, *This Sex*, 129, 131; Julia Kristeva, *Revolution*, 26.

12. Hélène Cixous, *La venue à l'écriture*, 245, 249.

13. Mikhail Bakhtin, *The Dialogic Imagination*, 345.

14. George Eliot, *The Mill on the Floss*, 432–33.

15. John Berger, *Ways of Seeing*, 47.

16. For a discussion of Kristeva's model of abjection and its relation to the material—its potential and danger for feminist theory—see Mary Russo's "Female Grotesques: Carnival and Theory," *Feminist Studies/Critical Studies*, ed. Teresa de Lauretis (Bloomington: Indiana University Press, 1986), 219–21; and Gayatri Spivak's critical response to Kristeva's work on the subject in "The Politics of Interpretations" (278).

17. As Staël writes in the chapter on love in *De l'influence des passions* (1796): "Oh women! you are the victims of the temple where they say you are worshipped, listen to me. It is true the love that women inspire gives them a moment of absolute power; but in life taken as a whole, even in the development of a feeling, their wretched fate reclaims its ineluctable dominion" *Oeuvres complètes* (Paris: Treuttel et Wurtz, 1820–21, 4: 169; translation is my own). The novel charts the taking back of the power that Corinne had exercised in her person. As Castel-Forte, Erfeuil, and Corinne herself had foreseen, returned to England, Oswald is released from the claims of the adored woman's charms.

The topography of the abyss [*l'abîme des douleurs*] is reminiscent of the metaphorics of *The New Eloise*, a novel central to Staël's remapping of eighteenth-century fiction. Her rewriting of the male precursor will be clearer in the invention of Julie-tte. The metaphors of the fall, of course, also recall "the romantic image of the artist" Maurice Shroder has emblematized in the figure of Icarus. But what happens when "the revolt of the son against his father" is carried out by a daughter? *The Image of the Artist in French Romanticism* (Cambridge: Harvard University Press, 1961), 56.

18. Colette, *The Vagabond*, 47–48.

Melancholia, Mania and the Reproduction of the Dead Father

Thanks for this article go to the participants in my graduate seminar on women novelists at New York University in the fall of 1990, and notably to Mary Helen McMurran, for her contributions on Staël and sensibility. Thanks also go to Margaret Waller, who kindly showed me her incisive chapter on *Corinne* in *The Male Malady* while the book was in manuscript form, and whose analysis of Oswald's melancholy has informed my own.

I have occasionally modified English translation (*Corinne, or Italy*, trans. Avriel Goldberger, Rutgers University Press, 1987) in order to render more literally linguistic nuances essential to my argument. When my discussion leans on a linguistic nuance evident only in French, I have included a reference to the French original along with the English translation (*Corinne ou l'Italie*, Simone Balayé ed., Gallimard, 1985). Translations of all other citations from French texts are my own.

1. Miller, *Subject to Change*, 174.

2. Corinne's performances, Staël stresses, excel for the strength of the response that they elicit in their audience; so, Corinne's first improvisation is above all notable for inspiring "an emotion in the listener as vivid as it is unexpected" (31).

3. I develop this argument in *Compromising Positions: The Literary Struggles Engendering the Modern Novel in France*. My published essays on the subject include a generic description of the sentimental social novel: "In Lieu of a Chapter on Some French Women Realist Novelists" (where I provisionally termed the "sentimental social novel" the "feminine social novel"). They also include an overview of the importance of gender in French novelistic struggles of the first half of the nineteenth century: "Women and Fiction in the Nineteenth Century."

4. See *Compromising Positions*.

5. Focusing on the father-obsessed *Le Père Goriot*, Sandy Petrey, for example, writes: "Paternal dissolution in *Le Père Goriot* is consequently a game with deadly implications, for the Name of the Father was associated, explicitly and interminably, with the survival of the state." See Petrey, *Realism and Revolution*, 90.

6. Kofman, *Mélancolie de l'art*, 44.

7. Balayé, *Madame de Staël*, 147.

8. Staël, *De l'Allemagne*, 2: 47.

9. Staël, *Essai sur les fictions*, 1: 128.

10. Lipking, "Aristotle's Sister: A Poetics of Abandonment," 98.

11. Allart, *Lettres sur les ouvrages de Madame de Staël*, 90.

12. Waller, *The Male Malady*, 64.

13. Freud, "Mourning and Melancholia" in *Standard Edition*, 14:251.

14. Ibid., 249.

15. Ibid.

16. Ibid.

17. Althusser's classic discussion of reproduction is found in "Ideology and Ideological State Apparatuses" in *Lenin and Philosophy*.

18. Waller, *The Male Malady*, 80. Waller continues, "the father figure's . . . absence means that his power is nowhere and therefore everywhere, impossible to combat" (82).

19. A rich bibliography exists on the complex relation of Staël's narrative to the French Revolution. Texts important to my understanding of the subject include the previously mentioned works by Balayé, Miller, and Waller, as well as Madelyn Gutwirth's *Madame de Staël, Novelist*.

20. Bonald, "Du style et de la littérature" (1806), in *Mélanges littéraires, politiques et philosophiques*, quoted in Margaret Iknayan, *The Idea of the Novel in France: The Critical Reaction 1815–1848*, 42. On Staël's view of England as the land of the bourgeoisie, see her comments in *De la littérature*.

21. Ménard, "Madame de Staël et la peinture," 261.

22. To explain France's continued subjection to the power of the dead king, it would be illuminating to pursue Robert Hertz's anthropological work on the difficulties of burying "those who die a violent death" (at moments, Oswald feels himself the murderer of his father). "They are often the objects of special rites," Hertz remarks; "their unquiet and spiteful souls roam the earth for ever; or, if they emigrate to another world, they live in a separate village, sometimes even in a completely different area from that inhabited by other souls." See Hertz, "The Collective Representation of Death," 85.

Hertz's analysis isolates a second social factor which could plausibly explain the difficulty of giving proper burial to the French king; the fact that when the head of a community dies, this death is accompanied by a socially destabilizing release of passion: "It often seems that the blow which strikes the head of the community in the sacred person of the chief has the effect of suspending temporarily the moral and political laws and of setting free the passions which are normally kept in check by the social order" (49).

23. Freud, 243, emphasis added.

24. Ibid., 253.

25. Ibid., 254, 255.

26. Ibid., 255.

27. Ibid., 254.

28. Gutwirth, *Madame de Staël, Novelist*, 203.

29. Freud, 254, 255.

30. Gutwirth writes: "Fathers represent not only public opinion and conscience, but seemingly fate itself" (225).

31. The adolescent failure of Corinne's relation to the fathers may itself reduplicate her father's absence during her childhood. But in applying psychoanalysis to a novel, we must, of course, stick to the details we are given about the characters; we cannot hypothesize that they have a life beyond the text.

32. On the power of the fathers in *Corinne*, Miller observes, "the novel . . . is a book about the fathers as an authorizing, all powerful location and body of intention; about the name of the father, about the fatherland, about the

organization of separate spheres in which the letter of the father's law compels the son's desire, and the daughter seeks to inhabit another, perhaps maternal space" (165–66).

33. Freud, 255.

34. Waller, *The Male Malady*, 68.

Staël's *Corinne:* The Novel's Other Dilemma

This essay first appeared in *Stanford French Review* 11 (1987): 77–87.

1. Naomi Schor, "Unwriting *Lamiel*," *Breaking the Chain*, 145.

2. On the end of the salon tradition, see Sophie Gay's *Salons célèbres*, (Dumont 1837). Gay viewed the salon of Suzanne Curchod Necker, Staël's mother, and that of Staël herself as the last true salons.

3. Georges May, *Le dilemme du roman*, 71.

4. Hélène Cixous, *La venue à l'écriture*, 61.

5. Ibid., 54.

6. Ibid., 55.

7. Haussonville, *Le salon de Madame Necker*, 1: 15. Haussonville provides much valuable information on Suzanne Curchod's youthful salon activities and on her *précieuse* writings.

8. Staël, *Journal de jeunesse*, 236.

9. Staël, *Lettres sur J.-J Rousseau*, 21; Jean-Jacques Rousseau, *Lettre à d'Alembert*, 138–39, n. 2 in *Oeuvres complètes*.

10. Cixous, *La venue à l'écriture*, 55.

11. Helen Borowitz, "The Unconfessed *Précieuse*," 36–38.

12. Sainte-Beuve, *Portraits*, 86; Madelyn Gutwirth, *Madame de Staël, Novelist*, 187.

13. Cixous, *La venue à l'écriture*, 55.

14. Gutwirth, *Madame de Staël, Novelist*, 173.

15. *Corinne ou l'Italie*, ed. Simone Balayé (Paris: Gallimard, 1985), 555. Subsequent parenthetical references are to the same edition. Translations are my own.

16. Staël, *Sapho* in *Oeuvres complètes*, 316.

17. Cixous, *La venue à l'écriture*, 55.

18. By putting lengthy citations from Necker's *Cours de morale religieuse* in the mouth of Oswald's dead father, Staël identified her own dead father with the fathers in her novel. Staël's composite paternal portrait may be more complex still, for elsewhere—most strikingly in the *Lettres sur J.-J. Rousseau*—she suggests an identification between Necker and Rousseau. On this point, see M. Gutwirth, "Madame de Staël, Rousseau and the Woman Question."

Voice as Fossil; Germaine de Staël's *Corinne, or Italy:* An Archaeology of Feminine Discourse

This essay, translated by Betsy Wing, first appeared in *Tulsa Studies* 6 (1987): 47–60.

1. See Christopher Herold, *Mistress to an Age*, 93.

2. See Simone Balayé, "Madame de Staël, Napoléon et la mission de l'écrivain," 125.

3. I remind the English reader that *femelle* in French is always pejorative.

4. Staël, *Lettres sur les écrits de J.-J. Rousseau* in *Oeuvres complètes*, 1: 1.

5. Sigmund Freud, "Hysterical Phantasies and their Relation to Bisexuality," *Standard Edition*, 9:159.

6. Charles-Augustin Sainte-Beuve, "Madame de Staël" in *Portraits de femmes, Oeuvres complètes*, 1061.

7. Pierre Kohler, *Madame de Staël et la Suisse*, 53.

8. Staël, *De l'Allemagne* in *Oeuvres complètes*, 2: 217.

9. *Lettres sur les écrits de J.-J. Rousseau*, 1: 1.

10. Staël, *Essai sur les fictions* in *Oeuvres complètes*, 1: 21. It may be according to this curious logic of the "extra" that women writers are referred to with the extra title "Madame" or with the mention of their first name, when the title "Monsieur" would sound ridiculous for a male writer.

11. Alain Girard, *Le journal intime* (subsequently cited in the text as *JI*), 23. *Journal de jeunesse* of Germaine de Staël was published in *Occident et Cahiers staëliens* 1–4 (1930–32). I further scrutinize this problematic question of the opposition of the public/private as contrasted to the Staëlian opposition public/particular in "Exclusion des femmes et modernité dans les écrits politiques de Germaine de Staël" in *Le Groupe de Coppet et l'Europe, 1789–1830.*

12. Sigmund Freud and Josef Breuer, "The Mechanism of Hysterical Phenomena," *Standard Edition*, 2: 13.

13. The name Delphine is in classical mythology "Delphyne," the name of a dragon—half-woman, half-snake—that was attached to the oracle of Delphi, whose original possessor was Gaia (the Earth). Later the oracle became the possession of Apollo, and the dragon seemed to have been replaced by a Sibyl, the inspired prophetess called Pythia. The word *pythia* uttered in ecstasy was often obscure and enigmatical, couched in ambiguous and metaphorical expressions that needed interpretation. The heroine Corinne, on the other hand, is often compared to the legendary Erythraean Sibyl who is supposed to have brought to Italy the Sibylline books of prophecy (a collection of oracular utterances in Greek hexameters. See O. Seyffert, *Dictionary of Classical Antiquities* (New York: Meridian Library, 1958).

14. Meant here is the ideological interpellation of the subject in Louis Althusser's sense. See "Idéologie et appareils idéologiques d'Etat" in *Positions* (Paris: Editions Sociales, 1970), 67–125.

15. Napoleon's line, reworked by Freud and commented on by Sarah Kofman, *L'Enigme de la femme,* 146.

16. See Simone Balayé, *Les carnets de voyage de Madame de Staël,* 16.

17. Robert de Luppé, ed., *Madame de Staël et J.B.A. Suard. Correspondance inédite* (letter of 9 April 1805), 25.

18. For the detailed analysis of this process of metaphorical substitution, see my book *Fictions féminines: Germaine de Staël et les voix de la Sibylle.*

19. *Corinne ou l'Italie,* ed. Simone Balayé (Paris: Gallimard, 1985), 57. Subsequent parenthetical references are to the same edition. Translation is my own.

20. Sigmund Freud, *Délires et rêves dans 'Gradiva' de Jensen,* 142. Kofman has analyzed the fictional dimension of Freud's reading in *Gradiva: Quatre romans analytiques* (Paris: Galilée, 1973), 101–33. It is to shed light on the

effect of this reading regarding the notion of author and voice that we discuss it here.

21. *Delusions and Dreams in Jensen's 'Gradiva', Standard Edition,* 9:90.

22. Ibid., 54.

23. Freud, "Hysterical Phantasies," 9:159.

24. Roland Mortier, in *La Poétique des ruines en France,* has brilliantly analyzed the thematic variations of the ruin motif. His work is reinterpreted from a psychoanalytic perspective here. In this light the melancholy attitude of the observer of ruins began to disclose the possibility of a connection to fetishism (cf. Freud, "Fetishism," *Standard Edition,* 21: 152–59). The lost object is, in fact, described in a contradictory manner in "Fetishism" as simultaneously the "mother's penis" and the mark "of the lack of a penis." The fetish is thus presented as a sort of ambiguous "memorial substitute." The indecidability of the melancholy memorial as it concerns sexual identity, implicit in Freud's text, is fully exploited in the Staëlian novel. The analysis of the fetishism of ruins is clarified elsewhere in Jean Baudrillard's study, "Fétichisme et idéologie: la réduction sémiologique," in *Pour une critique de l'économie politique du signe* (Paris: Gallimard, 1982), 93–113.

25. See Madame de Staël, *De la littérature* in *Oeuvres complètes,* 1: 170.

26. See Sigmund Freud's *L'Inquiétante étrangeté.* "It is a matter of returning to certain phases in the developmental history of the awareness of the Ego, a regression to the period in which the Ego was not yet clearly defined in relation to the external world and to others," 186–87. The relationship between mother and melancholy is developed by Melanie Klein in "Mourning and Its Relations to Manic-depressive States," in *Love, Guilt and Other Works* (New York: Delta Books, 1975), 186–95.

27. See Julia Kristeva, "Noms de lieux," in *Polylogue,* where putting the proper name or patronym into question is presented in the following manner: "This archaeology of naming (spatial marker, demonstratives, 'topic,' a person's name) and what is undecidable about the subject-object relationship accompanying it on the psychoanalytic level (potential space, primary narcissism, auto-eroticism, sado-masochism) will have a connection to the confused reflections of logicians on the semantics of proper names" (489).

28. We are establishing a parallelism between the strategies of Staëlian writing and those identified by Kristeva in Mallarmé: "what is it that the poet unearths from the paradoxical semiosis of the newborn, of that 'semiotic chora,' of that 'space' before the sign, the archaic organization of primary narcissism, in order to defy the closing off of senses" (Ibid., 479).

29. Ibid. This opens up an interesting question of the relationship of the feminine quest for the mother and the patriarchal ideology of "maternity" which was put in place, first during the 1789 Revolution by the republican, then by Napoleon's civil legislation. In this perspective see Madelyn Gutwirth's *The Twilight of the Goddesses: Women and Representation in the French Revolutionary Era.*

30. The notion of voice is taken here in the different senses set forth by Guy Rosolato in "The Voice," in *Essais sur le symbolique* (Paris: Gallimard, 1964). "Literary voice in the linguistic sense, linked to the system of pronouns or the verb system (passive, active, pronominal), or the 'relative' voice linked to the question of the 'Name of the Father' and finally the voice in the sense of origin that sustains the fantasies of a unity, ambisexuality and that in that case, becomes the 'not-lost object'" (304). Hélène Cixous and Catherine Clé-

ment stress the specific relationship to voice in what is described as "feminine writing" in *La Jeune née,* 170.

31. For theft and kleptomania defined in feminist theory as characteristically feminine, see *La Jeune née,* 178.

32. See Cixous's "Le rire de la Méduse" and also Demeter's laughter when faced with Baubo in Kofman, *L'Enigme de la femme,* 146.

33. François Auguste René de Chateaubriand, *Mémoires d'outre-tombe,* 3: 256.

Places of Memory: History Writing in Staël's *Corinne*

1. Recent discussions of Staël's history writing have focused primarily on this work. See, for example, Michel Delon, "Germaine de Staël and Other Possible Scenarios of the French Revolution" and Charlotte Hogsett, "Generative Factors in *Considerations on the French Revolution,* both in *Germaine de Staël: Crossing the Borders.* See also Linda Orr's "Outspoken Women and the Rightful Daughter of the Revolution: Madame de Staël's *Considérations sur la Révolution française*" and Charlotte Hogsett's *The Literary Existence of Germaine de Staël.*

2. English quotations of the text (referenced by the numbers in parentheses) are from Avriel Goldberger's translation and edition, *Corinne, or Italy* (New Brunswick, NJ: Rutgers University Press, 1987). Quotations in the original French are from Simone Balayé's edition, *Corinne ou l'Italie* (Paris: Gallimard, 1985).

3. On the social composition of the Idéologue milieu, see Martin Staum, "The Class of Moral and Political Sciences: 1795–1803."

4. Constantin-François Volney, "Les Leçons d'histoire," in *Oeuvres complètes de Volney.* Volney delivered these lectures at the newly founded Ecole normale, centerpiece of the Idéologues' educational project. The school's inauguration in 1794 was considered a major cultural event, and many of France's leading intellectuals—including Fourier, Bougainville, and Germaine de Staël—were in attendance. See Sergio Moravia, *Il Tramonto dell'illuminismo: filosofia e politica nella società francese 1770–1810* (Bari: Laterza, 1968).

5. One of the earliest and most original analyses of the relation of vision to subjectivity in travel writing is Mary Louise Pratt's "Scratches on the Face of the Country; or, What Mr. Barrow Saw in the Land of the Bushmen." See also Johannes Fabian, *Time and the Other: How Anthropology Makes its Object.*

6. "J'ai pensé que le genre des voyages appartenait à l'histoire, et non aux romans." Preface to *Voyage en Egypte et en Syrie.* The translation of Volney's text as well as those of Destutt de Tracy, Pierre Nora, and Simone Balayé cited below are mine.

7. "La première cause de toute erreur est l'imperfection des souvenirs" (*Eléments,* 3: 543).

8. "L'imagination dans le sens de mémoire vive qui prend ses souvenirs pour des impressions actuelles et réelles, c'est la mémoire unie à un jugement erroné" (*Eléments,* 3: 442).

9. See the very thoughtful explication of the novel's title in Marie-Claire Vallois' *Fictions féminines: Mme de Staël et les voix de la Sibylle.*

10. "La mémoire s'enracine dans le concret, dans l'espace, le geste, l'image et l'objet." Pierre Nora, "Entre Mémoire et Histoire: la problématique des lieux" in *Les Lieux de mémoire*, xix.

11. "Parce qu'elle est affective et magique, la mémoire ne s'accommode que des détails qui la confortent; elle se nourrit de souvenirs flous, télescopants, globaux ou flottants, particuliers ou symboliques, sensible à tous les transferts, écrans, censure ou projections. L'histoire, parce que opération intellectuelle et laïcisante, appelle analyse et discours critique. La mémoire installe le souvenir dans le sacré, l'histoire l'en débusque, elle prosaïse toujours" (*Les Lieux*, xix).

12. Sigmund Freud, *Civilization and its Discontents*, 16. Freud often compared the task of the analyst to that of an archaeologist. See, for example, his article "Construction in Analysis," *Standard Edition of the Complete Psychological Works of Sigmund Freud,* vol. 23.

13. Simone Balayé, "Corinne et la ville italienne: ou l'espace extérieur et l'impasse intérieure," 38.

14. See Linda Orr, "The Revenge of Literature: A History of History."

15. "Le vrai est souvent incomplet dans ces effets," (*Essai sur les fictions*, 42). The English translations from *Essai* are mine.

16. "Les circonstances marquantes que l'histoire consacre laissent d'immenses intervalles où peuvent se placer les malheurs et les torts dont se composent cependant la plupart des destinées privées" (*Essai*, 43).

Corinne: Political Polemics and the Theory of the Novel

1. The subsequent quotations refer to *Essai sur les fictions* and *De la littérature* in *Oeuvres complètes*, 1: 62–72, 196–334. Translations are mine.

2. Staël, *De la littérature,* part 1, chap. 4.

3. Ibid., chap. 8.

4. Ibid., chap. 9.

5. Robert Nelson, "The Quarrel of the Ancients and the Moderns," 364–69.

6. See her *Des Circonstances actuelles qui peuvent terminer la Révolution et des principes qui peuvent fonder la République en France.*

7. Staël, *Essai sur les fictions,* 67–69.

8. Staël, *De la littérature,* part 2, chap. 5.

9. Georges May, "The Influence of English Fiction on the French Mid-Eighteenth-Century Novel," 265–80.

10. Staël, *Essai sur les fictions,* 66–68.

11. Melvin Richter, *The Political Thought of Montesquieu,* 270–71.

12. *De la littérature,* part 1, chap. 15 and chap. 10.

13. *Corinne, or Italy,* trans. Avriel Goldberger, books 6–11, passim. Further parenthetical references are to this edition.

14. Richter, *Political Thought,* 214–19.

15. See Ellen Moers, "Performing Heroinism: The Myth of Corinne" in *Literary Women,* 173–210.

16. *Corinne,* book 2, chap. 2; book 4, chap. 2.

17. Ibid., book 4.

18. Staël, *Essai sur les fictions,* 66.

19. Ibid., 70.

20. Staël, *De la littérature*, 302.

Tracing a Sisterhood: Corilla Olimpica as Corinne's Unacknowledged Alter Ego

The author gratefully acknowledges the encouragement and constructive criticism of April Alliston, Josephine Diamond, and Karyna Szmurlo.

1. *Corinne, or Italy,* trans. Avriel Goldberger (New Brunswick, NJ: Rutgers University Press, 1987), 431. Translations of *Corinne* are primarily from this edition. All other translations from French and Italian texts are mine.

2. Corilla's crowning took place on 31 August 1776. Arcadia is the most representative literary institution of eighteenth-century Italy. At a time when academies and salons were the center of cultural life, Arcadia counted colonies in all the major Italian cities. In fact, membership in Arcadia outnumbered the cumulative membership of all other Italian academies of that time (Maylender, *Storia delle Accademie,* 270). For this reason Arcadia has been called the first national academy and the first cultural phenomenon to unify Italy (Natali, *Il Settecento,* 6). All the most prominent literary figures of the time, including Parini, Verri, Alfieri, and of course, Monti, belonged to it. Staël was made an honorary member of Arcadia on her 14 February 1805 visit to the Roman seat of the Academy. Corilla's activity belongs to what some historians have called the *seconda Arcadia;* that is, a second flourishing of the academy's prominence in the years 1770 to 1780 (see, for example, Dionisotti, "Ricordo di Cimante Micenio," and Felici, "L'Arcadia romana"). On Arcadia's poetics of enthusiasm, see also my forthcoming *Enlightenment, Arcadia and Corilla.*

3. Corilla was accused of obtaining the topics of her twelve improvisations in advance. Her coronation was contingent upon her satisfactory performance at these exams. There is a flagrant contradiction between these accusations and the subsequent events of Corilla's life. Some of the most distinguished members of the nobility and of the literary world published the acts of her coronation three years later, which included several dozens of sonnets and poems written in her honor. As a consequence of her renewed prestige, she received further honors from various crowns in Europe.

4. On *Corinne's* portrayal of the predicament of the woman of genius, see for example Miller, *Subject to Change,* 296, and Peel, "Contradictions of Form," 282. The sense of entitlement, the success, the achievement, and the recognition accorded Corinne by Italian society strikes some commentators as incongruous: "Ideal" or "utopian" or "a land of women" is the Italy that allows such a phenomenon to take place (see, for example, Gutwirth, *Madame de Staël, Novelist,* 211, 214–15; Moers, 187, 201 ff.; Miller, *Subject to Change,* 176; Peel, *Contradictions of Form,* 291). We shall argue that Staël's Italy is no utopia with respect to the place of Corinne in its society. Some critics comment positively on the use of improvisation as a medium of the protagonist's genius. Joan DeJean sees it as "the mark of Staël's literary heritage . . . a way of keeping the oral female web alive in literature ("Dilemma," 81). For others "it seems odd de Staël would devalue writing in a written work" (Peel 291) and "it is paradoxically when she is no longer performing that Corinne becomes the figure of the woman writer, that she comes finally . . . to writing" (Miller 194).

I shall argue that the issues at the heart of the novel do not hinge on the subordination of oral to written, of improvisation to writing.

5. Schlegel, "Une étude critique," 61. "The name of Corinne," Staël wrote, "should not be confused with that of Corilla, the Italian *improvisatrice* everybody has heard of; Corinne was a Greek woman well known for her lyric poetry; Pindar himself studied with her" (431).

6. Among the commentators who associated Corilla and Corinne are Schlegel, Casanova, Dejob, Ademollo, Vernon Lee, Gennari, Natali, Balayé, and Peel. It is also noteworthy that Casanova in his *Mémoires* (vol. 6, chap. 14) refers to Corilla Olimpica as "Corinne." See Natali, *Il Settecento*, 1: 165.

7. Blurbs on Corilla in recent anthologies (for example, Costa-Zalossow's) are ultimately based on Ademollo's 1887 biography, through the mediation of two twentieth-century bio-bibliographies (De Blasi 1934; Buti 1942).

8. Gennari, *Le Premier voyage*, 142.

9. See Staël's *Correspondance*, 501. During her visit of the academy, Staël could not have missed Corilla's bust, prominently displayed at the entrance of the Serbatoio d'Arcadia. Records of Staël's visit can also be found in the Roman chronicle *Diario* and in the *Atti Arcadici* for the year 1805.

For a list of Staël's readings during her trip to Italy, see Balayé, *Carnets*, 110. For details on the relationship between Cesarotti and Staël, see Luchaire, "Lettres de V. Monti," 244–45, and *Atti*, 58. Cesarotti is mentioned in *Corinne*'s chapter on "Italian Literature." Teresa Bandettini Landucci (1763–1837), together with Fortunata Sulgher (1755–1824) were the most famous performing improvisers at the time of Staël's trip to Italy in 1805. Corilla's last extant verses, a sort of poetic testament, were dedicated to Landucci, whom Corilla identified as the heir to her poetic laurels. A few of Staël's letters to Landucci are reported in her *Correspondance*.

10. In his November 1776 *Correspondance* Grimm wrote: "Prince Gonzaga, companion of Mme Corilla, the famous improviser he had crowned in Rome in spite of the *cabala* that opposed her triumph, has been here [in Paris] for a few days" (11: 365). When Corilla finds refuge in Florence there is Gonzaga with her, as Castel-Forte is with Corinne.

11. The *Atti* were, and still are, held by the library of the literary academy "Arcadia" in Rome. Staël probably had a copy made when she visited the Academy. A. W. Schlegel, who traveled with her, was aware of the existence of this document. Another document Staël might have consulted is the positively raving review of Corilla's crowning by Count d'Albon (249).

12. Balayé, "*Corinne* et la presse parisiennne," 6–7. For the general public's response to *Corinne*, see Balayé, "*Corinne* et les amis," 139–49.

13. The identification of Corinne with Germaine de Staël did not substantially alter the critics' final judgment of Corinne as an "ideal" character. See, for example, Constant, "De Madame de Staël," 3.

14. Schlegel, "*Une étude critique,*" 61 and 59; my emphasis.

15. Silvagni, *La corte e la società romana*, 235.

16. Ademollo, *Corilla Olimpica*, 413; Burney is quoted ibid., 129. For a study of Corinne as a Sapphic character, see DeJean, "Portrait of the Artist as Sappho," 127.

17. Corilla Olimpica (Maria Maddalena Morelli), *Corilla Olimpica, Pastorella d' Arcadia, a' dilettissimi suoi Cavalieri* (Siena 1761), 2.

18. "Con umiltade a lato / vi vuol nobile orgoglio / non sale in Campidoglio / chi ha in seno la viltà" (qtd. in Ademollo 272).

19. Corilla's will as well as some official documents bearing Corilla's literary name can be found in Ademollo (413, 410).

20. To attend to her niece's needs, Corilla refused a highly honorific position at the court of Catherine the Second of Russia. Later in life, as a widow and the head of a household of seven, Corilla adopted her niece and made her a universal heir. On eighteenth-century Italian legislation on women, see *Donne e diritto,* ix.

21. De Lauretis, "The essence of the Triangle," 22.

22. The hall is thus described in the *Atti:*

On the one end of the room there was a platform surmounted by a canopy. On the platform was a throne, and hanging over it, a portrait of the Pope. On a step leading up to the throne there were four seats for the Conservators of the Senate.... The chair for Corilla was on the step below the senator's. At the opposite end of the room, the chairs for the crowd, the common people. On the sides, seats for the noblemen and for the Arcadi.... Corilla knelt in front of the Conservators and she was crowned with laurel by the first among them." (*Atti*, 35–37)

Staël wrote:

At the far end of the reception hall stood the Conservators of the Senate and the senator who was to crown her. On the one side were all the cardinals and the most eminent women of the land: on the other, the men of letters of the Roman Academy. The opposite side of the room was filled by part of the immense throng that had followed Corinne. The chair meant for her was set on the step below the senator's. As custom decreed, before sitting down she bent her knee on the first step, in full view of the assembly. (*Corinne*, 22)

23. Abundant examples of the verbal war waged against and around the crowning can be found in the "Pizzi-Corilleide," a 1776 manuscript collecting indiscriminately libels against Corilla (including some defiling her name under her name/in her own persona), poems in her praise, and some of Corilla's own work.

24. Amaduzzi's letter is quoted in Ademollo 281. Indeed a crowd had gathered to take part in the ceremony: a document mentions at least three thousand people (299); the *Atti* mention an "innumerable crowd." Staël wrote that an "immense throng" had accompanied Corinne.

25. According to the *Atti,* the "poets of Rome" read a prose encomium, six sonnets and an ode in honor of Corilla. Many more would have wanted to pay tribute to Corilla, but it was appropriate to leave the floor to the crowned poet's improvisations. All of these unexpressed tributes to Corilla, and many more written afterwards, were published in an appendix to the *Atti:* dozens of sonnets and odes. On reading these poetical homages one shares *Corinne's* narrator's opinion that most of them were rather conventional.

26. Whether Godard was able to provide Staël with Corilla's work or just clues (according to the *Atti,* Corilla's *canzoniere,* now lost, was at the time preserved at the Academy), Staël interpreted Corilla's story according to her personal understanding of the woman writer's predicament.

27. For the topic of Corilla's improvising, see *Atti,* 74–76. Corilla commented on the significance of her crowning, at the request of the Custode d'Arcadia Pizzi, but her reflections on the subject have not been reported. We do have reports of Corilla's own defense of her right to the crown during the examinations which were part of the confirmation process (qtd. in Ademollo 272–74).

28. The Parisian correspondent for the Florentine gazette *Notizie del mondo*, for example, reports (9 April 1777) on the debate as it was taking shape in France (qtd. in Grigioni 272).

Ademollo, Corilla's biographer, likes to present the war over Corilla as a contest between Jesuits and anti-Jesuits for their preeminence over the Pope. In fact, her opponents cannot be easily categorized; they represent society's largest latent and patent gynophobia, if not misogyny.

29. See, respectively, Vitagliano's *Storia della poesia estemporanea;* Lancetti's *Memorie dei poeti laureati;* and, on Corilla, *Atti della solenne coronazione.*

30. Casanova, *Mémoires,* 2: 698–99 and 3: 796.

31. This at least was the expectation of her friends and supporters, which can be found in Corilla's correspondence (Amaduzzi, "Papers").

32. Corilla Olimpica to Giovanni C. Amaduzzi, 16 December 1776, 15 October 1776, and 14 January 1777, respectively; Amaduzzi, "Papers"); also partially qtd. in Grigioni, 267–68.

33. Corilla lived a rewarding, long life; she died at seventy-three years of age, still admired by many, the head of a household of seven. Her solemn funeral ceremony organized by the French General Miollis in 1800 took place in that very Hall of the Florentine Academy where Corinne pronounced her own spiritual testament. It included the reading of poetry and eulogies in her honor.

34. In her *Des circonstances actuelles* Staël addresses the issue: "What peace, what happiness can any court return to a woman attacked in the papers? Her family may be permanently disturbed; her husband may have lost his respect for her; a man who loved her may have left her because she has lost that affecting charm endowed by a quiet life devoted entirely to the object who took her gift. Finally, do these slanderers know the depths to which they have put life in turmoil? They accuse a gentle soul with their cruel opinion. They only hurt the souls they should be treating kindly" (119).

35. Gutwirth, *Madame de Staël, Novelist,* 292.

36. Corilla did not die of sorrow, but she wrote: "Excellent Roman fathers, it is not true that one can die of sorrow: it is the foolish deception of a passionate and insincere heart. If it were true, I would have perished of a broken heart." [Padri eccelsi del Tebro: oh non è vero / Che di dolor si muoia: E' folle inganno / Di cuor appassionato, e menzognero / Se fosse ver, morta sarei d'affanno, "Pizzi-Corilleide," 243]. Her poetic self did succumb though to the grueling trial months after her crowning. In another poem "Tornai del Tebro alla città Signora" [I Returned to the City of the Tiber, "Pizzi-Corilleide," 92] she reveals she returns to Rome to repossess the poetic gift that pain had taken away.

37. The novel does not deny the existence of patriarchy in Italy, and Corinne's statements about her country's "open mindedness" should be put in perspective: First, Corinne's comments frequently refer to her friends, who are a progressive elite. Even so, these friends are not said to have condoned her compromising behavior. Second, to avoid separation from Oswald, Corinne openly deceives him about her country's liberal nature and willingly lets Oswald compromise her (187).

38. In her combination of Southern imagination and a Northern metaphysical interest, Corinne embodies the new Arcadian poetics espoused by Pizzi, and by a group of Italian intellectuals to which Corilla belonged, and who were

instrumental to her crowning. (For this group's attempt to poetic reform, see Felici, esp. 174–75; and Cipriani, "Contributo per una storia politica," 133 ff. and my article "The Poetics of *Seconda Arcadia*," 55 ff.) Castel-Forte's praise of Corinne can be seen as modeled on Abbot Godard's 1776 prose eulogy of Corilla (cf. *Corinne* 23 with *Atti* 46–47, 57).

39. See Prince Castel-Forte's strong words of praise: "And to foreigners we say: 'Gaze on her, for she is the image of our beautiful Italy; she is what we would be except for the ignorance, envy, discord and indolence to which our fate has condemned us'" (25). On the increasingly conservative political situation, see Cipriani 148–51; Landes, *Women in the Public Sphere*, 169; Gutwirth, *Madame de Staël, Novelist*, 296.

40. Foscolo, *Saggo d'un gazzettino del bel mondo*, 364 and 362, respectively. Corilla's crowning was so well known, that one did not need to be a scholar of the caliber of Foscolo to make the connection. The unknown reviewer of *Corinne* for the *Giornale bibliografico universale*, for example, had done so in 1807.

41. Schlegel, "Une étude critique," 61. "Metaphysical" is synonymous with abstruse, obscure, incomprehensible, for Foscolo.

42. Peel, "Contradictions of Form," 290–91; Miller, *Subject to Change*, 194.

43. Ademollo, *Corilla*, xvi–xviii.

44. See Gutwirth, *Madame de Staël, Novelist*, 206–7. As DeJean has noticed, Staël subversively reinterpreted the patriarchal myth of the female enchantress by revealing her iconoclastic potential: she is feared as a threat to the patriarchal order ("Sappho," 129).

45. On Perfetti, see Bouvy, "L'improvisation," 8–9. On Corilla, Bonstetten is emblematic; he does praise Corilla for her "knowledge of the human heart, [and her] lovely and fine spirit," but not without having previously noted that Corilla had allegedly admitted to him the relative inferiority of her talent: "Do not pay too much attention to my talent: when one is a real poet, one writes, and does not improvise" (qtd. in Gennari 142).

46. Lancetti 356–57. Lancetti does not openly accuse Amarilli of having known the topics in advance (even if such a conclusion is left open to any reader to make), but only of having found a formidable match in the abbot, who by improvising as well as she (but the ambiguous Italian formulation could also be taken to mean "improvising her very same beautiful verses") had deserved the crown as much as she.

47. Instead of the strong, exceptionally talented and proud artist, convinced of her right to develop her gifts and bear them to the world (see "Corilla Olimpica a' suoi Cavalieri"), nineteenth-century novels and plays presented a Corilla who, as a model of bourgeois domestic virtue, refused the Capitol crown to humbly devote her life to her family (see Ademollo xxi).

Corinne and Female Transmission: Rewriting *La Princesse de Clèves* through the English Gothic

Revised and adapted from chapter 6 in *Virtue's Faults: Correspondences in Eighteenth-Century British and French Women's Fiction* (Stanford: Stanford University Press, 1996).

1. The general argument encapsulated here is developed more fully in *Virtue's Faults*.

2. On the primacy of the mother-daughter dyad in *La Princesse de Clèves*, see Hirsch, "A Mother's Discourse," and Kamuf, *Fictions of Feminine Desire*.

3. *La Princesse de Clèves*, 53. All references to this novel, abbreviated here as *PC*, are to the Garnier-Flammarion edition. Textual references to Staël's novel indicate Avriel Goldberger's translation, *Corinne, or Italy* (New Brunswick, NJ: Rutgers University Press, 1987), and occasionally, Simone Balayé's edition, *Corinne ou l'Italie* (Paris: Gallimard, 1985).

See also Nancy Miller, who notes the echo of *La Princesse de Clèves* in Lucile's entrance into the opera house as the focus of the collective gaze (*Subject to Change*, 183). Miller grounds her reading of *Corinne* in its revisions of *La Princesse de Clèves* and, with reference to Peterson's *The Determined Reader*, of the *Aeneid*: "Lafayette's exquisitely crafted novel of a daughter's desire and a mother's match would seem to be radically refigured through what might properly be called an epic of female vocation: the extravagant staging of a woman's performance (demonstration) of what she wants" (163). I take off from this reading of the novel as revising a French female tradition through the founding patriarchal epic of the Roman empire; the resonance of Staël's correspondences with Lafayette needs the third note, of the female Gothic, of women's writing from *Corinne*'s fatherland, to be fully heard.

4. See also Kamuf, *Fictions of Feminine Desire*, 75, 81.

5. The Princess's inheritance is represented as a maternal one, a mother's will doubly figured in the moveable property of the jewels, which require a match—the proper patronym—and the miniature portrait which requires the daughter to live up to the maternal image of feminine perfection. On the jeweler's shop scene in *La Princesse de Clèves*, see Kamuf, *Fictions of Feminine Desire*, 72–73; Miller, *Subject to Change*, 162–64.

6. Writing is in general associated with the will of the dead father throughout *Corinne*, as has also been observed by Miller (who argues that the novel opposes a new feminist writing to patriarchal writing; *Subject to Change*, 171, 195), as well as by Peel ("Corinne's Shift," 103) and Peterson (*The Determined Reader*, 48).

7. This interpretation is argued fully in *Virtue's Faults*.

8. Peel, "Corinne's Shift," 105.

9. A similar play on *mer* and *mère* in the characterization of a Gothic mother occurs in Boisgiron, 3: 1.

10. Further references to Lee's novel in the text of this essay are denoted by *R*.

11. See also Peel: "The novel shows that the Italy/England opposition is too simple" ("Contradictions of Form," 288).

12. Cf. Peterson, *The Determined Reader*, 42–44; Miller, *Subject to Change*, 186–87; Moers, *Literary Women*, 200–3.

13. Historically, Italy obviously was not part of the British Empire, but it was part of Napoleon's, the emperor who exiled Staël herself.

14. Reading the novel as a revision of the *Aeneid*, for example, Carla Peterson notes that Corinne alternates among the roles of the Cumaean Sibyl, of Dido, and of Aeneas (55). Staël's characters do not simply repeat, but rather combine and transform the personae of the texts they invoke, and they do so across traditional gender norms.

15. On Oswald performing both roles with Corinne, see Miller, *Subject to Change*, 166; with Lucile, see above, 3–4, and below.

16. Mullan, *Sentiment and Sociability*, 112.

17. On the association of sensibility and femininity, see, for example, Marshall, *The Surprising Effects of Sympathy;* Mullan, *Sentiment and Sociability,* and Todd, *Sensibility.* The "Man of Feeling" was of course well known in Mackenzie's work of that title, as well as in Sterne (*A Sentimental Journey*), Richardson (*Grandison*), and Rousseau (*Julie*'s St.-Preux), yet these, like Staël's Oswald, are clearly feminized heroes according to the codes of the time, standing in contrast both to rakes like Lovelace and to patriarchs like Wolmar.

18. "Interest," in the sense of expressing interest, being interested in someone, is a key word in the vocabulary of sensibility, where it expresses a sympathetic relation toward a person quite the opposite of those based on "interested" views.

19. See Balayé's edition (175), where it is Italy, and not Italians as in the translation, which has been deprived of independence.

20. For women in this period, and especially for heroines in the eighteenth-century tradition that intervenes between Lafayette and Staël, virtue consisted in practically nothing other than passivity, the avoidance of fault through the avoidance of action, even in the face of the severest trials of Providence. See Alliston, "The Values of a Literary Legacy," 113–14.

21. See also Moers, who sees Oswald as modeled upon Richardson's Grandison (201).

22. I know of only one French Gothic novel, which pre-dates *Corinne* slightly: Anne Mérard de Saint-Just's *Le Château noir, ou Les Souffrances de la jeune Ophelle* (Paris, 1799).

23. Moers, *Literary Women,* 200–203, 210.

24. See ibid., 202: "Both Oswald's values and the secret behind his melancholy derive from his worship of his dead father, as he explains to Corinne halfway up the slope of Mount Vesuvius, where 'all that has life disappears, you enter the empire of death, and only ashes shift beneath uncertain feet.'"

25. If, according to Terry Castle, *The Mysteries of Udolpho* represents "the spectralization of the Other," *Corinne* performs a spectralization of the self. The fact that this is true of other Gothic and sentimental fiction as well complicates, I think, her general claims.

26. Gilbert and Gubar, *Madwoman in the Attic,* 98–104.

27. Peterson, *The Determined Reader,* 38–39.

28. See also ibid., 44: "She has lost that sense of continuing relation with the mother, or with mother surrogates, that is so important to the maturing young woman."

29. Miller, *Subject to Change,* 186–87.

30. Moers, *Literary Women,* 209–10.

31. See Vallois, *Fictions féminines,* 110: "La fiction staëlienne, loin d'être, comme dans les romans romantiques contemporains, le lieu de l'épanchement lyrique de la personne, est . . . comme le lieu de sa dispersion ou de son exil."

32. See Peel, "Contradictions of Form," 285; Vallois, "Voice as Fossil," 52. Recent feminist psychoanalytic theory strongly supports the idea that the integration of the self has as much to do with separation as with connection, especially for daughters, who have more difficulty than sons in separating from the mothers they resemble. This model of separation seems a fruitful one to me for understanding fragmentation in women's fiction. See, for example, Chodorow, *In a Different Voice,* and Benjamin, *The Bonds of Love.*

33. Goldberger translates *sympathie* as "empathy," in accordance with modern English usage. "Empathy" does best convey to the modern reader the sense

of *feeling with* another person that is central to the eighteenth-century conception of sympathy; I retain the word "sympathy" in my discussion, however, because it represents a complex of literary resonances and philosophical ideas that are not included in the modern word, "empathy."

The suggestion that Corinne wants maternal love can be comprehended in the idea of sympathy, but to substitute the idea of maternal love for it is to idealize maternal love in a way that Staël and her predecessors quite emphatically do not. It is true that eighteenth-century gender discourse not only conceptualized sympathy as feminine, but sometimes specifically identified its feminine character with the immediacy of the mother-infant bond; nevertheless sympathy was never reduced to that particular connection, and more importantly women's fiction tends to represent the relation between mothers and marriageable daughters in patrilineage as one of specularity, the false double of sympathy (cf. Miller, Peterson).

34. Moers mentions that Staël invented the term "romanticism" (Moers, *Literary Women,* 206–7).

35. Compare Balayé, "Corinne et Rome": "Cependant, faire de Rome la ville d'une femme est une idée paradoxale. Rome est la ville des prêtres, elle a été la capitale d'un monde représenté couramment comme viril. Dans cette opposition puissance ancienne/faiblesse actuelle, le prêtre, le noble romain, le peuple, tout est devenu signe d'une féminisation dérisoire, accusation que portera plus tard Oswald" (46). See also Peel, "Contradictions of Form," 286.

36. On the perils of specularity in a feminine position see Miller, *Subject to Change;* Schor, "Portrait of a Gentleman"; Jacobus, *Reading Woman;* and Irigaray, *Speculum.*

37. "Inexprimable émotion, que la voix de ce qu'on aime! .... Ce soupir et l'accent mélancolique de sa voix causèrent à Corinne une vive joie" (Balayé 501).

38. On sound and inflection as a specifically maternal language in opposition to writing and signification, see Homans, *Bearing the Word.*

39. See also Miller, *Subject to Change,* 196.

40. See Moers on the reception of this example by women writers of the nineteenth century (Moers, *Literary Women,* 173–210).

41. The reliance on resemblance to the father as a mark of legitimacy goes back in literature to the *Odyssey,* where Telemachus is repeatedly reassured that he must indeed be his father's son because he resembles him (Fitzgerald, e. g. book 1. 20). There hardly exists a work in the Gothic tradition that does not centrally play upon the epic/romance topos of paternal resemblance (or sometimes, especially in the female Gothic, maternal resemblances also), from Lee's *The Recess,* where the twin heroines' sense of haunting begins when they notice their own uncanny resemblance to the portraits of an unidentified man and woman that ornament the Recess, to Radcliffe's *Mysteries of Udolpho,* where again the heroine's resemblance to the portrait of an unknown lady at first implies an illegitimate maternal resemblance, but is later explained as a legitimate paternal one (to a sister of the father; 661–63), to Collins's *The Woman in White,* where the final mystery (with its shadow of a doubt about the heroine's legitimacy) is again cleared up by "the test of personal resemblance" (Collins 436).

42. Cf. Peel, "Corinne's Shift," 108, and Gutwirth, *Madame de Staël, Novelist,* 252.

43. Mullan, *Sentiment and Sociability,* 223.

44. See Gutwirth, *Madame de Staël, Novelist* (254–56) and Peel, "Corinne's Shift," 108.

45. For a discussion of Corinne's revenge on Oswald in its Sapphic association, see DeJean, *Fictions of Sappho,* 185–86.

46. See also Miller, *Subject to Change,* 192, 195.

47. The importance of Staël's identifications with Necker and Rousseau in problematizing her coming to authorship are discussed by Gutwirth in "Madame de Staël, Rousseau, and the Woman Question" (esp. 103).

48. Other significant cultural influences would include the "backlash" against eighteenth-century feminism that followed the French Revolution in both England and France. I discuss this aspect in *Virtue's Faults.*

49. Peel's article, "Corinne's Shift to Patriarchal Mediation," is an insightful discussion of the same contradiction that is my focus here, between the heroine's wish to live on and to pass on her talents to other women, versus her destructive reliance upon "patriarchal mediation" (including her "possession" of Lucile and Juliette) in order to do so (see esp. 101, 104–6). My interpretation bears out Nancy Miller's suggestion that the performance of Corinne's last song may imply "a different sort of literary community and continuity of women: not the biological simplicity of the father and son rivals of our dominant cultural paradigms but a more complex legacy" ("Politics, Feminism, and Patriarchy," 194).

50. The pleasurable distancing of spectator from specter is characteristic of the Gothic. See also Wolstenholme on Radcliffe: "the reader assumes the position of voyeur from a safe perspective" (*Gothic (Re)Visions,* 18).

Corinne and the Woman as Poet in England: Hemans, Jewsbury, and Barrett Browning

We are grateful to William Bush, Madelyn Gutwirth, Margaret Higonnet, Roberta Rigsby, Robin Sheets, Karyna Szmurlo, and Joan Templeton for their comments on portions of this essay.

1. On these and other women poets of the Romantic period, see Stuart Curran, "Romantic Poetry: The 'I' Altered," 185–207, and Marlon B. Ross, *The Contours of Masculine Desire and the Rise of Women's Poetry,* 187–316. Essays on these poets are appearing regularly now, especially in vols. edited by, among others, Carol S. Wilson, Paula Feldman, and Harriet Linkin. The MLA is devoting a new *Approaches to Teaching* to Romantic women poets. Although unpublished, a 1974 dissertation written by Marcia Geib Kutrieh is a useful introduction and anthology (*Popular British Romantic Women Poets*). See also Andrew Ashfield's 1995 anthology, *Romantic Women Poets, 1770–1838.*

2. The record of that influence (which was not without its conflicts) has been "canonized" in the new text anthology, Duncan Wu's *Romanticism: An Anthology* (Oxford: Blackwell, 1994); see the poems by Landon on Hemans and by Barrett Browning on both (1092–95, 1103–05). Regrettably, Landon's work falls outside this study.

3. Simone Balayé discusses the meaning of exile in Staël's life in "Absence, exil, voyage."

4. Vivian Folkenflik, *Extraordinary Woman,* 1. See also Charlotte Hogsett *The Literary Existence,* 13, 140, 154. Marianne Spaulding Michaels gives a balanced account of Staël's feminism ("Feminist Tendencies," 231–32).

5. Moers, *Literary Women*, 314–15.

6. Textual references to *Corinne, or Italy* indicate Avriel Goldberger's translation (New Brunswick, NJ: Rutgers University Press, 1987).

7. Texts on the reception of *Corinne* include Charles-Augustin Sainte-Beuve ("Madame de Staël," 434–35), Gutwirth (*Madame de Staël, Novelist*, 259–309), and Moers, *Literary Women*, 263–319.

8. Gutwirth, "Woman as Mediatrix," 23.

9. Henry F. Chorley, *Memorials of Mrs. Hemans*, 1: 9–10. For other references by Hemans to herself as like Corinne, see Harriett Hughes (Hemans's sister), "Memoir of Mrs. Hemans" in vol. 1 of *The Works of Felicia Hemans*, ed. Harriett Hughes, 99.

10. Peterson, *The Determined Reader*, 45.

11. This analysis is indebted to Marlon Ross's study of Mary Tighe's aesthetics of transience (158–67) and is further developed by Sweet in "History, Imperialism, and the Aesthetics of the Beautiful: Hemans and the Post-Napoleonic Moment." Madelyn Gutwirth discusses the processional, specifically the triumphal feminine "cameo" which, she argues, prefigures Corinne's inauguration and configures the novel, from Corinne at the Capitol to Corinne abandoned. See her "*Corinne* et l'esthétique du camée," 174–82.

12. On *Corinne*'s oscillations, deferrals, and mobilities, see Miller, *Subject to Change*, 169, 173; Peterson, *Determined Reader*, 42. Interpretations of the novel's equivocal ending include these: revenge or revolt (Gutwirth, *Madame de Staël, Novelist*, 257); defeat (DeJean, "The Novel's Other Dilemma"); recuperation of the feminine through the construction of the author (Miller 195–96; and Peterson 60–61); and see Peel, "Corinne's Shift." For a thorough study of text and gender in *Corinne*, see Peterson 42–45, 49–51, and throughout.

13. On Hemans as a laureate *manquée*, see Ross, *Contours*, 233.

14. Further citations from Hemans, indicated parenthetically as *PW*, refer to *The Poetical Works of Mrs. Felicia Hemans* (Philadelphia: Grigg and Elliot, 1847). For a more extensive discussion of *The Restoration* and Hemans's other triumphs and odes, see Sweet, "History."

15. This poem is discussed at greater length by Sweet in *Approaches to Teaching British Women Poets of the Romantic Period*, ed. Stephen C. Behrendt and Harriet Kramer Linkin (New York: MLA, 1997), 101–5.

16. The nineteenth-century translation of *Corinne* by Isabel Hill reads more triumphantly, "the storm may in a moment dash down flowers that yet shall raise their heads again." *Corinne, or Italy*, trans. Isabel Hill, with metrical versions of the odes by L. E. Landon (New York: A. L. Burt, 1833), 53. The late twentieth-century translation by Goldberger reads more darkly: "it takes but a moment for a storm to crush flowers still holding their heads upright" (54). Perry Miller applies the date of 1807 to the undated Hill edition (xxi), and Gutwirth follows his dating (282). But since Landon collaborated in this translation and did not begin her adult career until 1824 with *The Improvisatrice*, a later date is probable; the earliest National Union Catalog date is 1833.

17. Staël's passage on the flowers "crushed . . . underfoot" alludes to Sappho's fragment on the crushed hyacinth; see Mary Barnard, trans., *Sappho: A New Translation* #34; see also #272 and #296.

18. Hemans's historical source in this and other poems is *Histoire des républiques italiennes du Moyen Âge*, by J.-C.-L. Simonde de Sismondi, who was Staël's friend and collaborator.

19. After 1819, however, Hemans's allusions to *Corinne* and Staël involve the darker implications of feminine vulnerability and displacement. (Five more allusions to *Corinne* can be traced, three to *De l'Allemagne,* and one to *Dix années d'exil.*) For example, Hemans's 1820 "The Maremma," whose headnote is from *Corinne,* puts Italy's poisonous powers at the command of a murderous husband rather than a vengeful widow. And for most readers, Hemans's 1830 lyric "Corinne at the Capitol" represents a retreat from Corinnian fame to a safe English hearth (*PW* 322): see Susan Wolfson, "'Domestic Affections' and 'the spear of Minerva': Felicia Hemans and the Dilemma of Gender" (159–60). Such a reading does, however, discount the equivocal rhetoric of Hemans's earlier work and pass over the poem's allusion to Tasso, whose story suggests even more strongly than Corinne's that the obscurity of a feminine home might harbor genius rather than work against it (cf. Hemans's 1828 "Tasso and His Sister," *PW* 280–81).

20. On Jewsbury, see Chorley 1: 167–71; Clarke, *Ambitious Heights,* 27–75, 82–97; Ross, *Contours,* 243–49, 259–64; and Wolfson, passim. References are to Jewsbury's *Phantasmagoria* (London: Hurst, Robinson; Edinburgh: Constable, 1825).

21. *The Athenaeum* 172 (February 1831): 104–5. On the struggles of Jewsbury and Hemans with "the incompatibility of womanliness and writing" in their setting, see N. Clarke, *Ambitious Heights,* 32–37.

22. Clarke, *Ambitious Heights,* 83. References in the text are to *The Three Histories* (London: Westley, 1830).

23. William Rossetti, introduction, *The Poetical Works of Mrs. Hemans,* 22–23. See also Clarke, *Ambitious Heights,* 82–83, and Ross, *Contours* 250–51.

24. On Landon, see William B. Scott, introduction, *The Poetical Works of Letitia E. Landon,* xi–xvi; Glennis Stephenson, *Letitia Landon: The Woman Behind L.E.L.;* and Ross, *Contours,* passim. For a more dubious assessment of the value of Hemans, Landon, Staël, and Barrett Browning to each other, see Dorothy Mermin, *Elizabeth Barrett Browning: The Origins of a New Poetry* (31–32).

25. Cora Kaplan in the introduction to her novel in verse: *'Aurora Leigh' and Other Poems* (London: Women's Press, 1978), 17. Subsequent references to the epic are to the same edition and indicate title, page, book, and line. Kaplan discusses in some detail how Barrett Browning borrows, and adapts, elements from *Corinne* (17–22). Although the heroines' roles are a mediated, distilled trope of the authors' roles, the texts are both still highly autobiographical. The autobiographical element of each text has been sensitively discussed, in the case of *Corinne,* by Madelyn Gutwirth (*Madame de Staël, Novelist,* passim) and Simone Balayé in her edition of *Corinne* (introduction, 18–19), and, in the case of *Aurora Leigh,* by Susan Stanford Friedman ("Gender and Genre Anxiety," 208) and Gardner B. Taplin (*The Life of Elizabeth Barrett Browning,* 313).

26. Sandra M. Gilbert and Susan Gubar, *The Madwoman in the Attic,* 580. Moers explains Dickinson's indebtedness to Barrett Browning and to *Aurora Leigh* in particular, 84–95. See Angela Leighton in *Elizabeth Barrett Browning* (11) and Helen Cooper, *Elizabeth Barrett Browning, Woman and Artist* (21).

27. Leighton, *Elizabeth Barrett Browning,* 26. Kaplan, in the ironically titled "Wicked Fathers," and Leighton give nuanced accounts of the nurturing and inhibiting effects Barrett Browning's father had on her.

28. See Kaplan, "Wicked Fathers," 201; Moers, *Literary Women*, 8.

29. Mermin, *Elizabeth Barrett Browning*, 174; Cooper, *Elizabeth Barrett Browning*, 4.

30. See Cooper, *Elizabeth Barrett Browning*, 5, 11; Mermin, *Elizabeth Barrett Browning*, 8.

31. Friedman discusses in more detail how Barrett Browning drew both on genres that were conventionally female and on those that were conventionally male. See Taplin's introduction to his edition of *Aurora Leigh* (xx–xxi) for an account of how shocking *Aurora Leigh* was thought to be for women readers in its day.

32. Mermin, *Elizabeth Barrett Browning*, 187, 190.

33. "'Art's a Service'," 121. For a discussion of Barrett's reading of Staël and others, consult Taplin, *The Life of Elizabeth Barrett Browning*, 97, 41, 20. Mary Jane Lupton reports that Barrett's poems about the risorgimento and slavery angered reviewers and struck them as unfeminine, *Elizabeth Barrett Browning*, 52. See also Mermin, *Elizabeth Barrett Browning*, 232.

34. Gilbert notes this in "From *Patria* to *Matria*," 204.

35. Leighton, *Elizabeth Barrett Browning*, 154; Cooper, *Elizabeth Barrett Browning*, 185–87; and Joyce Zonana in "The Embodied Muse."

36. See Taplin, *The Life of Elizabeth Barrett Browning*, chap. 17; Cooper, *Elizabeth Barrett Browning*, 146–48; as well as Elizabeth K. Helsinger, Sheets and Veeder in *The Woman Question*, 3: 41.

Nathaniel Hawthorne and *The Marble Faun:* Textual and Contextual Reflections of *Corinne, or Italy*

1. Whenever possible, I have used the volumes of *The Centenary Edition of the Works of Nathaniel Hawthorne*, ed. William Charvat et al. (Columbus: Ohio State University Press, 1962—): vol. 4, *The Marble Faun*, 1964; vol. 8, *The American Notebooks*, 1972; vol. 9, *Twice-told Tales*; vol. 14, *The French and Italian Notebooks*, 1980; vol. 17, *Letters 1853–1856*, 1987; vol. 18, *Letters 1857–1864*, 1987. Volume and page numbers for this series are cited parenthetically.

Because of the contextual nature of this inquiry, all references to *Corinne, or Italy* by Madame de Staël-Holstein are from an American edition published in New York by Burgess, Stringer & Co., 1847. Page numbers are cited parenthetically. Because there appears to be no indication of what version or versions Hawthorne knew, I use this translation as representative, maintaining the French spelling of characters' names. He might have read earlier translations during his youth, or read an original after he had studied French, as he became skilled enough in that language to read Voltaire, Montaigne, and Rousseau. Hawthorne may also have had access to various European versions of *Corinne* during his years abroad. The translator is not identified, but the translation seems to be the "most popular" version, Isabel Hill's, described by Avriel H. Goldberger in "Germaine de Staël's *Corinne:* Challenges to the Translator," 801. The title page attributes to "L. E. L.," or Letitia E. Landon, the translation of Corinne's poetry into "more or less iambic pentameter stanzas of unequal length" (Goldberger, "Challenges," 801). Curiously, when Hawthorne's daughter, Una, took ill with malaria, he noted that her fever made "the poor child talk in rhythmical measure, like a tragic heroine" (14:495).

2. *The Shape of Hawthorne's Career*, 213. Baym refers specifically to descriptions in Hawthorne's *English Notebooks*, but the *French and Italian Notebooks* are as richly detailed.

3. Bloom, *The Anxiety of Influence*, 5. I wish to thank Professor Higonnet for sharing with me the text of her paper, "Telling and Thieving: Engendering Authority," delivered at the MLA Convention, December 1989 (unpaginated manuscript). A longer version of her argument appears in "Telling Theft: Authenticity, Authority, and Male Anxieties." See Leland S. Person, Jr., *Aesthetic Headaches*, for a discussion of Hawthorne's strong female protagonists as expressions of this impulse. For an examination of Hawthorne's work in the context of his marketplace, see Milton R. Stern, *Contexts for Hawthorne*.

4. "Hawthorne's Literary Borrowings," 560. See also Carol Hanbery MacKay, "Hawthorne, Sophia, and Hilda as Copyists: Duplication and Transformation in *The Marble Faun*."

5. Jane Lundblad, *Nathaniel Hawthorne and the European Literary Tradition*. See also Harry Levin, "Statues from Italy: *The Marble Faun*"; Millicent Bell, *Hawthorne's View of the Artist*; and Claude M. Simpson's introduction to *The Marble Faun*.

6. The many articles on this topic include F. I. Carpenter's "Puritans Preferred Blondes: The Heroines of Melville and Hawthorne." See also Goldberger, "Challenges," 800.

7. Spender, *The Writer or the Sex?*, 140.

8. Gilbert, "From *Patria* to *Matria*: Elizabeth Barrett Browning's Risorgimento," 209.

9. In *The Blithedale Romance*, Hawthorne bases the vital Zenobia in part on Margaret Fuller, but in the romance mentions the real-life Fuller's resemblance to Zenobia's pale rival, Priscilla, perhaps as an attempt to confound those who would insist that Fuller and Zenobia are interchangeable identities. See Harry De Puy, "*The Marble Faun*: Another Portrait of Margaret Fuller?" 169.

10. Young, *Hawthorne's Secret*, 95. Moers, *Literary Women*, 207. For another consideration of *Corinne*'s feminism, see Ellen Peel, "Contradictions of Form."

11. Perry Miller, foreword, *Margaret Fuller: American Romantic*, xix.

12. "History and Romance, Sympathy and Uncertainty: The Moral of the Stones in Hawthorne's *The Marble Faun*," 160n. As Levin points out, Hawthorne may have known Charlotte Brontë's *Villette* (1853), in which the Protestant Lucy Snowe also confesses to a Catholic priest. Given Hawthorne's admitted admiration for Brontë's *Jane Eyre* and *The Marble Faun*'s other echoes of *Villette*—its hallucinatory masquerade scenes and its similar treatment of Cleopatra as an artistic subject—the correspondence seems more than coincidental, suggesting Hawthorne's further debt to European women authors.

13. Quoted in Morroe Berger's introduction to *Madame de Staël on Politics, Literature, and National Character*, 21. See also Berger, 22, and Van Wyck Brooks, *The Dream of Arcadia*, 16.

14. And unlike Miriam, the regal Corinne would never need to mend her own gloves, living as she does in an impressive, well-staffed villa (66).

15. Michael T. Gilmore, *American Romanticism and the Marketplace*, 10.

16. P. Miller, xxi. Louise Hall Tharp, *The Peabody Sisters of Salem*, 38. Herbert, *Dearest Beloved: The Hawthornes and the Making of the Middle-*

Class Family, 215. For detailed accounts of *Corinne*'s reception, see Moers, *Literary Women;* Madelyn Gutwirth, *Madame de Staël, Novelist;* and Goldberger's introduction to her 1987 translation of *Corinne, or Italy*, and her "Challenges." See also Young, *Hawthorne's Secret*, 95.

17. Gilmore, *American Romanticism*, 147.

18. Weisbuch, *Atlantic Double-Cross*, 11.

19. See Susan Coultrap-McQuin, *Doing Literary Business*, 14. See also Lawrence Buell, *New England Literary Culture*, 78.

20. Weisbuch, *Atlantic Double-Cross*, 9.

21. "Mrs. Hutchinson" in *Tales and Sketches*, 18–19. In his notebooks, Hawthorne typically uses the verb "scribble" when referring to drafting or sketching preliminary versions of his own fiction. Significantly, he addresses most of his famous diatribes against female scribblers to his editors, in part responsible for bringing these women into public view. For further discussions of Hawthorne and his female rivals, see Ann D. Wood, "The 'Scribbling Women' and Fanny Fern: Why Women Wrote"; Henry Nash Smith, "The Scribbling Women and the Cosmic Success Story"; and John T. Frederick, "Hawthorne's Scribbling Women." See also Raymona E. Hull, " 'Scribbling' Females and Serious Males: Hawthorne's Comments from Abroad on Some American Authors," 35.

22. Person, *Aesthetic Headaches*, 8–9; Wallace, "Hawthorne and the Scribbling Women Reconsidered," 221; Gilmore, *American Romanticism*, 5.

23. Larry J. Reynolds, *European Revolutions and the American Literary Renaissance*, 79.

24. Both passages quoted in P. Miller, *Margaret Fuller*, xix, xxi, 163. See Paula Blanchard, *Margaret Fuller: From Transcendentalism to Revolution;* James R. Mellow, *Nathaniel Hawthorne in His Times;* Arlin Turner, *Nathaniel Hawthorne: A Biography;* Perry Miller's introduction to *Margaret Fuller: American Romantic;* and several essays in Joel Myerson's edition of *Critical Essays on Margaret Fuller*, among others.

25. "American Literature" in P. Miller, 229, 249–50, 233. Quoted in Miller, xx. De Puy claims, "Miriam, then, *is* Margaret Fuller" (170), although many other real-life characters merge in Hawthorne's creation. See Patrick Brancaccio, "Emma Abigail Salomons: Hawthorne's Miriam Identified."

26. Tharp, *Peabody Sisters*, 38, 33.

27. Quoted in Turner, *Nathaniel Hawthorne*, 191.

28. Brooks, *The Dream of Arcadia*, 90.

29. Wallace, "Hawthorne and the Scribbling Women," 220.

30. *The American Narcissus: Individualism and Women in Nineteenth-Century American Fiction*, 195.

31. Quoted in Elaine Showalter's introduction to *Alternative Alcott*, xii. On Hosmer's intimacy with other women, see Lillian Faderman, *Surpassing the Love of Men*. Sculptor Louise Lander, a young American who literally rendered Hawthorne a "man of marble" served as a particularly troubling Corinne-figure for him. For a discussion of the intrigue between Lander and the Hawthornes, see especially Herbert, *Dearest Beloved*, 228–35.

32. Cora Kaplan, *Aurora Leigh*, 149; quoted in Kaplan, 146, 150.

33. In Italy, Sophia Hawthorne may have shared her husband's blind spot regarding Barrett Browning's identity as poet. Describing an evening with the Brownings and American poet William Cullen Bryant, she reported that the "three poets"—Browning, Bryant, and *Hawthorne*—talked literature, while

she and Barrett Browning discussed spiritualism, a topic which both husbands found unsettling (quoted in Tharp, *Peabody Sisters,* 261).

34. See Gary Scharnhorst, "Hawthorne and *The Poetical Works of Spenser.*"

35. I wish to thank Professor Bailey for sharing with me her mansucript, "'Like Another Wife': Cooper, Cole and the Italian Landscape," delivered in a modified form at the 1991 ALA convention.

36. Hillard, *Six Months in Italy,* 494; 530; 260–61. Earlier editions of the text read identically in these sections.

37. The Centenary edition corrects this manuscript misspelling (4:486n).

38. Moers, *Literary Women,* 178. Later editions of Hill's translation in fact transcribe "Nelvil" as "Nevil."

39. In this notebook entry, Hawthorne again misspells Nelvil's name, this time as "Nelville," approximating the name of another intimate he may have remembered while in Rome: Herman Melville. Ten years earlier, Melville, like Margaret Fuller, lauded Hawthorne as an American original who approached the greatness of Shakespeare. And like Fuller's, Melville's praise may have haunted Hawthorne as he plotted *The Marble Faun,* particularly as Melville had exhorted, not unlike the native Corinne, "[I]t is better to fail in originality, than to succeed in imitation.... [N]o American should write like an Englishman, or a Frenchman; let him write like a man for then he will be sure to write like an American." See "Hawthorne and His Mosses" in *Hawthorne: The Critical Heritage,* 120. By this logic, could a man who in any way wrote like a European woman be said to write like an American? Having failed to secure for the younger writer a lucrative political appointment like his Consulship at Liverpool, Hawthorne had last seen Melville in England, in yet another possible crossing of art, Americanism, finances, and fear of failure.

40. Person, *Aesthetic Headaches,* 167.

Marguerite Yourcenar: Daughter of Corinne

This closing essay is the last written on Staël by Charlotte Hogsett who passed away on 10 March 1996.

1. *Corinne, or Italy,* Avriel Goldberger, trans. and ed. (New Brunswick: Rutgers University Press, 1987), 19. Subsequent references are to the same edition. All other translations are mine.

2. This account is based on Josyanne Savigneau, *Marguerite Yourcenar: l'invention d'une vie,* 414–18.

3. *Discours de réception de Madame Marguerite Yourcenar,* 11. Further references are indicated as *DR.*

4. Unless otherwise noted, information on the French Academy is based on Daniel Oster, *Histoire de l'Académie Française.*

5. Consult Gilles Ménage, *The History of Women Philosophers.*

6. Goldberg Moses, *French Feminism in the Nineteenth Century,* 103.

7. *Oeuvres romanesques,* xiii–xxxiii. References to the same edition are indicated as *OR.*

8. See Staël's *Dix années d'exil* in *Oeuvres complètes,* 390, and Yourcenar, "Carnets de notes" for *Mémoires d'Hadrien* in *Oeuvres romanesques,* 525.

9. Campbell, *Life of Petrarch,* 203, and *Grand Dictionnaire Encyclopédique* (Paris: Larousse, 1982), vol. 3, 1758. See also Boulting, *Tasso and His Times,* 300–2.

10. See Gennari, *Le Premier voyage de Madame de Staël en Italie* and Balayé, *Les carnets de voyage*.

11. *De l'influence des passions sur le bonheur des individus et des nations* in *Oeuvres complètes*, 18–19. Translation is mine.

12. Ibid., 134–35.

13. Yourcenar discusses this early work with Matthieu Galey in *Les yeux ouverts* (Paris: Le Centurion, 1980), 51–52.

14. Staël, *De l'influence des passions*, 61.

15. Savigneau, *Marguerite Yourcenar*, 112–13.

16. "Le Succès Yourcenar: vérité et mystification."

17. Yourcenar, *Les yeux ouverts*, 53–54.

18. For three developments of this idea, see Balayé, *Lumières et Liberté*; Gutwirth, *Madame de Staël, Novelist*; and Hogsett, *The Literary Existence of Germaine de Staël*.

Bibliography

Ademollo, Alessandro. *Corilla Olimpica.* Firenze: C. Ademollo e C., 1887.

Albon, Comte d'. *Discours sur l'histoire, le gouvernement, les usages, la littérature et les arts de plusieurs nations de l'Europe,* 1779.

Allart, Hortense. *Lettres sur les ouvrages de Madame de Staël.* Paris, 1828.

Alliston, April. "The Values of a Literary Legacy: Retracing the Transmission of Value through Female Lines." *The Yale Journal of Criticism* 4, no. 1 (Fall 1990): 109–28.

———. *Virtue's Faults: Correspondences in Eighteenth-Century British and French Women's Fiction.* Stanford: Stanford University Press, 1996.

———. "Of Haunted Highlands: Mapping a Geography of Gender in the Margins of Europe." In *Cultural Interactions in the Romantic Age: Critical Essays in Comparative Literature,* edited by Gregory Maertz. Albany, NY: State University of New York Press, forthcoming.

Amaduzzi, Giovanni C. "Papers." Biblioteca della Rubiconia Accademia dei Filopatridi, Savignano di Romagna.

Ashfield, Andrew, ed. *Romantic Women Poets, 1770–1838: An Anthology.* Manchester: Manchester University Press, 1995.

Atti della solenne coronazione fatta in Campidoglio della insigne poetessa Maria Maddalena Morelli, pistoiese, tra gli Arcadi Corilla Olimpica. Parma, 1779.

Babitt, Irving. *Modern French Criticism.* Boston: Houghton Mifflin, 1912.

Bailey, Brigitte. "'Like Another Wife': Cooper, Cole and the Italian Landscape." Paper delivered at the ALA Convention, May 1991.

Bakhtin, Mikhail. *The Dialogic Imagination.* Edited by Michael Holquist. Austin: University of Texas Press, 1980.

Balayé, Simone. "*Corinne* et les amis de Madame de Staël." *Revue d'histoire littéraire de la France* 66 (1966): 139–49.

———. "*Corinne* et ses illustrateurs." *Versailles* 2e trimestre (1966): 16–25.

———. "Benjamin Constant, lecteur de *Corinne.*" In *Benjamin Constant, Actes du Congrès Benjamin Constant,* edited by Pierre Cordey and Jean-Luc Seylaz, 189–99. Genève: Droz, 1968.

———. "Madame de Staël et l'indépendance italienne." *Revue des sciences humaines* (January 1969): 47–56.

———. "Madame de Staël, Napoléon et la mission de l'écrivain." *Europe* 21 (1969): 124–37.

———. "Madame de Staël et Sismondi ou un dialogue critique." *Cahiers staëliens* 8 (1969): 33–46.

———. "Les livres des Italiens et les livres sur l'Italie dans la bibliothèque de Madame de Staël." *Cahiers staëliens* 10 (1970): 58–64.

———. "Absence, exil, voyage." In *Madame de Staël et l'Europe,* preface by Jean Fabre and Simone Balayé, 228–37. Paris: Klincksieck, 1970.

———. *Les carnets de voyage de Madame de Staël; contribution à la genèse de ses oeuvres.* Genève: Droz, 1971.

———. "Fonction romanesque de la musique et des sons dans *Corinne.*" *Romantisme* 3 (1972): 17–32.

———. "*Corinne* et la presse parisienne de 1807." *Approches des lumières. Mélanges offerts à Jean Fabre,* 1–16. Paris: Klincksieck, 1974.

———. *Madame de Staël: Lumières et Liberté.* Paris: Klincksieck, 1979.

———. "Corinne et Rome ou le chant du cygne." In *Thèmes et figures du Siècle des Lumières. Mélanges offerts à Roland Mortier,* edited by Raymond Trousson, 45–58. Genève: Droz, 1980.

———. "Corinne et la ville italienne ou l'espace extérieur et l'impasse intérieur." In *France et Italie dans la culture européenne. Mélanges à la mémoire de Franco Simone,* 33–50. Genève: Slatkine, 1984.

———. "Pour une lecture politique de *Corinne.*" In *Il Gruppo di Coppet e l'Italia,* edited by Mario Matucci, 7–16. Pisa: Pacini, 1988.

———. "Du sens romanesque de quelques oeuvres d'art dans *Corinne* de Mme de Staël." In her *Madame de Staël: écrire, lutter, vivre,* 111–35. Genève: Droz, 1994.

———. "Politique et société dans l'oeuvre staëlienne: l'exemple de *Corinne.*" *Cahiers de l'Association des études françaises* 46 (1994): 53–67.

Barnard, Mary. *'Sappho': A New Translation.* Berkeley: University of California Press, 1958.

Barrett Browning, Elizabeth. *'Aurora Leigh': A Poem.* Introduction by Gardner B. Taplin. Chicago: Cassandra Academy, 1979.

———. *Aurora Leigh and Other Poems.* Introduction by Cora Kaplan. London: Women's Press, 1978.

———. *Hitherto Unpublished Poems and Stories with an Inedited Autobiography.* Edited by H. Buxton Forman. 2 vols. Boston: Bibliophile Society, 1914.

Barzun, Jacques. *Simple and Direct.* New York: Harper & Row, 1975.

Baym, Nina. *The Shape of Hawthorne's Career.* Ithaca: Cornell University Press, 1975.

Beauvoir, Simone de. *The Second Sex.* Translated by H. M. Parshley. New York: Bantam Books, 1971.

Beldensperger, Fernand. *Sensibilité musicale et romantisme.* Paris: Presses françaises, 1925.

Bell, Millicent. *Hawthorne's View of the Artist.* New York: State University of New York Press, 1962.

Benjamin, Jessica. *The Bonds of Love: Psychoanalysis, Feminism and the Problem of Domination.* New York: Pantheon Books, 1988.

———. "A Desire of One's Own: Psychoanalytic Feminism and Intersubjective Space." In *Feminist Studies/Critical Studies,* edited by Teresa de Lauretis, 78–101. Bloomington: Indiana University Press, 1986.

Benveniste, Emile. *Problèmes de linguistique générale*. 2 vols. Paris: Gallimard, 1974.

Berdichevski, Maria. "Ecrits de Madame de Staël: révolte et soumission." Diss., Rutgers University, 1993.

Berger, John. *Ways of Seeing*. London and New York: Penguin, 1973.

Berger, Morroe. Introduction to *Madame de Staël on Politics, Literature and National Character*. New York: Doubleday, 1964.

Besser, Gretchen Rous. *Germaine de Staël Revisited*. New York: Twayne, 1994.

Blanchard, Paula. *Margaret Fuller: From Transcendentalism to Revolution*. New York: Lawrence, 1978.

———. "Corinne and the 'Yankee Corinna': Madame de Staël and Margaret Fuller." In *Woman as Mediatrix: Essays on Nineteenth-Century European Women Writers,* edited by Avriel H. Goldberger, 39–46. New York: Greenwood Press, 1987.

Bloom, Harold, *The Anxiety of Influence*. New York: Oxford University Press, 1973.

Boisgiron, Mme de. *Lettres de Mademoiselle de Boismiran*. Paris, 1777.

Bonald, Louis, G. A. "Du style de la littérature." In *Mélanges littéraires, politiques et philosophiques*. Paris: Adrien Leclerc, 1819.

Borowitz, Helen. "The Unconfessed Précieuse." *Nineteenth-Century French Studies* 11 (1982–83): 32–59.

———. *Impact of Art on French Literature, from de Scudéry to Proust*. Newark: University of Delaware Press, 1985.

Bosse, Monika. "*Corinne ou l'Italie*: Diagnostic d'un dilemme historique." In *Il Gruppo di Coppet e l'Italia,* edited by Mario Matucci, 83–107. Pisa: Pacini, 1988.

Boulting, William. *Tasso and His Times*. New York: Kaskell House, 1968.

Bourgeois, René. "L'inversion ironique: les faux comédiens." In his *L'ironie romantique. Spectacle et jeu de Madame de Staël à Gérard de Nerval,* 97–105. Grenoble: Presses universitaires de Grenoble, 1974.

Bouvy, Eugène. "L'improvisation poétique en Italie." *Bulletin Italien* 6 (1906): 1–20.

Brancaccio, Patrick. "Emma Abigail Salomons: Hawthorne's Miriam Identified." *Nathaniel Hawthorne Journal* 8 (1978): 95–103.

Brikett, Jennifer. "Speech in Action: Language, Society, and Subject in Germaine de Staël's *Corinne*." *Eighteenth-Century Fiction* 7 (1995): 393–408.

Brooks, Van Wyck. *The Dream of Arcadia*. New York: E. P. Dutton, 1958.

Bruschini, Enrico and Alba Amoia. "Rome's Monuments and Artistic Treasures in Mme de Staël's *Corinne* (1807): Then and Now." *Nineteenth-Century French Studies* 22 (1994): 311–47.

Buell, Lawrence. *New England Literary Culture*. New York: Cambridge University Press, 1989.

Burkhard, Marianne. "Love, Creativity and Female Role: Grillparzer's *Sappha* and Staël's *Corinne* between Art and Cultural Norm." *Jahrbuch fur Internationale Germanistik* 16, no. 2 (1984): 128–46.

Buti, Maria Bandini. *Poetesse e scrittrici*. Vol. 6. *Enciclopedia Biografica e Bibliografica Italiana*. Rome: E.B.B.I., 1942.

Byron, Lord. *Childe Harold's Pilgrimage. The Complete Poetical Works.* Edited by Jerome J. McGann and Barry Weller. 7 vols. Oxford: Clarendon, 1980–91.

Campbell, Joseph. *Hero with a Thousand Faces.* New York: Pantheon, 1949.

Campbell, Thomas. *Life of Petrarch.* London: Colburn, 1841.

Canonici Fachini, Ginevra. *Prospetto biografico delle donne italiane rinomate in letterature.* Venezia: Avisopoli, 1824.

Caramaschi, Enzo. "Le point de vue féministe dans la pensée de Mme de Staël." *Saggi e ricerche di letterature francese* 12 (1973): 285–352.

Carpenter, F. I. "Puritans Preferred Blondes: The Heroines of Melville and Hawthorne." *New England Quarterly* 9 (June 1936): 253–72.

Casanova, Jacques. *Mémoires.* Edited by R. Abirached. Paris: Gallimard, 1959.

Castle, Terry. "The Spectralization of the Other in *The Mysteries of Udolpho.*" In *The New Eighteenth Century: Theory, Politics, English Literature,* edited by Felicity Nussbaum and Laura Brown, 231–53. New York: Methuen, 1987.

Chateaubriand, René de. *Mémoires d'outre-tombe.* Paris: Flammarion, 1948.

Chodorow, Nancy. *The Reproduction of Mothering: Psychoanalysis and the Sociology of Gender.* Berkeley: University of California Press, 1978.

Chorley, Henry F. *Memorials of Mrs. Hemans.* 2 vols. London: Saunders and Otley, 1836.

Cipriani, Antonio. "Contributo per una storia politica dell'Arcadia settecentesca." *Accademia Litteraria Italiana. Arcadia: Atti e Memorie* 5 (1970): 101–66.

Cixous, Hélène. "Le rire de la Méduse." *L'Arc* 8 (1975): 39–54.

Cixous, Hélène and Catherine Clément. *La Jeune née.* Paris: Union Générale d'Editions, 1971.

Cixous, Hélène, Madeleine Gagnon, and Annie Leclerc. *La venue à l'écriture.* Paris: Union Générale d'Editions, 1977.

Clarke, Dorothy Clotelle. "An Hispanic Variation on a French Theme: Mme de Staël, Butor, Agudiez." *Symposium* 22 (1968): 208–14.

Clarke, Norma. *Ambitious Heights: Writing, Friendship, Love—The Jewsbury Sisters, Felicia Hemans, and Jane Carlyle.* London: Routledge, 1990.

Cohen, Margaret. "Women and Fiction in the Nineteenth Century." In *A Cambridge Companion to the Modern French Novel,* edited by Timothy Unwin. Cambridge: University Press of Cambridge, forthcoming.

———. *Compromising Positions: The Literary Struggles Engendering the Modern Novel in France.* Princeton: Princeton University Press, forthcoming.

Cohen, Margaret and Christopher Prendergast, eds. *Spectacles of Realism: Body, Gender, Genre.* Minneapolis: University of Minneapolis Press, 1995.

Coleman, Patrick. "Exile and Narrative Voice in *Corinne.*" *Studies in Eighteenth-Century Culture* 24 (1995): 91–105.

———. "Intimité et voix narrative dans *Corinne.*" In *L'invention de l'intimité au Siècle des Lumières,* edited by Benoit Melancon, 57–66. Nanterre: Université Paris X, 1995.

Colette, Sidonie Gabrielle. *The Vagabond.* Translated by Enid McLeod. New York: Farrar, Straus, and Giroux, 1980.

Collins, William Wilkie. *The Woman in White*. Edited by Harvey Peter Sucksmith. Oxford: Oxford University Press, 1973.

Colson, Lydia Catherine. "Etude de la société dans *Corinne ou l'Italie* de Mme de Staël." Diss., Case Western Reserve University, 1970.

Constant, Benjamin. "De Madame de Staël et de ses ouvrages." *Oeuvres*. Vol. 2. Paris: Gallimard, 1957.

Cooper, Helen. *Elizabeth Barrett Browning: Woman and Artist*. Chapel Hill: University of North Carolina Press, 1988.

Cordova, Sarah. "Poetics of Dance: Narrative Designs from Staël to Maupassant." Diss., University of California, Los Angeles, 1993.

Corilla Olimpica (Maria Maddalena Morelli). *Corilla Olimpica, Pastorella d'Arcadia, a' dilettissimi suoi Cavalieri*. Siena, 1761.

Cossy, Valérie. "Germaine de Staël, Jane Austen et leurs éditeurs. L'image de l'auteur à travers quelques éditions du XIXème siècle." *Etudes de lettres* juillet-septembre (1993): 69–86.

Coulet, Henri. "Révolution et roman." *Revue d'histoire littéraire de la France* 4 (1987): 638–60.

Coultrap-McQuin, Susan. *Doing Literary Business: American Women Writers in the Nineteenth Century*. Chapel Hill: University of North Carolina Press, 1990.

Curran, Stuart. "Romantic Poetry: The 'I' Altered." In *Romanticism and Feminism*, edited by Anne K. Mellor, 187–207. Bloomington: Indiana University Press, 1988.

Daemmerich, Ingrid G. "The Function of the Ruins Motif in Madame de Staël's *Corinne*." *Romance Notes* 15 (1973–74): 255–58.

Dal Bo, Katja. "La description problématique dans *Corinne*." *Cahiers staëliens* 43 (1991–92): 63–84.

David, Deirdre. "'Art's a Service': Social Wound, Sexual Politics, and *Aurora Leigh*." *Browning Institute Studies* 13 (1985): 113–36.

De Blasi, Yolanda. *Antologia della scrittrici italiane dalle origini al 1800*. Firenze: Casa Editrice Nemi, 1930.

———. *Le scrittrici italiane dalle origini al 1800*. Firenze: Casa Editrice Nemi, 1934.

De Lauretis, Teresa. "The Essence of the Triangle or, Taking the Risk of Essentialism Seriously: Feminist Theory in Italy, the U.S., and Britain." *Differences* 2 (1989): 3–37.

De Puy, Harry. "*The Marble Faun*: Another Portrait of Margaret Fuller?" *Arizona Quarterly* 40, no. 2 (Summer 1984): 163–78.

Decreus-Van Liefland, Juliette. *Sainte-Beuve et la critique des auteurs féminins*. Paris: Boivin, 1949.

DeJean, Joan. "Lafayette's Ellipses: The Privileges of Anonymity." *PMLA* 99, no. 5 (October 1984): 884–902.

———. "Staël's *Corinne*: The Novel's Other Dilemma." *Stanford French Review* 11 (Spring 1987): 77–88.

———. "Sappho in (Napoleonic) Italy." In her *Fictions of Sappho 1546–1936*, 167–97. Chicago, London: University of Chicago Press, 1989.

———. "Portrait of the Artist as Sappho." In *Germaine de Staël: Crossing the Borders*, edited by Madelyn Gutwirth, Avriel Goldberger, and Karyna Szmurlo, 122–37. New Brunswick, NJ: Rutgers University Press, 1991.

Dejob, Charles. *Madame de Staël et l'Italie.* Paris: Armand Colin, 1890.

Delon, Michel. "Corinne et Juliette." *Europe* 693–94 (1987): 57–63.

———. "Germaine de Staël and Other Possible Scenarios of the French Revolution." In *Germaine de Staël: Crossing the Borders*, edited by Madelyn Gutwirth, Avriel Goldberger, and Karyna Szmurlo, 22–33. New Brunswick, NJ: Rutgers University Press, 1991.

Deneys-Tunney, Anne. "*Corinne* by Madame de Staël: the Utopia of Feminine Voice as Music within the Novel." *Dalhousie French Studies* 28 (Fall 1994): 55–63.

Destutt de Tracy, Antoine. *Eléments d'idéologie.* 3 vols. Paris: Courcier, 1804.

Diario Ordinario. Roma: Cracas, 1805.

Didier, Béatrice. "Aspects de la musique italienne chez Mme de Staël et Sismondi." In *Il Gruppo di Coppet e l'Italia*, edited by Mario Matucci, 109–25. Pisa: Pacini, 1988.

Dionisotti, Carlo. "Ricordo di Cimante Micenio." *Accademia degli Arcadi: Atti e Memorie* 1 (1954): 94–121.

Doane, Mary Ann. "Woman's Stake: Filming the Female Body." *October* (Summer 1981): 23–36.

Donne e diritto: Due Secoli di legislazione—1796/1985. Edited by Agata Alma Capiello et al. Roma: Presidenza del Consiglio dei Ministri, 1988.

Dubé, Pierre H. *Bibliographie de la critique sur Madame de Staël (1789–1994).* Genève: Droz, 1998.

Eliot, George. *The Mill on the Floss.* New York: New American Library, 1965.

Ellis, Kate Ferguson. *The Contested Castle: Gothic Novels and the Subversion of Domestic Ideology.* Urbana: University of Illinois Press, 1989.

Fabian, Johannes. *Time and the Other: How Anthropology Makes its Object.* New York: Columbia University Press, 1983.

Faderman, Lillian. *Surpassing the Love of Man: Romantic Friendship and Love Between Women from the Renaissance to the Present.* New York: Quill, 1981.

Fauchery, Pierre. *La Destinée féminine dans le roman européen du dix-huitième siècle.* Paris: Armand Colin, 1972.

Felici, Luigi. "L'Arcadia romana tra illuminismo e neoclassicismo." *Accademia Letteraria Italiana. Arcadia: Atti e Memorie* 5 (1970): 167–92.

Folkenflik, Vivian. *An Extraordinary Woman: Selected Writings of Germaine de Staël.* New York: Columbia University Press, 1987; reprinted as *Major Writings of Germaine de Staël*, 1992.

Foscolo, Ugo. "Saggo d'un gazzettino del bel mondo." *Prose varie d'arte.* In *Opere*, 5: 358–67. Florence: Le Monnier, 1951.

Frederick, John T. "Hawthorne's Scribbling Women." *New England Quarterly* 48 (1978): 231–40.

Freud, Sigmund. *Standard Edition of the Complete Psychological Works of Sigmund Freud.* 24 vols. Edited by James Strachey. London: Hogarth Press, 1953–74.

———. *L'Inquiétante étrangeté.* Paris: Gallimard, 1933.

———. *Délires et rêves dans 'Gradiva' de Jensen.* Paris: Gallimard, 1949.

———. *Civilization and its Discontents.* Edited by James Strachey. New York: W. W. Norton, 1961.

Friedman, Susan Stanford. "Gender and Genre Anxiety: Elizabeth Barrett Browning and H. D. as Epic Poets." *Tulsa Studies* 5 (1986): 203–28.

Fuller, Margaret. "American Literature. Its Position in the Present Time, and Prospects for the Future." In *Margaret Fuller: American Romantic,* edited by Perry Miller, 227–50. Gloucester, MA: Peter Smith, 1969.

———. "Women in the Nineteenth Century." Abridged. In *Margaret Fuller. American Romantic,* edited by Perry Miller, 135–91. Gloucester, MA: Peter Smith, 1969.

Gallop, Jane. *The Daughter's Seduction.* Ithaca: Cornell University Press, 1982.

Gengembre, Gérard and Goldzink, Jean. "L'opinion dans *Corinne.*" *Europe* 693–94 (1987): 48–57.

———. "Républicain as-tu du style? ou écriture et politique dans les *Circonstances actuelles.*" *Cahiers staëliens* 43 (1991–92): 13–28.

Gennari, Geneviève. *Le Premier voyage de Madame de Staël en Italie et la genèse de 'Corinne'.* Paris: Boivin, 1947.

Gilbert, Sandra M. "From Patria to Matria: Elizabeth Barrett Browning's Risorgimento." In *Textual Analysis: Some Readers Reading,* edited by Mary M. Caws, 207–31. New York: MLA of America, 1987.

Gilbert, Sandra M. and Susan Gubar. *The Madwoman in the Attic: The Woman Writer and the Nineteenth-Century Literary Imagination.* New Haven: Yale University Press, 1979.

Gilmore, Michael T. *American Romanticism and the Marketplace.* Chicago: University of Chicago Press, 1985.

Giornale Bibliografico Universale 1 (1807): 18–87.

Girard, Alain. *Le journal intime.* Paris: Presses Universitaires de France, 1963.

Goldberger, Avriel H. Introduction to *Corinne, or Italy.* New Brunswick, NJ: Rutgers University Press, 1987.

———. "Germaine de Staël's *Corinne*: Challenges to the Translator." *The French Review* 63 (1989–90): 800–809.

Grigioni, Carlo. "Sedici anni della vita di Corilla Olimpica in un carteggio inedito (1776–1792)." *La Romagna* 17 (1928): 260–88.

Grimm, et al. *Correspondance.* Paris: Garnier, 1879.

Guichard, Léon. *La Musique et les lettres au temps du romantisme.* Paris: Presses Universitaires de France, 1955.

Giuli, Paola. "The Feminization of Italian Culture: The Poetics of *Seconda Arcadia* and Literary History." *NEMLA Italian Studies* 19 (1995): 51–68.

Giusti, Ada. "The Politics of Location: Italian Narratives of Mme de Staël and George Sand." *Neohelicon* 22, no. 2 (1995): 205–19.

Gutwirth, Madelyn. "Madame de Staël's Debt to *Phèdre: Corinne.*" *Studies in Romanticism* 3 (1964): 161–76.

———. "Madame de Staël, Rousseau and the Woman Question." *PMLA* 86 (1971): 100–109.

296　　　　　　　　　　BIBLIOGRAPHY

―――. "*Corinne* et l'esthétique du camée." In *Le Préromantisme Hypothèque ou Hypothèse?*, edited by Paul Viallaneix, 237–45. Paris: Klincksieck, 1975.

―――. *Madame de Staël, Novelist: The Emergence of the Artist as Woman.* Urbana, Chicago, London: University of Illinois Press, 1978.

―――. "Du silence de Corinne et de sa parole." In *Benjamin Constant, Madame de Staël et le Groupe de Coppet*, edited by Etienne Hofmann, 427–34. Oxford: Voltaire Foundation; Lausanne: Institut Benjamin Constant, 1982.

―――. "Forging a Vocation: Germaine de Staël on Fiction, Power, and Passion." *Bulletin of Research in the Humanities* 86 (1983–85): 242–54.

―――. "*Corinne* and *Consuelo* as Fantasies of Immanence." *George Sand Studies* 8, no. 1–2 (1986–87): 21–27.

―――. "Woman as Mediatrix: from Jean-Jacques Rousseau to Germaine de Staël." In *Woman as Mediatrix. Essays on Nineteenth-Century European Woman Writers*, edited by Avriel Goldberger, 13–29. New York: Greenwood, 1987.

―――. *The Twilight of the Goddesses: Women and Representation in the French Revolutionary Era.* New Brunswick, NJ: Rutgers University Press, 1992.

Gutwirth, Madelyn, Avriel Golberger and Karyna Szmurlo, eds. *Germaine de Staël: Crossing the Borders.* New Brunswick, NJ: Rutgers University Press, 1991.

Hansen, Helynne Holstein. "Marriage and the Feminist Spirit in the Works of Two Female Novelists of the Romantic Era: Madame de Staël and George Sand." Diss., University of Utah, 1990.

Harmon, Danuté. "The Antithetical World View of Madame de Staël: Ideology, Structure, and Style in *Delphine* and *Corinne*." Diss., The George Washington University, 1975.

Hatzfeld, Helmut. *Initiation à l'explication de textes français.* Munich: Max Hueber, 1975.

Haussonville, Gabriel-Paul Othenin d'. *Le salon de Madame Necker.* 2 vols. Paris: Calmann-Lévy, 1882.

Hawthorne, Nathaniel. *The Centenary Edition of the Works of Nathaniel Hawthorne.* Edited by William Charvat, et al. Columbus: Ohio State University Press, 1962—.

―――. "Mrs. Hutchinson." *Tales and Sketches.* Edited by Roy Harvey Pearce, 18–24. New York: Library of America, 1982.

Heller, Deborah. "Tragedy, Sisterhood, and Revenge in *Corinne*." *Papers on Language and Literature* 26, no. 2 (1990): 212–32.

Helsinger, Elizabeth K., Robin Lauterbach Sheets, and William Veeder. *The Woman Question: Society and Literature in Britain and America, 1837–1883.* 3 vols. New York: Garland, 1983.

Hemans, Felicia. *The Poetical Works of Mrs. Felicia Hemans.* Philadelphia: Grigg and Elliot, 1847.

Herbert, T. Walter. *Dearest Beloved: The Hawthornes and the Making of the Middle-Class Family.* Berkeley: University of California Press, 1993.

Herold, J. Christopher. *Mistress to an Age.* New York: Bobbs-Merrill, 1958.

Herrmann, Claudine. "Corinne, femme de génie." *Cahiers staëliens* 35 (1984): 60–75.

Hertz, Robert. "The Collective Representation of Death." In his *Death and the Right Hand*, 27–86. London: Cohen and West, 1960.

Higonnet, Margaret. "Suicide as Self-Construction." In *Germaine de Staël: Crossing the Borders*, edited by Madelyn Gutwirth, Avriel Goldberger, and Karyna Szmurlo, 69–81. New Brunswick, NJ: Rutgers University Press, 1991.

———. "Telling Theft: Authenticity, Authority, and Male Anxieties." *Literature Interpretation, Theory: LIT* 5 (1994): 119–34.

Hillard, George Stillman. *Six Months in Italy*. 16th ed. Boston: Houghton, Osgood, 1879.

Hirsch Marianne. "A Mother's Discourse: Incorporation and Repetition in *La Princesse de Clèves*." *Yale French Studies* 62 (1981): 67–87.

Hogsett, Charlotte. *The Literary Existence of Germaine de Staël*. Carbondale-Edwardsville: Southern Illinois Press, 1987.

———. "Generative Factors in *Considerations on the French Revolution*." In *Germaine de Staël: Crossing the Borders*, edited by Madelyn Gutwirth, Avriel Goldberger, and Karyna Szmurlo, 34–41. New Brunswick, NJ: Rutgers University Press, 1991.

Holland, Claude. "Structures of the Feminine Imagination: Mme de Staël's *Corinne* and Sand's *Mademoiselle Merquem*." Diss., Columbia University, 1983.

Holmström, Kirsten. *Monodrama, attitudes, tableaux vivants, 1770–1815. Studies on Some Trends of Theatrical Fashion*. Stockholm: Almqvist and Wiksell, 1967.

Homans, Margaret. *Bearing the Word: Language and Female Experience in Nineteenth-Century Women's Writing*. Chicago: University of Chicago Press, 1986.

Homer. *The Odyssey*. Translated by Robert Fitzgerald. New York: Doubleday, 1961.

[Hughes, Harriett.] "Memoir of Mrs. Hemans." *The Works of Mrs. Hemans*. 7 vols. Edinburgh: Blackwood, 1839.

Hull, Raymona E. "'Scribbling' Females and Serious Males: Hawthorne's Comments from Abroad on Some American Authors." *The Nathaniel Hawthorne Journal 1975*. Englewood, CO: Microcard Editions Books, 1975.

Hunt, Lynn. "Engraving the Republic. Prints and Propaganda in the French Revolution." *History Today* (October 1980): 10–17.

Iknayan, Marguerite. *The Idea of the Novel in France*. Paris, Geneva: Minard-Droz, 1961.

Irigaray, Luce. *Speculum de l'autre femme*. Paris: Minuit, 1974.

———. *This Sex Which is Not One*. Translated by Catherine Porter. Ithaca: Cornell University Press, 1985.

Jacobus, Mary. *Women Writing and Writing about Women*. Totowa, NJ: Barnes, 1979.

———. *Reading Woman: Essays in Feminist Criticism*. New York: Columbia University Press, 1986.

Janeway, Elizabeth. *Man's World, Woman's Place*. New York: Morrow, 1971.

Jewsbury, Maria Jane. *Phantasmagoria: or, Sketches of Life and Literature*. 2 vols. London: Hurst, Robinson; Edinburg: Constable, 1825.

———. *The Tree Stories*. London: Westley, 1830.

[Jewsbury, Maria Jane.] "Literary Sketches. No. 1. Felicia Hemans." *Athenaeum* 12 (February 1831): 104–5.

Johnson-Cousin, Danielle. "Lantier, Chaussard et Mme de Staël: des romans à sensation(s) à l'oeuvre créatrice, étude d'influences inconnues sur *Corinne* (1807) et sur *Sapho* (1811)." *Studies on Voltaire and the Eighteenth Century* 317 (1994): 161–80.

———. "L'orientalisme de Mme de Staël dans *Corinne* (1807): politique esthétique et féministe." *Studies on Voltaire and the Eighteenth Century* 317 (1994): 181–237.

Kadish, Doris. "Narrating French Revolution: The Example of *Corinne*." In *Germaine de Staël: Crossing the Borders,* edited by Madelyn Gutwirth, Avriel Goldberger, and Karyna Szmurlo, 113–21. New Brunswick, NJ: Rutgers University Press, 1991.

———. "Allegorizing Women: *Corinne* and *The Last Man.* In her *Politicizing Gender: Narrative Strategies in the Aftermath of the French Revolution,* 15–36. New Brunswick, NJ: Rutgers University Press, 1992.

Kamuf, Peggy. *Fictions of Feminine Desire: Disclosures of Heloise.* Lincoln: University of Nebraska Press, 1986.

Kaplan, Cora. "Wicked Fathers: A Family Romance." In *Sea Changes: Essays on Culture and Feminism,* 191–211. London: New Left-Verso, 1986.

———. "Aurora Leigh." In *Feminist Criticism and Social Change,* edited by Judith Newton and Deborah Rosenfelt, 134–64. New York: Methuen, 1985.

Kies, Albert. "*Corinne* ou l'obsession du spectacle." *Revue générale* 7 (1972): 47–53.

Kofman, Sarah. *L'Enigme de la femme.* Paris: Galilée, 1980.

———. *Mélancolie de l'art.* Paris: Galilée, 1985.

Kohler, Pierre. *Madame de Staël et la Suisse.* Paris: Payot, 1916.

Kristeva, Julia. *Polylogue.* Paris: Seuil, 1977.

———. *Pouvoirs de l'horreur. Essai sur l'abjection.* Paris: Seuil, 1980.

———. *Revolution in Poetic Language.* Translated by Margaret Waller. New York: Columbia University Press, 1984.

———. "Gloire, deuil et écriture. Lettre à un ami romantique sur Madame de Staël." *Romantisme* 62 (1988): 7–14.

Kutrieh, Marcia G. "Popular British Romantic Women Poets." Diss., Bowling Green University, 1974.

"La Pizzi-Corilleide o siano Compozitioni Diverse in Rima o in Prosa in Occasione della Corona Capitolina Data in Roma a Maria Maddalena Morelli detta Corilla Olimpica l'anno 1776, 31 agosto." Manuscript 45 of the Accademia litteraria italiana "Arcadia."

Ladurie, Emmanuel Le Roy. "Family Structures and Inheritance Customs in Sixteenth-Century France." In *Family and Inheritance,* edited by Jack Goody, et al., 37–95. Cambridge: Cambridge University Press, 1976.

Lafayette, Marie de. *La Princesse de Clèves.* Paris: Garnier-Flammarion, 1966.

———. *The Princess of Clèves.* Translated by Walter J. Cobb. New York: Penguin Books, 1989.

Lalande, Joseph Jérôme de. *Voyage en Italie.* Vol. 2. Yverdon, 1769.

Lamartine, Alphonse de. "Les destinées de la poésie." In *Oeuvres complètes.* 8 vols. Paris: Hachette-Furne, 1856.

——. *Souvenirs et portraits*. Paris: Hachette, 1871.

Lancetti, V. *Memorie dei poeti laureati*. Milano: Borroni and Scotti, 1839.

Landes, Joan. *Women in the Public Sphere in the Age of the French Revolution*. Ithaca: Cornell University Press, 1989.

Lang-Peralta, Linda. "Figures of Constraints and Strategies of Resistance in the Texts of Frances Burney and Germaine de Staël." Diss., University of California Irvine, 1990.

Le Gall, Béatrice. "Le paysage chez Mme de Staël." *Revue d'histoire littéraire de la France* 66 (1966): 38–51.

Lee, Sophie. *The Recess; or, A Tale of Other Times*. London, 1783–85.

Lee, Vernon. *Studies of the Eighteenth Century in Italy*. London: Fisher Unwin, 1887.

Lehtonen, Maija. "Le fleuve du temps et le fleuve de l'enfer: thèmes et images dans *Corinne* de Madame de Staël. *Neuphilologische Mitteilungen* 3–4 (1967): 225–42, 391–408; 1 (1968): 101–28.

Leighton, Angela. *Elizabeth Barrett Browning*. Bloomington: Indiana University Press, 1986.

Lepschy, Laura. "Madame de Staël's Views on Art in *Corinne*." *Studi francesi* 14 (1970): 481–89.

Levin, Harry. "Statues from Italy: *The Marble Faun*." In *Hawthorne Centenary Essays,* edited by Roy Harvey Pearce, 119–40. Columbus: Ohio State University Press, 1964.

Lewis, Bart. "Literature and Society: Madame de Staël and the Argentine Romantics." *Hispania* 69, no. 4 (1985): 740–46.

Lipking, Lawrence. "Aristotle's Sister: A Poetics of Abandonment." *Critical Inquiry* 10 (1983): 61–81.

——. *Abandoned Women and Poetic Tradition*. Chicago and London: University of Chicago Press, 1988.

Luchaire, Julien. "Lettres de V. Monti à Mme de Staël, pendant l'année 1805." *Bulletin Italien* 6 (1906): 227–45.

Lundblad, Jane. *Nathaniel Hawthorne and the European Literary Tradition*. Reprint. Ann Arbor: University of Michigan Press, 1983.

Lupton, Mary Jane. *Elizabeth Barrett Browning*. Old Westbury, NY: Feminist Press, 1972.

Macherey, Pierre. "Corinne philosophe." *Europe* 693–94 (1987): 22–37.

MacKay, Carol Hanbery. "Hawthorne, Sophia, and Hilda as Copyists: Duplication and Transformation in *The Marble Faun*." *Browning Institute Studies* 12 (1984): 93–120.

Marsan, Hugo. "Madame de Staël et Hélène Cixous." *Le temps de lire* 3 (1979): 55–56.

Marshall, David. *The Surprising Effects of Sympathy: Marivaux, Diderot, Rousseau, and Mary Shelley*. Chicago: University of Chicago Press, 1988.

Marso, Lori. "Detached Men and Passionate Women in the Novels of Jean-Jacques Rousseau and Germaine de Staël." Diss., New York University, 1994.

May, Georges. *Le dilemme du roman au XVIIIe siècle*. Paris: Presses Universitaires de France, 1963.

———. "The Influence of English Fiction on the French Mid-Eighteenth-Century Novel." In *Aspects of the Eighteenth Century,* edited by Earl Wasserman, 265–80. Baltimore: John Hopkins University Press, 1965.

Maylender, Michele. *Storia delle Accademie d'Italia.* Bologna: Cappelli, 1926.

McGill, Kathleen. "Women and Performances: The Development of Improvisation by Sixteenth-Century Commedia dell'Arte." *Theater Journal* 43 (1991): 59–69.

Mellow, James R. *Nathaniel Hawthorne in His Times.* Boston: Houghton Mifflin, 1980.

Melville, Herman. "Hawthorne and His Mosses." In *Moby-Dick,* 535–51. New York: Norton, 1967.

Ménage, Gilles. *The History of Women Philosophers.* Translated by Beatrice Zedler. Lanham, MO: University Press of America, 1984.

Metcalf, Beate. "La Théorie du roman chez Madame de Staël." *Europe* 693–94 (1987): 38–48.

Ménard, Jean. "Madame de Staël et la musique, avec des documents inédits." *Revue de l'Université de l'Ottawa* July–September and October–December (1961): 420–35 and 552–63.

———. "Madame de Staël et la peinture." In *Madame de Staël et l'Europe,* 253–62. Paris: Klincksieck, 1970.

Mérard de Saint-Just, Anne. *Le château noir ou les souffrances de la jeune Ophelle.* Paris, 1799.

Mercken-Spaas, Godelieve. "Death and the Romantic Heroine: Chateaubriand and de Staël." In *Pre-Text, Text, Context,* edited by Robert L. Mitchell, 79–86. Columbus: Ohio State University Press, 1980.

Mermin, Dorothy. *Elizabeth Barrett Browning: The Origins of a New Poetry.* Chicago: University of Chicago Press, 1989.

Michael, John. "History and Romance, Sympathy and Uncertainty: The Moral of the Stones in Hawthorne's *The Marble Faun." PMLA* 103, no. 2 (1988): 150–61.

Michaels, Marianne Spaulding. "Feminist Tendencies in the Work of Mme de Staël." Diss., University of Connecticut, 1976.

Miller, Nancy K. *Subject to Change: Reading Feminist Writing.* New York: Columbia University Press, 1988.

———. "Politics, Feminism, and Patriarchy: Rereading *Corinne."* In *Germaine de Staël: Crossing the Borders,* edited by Madelyn Gutwirth, Avriel Goldberger, and Karyna Szmurlo, 193–97. New Brunswick, NJ: Rutgers University Press, 1991.

Miller, Perry. Foreword to *Margaret Fuller: American Romantic.* Edited by Perry Miller, ix–xxviii. Garden City, NY: Doubleday, 1963.

Moers, Ellen. "Madame de Staël and the Woman of Genius." *American Scholar* 44 (1975): 225–41.

———. *Literary Women: The Great Writers.* New York: Doubleday, 1976.

Moore de Ville, Chris. "Women Communicating in Three French Novels: The Portrait of the Artist as a Young Woman." *Romance Notes* 36, no. 2 (1996): 217–24.

Mortier, Roland. *La Poétique des ruines en France.* Geneva: Droz, 1974.

Mortimer, Armine Kotin. "Male and Female Plots in Staël's *Corinne*." In *Correspondances: Studies in Literature, History, and the Arts in Nineteenth-Century France*, edited by Keith Busby, 149–56. Atlanta, Amsterdam: Rodopi, 1992.

Moses, Claire Goldberg. *French Feminism in the Nineteenth Century*. Albany: State University of New York, 1984.

Mueller-Vollmer. "Guillaume de Humboldt, interprète de Madame de Staël; distances et affinités." *Cahiers staëliens* 37 (1985–86): 80–96.

Mullan, John. *Sentiment and Sociability: The Language of Feeling in the Eighteenth Century*. Oxford: Oxford University Press, 1988.

Myerson, Joel, ed. *Critical Essays on Margaret Fuller*. Boston: G. K. Hall, 1980.

Natali, Giulio. *Il Settecento*. In *Storia letteraria d'Italia*. Milano: Vallardi, 1936.

Naudin, Marie. "Madame de Staël, précurseur de l'esthétique musicale romantique." *Revue des sciences humaines* 139 (1970): 391–400.

Nelson, Robert. "The Quarrel of the Ancients and the Moderns." In *A New History of French Literature*, edited by Denis Hollier, 364–69. Cambridge: Harvard University Press, 1989.

Ness, Béatrice. "Le Succès Yourcenar: vérité et mystification." *French Review* 64 (1991): 794–803.

Omacini, Lucia. "Quelques remarques sur le style des romans de Mme de Staël d'après la presse de l'époque (1802–1808)." *Annali di Ca' Foscari* 10 (1971): 213–38.

———. "Pour une typologie du discours staëlien: les procédés de la persuasion." In *Benjamin Constant, Madame de Staël et le Groupe de Coppet*, edited by Etienne Hofmann, 371–91. Oxford: The Voltaire Foundation. Lausanne: Institut Benjamin Constant, 1982.

Orr, Linda. "The Revenge of Literature: A History of History." *New Literary History* 18 (1986): 1–22.

———. "Outspoken Women and the Rightful Daughter of the Revolution: Madame de Staël's *Considérations sur la Révolution française*." In *Rebel Daughters: Women and the French Revolution*, edited by Sara Melzer and Leslie Rabine, 121–36. Oxford: Oxford University Press, 1992.

Oster, Daniel. *Histoire de l'Académie Française*. Paris: Vialetay, 1970.

Ovid. *Metamorphoses*. Translated by Rolfe Humphries. Bloomington: Indiana University Press, 1955.

Peel, Ellen. "Contradictions of Form and Feminism in *Corinne ou l'Italie*." *Essays in Literature* 14 (1987): 281–98.

———. "Corinne's Shift to Patriarchal Mediation: Rebirth or Regression?" In *Germaine de Staël: Crossing the Borders*, edited by Madelyn Gutwirth, Avriel Goldberger, and Karyna Szmurlo, 101–12. New Brunswick, NJ: Rutgers University Press, 1991.

Person, Leland S., Jr. *Aesthetic Headaches: Women and Masculine Poetics in Poe, Melville, and Hawthorne*. Athens, GA: University of Georgia Press, 1988.

Peterson, Carla. *The Determined Reader: Gender and Culture in the Novel from Napoleon to Victoria*. New Brunswick, NJ: Rutgers University Press, 1986.

Petrey, Sandy. *Realism and Revolution*. Ithaca: Cornell University Press, 1988.

Plutarch. *Plutarch's Lives*. Translated by John Langhorne and William Langhorne. Cincinnati: Applegate, 1856.

Porter, Laurence. "The Emergence of a Romantic Style: From *De la littérature* to *De l'Allemagne*." In *Authors and Their Centuries*, edited by Philip Crant, 129–42. Columbia: University of South Carolina Press, 1974.

Poulet, Georges. "The Role of Improvisation in *Corinne*." *English Literary History* 4 (1974): 602–12.

———. "*Corinne* et *Adolphe*, deux romans conjugués." *Revue d'histoire littéraire de la France* 78 (1978): 580–96.

Pratt, Mary Louise. "Scratches on the Face of the Country; or, What Mr. Barrow Saw in the Land of the Bushmen." *Critical Inquiry* 12 (1985): 119–43.

Pratt, T. M. "Madame de Staël and the Italian Articles." *Comparative Literature Studies* Winter (1985): 444–54.

Principato, Aurelio. "L'inscription du dialogue dans *Corinne* et dans *Adolphe*." In *Il Gruppo di Coppet et Italia*, edited by Mario Mattuci, 191–210. Pisa: Pacini, 1988.

Radcliffe, Ann. *The Mysteries of Udolpho*. Edited by Bonamy Dobrée. Oxford: Oxford University Press, 1966.

Radeley, Virginia L. *Elizabeth Barrett Browning*. New York: Twayne, 1972.

Reynolds, Larry J. *European Revolutions and the American Renaissance*. New Haven: Yale University Press, 1988.

Richter, Melvin. *The Political Thought of Montesquieu*. Cambridge: Harvard University Press, 1977.

Rosbottom, Ronald C. "A Blurred Voice." *Eighteenth Century: Theory and Interpretation* 31, no. 2 (1990): 161–68.

Ross, Marlon. *The Contours of Masculine Desire and the Rise of Women's Poetry*. New York: Oxford University Press, 1989.

Rossetti, William. Introduction to *The Poetical Works of Mrs. Hemans*, 11–24. London: Moxon, 1873.

Rousseau, Jean-Jacques. *Lettre à d'Alembert*. Edited by M. Fuchs. Geneva: Droz, 1948.

Rousset, Jean. *L'Intérieur et l'extérieur*. Paris: José Corti, 1968.

Sainte-Beuve, Charles-Augustin. "Madame de Staël." *Revue des Deux Mondes* 2 (1835): 265–301, 416–42.

———. *Portraits de femmes*. Paris: Garnier, 1845.

———. *Causeries du lundi*. 2d ed. 15 vols. Paris: Garnier, 1856–62.

———. *Oeuvres complètes*. Paris: Pléiade, 1960.

Salvagni, David. *La corte e la società romana nei secoli XVIII e XIX*. Roma: Forzani, 1885.

Savigneau, Josyanne. *Marguerite Yourcenar: l'invention d'une vie*. Paris: Gallimard, 1990.

Scharnhorst, Gary. "Hawthorne and *The Poetical Works of Spenser*: A Lost Review." *American Literature* 61, no. 4 (December 1989): 668–73.

Schlick, Yael. "Beyond the Boundaries: Staël, Genlis, and the Impossible Femme Célèbre." *Symposium* 50, no. 1 (1966): 50–63.

Schlegel, August W. "Une étude critique de *Corinne ou l'Italie*." *Cahiers staëliens* 16 (1973): 57–71.

Schor, Naomi. *Breaking the Chain: Woman, Theory, and French Realist Fiction.* New York: Columbia University Press, 1985.

———. "Portrait of a Gentleman: Representing Men in (French) Women's Writing." *Representations* 20 (Fall 1987): 113–33.

———. "*Corinne*: The Third Woman." *L'Esprit Créateur* 34 (1994): 99–106.

Sheriff, Mary D. "Germaine, or Corinne." In *The Exceptional Woman: Elisabeth Vigée-Lebrun and the Cultural Politics of Art,* 243–61. Chicago, IL: University of Chicago Press, 1996.

Showalter, Elaine. *A Literature of Their Own: British Women Novelists from Brontë to Lessing.* Princeton, NJ: Princeton University Press, 1977.

———. Introduction to *Alternative Alcott.* New Brunswick, NJ: Rutgers University Press, 1988.

Showalter, English. "Corinne as an Autonomous Heroine." In *Germaine de Staël: Crossing the Borders,* edited by Madelyn Gutwirth, Avriel Goldberger, and Karyna Szmurlo, 188–92. New Brunswick, NJ: Rutgers University Press, 1991.

Sismondi, Charles Simonde de. *Histoire des républiques italiennes du Moyen Âge.* 5th ed. 8 vols. Brussels: Société typographique belge, Ad. Ahlen, 1858.

Smith, Henry Nash. "The Scribbling Women and the Cosmic Success Story." *Critical Inquiry* 1 (1974): 47–70.

Spacks, Patricia Meyer. *Desire and Truth: Functions of Plot in Eighteenth-Century English Novels.* Chicago: University of Chicago Press, 1990.

Spender, Dale. *The Writer or the Sex?* New York: Pergamon Press, 1989.

Spivak, Gayatri. "The Politics of Interpretations." *Critical Inquiry* 9 (September 1982): 259–78.

Staël, Germaine de. *Oeuvres complètes.* 17 vols. Strasbourg and London: Treuttel and Würtz, 1820–21. Reprint in 2 vols. Genève: Slatkine, 1967.

———. *Corinne, or Italy.* 3 vols. London: Tripper, 1807.

———. *Corinne, or Italy.* Translated by Isabel Hill, with metrical versions of the odes by L. E. Landon, New York: Brut, [1833].

———. *Corinne, or Italy.* American ed. New York: Burgess, Stringer and Co., 1847.

———. *Corinne ou l'Italie.* 2 vols. Edited by Claudine Herrmann. Paris: Editions Des femmes, 1979.

———. *Corinne ou l'Italie.* Edited and introduced by Simone Balayé. Paris: Gallimard, 1985.

———. *Corinne, or Italy.* Translated and introduced by Avriel H. Goldberger. New Brunswick, NJ: Rutgers University Press, 1987.

———. *Journal de jeunesse. Occident et Cahiers staëliens* 1–4 (June 1930; July 1931; October 1932): 76–80, 157–60, 235–42.

———. *Mon Journal.* Edited by Simone Balayé. *Cahiers staëliens* 28 (1980): 55–79.

———. *De la littérature.* Edited by Paul Van Tieghem. Genève: Droz, 1959.

———. *De l'Allemagne.* Edited by Jean de Pange, introduction by Simone Balayé. 5 vols. Paris: Hachette, 1958–60.

———. *Madame de Staël et J. B. A. Suard. Correspondance inédite.* Edited by Robert de Luppé. Genève: Droz, 1970.

————. *Des circonstances actuelles.* Edited by Lucia Omacini. Genève: Droz, 1979.

————. *'Essai sur les fictions' suivi de 'De l'influence des passions sur le bonheur des individus.'* Paris: Ramsay, 1979.

————. *Considérations sur la Révolution française.* Edited and introduced by Jacques Godechot. Paris: Tallandier, 1984.

————. *Correspondance générale. Le Léman et l'Italie.* Vol. 5, Part 2. Edited by Béatrice W. Jasinski. Paris: Hachette, 1985.

————. *Correspondance générale. De 'Corinne' vers 'De l'Allemagne.'* Edited by Béatrice Jasinski. Vol. 6. Paris: Klincksieck, 1993.

Starobinski, Jean. *Portrait de l'artiste en saltimbanque.* Genève: Skira, 1970.

Staum, Martin. "The Class of Moral and Political Sciences: 1795–1803." *French Historical Studies* 11 (1980): 371–97.

Stern, Milton R. *Context for Hawthorne: 'The Marble Faun' and the Politics of Openness and Closure in American Literature.* Urbana: University of Illinois Press, 1991.

Stephenson, Glennis. *Letitia Landon: The Woman Behind L.E.L.* Manchester: Manchester University Press, 1995.

Surridge, Lisa. "Madame de Staël Meets Mrs. Ellis: Geraldine Jewsbury's *The Half Sisters.*" *Carlyle Studies* (1995): 81–95.

Swallow, Noreen J. "The Weapon of Personality: A Review of Sexist Criticism of Madame de Staël." *Atlantis* 8 (1982): 78–82.

Sweet, Nanora. "History, Imperialism, and the Aesthetics of the Beautiful: Hemans and the Post-Napoleonic Moment." In *At the Limits of Romanticism: Essays in Cultural, Feminist and Materialist Criticism,* edited by Mary A. Favret and Nicola J. Watson, 170–84. Bloomington: Indiana University Press, 1994.

Szmurlo, Karyna. "Le jeu et le discours féminin: la danse de l'héroïne staëlienne." *Nineteenth-Century French Studies* 1–2 (1986–87): 1–13.

————. "Germaine Necker, Baronne de Staël (1766–1817)." In *French Women Writers,* edited by Eva Sartori and Dorothy Zimmerman, 463–72. New York, Westport: Greenwood Press, 1991.

————. "Germaine de Staël." In *A Critical Bibliography of French Literature: The Nineteenth Century,* edited by David Baguely, 51–60. Syracuse: Syracuse University Press, 1994.

————. "Speech Acts: Staël's Historiography of the Revolution." In *Literate Women and the French Revolution of 1789,* edited by Catherine Montfort, 237–52. Birmingham, AL: Summa Publications, 1994.

————. "Pour une poétique des langues nationales: Germaine de Staël." In *Le Groupe de Coppet et l'Europe,* edited by Kurt Kloocke, 165–79. Lausanne, Institut Benjamin Constant; Paris: Jean Touzot, 1994.

————. "Vers la théorie du performatif: Germaine de Staël." In *Le Groupe Coppet et le monde moderne,* edited by Françoise Tilkin, 377–93. Genève: Droz, 1998.

Taplin, Gardner B. *The Life of Elizabeth Barrett Browning.* New Haven, CT: Yale University Press, 1957.

Tenenbaum, Susan. "Liberating Exchanges: Mme de Staël and the Uses of Comparison." In *Literate Women and the French Revolution of 1789*, edited by Catherine Monfort, 225–36. Birmingham, AL: Summa Publications, 1994.

Terzian, Debra. "Growing up Female in Fiction: Reading Women's Developmental Narrative in Madame de Lafayette, Germaine de Staël, and George Sand." Diss., Brown University, 1993.

Tharp, Louise Hall. *The Peabody Sisters of Salem.* Boston: Little, Brown, 1950.

Thibaudet, Albert. *Histoire de la littérature française.* Paris: Libraire Stock, 1936.

Todd, Janet. *Sensibility: An Introduction.* London: Methuen, 1986.

Trouille, Mary. "A Bold New Vision of Woman: Staël and Wollstonecraft Respond to Rousseau." *Studies on Voltaire and the Eighteenth-Century* 292 (1991): 293–336.

Turner, Arlin. "Hawthorne's Literary Borrowings." *PMLA* 51 (June 1936): 543–62.

———. *Nathaniel Hawthorne: A Biography.* New York: Oxford University Press, 1980.

Vallois, Marie-Claire. *Fictions féminines. Mme de Staël et les voix de la Sibylle.* Stanford: Anma Libri, 1987.

———. "Old Idols, New Subjects: Germaine de Staël and Romanticism." In *Germaine de Staël: Crossing the Borders,* edited by Madelyn Gutwirth, Avriel Goldberger, and Karyna Szmurlo, 82–97. New Brunswick, NJ: Rutgers University Press, 1991.

Vitagliano, Adele. *Storia della poesia estemporanea nella litteratura italiana dalle origini ai nostri giorni.* Roma: Loescher, 1905.

Viveash, C. F. "Jane Austen and Madame de Staël." *Persuasions* 13 (1991): 39–40.

Volney, François. "Les Leçons d'histoire." In *Oeuvres complètes* with a Notice by Adolphe Bossage. 2d ed. 8 vols. Paris: Parmentier Librairie, 1825–26.

———. *Voyage en Egypte et en Syrie.* Edited by Jean Gaulmier. Le Monde Outre-Mer Series. Paris: Mouton, 1959.

Wallace, James D. "Hawthorne and the Scribbling Women Reconsidered." *American Literature* 62, no. 2 (June 1990): 201–22.

Waller, Margaret. "The Melancholy Man and the Lady with the Lyre: The Sexual Politics of Genius in Early Romantic Fiction and Painting." In *Correspondances: Studies in Literature, History, and the Arts in Nineteenth-Century France,* edited by Keith Busby, 223–37. Atlanta, Amsterdam: Rodopi, 1992.

———. *The Male Malady: Fictions of Impotence in the French Romantic Novel.* New Brunswick, NJ: Rutgers University Press, 1993.

Warren, Joyce. *The American Narcissus: Individualism and Women in Nineteenth-Century American Fiction.* New Brunswick, NJ: Rutgers University Press, 1984.

Weisbuch, Robert. *Atlantic Double-Cross.* Chicago: University of Chicago Press, 1986.

Wilkes, Joanne. "When Gentlemen Preferred Blondes: Madame de Staël's *Corinne* and the Works of George Eliot." In *Imperfect Apprehensions: Essays in English Literature,* edited by Geoffrey Little, 248–59. Sydney: Challis, 1996.

Wilson, Clotilde. "*La Modification,* or Variations on a Theme by Mme de Staël." *Romanic Review* 55 (1964): 278–82.

Wittig, Monique. "The Straight Mind." *Feminist Issues* 1 (1980): 103–12.

Wolfson, Susan J. "'Domestic Affections' and "the spear of Minerva": Felicia Hemans and the Dilemma of Gender." In *Re-Visioning Romanticism: British Women Writers, 1776–1837,* edited by Carol Shiner and Joel Haefner, 128–66. Philadelphia: University of Pennsylvania Press, 1994.

Wolstenholme, Susan. *Gothic (Re)visions: Writing Women as Readers.* Albany: State University of New York Press, 1993.

Wood, Ann D. "The 'Scribbling Women' and Fanny Fern: Why Women Wrote." *American Quarterly* 23 (1971): 3–24.

Wu, Duncan, ed. *Romanticism: An Anthology.* Oxford: Blackwell, 1994.

Yeager, Patricia. "The Dialogic Imagination." *PMLA* 99 (1984): 953–73.

Young, Philip. *Hawthorne's Secret.* Boston: Godine, 1984.

Yourcenar, Marguerite. *Les yeux ouverts.* Paris: Le Centurion, 1980.

———. *Discours de réception de Madame Marguerite Yourcenar à l'Académie Française et Réponse de Monsieur Jean d'Ormesson.* Paris: Gallimard, 1981.

———. *Oeuvres romanesques.* Paris: Gallimard, 1982.

Zonana, Joyce. "The Embodied Muse: Elizabeth Barrett Browning's *Aurora Leigh* and Feminist Poetics." *Tulsa Studies* 8 (1989): 242–62.

Index

ADX-748